GODS GALORE

GODS
GALORE

RUPERT STANBURY

Matador
9 Priory Business Park,
Wistow Road, Kibworth Beauchamp,
Leicestershire. LE8 0RX
Tel: 0116 279 2299
Email: books@troubador.co.uk
Web: www.troubador.co.uk/matador
Twitter: @matadorbooks

ISBN 978 1 8004 6530 5

British Library Cataloguing in Publication Data.
A catalogue record for this book is available from the British Library.

Printed and bound in Great Britain by 4edge Limited
Typeset in 11pt Minion Pro by Troubador Publishing Ltd,
Leicester, UK

Matador is an imprint of Troubador Publishing Ltd

This book is dedicated to my late mother and father, Coora and Ronald Stanbury, who inspired my love of books.

CONTENTS

PRINCIPAL CHARACTERS

Zeus's Realm

Aphrodite – Goddess of Love

Apollo – God of Archery, Dance, Music and much more; Artemis's twin

Artemis – Goddess of the Hunt; recently developed an interest in feminism and equality matters

Athene – Goddess of Wisdom

Bacchus – God of Wine; also proprietor of the Dog and Duck public house

Beetle – A tortoise, resident at the Dog and Duck

Mr Bumble – Beadle; member of Zeus's and Hera's household

Mrs Bumble – Housekeeper to Zeus and Hera

Fearless Frupert – A six-year-old boy

Florence Nightingale – A nurse

Hebe – Servant Goddess; often visits Hades' and Poseidon's realms.

Hephaestus – Builder God

Hera – Goddess; Zeus's wife

Hermes – Messenger God; currently spending most of his time studying nuclear thermodynamics

Iris – Messenger Goddess

Lennie – An eagle, resident at the Dog and Duck
Marie Antoinette – Former queen of France; now Hera's maid
Mars – God of War
Norbert ('Nobbly Butt') – Builder working for Hephaestus
Mistress Quickly – Hostess of the Dog and Duck
Zeus – King of the Olympian Gods

Hades' Realm

Mrs Aggycraggywoggynog ('Aggy') – Head cook in charge of
    the Kitchens
Attila – Former King of the Huns; now works in the Torturing
    Department
Cerberus – A three-headed dog
Death – A 'being' who transports people to the Underworld
Genghis Khan – Former Mongol King; now works in the
    Torturing Department
Gigliola – Works in the Kitchens
Hades – God; King of the Underworld
Homer – Once a writer, now Head Librarian
Ivan the Terrible – Former King of Russia; now works in the
    Torturing Department
Ming – Vesta's friend; works in the Kitchens
Nelson – Works in the Kitchens
Persephone – Goddess, Queen of the Underworld and Hades'
    wife
Satan – Director of the Torturing Department
Sisyphus – A former king who pushes a boulder up a hill
Vesta – A newly arrived girl in the Underworld
Virgil – Once a writer, now Assistant Librarian
Vlad – Formerly known as Vlad the Impaler when he was King
    of much of Eastern Europe; now works in the Torturing
    Department

Mr Wong – Works in the Kitchens, having once run a Chinese restaurant in Alderley Edge, England

Poseidon's Realm

Amphitrite – Goddess; Queen of the Seas and Poseidon's wife
Bettina – A small whale; Moby's fiancée
Dolores – Housekeeper to Poseidon
Gerrard and Suki – Two whales who are friends of Moby's
Hashimoto – Poseidon's butler
Kinky, Linky, Minky and Pinky – Mermaids living in the Sea Cavern
Moby – A large white whale
Poseidon – God; King of the Seas
Totty Turniptoes – Hair stylist, beautician and fitness instructor; used to live in Romford, Essex

Hamburg

Fritz – A man who lives under a tarpaulin; claims to be the Kaiser
Gropuddle – Fritz's dog
Inga and Judit – Two young ladies 'working' in the docks area

Monaco

Ahmed – A guest on the *Princess BoomBoom* yacht
Kirsty – A PA on the yacht
Jade, Chloe, Marie and Nicky – Party girls on the yacht with Totty

Yorkgate

Albert Titebotham – Stanley's son; a butcher

Angie Rowbotham – Stella's niece, for whom she works

Doreen Higginbotham – Runs a clothes shop

Eustace Uselessbottom – An English cricketer, playing in a test match at Headingley

Kasia, Gosia, Svetlana and Viktoria – Employees in Doreen's workshop

Mervyn Loosebottom – Trevor's cousin; a technology genius

Oswald Titebotham – Stanley's grandson; a schoolboy

Stanley Titebotham – A butcher

Stella Sidebottom – Hairdresser and beautician

Trevor Loosebottom – Runs the general store; friend of Hebe's

INTRODUCTION

HOMER IS THOUGHT TO HAVE WRITTEN THE *Iliad* and the *Odyssey* in the eighth century BC, while Virgil wrote the *Aeneid* about seven hundred years later in the first century BC. Both writers were concerned with the fall of Troy towards the end of the second millennium BC and the events which took place subsequently.

I first read these three ancient classics as a young adult. Many years later I decided it was time for a re-read, which triggered a renewed fascination in the various Olympian gods that are central to the three stories. This got me thinking about what these gods might be up to three thousand years later and so I decided to record various tales of their adventures in this small book called *Gods Galore*.

By way of background, we need to go back to the time before Troy fell when three gods, who were also brothers, drew lots to decide who should reign in the various parts of their joint empire. Poseidon drew the Sea, Hades claimed the Underworld and Zeus became God of the Sky, which also included the Land. Since Mount Olympus was in the sky, this became Zeus's home and it was also the place where many of the other gods lived.

It should come as no surprise that over the past three thousand years, many of these gods have both changed and developed in parallel with humankind. In *Gods Galore* we now find that Bacchus is no longer just the God of Wine but has also taken responsibility for all alcoholic drinks, especially beer. Additionally, he runs a pub which is at the heart of much of Olympus's social life. The goddesses Iris and Hebe have decided not to live in grand palaces but in a modern bungalow, where live Premier League football matches are regularly screened. Artemis, while still the Goddess of the Hunt, has become an ardent feminist as well as a supporter of other progressive causes, including 'new' political concepts such as democracy.

Some things, however, never change. Zeus still has his thunderbolts and continues to chase after attractive females. Wherever there are references to 'hanky panky' or 'extra-curricular activities', Zeus will inevitably be involved. Mars, as the God of War, continues to create trouble and strife both in the world and on Olympus, often to the general consternation of many of his fellow gods.

The relationships between the gods and humankind are at the heart of these tales. The Underworld is filling up all the time and Hades needs to find useful employment for the new arrivals. Historical figures such as Attila the Hun and Genghis Khan are able to employ their former skills in the Torturing Department. Others work in the kitchens, the mines and on building sites. A few people are seconded from the Underworld to Olympus or Poseidon's realm to assist the gods. Bacchus is fortunate to have Mistress Quickly from Shakespeare's historical plays to act as hostess of his pub; the former French queen Marie Antoinette and Dickens's Mr Bumble, together with his wife, are members of Zeus's household, and Poseidon's cavern has a Japanese butler and a South Carolinian maid working there. In addition, there are a number of other new characters, many of whom turn out to be particular catalysts for change, especially in the lives of the older gods.

As a number of readers will be aware, most gods have both Greek and Roman names. I have decided to use their Greek names with two exceptions. These are Mars, the God of War, and Bacchus, the God of Wine, where I have used their Roman names because, on balance, I believe they are more generally recognised than their Greek equivalents of Ares and Dionysus.

Finally, I recognise that there may be some classical scholars who might take exception to my portrayal of various gods and goddesses. This could relate to their personalities, their roles or even their powers. I would ask such critics to accept that *Gods Galore* is about the gods in the twenty first century AD, and that the changes to humankind in the past three thousand years will in part be mirrored in the lives of the gods. I wrote this book with the sole purpose of it being an entertaining read; if it achieves that objective, it has done its job. Put another way, I do not claim to have written the fourth great classic about the ancient world, although if it is still being read in another thousand years, perhaps its status could be revised then. However, that is for future generations.

Rupert Stanbury

I

BEFORE THE
COUNCIL MEETING

———

Mr Bumble, the beadle, was pacing to and
fro in front of the Council Chamber ringing his
bell. He was a portly chap who wore a blue frock
coat over a blue waistcoat with blue trousers and a blue beadle's
hat. This mass of blue was complemented by a very red face
with a large red nose and two bright red ears.

"Council Meeting, Council Meeting; all gods to the Council
Meeting," his pompous voice boomed. "Please hurry up,
everyone. Council Meeting begins soon."

As a number of gods approached the Chamber's portico,
Mr Bumble stopped ringing his bell, put it down on a nearby
ledge and took hold of a large parchment with a list of the
invited gods, which he proceeded to tick off.

"Apollo" – tick.

"Artemis" – tick.

"Iris" – tick.

He took up his bell again and continued his ringing. "Council Meeting, Council Meeting; all gods to the Council Meeting. Council Meeting, Council Meeting; will—"

"Hello," said a voice interrupting him from the left.

Mr Bumble stopped ringing as he looked at a fresh-faced young man wearing jeans, a dirty white T-shirt and mud splattered boots.

"Is this where the Council Meeting is?" asked the fresh-faced young man.

Mr Bumble gave him a puzzled look. "And you would be?" he enquired after several seconds of puzzlement.

"I'm Norbert" was the response.

Mr Bumble looked at his parchment. "Nobbly Butt," he muttered as he went down the list. "You don't seem to be here. Are you a new god who's just arrived?"

"Ha; that's a laugh. Me – a god."

"So, are you or aren't you?"

"Yea, if you like."

"It's not what I like. You're either a god or you're not," said Mr Bumble in a slightly exasperated tone.

"My mum always kept saying 'my god, my god' when I was around."

"She did?"

"Especially when I did things like put frogs in my big sister's bed or hid all her bras just before she went out to work."

The beadle ignored the comments about frogs and bras. The fact that the word 'god' had been used was what interested him. He would delve further.

"And your mother was?" he enquired.

"Nora; she cleaned the toilets at the Hungarian Ministry of Finance."

Mr Bumble frowned. This was not a promising answer; toilet cleaning mothers were not a normal source of supply of Olympian gods. However, there was one exception and the beadle decided to explore if this exception applied to the new arrival.

"And who was your father?"

"Dunno. My mum would never say."

Mr Bumble took a deep breath and let it out slowly. This seemed to be one of those cases where the exception might well apply.

"That piece of information is very revealing. Very revealing indeed," he muttered.

"Is it?"

"Most definitely. You're probably another one of Zeus's children."

"Am I? So, my dad's Zeus, is he?"

"Very likely, My Lord Nobbly Butt. You're a product of what I would call Zeus's extra-curricular activities. That's probably why you're here."

"Cor blimey. No wonder my mum never told me."

"Does Lady Hera know about you?"

"Dunno. Does it matter?"

"Does it matter? Of course it matters! She's Zeus's wife and is not at all pleased when her husband provides her with sudden additions to their already large extended family."

"You mean cos of his hanky panky on the side?"

"A crude but accurate description, My Lord Nobbly Butt. A considerable amount of upset tends to arise when new family members are suddenly introduced to her. We will need to proceed with great caution. Great caution, indeed."

Mr Bumble tapped his nose with a finger as he looked around furtively. Norbert's eyes followed Mr Bumble's, unsure what he was looking for but thinking it was wise to follow suit.

"Perhaps we should ask Mr H?" he said pointing to a tall, broad-chested male who was walking towards them.

Hephaestus was the Builder God. He was a master craftsman and spent his time carrying out the construction work on Mount Olympus. He had a warm-hearted personality and was imposing to look at with his curly black hair, large beard and immense muscles in both his arms and legs. Today he was wearing his best robe for the Council Meeting, although normally he was bare chested as he worked away with his hammers, saws and other tools.

"Good day, gentlemen," he said with a smile as he stopped to talk.

"High fives, Mr H," said Norbert, pushing out his right palm.

"High fives, Norb," the god replied with a smile. "Good to see you and Mr Bumble have got to know each other. I hope you'll become firm friends."

"My Lord Hephaestus," Mr Bumble began in a rather anxious tone, "it appears that My Lord Nobbly Butt, whom I take it you already know, is in a rather delicate position."

"Is he?"

"Indeed he is and I wondered if you could perhaps give some advice as to how we might proceed?"

"Sounds perplexing but I'll try. Could we, though, just clear up one matter – who is Lord Nobbly Butt?"

"That's my new name, Mr H," said Norbert. "Given to me by this here Mr Bumble, who's name I've only just learned myself."

Hephaestus roared with laughter. "Nobbly Butt; do you mind, Norb?"

"Well, I quite like Norbert cos I'm used to it, but I suppose if some people want to call me Nobbly Butt, that's okay, especially if I get to be a lord."

"A lord, you say?"

"Not only a lord, but I'm also a god."

"Are you? Who said so?"

"Mr Bumble here. He also told me that my dad's Zeus,

which he thinks could be a problem with his wife cos she's not my mum."

Hephaestus looked hard at the two of them and he then focused on the beadle for several seconds before speaking. "Mr Bumble, I would have to admit that I'm somewhat confused by this conversation. I do recognise that the position you hold in Zeus's household puts you at the centre of affairs on Olympus, but I'm amazed at what I've just learned in the last few minutes. It seems to be an extraordinary coincidence that a former Hungarian builder, who's been lent to me from the Underworld to assist with my workload, should somehow turn out to be one of Zeus's long-lost sons as well as being a member of the deity."

Mr Bumble's jaw dropped as he slowly repeated the words "Hungarian builder?"

"You didn't know?"

Mr Bumble shook his head.

"Do you think there might have been a bit of a misunderstanding?"

"I think there has, My Lord."

"Does that mean Zeus isn't my dad and I'm not a god or even a lord then?" asked Norbert.

"No, Norb, I'm afraid not," Hephaestus chuckled. "But don't be concerned about it. It means you won't get into any trouble with his wife Hera, who, by the way, happens to be my mother. Anyway, I must go into the meeting now. Remember, Mr Bumble, I'm relying on you to be a good friend to Norb while he's here."

Hephaestus walked into the Council Chamber and Mr Bumble began to ring his bell again as he continued to tick off the arriving gods. He tried to ignore his newly appointed Hungarian friend who stood a few feet away from him watching proceedings.

"Thetis" – tick.

"Hermes" – tick.

"Leto" – tick.

A tall, beautiful woman followed. She had long auburn hair and shining blue eyes. Wearing a goat-skin cloak and golden sandals, she carried a silver spear in her hand. Her gracious smile at Mr Bumble was not seen by him as he was bowing as low as his portly body would allow.

"Why did you bow to her and not the others?" Norbert asked as Mr Bumble's spine slowly unwound.

"That," replied the beadle, "is My Lady Athene. She is wonderful in every sense."

"Oh, you fancy her, do you?"

"Don't be ridiculous," he snapped. "She is the most charming, gracious, helpful, courteous and intelligent of all the gods and goddesses. She is wisdom personified."

"Nice looker too."

Mr Bumble ignored Norbert's comment and picked up his bell once more.

"Council Meeting, Council Meeting; Council Meeting about to begin. Hurry up, everyone."

"Demeter" – tick.

"Hebe" – tick.

"Paean" – tick.

"Blimey; who's this little cracker?"

Norbert was looking at Aphrodite, the Goddess of Love. She had shapely calves, a tight waist, large boobs and a gorgeous face, topped off with long, gleaming blonde hair. She was in high heels and wore a golden-coloured mini-skirt, a bright red T-shirt and a black leather jacket. Her model hips swayed provocatively as she walked over to the two of them.

"Hello, Honey Bumbs," she purred at the beadle. "Is Mrs Bumble still performing her wifely duties for you on a nightly basis? Any probs in that area, just let me know and I'll have a little word with her."

Aphrodite pouted her lips at Mr Bumble but got no response. His mouth opened and closed but no words came out; his red face became beetroot-coloured and torrents of perspiration ran down his cheeks. Eventually a very slight nod of the head took place, although whether this was an answer to Aphrodite or a nervous affliction was unclear.

"Lucky you," she said. "Now, Honey Bumbs, will you please try and open this for me? It's so stiff that I feel I need a real man to help me." She pulled out a bottle of French perfume from her designer bag and tried to turn the top with no success.

"I'll try, My Lady," said Mr Bumble who had now got his voice back. He put his bell down and took the bottle from her. Taking a deep breath, he tried to open it, but the black top just wouldn't move. He gritted his teeth, bent forward and tried again. As he strained and strained, his beetroot face became doubly beetroot in colour, perspiration again ran down his face, and he started wheezing and panting as if he'd just run a marathon.

"Ahem." Norbert coughed, thinking it was time to intervene. "Perhaps I could help?" He put his hand out to take the bottle from Mr Bumble, who was only too willing to relinquish it so he could get his breath back.

"Oh, could you please?" Aphrodite purred. "I'd be ever so grateful. I do want to have the right scent for the Council Meeting."

Norbert took hold of the bottle with his left hand and immediately turned the top round with his right. He handed the open bottle to an astonished Aphrodite with an equally astonished Mr Bumble next to her.

"You're a genius," the goddess said, and planted a kiss on Norbert's cheek. "But, Mr Bumble, who is this wonderful friend of yours? I've never seen him on Olympus before."

By now Mr Bumble's astonishment had turned to something approaching jealousy. "He's called Nobbly Butt," he peevishly replied. "A common workman, assisting Lord Hephaestus on a temporary basis."

"Well, I'm impressed, Nobbly Butt. How did you open my bottle?"

"Righty tighty, lefty loosey," was the reply.

"Sounds a bit naughty to me."

"Very simple, really. You and Mr Bumble here were trying to turn the top to the right, which just tightened it up all the more. You should have turned it to the left. Righty tighty, lefty loosey – that's what we say."

"I'll remember that, as I'm sure you will, won't you, Honey Bumbs?"

"Hmm," was the beadle's response as he gave Norbert an unfriendly look.

"Must go now," said Aphrodite. "I want to get in there before Mars. You come and see me one of these days, Nobbly Butt. Perhaps we can work on this righty tighty, lefty loosey thing together?" Aphrodite gave Norbert a saucy look, winked and walked into the Council Chamber.

Before relations had a chance to be sorted out between the beadle and the builder, heavy footsteps were heard approaching. They both looked down the hill and saw a monster of a man coming towards them. He was wearing heavy bronze armour, which clanged as he walked along. His ferocious-looking helmet was inscribed with a death's head, which covered a slightly balding scalp, and a mean-looking face with multiple scars on both cheeks.

"Is this Mars?" Norbert asked in a whisper as the monster approached.

Mr Bumble nodded and ticked off the name on his list. "Stand back," he muttered, and the two of them retreated a couple of paces as Mars grew level with them. Norbert was a confident chap generally, but he didn't like the look of this god, so he followed Mr Bumble's example of making a large bow.

When he looked up after a few seconds, he found Mars had made a detour towards him and Mr Bumble. He was staring directly into the beadle's face from a distance of no more than twelve inches.

"Bum," growled Mars.

"Yes, My Lord," croaked Norbert's companion nervously.

"A present for you."

A crushing right fist went into Mr Bumble's solar plexus, causing him to double up and fall to his knees, his head sagging in front of him. Mars stood over him for a few seconds reviewing his handiwork before turning around and marching through the doorway to join his fellow gods.

The beadle groaned and stayed on his knees, holding his chest. As soon as Mars moved away, Norbert went over to his new friend and tried to lift him to his feet.

"You okay, mate?"

Mr Bumble shook his head.

"Not surprised. Come on, let's get you up." Norbert was a strong man and managed to haul the beadle to his feet. He held him up and made him take deep breaths. After a few minutes, there was a noticeable revival.

"Thank you," said Mr Bumble when he eventually got his breath and voice back. "Thank you, Nobbly Butt."

"I take it that Mars is what you would call a Right Bloody Bastard?"

Mr Bumble nodded.

"Best avoided, eh?"

"Best avoided," the beadle agreed.

No more gods arrived over the next few minutes, allowing Mr Bumble to review his parchment.

"I think that's probably it. I'd better go in and report to Lord Zeus."

"Right, I'll follow you. Perhaps you can show me where to sit."

Mr Bumble, forgetting Norbert's recent assistance, looked at him in a superior manner. "Where to sit! Where to sit! You don't sit anywhere," he stated very firmly.

"Okay, I'll stand then."

"Stand! You don't stand anywhere. Only gods are allowed into the Council Chamber."

"Well, you're going in and you're not a god."

"I'm going in to give my report to Lord Zeus and then I have to leave. You see those two big doors?" And he pointed to two large grey metal doors underneath the portico. "They are locked shut once I leave and no one can enter while the gods discuss their godly business."

"Well, it doesn't seem very democratic to me," grumbled Norbert.

"Democratic! Democratic!" exclaimed the beadle. "This is Olympus. We don't do democracy here. What do you think the God's Council is – the British Houses of Parliament?"

After making this pointed statement, Mr Bumble turned his back on Norbert and strode up the steps into the Council Chamber.

II

GOING
UNDERGROUND

———

THE FERRYBOAT WAS A CROSS BETWEEN A Venetian gondola and a Cambridge punt. It was jet black and moved slowly along the river, edging towards the near shoreline. From a distance, the two figures looked identical. Both were wearing black cloaks with hoods: one of them standing at the back pushing on his pole, the other sitting impassively in the middle holding a long scythe. As the boat got nearer, the ferryman's features became clearer, showing a tired, worn-out, colourless old face. His passenger also became distinct, his head nothing but a skull atop a dirty white skeleton. No flesh or muscles, just bones and cartilage.

As the ferry gently nudged against the shoreline, a small head suddenly appeared looking over the side. It was a mass of mousy brown curls on top of a rosy-cheeked face with bright blue eyes, which inquisitively looked hither and thither.

"Here we are," said Death as he stood up and stepped onto the jetty, which represented a small dock. He turned towards the man at the back and threw him a coin.

"It should be the girl making the payment," was the growled reply.

"This time it's me," was the response.

"It's not right."

"No complaints. You've been paid, so shut it." Death and the ferryman stared aggressively at each other until the latter averted his gaze and busied himself with pocketing his fee.

The cloaked skeleton now turned to the young passenger. "Come on, little girl," he said, putting out his hand.

"I'm not a little girl," was the defiant response. "I'll be fourteen next week and I'm perfectly capable of getting out myself." She promptly stood up and hopped onto the jetty.

"I've also got a name – Vesta. Please call me Vesta and not little girl."

"Huh," Death grunted.

"So, what happens now?"

Before Death could reply, there was a series of loud, aggressive barks as a huge dog came running towards the boat. It was more than five feet high, black, like much else in the Underworld but unique in having three large heads. They were not attractive heads, each with four large fangs protruding from its mouth, the skin all wrinkled and the three large round noses filled with straggly hair coming out of the nostrils. The chins were square and scarred with torn skin but no obvious bleeding; the eyes were bloodshot, giving a manic look to the creature. The body was all muscle, as were the legs; at the back there was a long tail which ended in a serpent's head.

"Get away," yelled the ferryman brandishing his pole as the dog bounded up to him. "Get away, you brute." That made the dog bark and snarl all the more, but his adversary knew him of old and kept fending him off with his pole as he got close by.

"Bark, bark, growl, snarl, woof, snarl, bark, bark, growl, growl," went the dog.

Poke, poke. "Horrible brute." Poke, poke. "Ugly beast, filthy bastard." Poke, poke, was the response.

As this battle was continuing, Death stood impassively watching a scene which he had seen many times before.

"Don't," said Vesta, suddenly moving towards the ferryman. "He's just trying to be friendly."

"No, he's not," the ferryman replied, and poked the dog again with his pole. The animal turned away from the pole as a delayed reaction to Vesta's voice set in. All three heads looked at her with a degree of puzzlement.

"Give us a Mars bar or I'll bite yer bum," he growled.

"That's not very nice," replied Vesta.

"Snarl, snarl, growl, growl."

At that instant, Death pulled out a small object from his cloak. "Here you are. No biting today." He threw the Mars bar at the open mouth on the left which caught it cleanly.

"It's still got the wrapping on," exclaimed Vesta.

"He doesn't care," said Death. "Look at him."

The dog was greedily munching away and soon finished the bar off.

"Give us another or I'll bite yer bum," he said, looking again at Vesta.

"Shut it," Death intervened.

Vesta again slowly moved towards the animal. "Hello, doggy," she said. "Can I stroke you?"

"Watch out," warned Death. "He's dangerous."

"He won't bite me. I like animals." As she got closer to the dog, she smiled. "Nice doggy, nice doggy, you won't hurt me, will you?" she said. "Come on, nice doggy, let me give you a gentle stroke on one of your heads."

The dog was puzzled. No one had ever called him nice doggy before, let alone stroked the top of any of his heads. He stopped barking and snarling and watched the girl as she gently moved her hand to touch the back of his left head.

"There you are," murmured Vesta. "Nice doggy, nice doggy, are you enjoying that?" as she stroked away. "Nice doggy; is that good?"

Now, the anatomy of three-headed dogs is both straightforward and complex. Straightforward because each head has its own brain, complex due to the fact that the three brains can communicate with each other without any obvious sound. The day's new experience set off an immediate internal dialogue along the following lines:

Brain 1: "Who is this nutter? Nice doggy, nice doggy; we've never been called that before. Is she some sort of crackpot or something?"

Brain 2: "Probably been smoking something she shouldn't have."

Brain 1: "Ain't no hope without dope."

Brain 2: "Yea, that's it. What is dope, by the way?"

Brain 1: "Dunno. It's what people say."

Brain 2: "Yea right."

As Head 3 gave a gentle sigh, Brain 3 decided to participate: "That's so nice, so nice. Keep going, little lady. Never had a feeling like this before."

Brain 1: "So what's the feeling like?"

Brain 3: "Wonderful; wonderful."

Brain 1: "Is it better than sex?"

Brain 3: "Oh yes," followed by a further sigh.

Brain 2: "What's sex?"

Brain 1: "Dunno that either. Another one of those things people say."

Brain 2: "So how do you know it's better than sex, Brain 3?"

Brain 3: "It's wonderful, wonderful. It must be."

Brain 1: "Perhaps it is sex?"

Brain 3: "It must be. Wonderful, wonderful." Another long sigh.

Brain 2, sceptically: "I think there are a lot of things we don't know."

Brain 1: "Yea, right."

As the brains were actively engaged, other parts of their upper anatomy cranked into action.

Head 1: "Woof, woof; I want a stroke."

Head 2: "Woof, woof, woof; so do I."

Head 3: "Don't stop. It's wonderful, wonderful."

Head 2: "Woof, woof, woof!"

Vesta stood back and looked at the three heads. "I can't give you all a stroke at the same time. You've got to take it in turns. Twenty seconds each, okay?"

All three heads nodded as she moved round to the right head, which she began to pet.

Head 2: "I'll count. One, two, nineteen, twenty. My turn!"

Head 1: "Woof, growl, growl, woof, growl."

Vesta, looking at Head 2: "That's cheating and very naughty. You miss a turn."

Head 2: "Woof, woof; not fair; sorry, sorry; woof; not fair; woof, woof."

Vesta again stood back and looked sternly at Head 2: "You promise not to do that again?"

Head 2, in a quiet, whimpering tone: "Yes."

"Okay, I'll let you off this time. I do the counting in my head and my decision's final. Is that understood?"

Head 2 nodded.

"And you other two?"

Heads 1 and 3 both woofed and nodded their heads.

"Cool, then I'll continue."

While all this bonding was taking place, Death was scratching his head, feeling perplexed. After a while, he moved over to the ferryman, as he needed to communicate with someone moderately sane. The ferryman was not really sociable, viewing his transport role as merely moving cargo from A to B. It didn't matter to him whether he was moving tins of sardines, bags of cement or human beings. Death, on the other hand, felt he had an important social role. He was meeting new people every day and had to settle them into their new status of being dead – some of them were rather shocked and even got a bit upset. He then had to organise their journey to the Underworld and ensure a proper handover to the relevant authorities. An important job, but one which was best done with a human touch – although the skeleton was unsure if he could actually claim to be included in most definitions of humanity.

Death, first of all, wanted to check that he was not in a dream; the ferryman concurred by shaking his head. Next, it was important to establish that this had never been seen beforehand; his companion agreed. The dog's status then had to be confirmed. Both agreed that the term 'nice doggy' had not been a term used until now; instead words like vicious brute, nasty beast, horrible animal had been viewed as more accurate descriptions. Death was particularly keen on stressing that he was very confused and wondered if he was going down sick; his companion owned up to being equally confused, but hadn't felt any physical symptoms relating to illness. At the suggestion that Vesta might actually be a goddess in disguise with unique powers over aggressive dogs, the ferryman felt this was a matter above his pay grade – he was just unable to pass comment on it.

Meanwhile, Vesta was learning a lot about the nice doggy as she continued to stroke him.

"So, what's your name, doggy?"

"Cerberus."

"That's a good name. Mine's Vesta."

"Woof. That's a good name too."

"Tell me, what do you do?"

"I eat Mars bars and bite people on the bum."

"That's not nice!"

"So what? It's the best way to get a Mars bar."

Vesta decided to change the subject. She and Cerberus clearly didn't see eye to eye on the issue of bites on the bum.

"What I don't understand is why you've got three heads?"

"Because I have."

"But why? Do they do different things?"

The middle head had been doing most of the talking and continued to do so.

"Let me explain how it works," he said in a slightly pompous tone. "We can all do everything – talk, bark, bite, eat, sniff, lick, hear – you name it, we can do it. But over time, our separate abilities have developed. I'm Middly and happen to be the best talker, so I do most of the talking. Lefty here is really good at eating, so he's the one who consumes the food."

"Especially Mars bars," interrupted Lefty.

"Whereas Righty is the best barker and biter, aren't you?" Middly said, looking to his right.

"Woof," said Righty, "especially on the bum."

"So, are those your names – Middly, Lefty and Righty?" Vesta enquired.

"Woof, woof, woof!" went all three heads.

Death had now moved away from the ferryman and approached the two conversationalists.

"Time to go now, little girl. I have to take you to meet Hades."

"Not little girl! I'm called Vesta!" was the snapped reply. Even Cerberus growled at Death.

The skeleton sighed. "Alright. Vesta then."

"That's better. Anyway, who's Hades?"

"The King of the Underworld."

"Woof. He's the boss," Cerberus added helpfully.

"Cool," said Vesta. "Let's go. Bye, Mr Ferryman; hope to see you again." She waved at the hooded figure on the boat, who just stared back. He wasn't ignoring Vesta; indeed, all his attention was firmly fixed on her. It's just his brain worked very slowly and he was still trying to process the suggestion that she might be a goddess in disguise.

"I'm coming too," woofed Cerberus.

"Then make sure you behave," Death responded.

Cerberus had now run in front of the pair and, turning round, looked at Death. "Give us a Mars bar or I'll bite yer bum," he said hopefully.

"Shut it!"

III

THE GODS' COUNCIL

ZEUS WAS TOP GOD. HE SAT ON A THRONE PERCHED on a raised platform holding a small thunderbolt. His cloak was white and he wore a crown of oak leaves. His wife, Hera, sat on her own throne next to his. She was in a pale blue dress and had a small diamond tiara on her head. Her pointy, stern face looked around the Council Chamber as she waited for proceedings to begin.

In front of Zeus and Hera were semi-circular rows of thrones for the other gods, who were gradually taking their seats in a babble of conversation. There was no seating priority in the chamber; gods would sit where they liked.

Mr Bumble was standing next to Zeus with his parchment, which the two of them were studying intently.

"I have listed the names of all the gods on the left-hand side, My Lord Zeus," Mr Bumble explained in his pompous voice. "On the right-hand side I have placed a tick by the names of those gods who have entered the Chamber. For those gods who were given special dispensation by you not to attend, I have placed a horizontal line. You will recall giving me their names yesterday evening, My Lord. Finally, for the remaining gods who have neither a tick nor a horizontal line, I have placed a large cross."

"A very good system, Mr Bumble," replied Zeus, studying the parchment.

"Thank you, My Lord," Mr Bumble beamed. "You will see that there are three names with crosses."

"I'm looking at them now. As usual, my two brothers Hades and Poseidon are absent. No change there, but I have to accept they've got their own kingdoms to run. We should keep inviting them, though."

"There is a third name as well, My Lord."

"I'm looking at it now," Zeus said with a touch of anger in his voice. "Bacchus! Where's Bacchus? Why isn't he here? Where is he?"

"Regrettably, I don't know," Bumble answered.

Zeus looked at his wife. "Do you know where Bacchus is, Hera?" he asked.

"How should I know?" was the unhelpful response. "He's your son, not mine."

Zeus ignored Hera's dig at his former escapades and looked up again at the beadle. "Are you sure Bacchus isn't here?" he asked.

The two of them looked around the room, both shaking their heads.

"I will make enquiries," Mr Bumble said in due course. He moved to the front of the platform and tapped the floor hard a few times with his staff. The chatter died down and all eyes were turned towards the beadle.

"Is Lord Bacchus here? Has anyone seen Lord Bacchus?" Mr Bumble asked in a loud voice.

There were various mutterings from the assembled group as they looked around the room. A helpful comment from the left-hand side suggested he was 'pissed somewhere,' causing some muted laughter.

At the back, Artemis's little gang of younger gods sat together.

"Have a look to see if he's under your throne, Aphy," Artemis said to Aphrodite, who took her quite literally and got on her hands and knees to look for Bacchus.

"No, Arty," Aphy said after having had a good look round. "Not here. What about under yours, Apo?" she said, popping her head up to speak to Apollo, who sat on her other side.

"Have a look for me, darling."

Aphrodite peered under Apollo's throne and then popped her head up again. "No," she said, shaking her head. "Is he under you, Herm?" she enquired, looking at Hermes, who was sitting further along from Apollo.

"No," was the prompt response from the sensible member of the group.

Aphrodite pulled herself up and again sat on her throne. "Not here, Arty," she said in a serious voice, looking at her friend.

"You'd better tell Bumble," was the advice, which Aphrodite again took seriously and shouted out across the chamber with the other gods wondering why she had to say anything.

By now Zeus and the beadle had concluded that Bacchus had gone AWOL. Mr Bumble had to explain to the Top God that this was a British army expression, meaning 'Absent Without Leave'. The two decided there was nothing more to be done about it at that time, so the beadle was given permission by Zeus to leave. He duly marched out of the Council Chamber, bowing as appropriate to various gods and closing the doors firmly behind him.

Meanwhile Hebe was having an altercation with Mars.

Hebe was the Servant Goddess. This did not mean she was

actually a servant, but she carried out various tasks when there were no helpers from the Underworld around. This meant that she was a proper working god and was always on the go – a real busy bee. She was youthful looking with blonde hair in a bun and rosy cheeks. She was small and it would have been possible for about four Hebes to fit into one Mars.

The God of War was sitting next to Hephaestus in the front row. The two of them, together with Hebe, were the children of both Zeus and Hera, so they had been brought up in the same household. Their personalities were, however, very different.

"I don't want white wine," growled Mars as Hebe began to pour him a glass from her jug.

"Well, that's all we've got," Hebe replied.

"I said I don't want white wine. Fetch me some red."

"No!" was the firm response. "You either have white wine or nothing."

"I don't want white wine!" Mars shouted.

"Tuff buns! You'll get nothing then!" Hebe shouted back.

"I said I wanted red wine!"

"Listen, dimwit. There isn't any red wine!"

"But I want some."

"There isn't any, so shut your gob!"

Mars lunged forward to grab hold of his sister, but she side-stepped him. At this stage Hephaestus intervened and restrained Mars. "Hebe," he said. "I'd like a glass of white wine and if you leave a second one here, Mars can try it if he gets thirsty."

"But—" Mars was about to explode, but his brother held him tightly.

"No," said Hephaestus firmly. "Enough!" The two brothers looked at each other and Mars eventually settled back on his throne. Hephaestus was the only god who knew how to control him and they both knew it.

"Thanks, Hebe," the Builder God said after she'd poured the wine and skipped off.

Zeus had been watching his three children and gave a slight sigh of relief when matters had calmed down. He'd seen this scenario play out thousands of times. Mars, angry and violent, was always looking for a fight; Hebe, the pocket-rocket, was forever prepared to take him on; and Hephaestus, the steady and powerful builder, had to intervene to break them up.

"Time to begin," Hera whispered to Zeus, and handed him her sceptre.

Zeus tapped loudly on one of the arms of his throne. The humming of voices died down as the gods looked towards the two thrones on the raised platform.

"Order, order," Zeus said in a loud voice. "I bring the Council Meeting to order. We have a lot to get through today and you should all have an agenda on your thrones." Various voices confirmed this, as did a number of nodding godly heads. "In accordance with normal procedures," Zeus continued, "we will have an open discussion on each agenda item and then I will decide what we will do."

There was a certain amount of muttering in the room, which Artemis took advantage of.

"Aphy, shout out that we want a vote," she whispered to Aphrodite.

"Do we?"

"Yes."

"Okay." Then in a loud voice, she called out, "We want a vote!" She looked at Apollo, who also followed with, "We want a vote!" The two started chanting away while clapping their hands: "We want a vote! We want a vote! We want a vote!" After a few seconds it was clear none of the other gods were joining in, with a number of them looking disapprovingly at the small group on the back row.

Before the chant for democracy had a chance of fading out naturally, Zeus threw his small thunderbolt at Aphrodite. It landed under her throne, let off a loud bang and scorched her legs for a few seconds. She cried out in surprise, tears started flowing and, turning to Artemis, she was given a large hug and help rubbing her calves. Apollo, who was unharmed, immediately stopped his chanting and sat meekly back on his throne.

"Quiet, you children," shouted Zeus angrily at the back row. "To repeat – we will have an open discussion on each agenda item and then I will decide what we do. That means I, Zeus, Top God, no one else. Do I make myself clear?" His fierce eyes looked around the room, which was silent except for a few very quiet sobs from Aphrodite in Artemis's arms. "Good," said Zeus after an appropriate time. "Let's get on."

The Council Meeting then spent a considerable amount of time discussing a vast range of matters. These included relations between Olympus and the Underworld, relations between Olympus and the Seas, the melting of the polar icecaps, the question of whether Andorra should declare war on the United States, China and Russia at the same time. Mars was particularly keen on starting this fight, but better counsels prevailed. He was, however, allowed to continue supporting the activities of various guerrilla movements in both South America and Africa. The plans for a new palace for Demeter were discussed, with Hephaestus giving a detailed presentation with architectural drawings and sundry surveyors' reports. Who should become the next Prime Minister of Bulgaria involved a heated debate between supporters of the two main political parties, whereas the election of the next President of the United States surprisingly involved near total agreement.

Meanwhile Aphrodite recovered from the shock of the thunderbolt very quickly.

"You didn't join in," she whispered indignantly to Artemis.

"I didn't need to, Aphy. You did a really brilliant job without me."

"Did I?"

"Absolutely," said Artemis reassuringly. "You were brilliant. Anyway, we need to split our resource, not involve all our troops in one go."

"What do you mean, Arty?"

"You'll see. I'll take the lead next time. Just remember you were fab today."

"Thanks, you're a real friend."

After a long discussion on whether Six Mile Bottom, a hamlet near Cambridge in England, should be allowed to declare independence as a sovereign nation, the Council addressed the final agenda item.

This coming Sunday the Men's World Cup Final was being played between the German and Brazilian football teams. This was a matter of intense interest to a number of the male gods, who viewed it as the most important item on the Council's agenda that day. Many of the female gods, though, couldn't care less. Artemis was not one of them, since she considered the final as having important points of principle associated with it, which she intended to exploit.

As soon as Zeus introduced the subject, Artemis was on her feet.

"My Lord Zeus," she said. "Could you please tell us if the referee for this final will be a woman?"

The Top God looked perplexed, unsure what the point of the question was. However, any confusion he had was superseded by a roar from Mars who was also on his feet.

"What a bloody stupid question that is!" he screamed aloud. "Of course the referee won't be a woman! This is a man's game; nothing to do with women! The best place for women is at home in the kitchen and they should keep out of men's affairs. What's more, Zeus, you shouldn't allow the female gods to say anything about this match; it's male god business and the females should just shut up. We males don't get involved in their affairs, like knitting and cooking, so they shouldn't poke their noses into ours!"

By the time Mars had finished his face was bright red. The response in the room was precisely what Artemis had hoped for, expecting that Mars or someone else would voice such views. There was general uproar from many of the female gods as Mars was called a fascist, a male chauvinist, a pig and many other such 'friendly' names. Hera, in particular, was most indignant at her son's comments and voiced her displeasure at him, which he ignored. A number of the male gods such as Hermes also disagreed with the God of War's opinions. Even his brother, Hephaestus, was seen to be shaking his head as Mars spoke.

Mars angrily sat down and folded his arms in defiance at the din he had caused. After an appropriate time, Zeus called the meeting to order. Artemis had stayed on her feet during Mars's rant, looking very calm. Zeus eyed her before speaking.

"Do you want to reply to what you've just heard, Artemis?"

"Thank you, My Lord Zeus," she responded politely. "I won't waste any time on addressing the absurd sexist comments made by my half-brother." Mars tried to leap up and shout, but Hephaestus held him back. "My reason for asking the question about the referee is that we did decide many months ago to permit female officials to be involved in these finals and I was just making the natural enquiry as to whether one would be the referee in the last game. Furthermore, I'd like to enquire if the women officials are paid the same amount as the men?"

"Of course they're not!" shouted Mars angrily before his brother put a hand over his mouth and whispered, "Shut up; enough!"

"Well, I don't really know. Does anyone else know?" said Zeus, looking around the Chamber. There was a lot of shaking of heads and mumblings of the word 'no'.

Throughout this entire discussion, Athene had sat quietly

in her normal place on the right-hand side of the Chamber. She knew exactly what Artemis was trying to do and felt it was time to intervene.

"My Lord Zeus," she said, addressing her father as she stood up. "Perhaps I could say a few words?"

"Certainly, Athene," replied the Top God, relieved that his most intelligent daughter should decide to contribute.

"Thank you," Athene answered. "It seems to me that we have a short-term issue about this game on Sunday, and a longer-term matter, which I'll come on to later. For Sunday's game, I suggest we let the World Cup authorities make the decision about who will referee the match without any involvement by us. This should be fairly easy for all sides to accept because, while Artemis is quite right about the role of women officials in this tournament, neither of the two lady referees initially chosen are available. One of them ran into a goalpost and fractured her skull in the first five minutes of her inaugural match – I believe she's only just got out of hospital, still heavily bandaged up. The other one in her first match proceeded to red card all twenty-two players before half an hour had elapsed; this caused huge embarrassment to the authorities and she herself was subsequently red-carded and sent home early. So, whatever we think, there are only men available to referee the match."

Zeus decided to leap in at that stage. "Right," he said firmly. "That's clear. No need for further debate on the referee. We leave it to the authorities to decide, accepting it will have to be a man." He looked at Artemis, who had by now sat down. She smiled and nodded her head.

All eyes now turned to Athene once more since she was still on her feet.

"Perhaps I may continue," the goddess spoke. "I now come to the longer-term considerations. It's clear Artemis is raising some very relevant points about men and women's sport. In fact, these are matters which really apply to all aspects of society, but I propose just to focus on sport in my comments. Questions such as the involvement of men and women in each other's sports, the status of women's games vis a vis men's – are they equal, should they be equal and so on? Finally, should women be paid the same as men? All these are important matters, which need to be addressed, but I would suggest in a different forum."

"What forum would you suggest?" asked Zeus.

"I would propose a small working party to address all these matters and then to come back and make a presentation to another Gods' Council in a few months' time. Although the focus should be on sporting matters, it is inevitable that wider societal issues may also be addressed. I believe Artemis would be the ideal chairperson for this group, which should be no more than six or eight gods. My Lady Hera, if she is willing, should sit on this group as Artemis's counsellor. I think the two of them could jointly decide on the other members of this working party. In my view, this should also consist of some of our male gods, but perhaps in a minority role. That is my proposal, My Lord Zeus."

The whole Chamber had listened to Athene in respectful silence and at the end of her speech there was a lot of head nodding, and general murmurings of assent. This did not include Mars, who was still silenced by Hephaestus's hand over his mouth.

Following a quick glance from Zeus, Hera responded, "As usual, Athene, you have come up with a very wise suggestion and I agree wholeheartedly with your proposal. Artemis, have you any comments?"

Artemis smiled and said she agreed. She had got exactly what she wanted – a forum to press women's rights and equality, all achieved without any prior discussion with Athene, whom she was slightly afraid of because of her standing in the Olympian hierarchy.

Athene had remained on her feet, and after Hera and Artemis had spoken, all eyes focused on her again.

"One final point, My Lord Zeus. We haven't yet discussed who should win Sunday's match between Germany and Brazil. I myself am neutral between the two, but there is a tradition in football that says something about it being a simple game, consisting of twenty-two men chasing a ball for 90 minutes, which always ends with the Germans winning. I believe in upholding tradition, so I propose that Germany wins."

Athene then sat down and said no more as the Chamber started a long debate on the desired outcome of the match. At the end of two hours of contradictory discussion, Zeus made his decision: "Tradition says that *Germany wins.*"

After the Council meeting, Zeus called Iris over to him. Iris was the Messenger Goddess. She had long auburn hair and wore an elegant flowing dress with the seven colours of the rainbow. Her cloak was golden with wings on either side.

"Swift-footed Iris," said Zeus as she approached him. "Kindly find Bacchus and give him this message from me."

"You look annoyed, Zeus. I suspect Bacchus isn't going to like this," Iris commented with a wry smile.

"Hear me out..." He paused before continuing: "'Subject – Non-attendance at Council Meeting: I am Zeus, most powerful of all the gods; I rule over Olympus, the earth, the moon, the planets, the stars and the entire universe. All other gods quiver and shake in my presence. I am great and mighty, for I can bring disaster and destruction to any who oppose me. My word is law and I will not be defied by any other, especially a lazy, good-for-nothing, son of a skunk, junior god such as you. I therefore demand that you attend me at my palace before sunset today, when you will humbly acknowledge your wicked defiance and crave my forgiveness. If you do not do this, I will deliver terrible punishments on you. Your stomach and bowels will be filled with flesh-eating serpents, your ears and nose with cockroaches and spiders, your eyes will be torn out by immense rats, vultures will tear at your arms and legs which will be visited with terrible diseases, your groin will be fed on by crocodiles and your hair will be permanently on fire. All this will cause great pain and you will scream with agony, begging for my forgiveness, which I will never give. These punishments will continue for eternity, after which time you will be sent to the Underworld. There, each day, you will be impaled on sharp spikes and have your legs and arms torn off while your belly will be opened up and fed to hyenas and jackals. All this, I, Zeus, will do to you, if you again defy my command to attend me, the most powerful of all the gods whose rule is absolute.'"

"Have you got that?" continued Zeus.

Iris nodded before replying, "Three points of detail, Zeus."

"What?"

"Firstly, who's the skunk?"

"What skunk?"

"You called Bacchus the son of a skunk. I wondered if you, as his father, were the skunk, or was it his mother, or have you decided Bacchus isn't your son, so the skunk refers to his mystery dad?"

"Did I call him the son of a skunk?"

"Yes."

"Oh, well, take that bit out."

"Fine. Secondly, I don't quiver and shake in your presence, so you can't say all other gods are quiverers and shakers, unless you only mean male gods."

"Are you sure you don't quiver and shake, Iris?"

"Quite sure."

"Um…" mused Zeus. "I'm sure you do really, you just don't know it."

"What do you mean?"

"It's psychological. You're doing it, but you're not aware of it."

"I think I would be."

"I'm sure deep down you do."

"Psychological, you say. Well, I'd better tell the other gods who don't know they're quiverers and shakers."

"Who would they be?"

"All of them."

"What!"

"Third point. Eternity lasts for ever, so you can't talk about all these punishments after eternity."

"Can't I?"

"No."

"Well, just keep it in. Bacchus won't notice."

"Right. Now, a more general point, Zeus. Isn't the objective of all of this to make sure Bacchus attends future Council Meetings and any other appointments? If so, wouldn't it be better if you popped round to see him later today to have a friendly father-and-son chat, instead of making all these threats? I don't think he deliberately missed today's meeting; he was probably busy or pissed as someone said. If you really want to ensure he attends future meetings, create a system. I'd suggest telling Nell Quickly and she'll deliver him in person if necessary."

"Certainly not, Iris," Zeus replied. "I know how to handle Bacchus. What's more, I will inflict those terrible punishments on him, if he isn't grovelling at my feet before sunset."

Iris viewed Zeus sceptically for a full fifteen seconds.

"Then I'd better be going," she eventually said.

"Yes."

"Right. Before I go, how about slightly modifying your message? Change some words, tone it down a bit?"

"No."

"Sure?"

"Quite sure?"

"Okay; I'll be off then."

"Good."

"Before going, I just want to check you're quite, quite certain about your message?"

"Yes."

"Fine. I'm going." Iris didn't move. "Not just one or two teeny-weeny changes?"

"No."

"I see. Well, I'll be off." She started moving away and then turned round. "Last chance?" she said hopefully.

"Iris, please go!" Zeus replied with some force – so she did.

IV

THE DOG
AND DUCK

THE DOG AND DUCK TAVERN OR PUBLIC HOUSE was on the south side of Mount Olympus within walking distance of the gods' palaces. It was a stone and timber-built structure with dark wooden beams between white walls and small latticed windows. It stood in a pleasant cherry orchard of half a dozen acres. The tavern had been built many years ago by Hephaestus for Bacchus, the God of Wine and general intoxication, who was the proprietor. Most of the detailed overseeing was, however, carried out by Mistress Quickly since Bacchus was invariably either recovering from a hangover or in the process of getting another one. Getting hangovers was viewed as being Bacchus's main function in the efficient running of the tavern.

Mistress Quickly was a tall, slim lady of uncertain years. She had a narrow face, a narrow neck, a narrow body with narrow arms and narrow legs. Her hair was a mixture of white and grey but always kept in a tidy bun at the back. She usually wore a pink dress with a light blue apron and a pair of elegant silver sandals which Bacchus had once given her as a sign of his appreciation for all her hard work. At the time, she was also about to hit him over the head with a frying pan for being sick all over the kitchen floor, but this unexpected token slowed the pan's descent to a full stop about three inches above the god's head.

The Dog and Duck was an important part of Olympian social life. Bacchus had always insisted that it should be a place where all gods and mortals could mix freely. The mortals were not actually mortal anymore but were inhabitants of the Underworld who had come to work for the gods on Mount Olympus. Some had become permanent residents, such as Mr and Mrs Bumble and Mistress Quickly, while others like Norbert were on temporary assignments. Now, it was generally accepted amongst the gods that Mistress Quickly was the most competent of all the no-longer-mortal mortals. Not only did she keep Bacchus in order, at least some of the time, but she also ensured the efficient running of the tavern. She had had previous experience in the hospitality sector, having been the hostess of the Boar's Head Tavern down Eastcheap in the City of London. In this former role she had come across all sorts of villains and ruffians and considered the clientele of the Dog and Duck to be little different to that in her former life.

On the day of the Gods' Council, a handsome golden eagle was standing in front of the tavern drinking prosecco from a large bowl on the ground.

"Are you alright, Lennie?" asked Mistress Quickly as she came out of the front door holding a watering can for the rose beds under the windows.

"I'm on strike," said the eagle, looking up.

"Oh, why's that?"

"I'm protesting against the name of this establishment."

"Why? What's wrong with it?"

"It's called the Dog and Duck, that's what's wrong with it."

"Seems to me to be a perfectly good name. Lots of pubs and taverns are called the Dog and Duck. It's like the George and Dragon, the Crown and Anchor, the Red Rose – very common names for drinking establishments in London Town when I worked there."

"Huh!" replied Lennie. "You're just being difficult. You know it's not right."

"What I do know, Lennie, is this is the ninety-seventh time you've been on strike on this matter since I came to Olympus. It's a waste of time. Nothing ever happens, so give it a break."

"This time it's different."

"Why?"

"You'll see."

"What will I see?

Lennie looked suspiciously at Mistress Quickly. "I'm not sure which side you're on in this dispute, so I'm not going to disclose the strike committee's plans. You might pass them on to Bacchus."

"Suit yourself." Mistress Quickly shrugged and moved over to the rose beds with her watering can. "What do you think, Beetle?" she said to a small tortoise eating a lettuce in one of the beds.

"Don't say anything, Beetle," shouted Lennie, hopping over. "Nell Quickly's a spy."

"I thought we were all friends," said the tortoise, looking up.

"Not today," was the eagle's response.

"Are you on strike too?" asked the hostess.

"Yes!" Lennie firmly answered on Beetle's behalf.

"Am I?"

"Yes."

"Oh, okay, if you say so. I don't mind."

"Do you know why you're on strike, Beetle?" asked Mistress Quickly.

"No."

"Yes, you do," snapped Lennie.

Beetle took another mouthful of lettuce and then looked up. "Can you remind me please, Lennie? I've forgotten."

Lennie's exasperation levels were beginning to mount. He pointed with his beak at the tavern entrance. "Look up at that sign over the door. What do you see? Don't answer. You see a fine painting of you, a tortoise, and me, an eagle. Then look above it. Look at the words. What do they say? I'll tell you – they say the Dog and Duck."

"So, what's wrong?"

"What's wrong? What's wrong? I'll tell you what's wrong!" the eagle shouted. "I'm an eagle, who's been named after a lion, but I'm called a duck! You, Beetle, you've been given the name of an insect, but you're actually a tortoise although you're called a dog! That's what's wrong! Do you understand now?"

Beetle looked up at Mistress Quickly for some help. "It's all very confusing," he muttered. "I thought I was a dog."

"I give up!" screamed Lennie. "There's no use me talking to the two of you! I give up," and he hopped back to the prosecco bowl to take a long sip.

Mistress Quickly thought it was time to bring the strike to an end. "Look, Lennie," she said firmly. "You know and I know you're an eagle. We also know Beetle's a tortoise. But Bacchus thinks you're a duck and, since he's a god, if he says you're a duck, then you're a duck. It doesn't do any harm, so just accept it."

"No," was the response.

"Why not?"

"Reason one. Ever heard of the saying, 'if it looks like a duck, walks like a duck, quacks like a duck, then it probably is a duck'?"

"So what?"

"Well, I don't look, walk and quack like a duck. That's because I'm an eagle, not a duck. *Comprenez vous?*"

"So what's your second reason? And don't speak in foreign to me. I'm a London lass, born and bred."

"The second reason is very simple. We can easily change the name of the tavern to the Eagle. You know that just like all these other names you reeled off, the Eagle is a very common name for a public house. In fact, the Eagle pub is one of the most famous places in Cambridge; it's where all these scientists announced the discovery of the double helix. Don't you remember?"

"I don't know what you're on about. Double helix, never heard of it. It wasn't in any of Mr Shakespeare's plays, was it?"

"Never mind," said Lennie. "All I'm saying is we should change the name of the pub to the Eagle."

"And what about Beetle? I've never heard of a tavern being called the Eagle and Tortoise before. It doesn't sound right at all."

"Can we forget the Tortoise bit and just call it the Eagle?"

"No, Lennie; no. We're called the Dog and Duck and that's our name. It's not going to change whatever you do or say. So, *comprenez vous* too? Come on; let's just stop all this nonsense and call off the strike now and get back to normal."

"None of our demands have been met. Our labour continues to be withdrawn. No surrender!"

"Can you please tell me, Lennie, what this labour is? What do you actually do all day other than eat, drink and fly around from time to time?"

"I find your question so insulting that I refuse to answer it."

"So, you're going to continue with your strike?"

"Yes!"

"What about you, Beetle?"

"Yes, he is," Lennie answered on his behalf.

"Very well then. If you withdraw your labour, you'll receive no wages. So, I'll be taking this bowl of prosecco away and you won't be eating that game pie I've been baking for you. As far as you're concerned, Beetle, there'll be no more lettuce for you." Mistress Quickly took hold of the bowl and started walking to the tavern door.

"I'm no longer on strike," said Beetle.

"Typical unfair, mean, bullying capitalist behaviour," shrieked Lennie as Mistress Quickly continued to walk away. As she got to the porch, he continued, "However, in the circumstances, the strike is temporarily suspended pending further union consultations."

"Very glad to hear it," said Mistress Quickly, turning round and replacing the prosecco bowl. "I'll go and get that game pie; also, some more lettuce for you, Beetle."

"Thank you," the tortoise courteously replied.

Mistress Quickly had only been in her kitchen five minutes when there was a loud screech at the window. Looking up, she saw Lennie hovering with his wings outstretched trying to catch her attention.

"What is it, Lennie?" she asked.

"Iris is coming."

"I'll come."

By the time Mistress Quickly was out of the front door, Iris, who was wearing a golden cloak with golden wings, was slowing down, having run all the way at speed from the Council Chamber.

"Hi, Nell; is Bacchus around?" she said.

"Why do you always run everywhere, Iris? Being a goddess, you can whoosh around the place in a couple of seconds."

"I know, but I only like whooshing when I have long journeys to take. That's actually true of most of us gods. Around Olympus, I prefer to run. It keeps me fit. Also, I've got a new pair of trainers Hebe brought me from her last trip."

"Very stylish," Nell Quickly said, looking at Iris's red running shoes. "Do you want a drink of anything?"

"Nah, thanks. I'd better see Bacchus pronto. Zeus is on the warpath."

Mistress Quickly sighed. "Now what's he done?"

"You'll hear soon enough. Where is he?"

"Over in the orchard, no doubt fast asleep."

"Had a few too many?"

"Very likely a lot too many."

"I'll go and look for him."

The eagle shrieked. "I'll come with you," he said.

"I will too," Beetle added.

Iris smiled. "Hi, Lennie; hi, Beetle. Sorry, I didn't see you earlier. Best if you stay here with Nell. This is gods' business."

"Top secret, is it?" the tortoise enquired.

"Top secret," Iris agreed, laughing as she set off on a light jog towards the orchard. "Bye, everyone," she said with a wave.

When Bacchus had been a young god, he was clean-shaven with long light brown hair. He had had a slim physique, which was little affected by all the wine he drank. As he got older, he began to grow a beard while becoming short-haired on top. This was kept in order by Mistress Quickly shaving his head on a weekly basis, although he wouldn't let her near his beard. The result was a head that was tidy on top but a bit like a dense forest in the jungle down below. Overall, he looked a bit of a mess.

The other obvious change in Bacchus was the weight he had put on. He was now definitely plump with a large pot-belly. This change had started when he decided that he wouldn't just be the God of Wine but also the god of all the other drinks available. In particular, he discovered beer, which he proceeded to sample in great quantities, much of it remaining in his expanding torso. He was especially fond of north European beers from Germany, Denmark, Holland and, what he still referred to as, Britannicus.

The previous evening, a new beer had been delivered to the

Dog and Duck. It was called Hanseatic Headbanger and was promoted as having a very high alcohol content. That morning Bacchus had decided to sample it before releasing it for general consumption to the rest of Olympus. It was a beautiful day, so he and Mistress Quickly had carried a number of jugs into the cherry orchard, where he sat down on his favourite deckchair. He also brought a large poster which had been provided as marketing material. It was a picture of two young blonde German frauleins in bikinis each holding a large glass of beer under the slogan 'Want A Bang, Get a Headbanger'. Sitting peacefully holding a large beer glass with the poster in front of him, Bacchus set to work.

Iris found him many hours later, fast asleep and snoring like a rhinoceros.

"Wake up, Bacchus," she said, standing over him.

There was no answer, so she raised her voice and repeated, "Wake up, Bacchus."

There was still no response, so now she shook him hard and shouted in his ear, "Wake up, you silly fool! Wake up!"

This time Iris got a response as he jolted forward, waving his arms around. "What's going on?" he asked all bleary-eyed. "Oh, it's you, Iris. What do you want?"

"I've got a message for you from Zeus."

"Let me get up first." He pulled himself up from his deckchair and immediately toppled forwards onto the poster of the two German frauleins. Iris had to help him get off the ground and steady himself. "I need a drink," he said, moving over to the table with all the beer jugs."

"What is it?" Iris asked.

"It's called Hanseatic Headbanger. Look at the poster on the ground. It's a new beer which arrived yesterday and I've been trying it out. I have to say, Iris, it's bloody marvellous. Best beer I've had in years."

"So how much have you had?"

Bacchus looked in the jugs. He had started out with six and only one was left, half full.

"Only this one left and there's just enough for a pint each for the two of us."

"Not for me." Iris waved it away. "So, you've had five jugs yourself?"

"Five and a half, to be precise," responded Bacchus.

"And how many pints are in a jug?"

"Four."

"Four! That means you've drunk twenty-two pints! How can you, you nutter?"

"It's my job. I'm used to it."

"Tosh!"

"Look, Iris, don't get annoyed. I've had a hard day. Come and sit down next to me and tell me what Zeus wants."

The messenger perched on a second chair next to Bacchus, took a deep breath to calm herself and then continued with the business in hand. "You do know there was a Gods' Council meeting today?"

"I have a vague recollection," replied Bacchus.

"And you weren't there?"

"No, I was busy here."

"And you never thought of letting Zeus know beforehand, checking with him that it was okay not to be there?"

Bacchus yawned. "So, what's Zeus's message?" he asked, closing his eyes.

"I'll give it to you word for word... 'Subject – Non-attendance at Council Meeting: I am Zeus, most powerful of all the gods; I rule over Olympus, the earth, the moon, the planets, the stars and the entire universe. All other gods quiver and shake in my presence. I am great and mighty for I can bring disaster and destruction to any who oppose me. My word is law and I will not be defied by any other, especially a lazy, good-for-nothing junior god such as you."

Bacchus's left eye opened.

"I demand that you attend me in my palace before sunset today, when you will humbly acknowledge your wicked defiance and crave my forgiveness. If you do not do this, I will deliver terrible punishments on you. Your stomach and bowels will be filled with flesh-eating serpents, your ears and nose with cockroaches and spiders, your eyes will be torn out by immense rats, vultures will tear at your arms and legs which will be visited with terrible diseases, your groin will be fed on by crocodiles and your hair will be permanently on fire."

The right eye now opened.

"All this will cause great pain and you will scream with agony, begging for my forgiveness, which I will never give. These punishments will continue for eternity, after which time you will be sent to the Underworld."

The two eyes rolled.

"There, each day, you will be impaled on sharp spikes and have your legs and arms torn off while your belly will be opened up and fed to hyenas and jackals. All this, I, Zeus, will do to you, if you again defy my command to attend me, the most powerful of all the gods whose rule is absolute.'"

"Is that all?" Bacchus enquired nonchalantly.

"Isn't that enough?"

"Right; here's my message to Zeus. 'Subject – Response: I am the great Lord Bacchus, god of wine, beer, cider, spirits and all other alcoholic beverages. All other gods quiver and shake in my presence when they have consumed too much of my fine products. Zeus is a grizzled, pompous old tosspot with a face like a hippopotamus who can go stick his head up his own backside. I am busy working today and haven't got time for any of his stupid nonsense. What's more, no more threats from now on. If I get any further messages from him, he will be banned from the Dog and Duck indefinitely, so there'll be no further opportunities to chat up new female crumpet from the

THE DOG AND DUCK

Underworld. In addition, all future deliveries of fine wines to his palace will be cancelled.' Tell him that."

"Are you sure?" asked Iris. "Wouldn't it be better to go and see him and say, 'Sorry, Dad,' then hand him a decent bottle of wine and suggest the two of you open it and have a nice friendly chat?"

"No! I know how to handle him. It's about time he was told what we all think of him."

"You mean what you think of him."

Bacchus shrugged.

"On a matter of detail, how are you going to do these things to Zeus if your stomach and bowels are being attacked by flesh-eating serpents, you've got rats tearing out your eyes, and you're sitting on a spike with no arms and legs?"

"That's just a detail," Bacchus replied.

"Well then," Iris said as she stood up. "I'd better be off to see Zeus. No second thoughts?"

Bacchus shook his head.

"Sure?"

"I'm sure."

"Last chance?"

Again a shake of the head.

"Another last chance?"

"No."

"Third and final last chance?"

"No."

"Okay. Bye. Best of luck," Iris said hopefully before turning round and running off at speed to deliver Bacchus's message.

V

THE KING OF THE
UNDERWORLD

IT TOOK ABOUT TWENTY MINUTES TO WALK TO Hades' palace. Vesta spent this time looking around at her new home. The Underworld was a fairly dismal place, full of large barren rocks with no greenery. The sky was completely covered in grey clouds, but there were streaks of red, as if parts of it were on fire. Vesta assumed the red streaks must provide the light, but there wasn't much of it. Dusk was a permanent feature of the Underworld.

During the walk, she learned from Death that people came to the Underworld in the same condition they were in before they died. This explained why, for example, anyone who was killed in a house fire showed no signs of burns. Similarly, if your head had been chopped off, it was restored to the rest of your body in the afterlife.

After emerging through a narrow passage of high stones, Hades' palace came into sight.

"Wow!" Vesta exclaimed as she looked at a huge golden building in front of her. "Is that where Mr Hades lives?"

"Best for you to call him Lord Hades," Death replied. "But yes, that's his palace."

"Woof, woof," went Cerberus. "Big house; that's because he's the boss."

The three walked up the steps leading to a large golden archway. Once inside, they were in a spacious hall, illuminated by candles. Death led the way to an open doorway at the far end, followed by Cerberus with Vesta in the rear, looking around her with a mixture of interest and amazement. Everywhere was made of gold – the walls, ceilings, floors, windowpanes. She had never seen so much gold in her short life.

"You've not spoken to me yet," a voice suddenly hissed.

Vesta looked in front of her and saw the head of Cerberus's tail a couple of feet from her face. She didn't really like snakes, but this one smiled and winked at her.

"Oh, I'm sorry," she said in reply. "Do you have a name?"

"I do, but it's a proper name, not like Lefty, Righty or Middly."

"That's good. Are you going to tell me what it is?"

The snake smiled again and then replied, "I'm called Audrey."

"Audrey!" exclaimed Vesta. "But I thought you were a boy dog, not a girl dog."

"I ... we are, but that doesn't stop me being called Audrey."

"I suppose not," muttered Vesta, not entirely convinced.

"Anyway," Audrey continued. "I want you to know that I'm the real brains of the whole outfit."

"That's cool. Do the others know?"

"Ssh! ... No one knows. It's a secret, just between you and me."

"Cool."

By now, they had all walked into the throne room. It was

a large open space with nothing in it but a throne on a raised platform at the far end. Directly opposite was a small stool about ten feet away.

Hades sat bolt upright on the throne staring directly ahead at the three entrants to the room. He wore a grey tunic with a golden robe. He was of medium build but muscular. His long grey hair and beard were in curls but tidily kept. His face was stern, with penetrative eyes and a pale complexion. Not an unkind-looking god, but one who could be very firm.

As the three approached the throne, Cerberus bounded forward and began barking at Hades.

"Woof, woof. Give us a Mars bar or I'll bite yer bum," he said hopefully.

The god turned his gaze towards the dog and stared at him. Cerberus stared back and gave another woof. Hades continued to look at him but remained silent.

"Woof, woof," went Cerberus again, flinching, as he turned round and slunk back. "Just joking, boss. Just joking."

"Not a clever strategic move," Audrey murmured to Vesta as the tail wagged in her direction. "No brains, these heads."

Hades looked back at the group.

"This is Vesta, Hades," Death said. "Newly arrived."

"Ah yes," the god replied, looking into Vesta's face. "We've been expecting you, Vesta. I have your report here." He pulled a large parchment from his tunic and opened it up.

For the first time since arriving in the Underworld, Vesta began to feel nervous. The fact that Hades already had a report on her was really worrying and suddenly a whole mass of thoughts went through her head. Who could have written it? What was in it? Was she going to be punished for all the naughty things she had done in her nearly fourteen years on earth? In fact, what were all the naughty things she'd done? The list seemed endless. She was interrupted from these contemplations by Hades continuing to speak.

"Please sit down," he said, pointing to the stool. "We need to have a little chat."

"Thank you, sir," murmured Vesta, taking her seat. She looked around and saw that Death had left, but Cerberus was sitting quietly on the floor between her and the throne.

"Death always departs quietly, with no ceremony, once he's brought new arrivals to me," Hades said, realising that Vesta had noticed his absence. "You're very unlikely to meet him again. People only die once." At this point Hades leant forwards and, for the first time, smiled at Vesta. "Now, what I'd like you to do is explain in your own words the events which caused you to come to my Kingdom."

"Woof, woof," Cerberus barked, "I can answer that one. Vesta came here on the ferry with Death and the ferryman."

Hades sighed. "Thank you, Cerberus. I know that. What I want to know is—"

"I know what you mean," Vesta interrupted, feeling a bit more confident. "You want to know how I came to meet Mr Death."

"Precisely," said Hades, giving Cerberus a look, which equated to Death saying 'shut it.'

"Another strategic cock-up by the three heads," Audrey again muttered to Vesta.

"Well," Vesta began, "I was on this school trip to Iceland and one day we decided to go in a hot air balloon. I was the first into the basket, but before the others could get in with the pilot, there was a massive gust of wind. The rope wasn't tied up very well, so the balloon set off with only me in it. I didn't have a clue how to operate it, so it just blew towards this volcano in the distance and I couldn't do anything about it. Eventually, it was right over the volcano and then began to lose height. We were told this was a volcano that hadn't blown up for over a hundred years, but just as I was going down, it decided to erupt. The next thing I knew was Mr Death was helping me to my feet and then bringing me here."

Hades nodded. "I'm sorry, but thank you for telling me, Vesta," he said.

"Woof, woof," went Cerberus, deciding to contribute once more. "You won't do that again."

There was a dead silence as Hades and Vesta stared at Cerberus in some bewilderment.

"Very helpful, Cerberus," the god said sarcastically, and Cerberus once more got the feeling that his involvement had not quite hit the mark, a matter again confirmed in whispers by Audrey.

"Let's progress," continued Hades, pulling out a second parchment from his tunic. "We've got to decide what you're going to do between now and forever."

"What do you mean?" enquired Vesta.

"What job you're going to do. Everyone in the Underworld has to work. Let me see what vacancies are currently on offer." Hades looked at the new parchment for a while. "How about torturing?"

"Torturing!" shrieked Vesta. "What's that?"

"Working in the Torturing Department. Doing things like burning people, pulling their limbs off, impaling them on sharp spikes, boiling them in water or oil. That sort of thing."

Vesta shuddered. "I don't think I'd like that," she muttered.

"Let's look for something else then," said Hades, continuing to look at his parchment. "We've got a number of requirements for miners."

"Miners?"

"Yes. With all the new arrivals, there's a never-ending need to provide them with accommodation and that sort of thing. You could work either underground in the tunnels or in one of the quarries. The work's quite demanding, hacking away at rock faces all day. Alternatively, you could be part of the transport network carrying large rocks from the mines to the building sites."

"How big are the rocks?" Vesta asked.

"About the size of Cerberus, probably weighing three times as much."

"I'm only little," said Vesta. "I don't think I'm strong enough."

"You could be right," Hades agreed, eyeing her small frame. "I suppose that also precludes working on a building site; currently the only roles vacant are carrying large iron girders around."

"I don't think I could do that."

Hades again looked at his parchment. "Here's something you might be able to do," he said after a minute. "You could join the trapeze group."

"What's that?" enquired Vesta hesitantly.

"There's an idea we should set up a trapeze group to provide some light entertainment. You must have seen them at a circus, where people swing through the air from one trapeze to another. It's best to be small; fat people seem to fall to the ground a lot."

"Do they have nets underneath them?"

"No," replied Hades. "They're already dead, so they can't die again. It hurts when they fall a hundred feet to the ground, but I can patch them up afterwards."

Vesta thought carefully for a while. She worried that she was turning down all sorts of jobs and that if she didn't choose one, she'd be allocated something even worse. However, the idea of falling off a trapeze every day was just too much to bear, so she shook her head. "I'm sorry, sir," she said. "I can't take heights after my experience with the balloon."

Hades looked again at his parchment. "Alright, you'd better go to the Kitchens. Do you like cooking?"

Vesta breathed a sigh of relief. "I'm not very good at it," she replied. "But I'm keen to learn."

"Agreed then. I'll arrange for you to be taken to the Kitchens tomorrow morning. Now, I think it's time for you to go to the Girls' Quarters. Cerberus will take you."

"Woof," the dog barked, looking up.

"Can I please ask a question before I go?"

Hades nodded.

"Is Cerberus your pet?"

"No," replied Hades.

"Can I have him then?"

"No. He's no one's pet. His job is to guard the gate to the Underworld. Anyone who tries to leave gets bitten."

"On the bum," Cerberus added.

"Then can I be his friend?" Vesta asked.

"He doesn't have any friends. He doesn't need them."

"What's a friend?" Cerberus asked.

"Someone you're nice to," Vesta replied.

"Why do I want to be nice to people?"

"Because they're nice back. They give you Mars bars and stroke you on the head."

"Woof, woof. I like that."

"Look, Vesta," Hades interrupted. "No one wants to be Cerberus's friend. He doesn't need a friend. He's got a job to do and that's why he's here. If you want to be nice to him, that's acceptable to me, but don't expect him to be nice back. He doesn't like people. He bites them and he's good at it."

"On the bum," Cerberus once more contributed.

"Cool," said Vesta pensively. She thought for a while and then looked up again at Hades. "Can I ask another question, sir?"

"One more and that's it," Hades responded patiently.

"If Cerberus's job is to guard the gate, what happens when he's not there? Who's stopping loads of people leaving right now as we're sitting here?"

There was a dead silence as Hades and Cerberus looked at each other. In thousands of years Cerberus had been running around the Underworld carrying out all sorts of errands for Hades and neither of them had thought of this matter. Then some girl, who's not yet fourteen, comes along and asks the most obvious of questions.

"Woof; that's a good question," Cerberus eventually said.

Hades breathed out slowly, thinking how to respond. He decided to establish some accountability in the room. "So, what's the answer, Cerberus?" he asked.

"Woof, woof. Isn't that a question for you, boss?" was the hopeful response.

"Aren't you Head of Internal Security?" Hades snapped back.

"Am I?" Cerberus asked sheepishly.

"Yes. This is your responsibility."

"Woof, woof, woof," Cerberus barked for want of anything else to reply. He looked from Hades to Vesta and then back to Hades again. "Woof, woof." He didn't know the answer and wished Vesta hadn't asked the question.

"I think no one's guarding the gate at this moment," Vesta interjected, deciding to help the other two in the room. "So, you need to introduce new procedures."

"Woof," Cerberus went. "Just what I thought."

Hades was focused on today's new arrival. "What would you suggest, Vesta?" he asked.

"There are probably lots of things, but I've got a couple of initial ideas."

"Carry on."

"Well, the first one is to put up a large notice which says something like 'Dangerous Dog – Beware'. It will remind people of Cerberus and if they don't see him, they won't know if he's hiding behind some boulder and will run out and bite them."

"On the bum!" Cerberus added.

"The second one is to put some dangerous fish in the river, which will bite anyone who enters it. Again, put up a large notice; the aim is to discourage people from trying to escape because they'll get hurt."

"Piranha fish," said Hades, nodding his approval. "Nasty things. They'll strip the flesh off a living creature in a matter of minutes. That will put people off trying to escape."

"Woof," Cerberus agreed. "That's what we need – banana fishes."

Shortly afterwards, Vesta and Cerberus left for the Girls' Quarters, Hades having agreed to Vesta's two proposals. As he sat on his throne alone reflecting on their conversation, Hades wondered if he was getting stale, too set in his ways. He'd been running the Underworld for thousands of years and no longer questioned things. Everyone did what they'd always done and new arrivals were merely slotted into the current arrangements. Perhaps the whole place needed shaking up under new management. He wondered if the same applied to the two kingdoms run by his brothers, Zeus and Poseidon. It probably did, but it would no doubt take a thousand years to get them to agree to a job swap. Meanwhile, he'd have to carry on but start listening more to the people, especially the new ones. Vesta seemed a smart girl, someone to take an interest in, he decided.

VI

FATHER
AND SON

I RIS WAS STANDING IN FRONT OF ZEUS IN THE conservatory of the Top God's palace, which he shared with his wife Hera. His eyes were flashing to the left and right very rapidly and his face had developed a deep purple colour.

"Please repeat Bacchus's message, Iris."

"Word for word?"

Zeus nodded.

"Fine. Here goes ... 'Subject – Response: I am the great Lord Bacchus, god of wine, beer, cider, spirits and all other alcoholic beverages. All other gods quiver and shake in my presence when they have consumed too much of my fine products. Zeus is a grizzled, pompous, old tosspot with a face like a hippopotamus who can go stick his head up his own backside."

Zeus's teeth clenched.

"I am busy working today and haven't got time for any of his stupid nonsense. What's more, no more threats from now on. If I get any further messages from him, he will be banned from the Dog and Duck indefinitely, so there'll be no further opportunities to chat up new female crumpet from the Underworld."

Now the hands clenched.

"In addition, all future deliveries of fine wines to his palace will be cancelled. Tell him that.'"

"Thank you, Iris," said Zeus when she had finished, his whole body now clenched. "You may go now."

Iris did not move. Instead, she said by way of an understatement, "You look a bit peeved, Zeus. I did try to dissuade him from sending the message."

"Unsuccessfully, I see."

"Just as I counselled you not to send your missive in the first place."

"Mine was entirely justified," Zeus growled. "His was not. It's an abomination. An abomination, I say!"

"And so was yours," Iris responded pluckily. "But we are where we are. What are you going to do?"

"I'll deal with it."

"You're not going to do all those terrible things involving flesh-eating serpents and gigantic rats, crocodiles, hyenas and the like?"

"Leave it to me."

Iris folded her arms and stared long and hard. "All I can say is don't do what you're thinking of doing," and she turned round and walked out.

Zeus continued to fume in his chair, but after a few minutes he got up, walked into the entrance hall and unlocked a cupboard with the word 'Thunderbolts' etched on the outside.

*

Meanwhile everything was peaceful at the Dog and Duck. Bacchus had replenished a couple of jugs of Hanseatic Headbanger and, after having consumed one of them, was snoring peacefully on his deckchair. The recent labour strike had been called off. Lennie's focus was now on a further full bowl of prosecco with a large piece of game pie, while Beetle had two large lettuce leaves that he was munching away at. Mistress Quickly was in her kitchen washing a few last tankards in preparation for the evening's customers.

This tranquil scene was interrupted by a sharp flash of light. Nell Quickly frowned when she saw it fly past her kitchen window and frowned even more when she heard a large bang from the direction of the orchard. A few seconds later there was a loud scream, followed by another and then another, until pandemonium reigned as continuous screaming and shouting emanated from the same location. Mistress Quickly shot through the bar and out of the front door to witness mayhem on the near horizon.

Bacchus was running from the orchard to the tavern hollering for all it was worth. His pants were on fire and he was waving his arms all over the place as he tried to put the flames out, but with no success. Lennie was in the air near him, squawking away and flapping his wings in great agitation, hoping they would extinguish the fire. Unfortunately, all his flapping merely fuelled the flames and Bacchus was yelling to him to go away.

Mistress Quickly immediately realised what had happened. That flash of light was a thunderbolt aimed at Bacchus by Zeus. She ran back into the kitchen and returned in no time with a large bucket of water. She ran with it towards Bacchus, who was running towards her, screaming, "My dangly bits! My dangly bits!" Lennie meanwhile, with the best of intentions, continued to make things worse with all his flapping.

Beetle was also stirred into action. Bacchus was his great friend and he was in trouble. Beetle had three friends: Nell Quickly, who was like his mother; Lennie, who played the part of a naughty brother; and Bacchus, a much-loved uncle. He, Beetle, was determined to help. His four short legs were racing at top tortoise speed as he tried to close the gap between him and Bacchus.

"I'm coming, Bacchus," he shouted. "Beetle will save you."

As the distance closed between Bacchus and Beetle, Mistress Quickly pounded past him with her bucket. As she got close to Bacchus, he seemed to open his arms to her, shouting, "My dangly bits! My dangly bits! Save my dangly bits, Nell!" Mistress Quickly stopped a few feet from him and, as he continued to advance, she heaved the bucket of water directly at his dangly bits. The god came to a shuddering halt and then screamed "I'm still on fire!" Lennie was still flapping his wings and squawking, and Beetle was also pounding his legs at great speed. Mistress Quickly spent no time reviewing her handiwork but turned round with the empty bucket and ran back into the kitchen. By the time she returned with a second full bucket, Bacchus was nearly at the pub's front door and, with a final heave, a further torrent of water hit him in the midriff. This one did the trick and put the final flames out.

Bacchus was now reduced to tears and moaning with pain. Lennie continued to squawk and flap, continuously shouting out, "Missile attack! Missile attack! Prepare to repel invaders!" Beetle had found that his efforts had been in vain since Bacchus had run past him back to the pub, so all he could do was turn round and trace his steps at a more leisurely pace.

"Look, Nell, look," Bacchus moaned pulling his trousers down. "My dangly bits are all burnt."

Now Mistress Quickly had been a woman of the world before relocating to the realm of the gods. She was therefore not shocked by many things, even men's dangly bits, but seeing the complex mixture of Bacchus's blue, black and red burnt flesh was something to behold.

"Oh, my gosh," was all she could say.

"Help me, Nell. Help me!" Bacchus cried in agony.

Just at that moment there was a flash of light and Zeus appeared in front of them all.

"Ah!" he exclaimed, looking at Bacchus. "The miserable wretch has got his just deserts."

"Dad, Dad. Make it stop! The pain; the pain!" screeched Bacchus. "What have I done?"

Before Zeus had a chance to respond, Mistress Quickly went up to him and started jabbing him in the chest. There then came the following lecture from a very angry hostess: "What a disgrace you are, Lord Zeus. An absolute disgrace! Firing a thunderbolt at your own son, your own flesh and blood. How can you do such a thing? Look at his dangly bits. Look at them. All burnt to a cinder. Call yourself a father? You're no father. You're a monster. A monster, that's what you are. Now heal him quickly or I'll take my frying pan to your head!"

Zeus looked at Mistress Quickly open-mouthed as she spoke. "Do you know who I am, Nell?" he said when she had finished.

"Of course, I do. You may be Top God or whatever, but as far as I'm concerned you're a monster who's just attacked his own son. We've known each other a long time, Zeus, and the one thing you should have learned by now is I speak my mind. That I do, no matter if you're Top God, Middle God, Bottom God or just a normal person. You'll get no fear or favour from Nell Quickly, that you won't."

Just as he was thinking of a response to give this formidable lady, Bacchus screamed again about his dangly bits.

"Heal him now, Zeus," Mistress Quickly snapped at the Top God, while giving him another jab in the chest.

"Yes, alright," he mumbled, and, turning round to Bacchus, he raised his arm. There was a slight flash of light and Bacchus was suddenly covered in a cloud from which he shortly emerged with his trousers pulled up.

"That's a lot better," he sighed. "But it's still painful and…" he pulled his trousers open at the front and looked at his groin, "my dangly bits are bright pink."

"I've healed you about eighty per cent," replied Zeus, more confidently when addressing Bacchus than when he was conversing with Nell Quickly.

"What about the other twenty per cent?" Bacchus asked.

"That will depend on the talk you and I are about to have."

"Thank you, Lord Zeus," Mistress Quickly interrupted. "I didn't mean to be hard on you, but I believe in right and wrong, I do. When I see wrong, I speak my mind. Always have done; always will."

Zeus gave a smile. "You never bothered to ask why I threw a thunderbolt at him."

"No need to. I'm sure Bacchus did something foolish to start with. He just didn't deserve a great big thunderbolt between his legs."

"Even if he called his father 'a grizzled, pompous, old tosspot' and a lot more? Do you think that's appropriate?"

"Best if I don't comment, Lord Zeus. I've had my say and there's no need to add insult to injury. Anyway, I must go back to the kitchen. I've still got work to do."

Nell Quickly turned round and walked off, leaving Zeus rather perplexed at her answer.

"Let's go and have a drink in the orchard, Father," Bacchus said, leading Zeus away from the tavern.

During this interchange between the two gods and Mistress Quickly, Lennie had been flying around at great speed as he prepared his battleplan. "Missile attack! Missile attack! Prepare to repel invaders!" he squawked again when the plan had been formulated. This was just as peace had broken out on the ground, which Lennie had failed to observe.

"Allied Commander Lennie to General Beetle – ground force attack now on Zeus's legs. SAS Commander Nell Quickly – return with frying pan and lead assault on left flank. Royal Navy – all ships to battle stations; Ark Royal to commence shelling enemy target and launch bomber squadron."

Lennie himself flew towards Zeus and zoomed about a foot over his head, shouting out, "Rat a ta tat, rat a ta tat. Rat a ta tat." He circled and came round for another attack, again going "Rat a ta tat, rat a ta tat."

"Sorry, Father," said Bacchus. "I think Lennie's lost the plot."

"I'll deal with it," replied Zeus.

As Lennie again flew just over Zeus's head, the god put up his hand and Lennie came to a shuddering halt, suspended in the air. He flapped his wings, but nothing happened.

"What have you done, Zeus?" he shouted. "You're not playing by the established rules of war. You're in breach of the Geneva Convention. Put me down now. I insist!"

"Are you sure, Lennie?" Zeus enquired.

"I insist!" Lennie exclaimed again.

"Very well." Zeus put his hand up again and Lennie flopped perpendicularly to the ground.

"Ouch!" he screeched. "I didn't mean like that. My front's all bruised."

"You forgot the First Law of Warfare, Lennie."

"What's that, Zeus?"

"Never fight an army that's stronger than yours."

"Huh!" responded Lennie. "What's the Second Law of Warfare?"

"Never fight an army that's stronger than yours."

"And the Third?"

"Never fight an army that's stronger than yours."

"I suppose you're quite attached to that piece of advice?"

"I am."

"Then I will go and discuss it with my fellow military commanders prior to any future battles."

"Good idea, Lennie," said Zeus as the eagle waddled over to his bowl of prosecco for additional sustenance after his exertions.

In the orchard, Bacchus poured out two tankards of Hanseatic Headbanger.

"This is quite a beer," Zeus enthused after a few sips. "What is it?"

"Hanseatic Headbanger. Newly arrived."

"Very tasty. And who are these delightful young ladies?" asked Zeus, looking at the poster of the two young blondes with the headline 'Want a Bang, Get a Headbanger'.

"Models hired for marketing purposes, I suppose."

"Have you got their names and addresses?"

"Of course not, Father. They're just two girls on the poster."

"But very nice girls, I must say," said Zeus, continuing to stare at the poster. "You don't know which town they live in, by any chance?"

"Headbanger's head office is in Hamburg, so you could try there if you're really interested."

"Ah yes, Hamburg, port city, caters for the sailors. I've spent many a happy evening in the Reeperbahn. Have you ever been there?"

Bacchus shook his head. "Let's sit down and enjoy the beer," he said.

After the two had settled into their deckchairs and sipped at their tankards in tranquil silence for a couple of minutes, Bacchus turned to Zeus and said, "Sorry, Dad. I plain forgot about the Council Meeting."

"Perhaps I over-reacted a bit, son. That message of mine was a bit hard. And before you say anything, I'd like to suggest that your response was also a bit over the top."

"Let's drink to that," Bacchus replied, and they both tapped their tankards before draining them. He then got up and quickly poured out a couple of refills. As he sat down, Zeus raised his arm again, resulting in a flash of light and another temporary cloud around Bacchus.

"That's the final twenty per cent," said Zeus. His son peered inside his trousers and smiled. "Back to normal, I hope?"

"Back to normal," Bacchus agreed. "Thanks."

"Good, because if we're to have a proper chat, then I need you to be a hundred per cent," said Zeus. "You're one of the few people I can have an honest talk with, Bacchus, and I feel a great need for one now."

"Why? What's up?"

"Everything," replied Zeus. "It's not easy being Top God. All the problems end up at my door and normally there aren't any easy solutions; sometimes there are no solutions at all."

"I'll send you a barrel of Headbanger, Father. That will get rid of your problems. Of course, it will give you a mighty hangover problem the next morning when you wake up, but then I'll send you a second barrel for that."

"Can we please be serious for a few minutes?"

"Sorry," Bacchus replied. "Tell me about your problems."

"Where do I begin?" replied Zeus pensively. "Let's start with my two brothers. I always invite them to Council Meetings, but they never come. I understand it's a long trip for both of them and they have other priorities, but they never reply to any of my messages. I haven't seen Poseidon for over three hundred years and Hades for even longer."

"Does it matter? You always have massive rows and slanging matches when you get together. It's more peaceful if you stay apart."

"I know, but they are my brothers. I'd like to know how they're getting on. Sometimes Hebe gives me snippets of information when she visits them, but it's not the same."

"Why don't you visit them?"

"I've not been invited, Bacchus. It would feel all wrong just turning up unannounced on their doorsteps. Not very dignified either."

"Then why not send an ambassador to go and spend some quality time with both of them? Someone they like and respect who can try and engineer a meet-up between you all?"

"I suppose I could ask Iris or Hebe to go, but they've both got lots of other duties."

"I'm thinking of Athene; she'd be the best of all of us."

Zeus slapped his own leg. "That's a rather good idea, Bacchus. Yes, really rather good. Both Hades and Poseidon have always got on well with Athene. Let me think about how to pitch it to my brothers and then I'll speak to her. You do have a brain in there, son; either that or it's this Headbanger stuff."

"Probably both," Bacchus replied. "Let's have a top-up and you tell me about your next problem."

"Mars," growled Zeus. "He goes around Olympus hitting people, especially Bumble and other helpers from the Underworld."

"What about gods?"

"Once he thumped Apollo, but Artemis intervened and shot him with an arrow. Other than that, I don't know, but everywhere he goes, he just has rows and bullies whoever's around. I've laid the law down to him many times, as has Heph, but it never does any good."

"Mars is a problem we've always had, Father. Can't you encourage him to go and start some more wars down below? That will preoccupy him. It's worked in the past."

"I've thought about it, but there's a pacifist sentiment that's developed in many of the younger gods. Any new wars and multiple deaths just get the Artemises and Apollos of the world giving me nothing but grief on a daily basis."

"Not easy, I agree. I could send him a daily barrel of Headbanger, if you want?"

Zeus smiled ruefully. "It would probably make him more

aggressive," he said. "I think I'll go and have another chat with Heph about the situation. He's about the only person who can exercise any control over his brother. Even then, it only lasts for a few days. Let's move on. My next problem is Artemis and her little gang."

"Oh, what's all that about?"

"You need to come to Council Meetings and then you'll see. Put simply, Artemis is a cunning little minx and—"

"She is your daughter, Zeus," Bacchus helpfully interrupted.

"Thank you. I'm only too aware of that. Anyway, because she's cleverer than most, she leads a little gang of Apollo, Aphrodite, and sometimes Hermes. They've currently adopted what can only be described as liberal causes such as democracy, equality, women's rights. Everything to upend the current order which has served us well for thousands of years."

"What's democracy, Father?"

"A horrid idea which involves giving everyone a say, normally by way of a vote. Aphrodite, at Artemis's prompting, even shouted out at today's meeting that we should vote on issues. Absolutely extraordinary. It's a lunatic idea."

"Remind me, Father, how do we do it now?"

"I make all the decisions, of course. That way we get the right answer."

Bacchus didn't reply for a while as he contemplated this idea of democracy. It seemed quite attractive to him and he made a mental note to speak sometime with Artemis on the matter. He realised Zeus was against it and, since he and his father were getting on well at the moment, he felt it prudent not to get involved.

"As you say, Father. All absolutely extraordinary," he eventually said.

"I'm glad you agree. I would have expected nothing less from a sensible fellow like you, Bacchus. At today's meeting they got me to agree to some sort of working party to consider equality issues and then make a presentation to some future Council Meeting. I only agreed to it because it was Athene's proposal, made no doubt to defuse a rather tense stand-off between Artemis and Mars. I don't know what they're really going to discuss, but I'd be greatly comforted if you would sit on this group."

"Me?" exclaimed Bacchus. "What can I add? I run a pub. What's more, as far as equality is concerned, it certainly doesn't exist at the Dog and Duck. Females, as represented by Nell Quickly, are right at the top, followed by the animals and then males, whether gods or men, clearly being at the bottom of the social structure. Equality definitely won't happen here, nor should it. Current arrangements work and that's what's important."

"In answer to your question, you can contribute common sense. Hera and Artemis are working out who should sit on this group, but I'll get you on somehow. You'd be doing me a great favour if you said yes, son."

Bacchus sighed. "Very well," he said.

"Thank you. Next, I'm worried about Aphrodite. She's really unhappy. She's the Goddess of Love but can't find the right partner for herself."

"Hasn't she tried just about everyone? I could be flippant and suggest getting her together with Mars, but they've tried that already, haven't they?"

"Yes, with disastrous results. Have you any ideas?"

"Not me!" replied Bacchus firmly. "She hasn't tried me and I don't want her to. I'll go on your equality group, Zeus, but I'm not being paired off with Aphrodite, gorgeous as she is."

"I wasn't thinking of you, Bacchus. Even I know that's a silly idea. I just hoped you could think of someone."

"All I can suggest is someone from the Underworld. Get a few eligible men up here and see what she thinks of them. Hasn't Heph recently employed a new builder to assist him?"

"He has," replied Zeus. "It's worth trying. Another matter for me to speak to him about."

"Any more problems, Father?"

"Hera. I know she's not your mother, but you and she have always seemed to get on reasonably well."

"I think I'd say that she tolerates me, unlike a number of her other stepchildren," Bacchus interrupted.

"Well, we both know what we mean. The problem is that she just seems to be unhappy and dissatisfied all the time."

"Hasn't she always been like that? Isn't that the way she was created?"

"I like to think she was happy for a while when we first got married and also when Heph, Hebe and Mars were children. If she were human, I'd say she was going through some sort of mid-life crisis or the menopause, if you know what I mean."

"But we're not humans, Father; we're gods and these things don't happen to us. Can you be more specific on the sort of things she's unhappy about?"

"Let's take our household as an example," Zeus replied. "It's actually run pretty well by the Bumbles and even Hera accepts that. The problem is that she does insist on having a lady's maid to help her get ready in the morning, do her hair and nails, look after her wardrobe, and everything else that maids do. It's really quite a personal relationship, but Hera just can't get the right one, and it causes all sorts of rows and tensions."

"Can't Mrs Bumble also act as a lady's maid?"

Zeus shook his head. "She's the housekeeper," he replied, "and is busy enough; also she's no experience of being a lady's maid. The trouble is that Hera insists on employing ladies who've all had maids but have never actually done the work themselves. Take the current one, Marie Antoinette – used to be the French queen and so knows what's required but not how to do it. After five minutes of trying to do Hera's hair, she gets a headache and has to lie down for a couple of hours. Then Hera shouts at her and she gets another headache and that's another two-hour siesta. She'll have to go, but we're running out of candidates."

"Who did you have before?"

"Egyptian girl called Cleopatra and before that a couple of English queens who had their heads chopped off by the same husband. I think their names were Anne Boleyn and Catherine Howard."

"Father, don't you draw up the shortlist from which Hera decides?"

"I do, but she always sets out what criteria I'm to consider. It always seems to be queens."

"Young, attractive queens, if you don't mind me mentioning. Your list wouldn't be influenced by ideas of hanky panky, would it, Father?"

"How can you suggest such an idea?" replied Zeus defensively, turning red.

"I won't press it. What Hera really needs is someone like Nell Quickly. Clearly not Nell, because I need her here and also she doesn't know how to be a lady's maid, but that type of personality. By the way, thank you for not reacting to the telling-off she gave you earlier."

Zeus smiled. "I was applying the First Law of Warfare, 'Never fight an army that's stronger than yours.' I wouldn't have been wholly confident of coming out on top in any battle against Nell."

"Thanks, anyway."

"Oh, Nell Quickly and I have known each other a long time. I don't know if I ever told you, but whenever I visited London in her day, I often went drinking at her pub, the Boar's Head. Her clients were good fun but a bunch of rogues. One of them, Harry, became King of England after a few years. He sobered up a lot once he got crowned."

"Presumably you made him king?"

"Only indirectly. I organised for his father to win an earlier battle for the crown, so when he died, Harry took over. Yes, they were interesting times and Nell remains the same formidable woman she was then."

"Did you ever…?"

"No," Zeus replied. "I was never good enough for her." He took another sip of Headbanger and then continued, "But what about you, Bacchus? I'd like to see you settle down. Nell would be good for you; have you ever thought of asking her to marry you?"

"I thought you discouraged marriage between gods and humans? Relationships, yes, but not formal marriage."

"I'd make an exception for you and Nell, and I have no doubt the other gods would agree. What about it?"

Bacchus shook his head. "Like you, I'm not good enough for her," he replied. "Let's leave things as they are. They work."

"Nell used a phrase a lot in her Boar's Head days: 'If it ain't broke, don't fix it.' I suppose that's what you're saying?"

"Precisely," agreed Bacchus.

VII

THE TORTURING
DEPARTMENT

———————

T HE NEXT MORNING, VESTA WAS MET BY CERBERUS
outside the Girls' Quarters. His left face was covered
with streaks of red as if he'd been in a fight.

"Woof. Come on," said Cerberus. "We've got a busy day."

"I was just going with the other girls to breakfast," replied
Vesta. "Are we going to the Kitchens? Anyway, what's happened
to your face?"

"I'll tell you later. Hurry up, lots to do. No time for breakfast
and Kitchens are for tomorrow. Here's a Mars bar for you."
Cerberus turned Righty's head towards Vesta, holding a Mars
bar between his teeth.

"Thanks," said Vesta, taking the chocolate and eating it as
they went along.

Cerberus bounded along with Vesta having to walk very
fast to keep up. Eventually, they reached the jetty where the

ferry arrived daily with the new arrivals. In front of it were two large signs painted in red ink.

BEWAR OFF ZE DOGGE
EE IS DONJERUS ANND
BITES YU ON ZE BUMM

DONJERUS BANANAS FISSHES
VEY EETS YU DED OR ALIFFE

"Really cool," Vesta said. "Who painted them?"

"Woof, woof, I did," replied Cerberus, who began to wag his tail at Vesta's approval. "Over here." He took Vesta to a nearby rock, behind which was a pot of red paint and a brush. "Lefty held the brush between his teeth."

"Which explains why you've got that red all over your face."

"And I told him how to spell the words," added Audrey smugly, bending round to speak.

"Woof, woof," agreed Cerberus. "Now come along. We've got to go to the Torturing Department."

"What!" shrieked Vesta. "Why am I going to the Torturing Department? Hades said I should go to the Kitchens. Have I done something wrong?"

"Don't worry," said Cerberus. "Everyone goes to the Torturing Department on their first day for a look round and to find out about their punishment. Hades forgot when he spoke to you yesterday."

"What punishment?" Vesta said, refusing to move. "I don't want to go. I'm scared."

"Woof, woof. Don't worry. Everyone has a punishment in the Underworld. Hades likes you, so he's bound to have made sure it won't hurt too much. Believe me, I'm your friend. I promise I'll stay with you."

Vesta very reluctantly followed Cerberus, who had to keep

running behind her to hurry her up. Eventually they arrived at a large black building with no windows. The door had a sign on it which said 'TORTURING DEPARTMENT – DIRECTOR: MR SATAN'. Cerberus pushed the door open with his three noses and he and Vesta walked in.

Satan was sitting at a large desk opposite the door, smoking a cigarette. He was a small bald man, very pale with long pointed ears and two orange horns growing from the top of his head. He was dressed in evening wear and was busy writing on a parchment in front of him.

Cerberus growled and Satan raised his head. On seeing a young girl in front of him, he immediately stood up and moved round the desk to greet her. He was slightly hunchbacked and walked slowly because of a limp.

"My dear, welcome. Welcome, my dear," he spluttered as he approached Vesta. "I'm delighted to meet you. Delighted. You must be Vesta? Yes, Vesta, a most beautiful name. You are eagerly awaited. Most eagerly."

Satan put his hand out to shake Vesta's. It was cold and greasy, and Vesta slightly shuddered, especially when she looked into his face and saw broken black teeth and then smelt his breath, which rivalled the worst rubbish dump in the universe.

"My name is Satan," continued the hunchbacked man, still shaking Vesta's hand and spluttering as he spoke. "Yes, Satan is my name. I am the Director of the Torturing Department. This is my little fiefdom where you pay a price for all your past little misdemeanours. Yes, my dear, a price for misdemeanours; each misdemeanour has a price. Only fair, my dear. Yes, only fair. Do you understand? Do I make myself clear? *Comprenez vous?* as they say in France. *Vous comprenez?*"

During Satan's monologue, Vesta had stood transfixed, trying to concentrate on what he was saying. However, all this talk about misdemeanours and price caused her to suddenly blurt out, "So what's my price, Mr Satan? What punishment are you going to give me? I'm scared, you know, and don't mind admitting it."

Satan let go of Vesta's hand and stood back. "My dear, no need to be scared. No need. Today is not about your price; today is about getting to know the Torturing Department. Yes, getting to know. A guided tour is what is planned. That is a tour in which we guide you through our various activities. We are first and foremost a service department. We provide a valuable service – yes, most valuable. If at any time when using our service, you have a complaint, you must come and tell me. Yes, tell me you must. We pride ourselves on our service and any slight fall in standards – that is, standards that are not five-star – I must ask you to draw to my attention. My attention needs to be drawn. If it is not five-star, drawn to me it must."

"Yes," said Vesta for want of anything else to say once Satan had stopped talking.

Cerberus had been sitting in a corner all this time staring aggressively at Satan. While he had stayed quiet, he continued to emit an almost inaudible growl. The reality was that Cerberus detested Satan, who never gave him any Mars bars or indeed any form of chocolate before Mars bars were created. In the early days of their acquaintance, he had tried to take revenge on Satan by biting his bum, but whenever he got close to him, a large baseball bat suddenly appeared and crashed down on one or more of his heads. So, he had become wary of the fiend but was determined to get even with him one day. He was just waiting for the opportunity when Satan was not on his guard. Cerberus sensed today was not that day.

There was also another person in the room during this time, standing quietly in a corner to Satan's right. He was of medium height, but with a broad chest. His hair was long, tied into a ponytail at the back and he had a thin grey beard. He was dressed as a Central European fifth century warrior with flared, light brown trousers and a series of freely flowing tops; on his head was a fur and iron helmet. Satan now turned to him.

"Vesta, my dear," he spluttered. "Let me introduce you to one of my four very able assistants. Yes, very able. This is Mr Attila; indeed, the original Mr Attila the Hun. A man of ferocious savagery while alive and so we have been able to utilise his excellent skills in the Torturing Department. Excellent skills, I say. Yes, most excellent. Mr Attila has kindly volunteered to show you around today. Around, you will be shown. View him as your Client Service Manager to use the latest jargon, the latest jargon I use. A most excellent choice, a choice most excellent."

"Pleased to meet you," said Vesta, nervously walking over to Attila and putting out her hand. Attila didn't shake hands but nodded and gave her a reassuring smile.

"Let's go," he said, abruptly moving towards an opening to his right.

Suddenly, Cerberus decided to participate. "Woof, woof," he went as he got up. "I'm coming too."

"You are not!" spluttered Satan. "I am not having animals in the Torturing Department."

Cerberus snarled at him. "I'm going with Vesta. I promised her."

"No!" Satan exclaimed. "I am Director of the Torturing Department and I forbid you to go past my desk."

"Growl, growl, snarl, snarl, growl, snarl. I can go anywhere," Cerberus replied after having thought about how to respond. "I'm Head of the Underworld's Internal Security Department – not just a Director, but Managing Director."

"What!" screeched Satan. "You a Managing Director?"

"Woof."

"Cerberus," Vesta intervened, deciding to trust Attila. "I'll be alright. I'll go with Mr Attila myself and meet you outside when we're finished."

Cerberus continued to protest but was eventually persuaded by Vesta to let her go alone.

Attila walked silently with Vesta along a dark corridor before taking her into a small room to the left. It was quite light with many candles along the walls. There was a table with two goblets and a jug of water, and once the two of them had got inside, Attila turned round and gave Vesta a broad smile. He also poured the water into the two goblets and handed her one.

"Have a glass of water, Vesta, because it gets hot in this place. Now, before we start on the tour, three things. Number one, call me Attila, not Mr Attila. Number two, you're probably going to be shocked by a lot of what you see here, but since you're in the Underworld, you need to know what goes on. Finally, and this is the most important – Satan is a complete and utter prat."

Vesta burst out laughing. "He talks in a really strange way," she said.

"He thinks in a strange way as well, but despite being a prat, he's cunning and dangerous, so take care when he's about. Come on, drink up. Let's get started."

The two went out of the room and down a steep pair of steps to the cellars. There were four doors at the bottom and Attila opened the first. He and Vesta walked into an immense room full of people sitting on sharp spikes, with blood running down their legs. Many were moaning, some seemed unconscious, one or two were holding a conversation.

"This is Vlad's room. He spends most of his time impaling people. Learnt it a long time ago in what's now Romania. He's over there," and he pointed to a tall man, trying to lift a fat old woman onto a spike.

"Just you watch me piles," shrieked the old woman. "I've got terrible piles and I don't want you stirring 'em up again."

"This will take your mind off your piles, Fatima," Vlad replied. "Just stop struggling and it will be better for all of us."

"I can't 'elp it, can I? You try sitting on a sharp spike all day,"

Fatima shouted back. Just at that moment Vlad got her directly over the spike and dropped her onto it. "Oooh! *Ouch!* Ouuch! Oooh! You pig. Me piles are even worse now."

"You're okay now, Fatima. Stop wriggling around."

Vlad came over and was introduced to Vesta. "They're not all like Fatima," he said. "Come and meet William and Harold. They settled down to the torture a few centuries ago."

The three walked over to two old men singing 'One Man Went to Mow' in unison. They broke off when company arrived.

"*Enchanté, Mademoiselle,*" said William, putting Vesta's right hand to his lips when she had been introduced.

"My dear," said Harold, making a small bow. "Do you know the song we're singing?"

"I think I've heard it once."

"Let me give you the opening lines," Harold continued. "It goes like this:

'One man went to mow
Went to mow a meadow
One man and his dog
Went to mow a meadow

Two men went to mow
Went to mow a meadow
Two men one man and his dog
Went to mow a meadow'"

"Oh yes," said Vesta. "I remember it now. How many men are you up to?"

"Quite a lot," replied Harold. "Every time we're brought in here, we pick up where we last left off. William will know."

"Seventeen million, three hundred and fourteen thousand, four hundred and twenty-six men," William promptly stated.

"William's got a much better memory than I have," said

74

Harold. "He even remembers that battle we fought a long time ago."

"Ten Sixty-six," William said proudly.

"He won," added Harold. "But we've settled our differences and become good friends since then."

"*Mais oui, mon ami*," the Frenchman said. "But come, we must continue. *Enchanté, Mademoiselle*," and the two continued with their men and the dog.

Attila and Vesta then moved on to the second room, which was equally large, but hotter because of numerous fires burning. It consisted of two halves. On the left side were huge cauldrons of water being heated up. They all had lids on them, but these were full of holes with people's heads sticking out of the top. On the right were a mass of bodies on large spits which were over hot fires.

"Ugh!" exclaimed Vesta. "This is horrible. People are being boiled and roasted."

"We're in Ivan's section now," Attila responded. "He used to do this when he ran Russia. I don't think we should interrupt him because he looks as if he's run off his feet at the moment."

When Ivan had been tsar of Russia he had had a whole army of people to carry out his orders, whereas in the Torturing Department, he had to do everything himself. Although an imposing and ferocious man who had been doing this for many hundreds of years, he was continuously harassed. Vesta watched him racing around the room, dealing with one torture after another.

"Hurry up," a voice shouted from one of the spits. "This side's done. Turn me over or part of me will be undercooked."

"I'm coming, Michael. I'm coming," said Ivan, hurrying over to the spit and turning it over.

A group of women in one of the cauldrons now started shouting. "Get over here, Ivan. This water's freezing. Heat it up more. We're all getting goose-pimples," a blonde woman screamed.

"Regina, I'm doing my best," Ivan shouted back as he ran to the cauldron and started stoking the fire underneath. "You'll be complaining it's boiling next."

"Isn't that the whole point?" Regina retorted. "I've got used to the heat over the years; I don't like the cold now."

"I'll make sure you boil away for a good long time then," said Ivan sarcastically.

"Better than freezing," was Regina's response, determined to have the last word.

"My good man, do come over here," an aristocratic English voice called from another cauldron.

"What do you want now, Lord PompousAss?" Ivan sighed, moving over to him.

"I'm worried about my suit getting stretched in this very hot water. Can't you turn the temperature down a touch?"

"No, I bloody well can't!" shouted Ivan. "I told you to put your swimming trunks on, not your best suit, you idiot!"

"There's really no need to take that tone, old chap. I was only—"

"Let's go and see Genghis," Attila said to Vesta, deciding little purpose would be served witnessing any further discussion between Ivan and the English Lord.

The third room was far more peaceful than Ivan's. Genghis Khan was busy polishing a number of large racks, while in the room, stretching as far as the eye could see, were bodies lying on the ground without any limbs. Many were snoring, a few were talking to each other; one pair was even playing a game of I spy. Along the wall on the right were stacks of arms and legs, all jumbled up and piled as high as the ceiling.

"Morning, Attila," Genghis said, walking over to Vesta and the Hun. Genghis was a thick set man, with a goatee beard and small moustache. He was dressed in traditional Mongol wear and had a tight iron helmet on his head.

"It's a pity you weren't here earlier. I'm pretty well finished for the time being unless any late arrivals turn up," Genghis said after the introductions were made. "You could have seen how these machines work, Vesta." He pointed at the large racks. "Of course, when I was riding the steppes, we didn't need racks; we used four horses instead. Anyway, needs must; we've no horses in the Underworld, so we make do with these contraptions."

By now Vesta had started to become immune to all the terrible tortures she'd been witnessing during the day. Being inquisitive by nature, she decided to ask some questions.

"What I don't understand is what happens to all these people who've been tortured," she said. "Take the people here. Are they left on the ground with no arms and legs for ever? Likewise, do the people on the spikes just sit on them until eternity, the same with the ones next door in the pots or being roasted?"

"No, no," Attila replied, laughing. "Let's explain how it works."

Between them, Attila and Genghis gave a comprehensive account of the role of the Torturing Department in Underworld society, as well as the power of the gods. Upon arrival in the Underworld, each person was given a punishment, depending on what they'd done while alive. Neither of Satan's two assistants quite knew how this was determined, but Hades always made the final decision. Someone like Fatima in the first room had poisoned her husband so she could take all his money and settle down with a younger man. This resulted in a punishment of sitting on a spike for a day every so often. The rest of the time, she was in the tailoring department mending clothes.

"But all these people are badly injured after their tortures," said Vesta. "How are these injuries healed? Also, how do the people in here get their arms and legs back?"

"Ah," replied Genghis. "That's where the gods come in. At the end of each day, Hades comes round and he's able to heal everyone. So, people who've sat on spikes, been boiled or roasted, can have their wounds fixed in an instant. In my area, that includes reattaching limbs. None of us know how he does it because when he sets to work a dense cloud develops and, hey presto, people are put back together again. It's a skill which he, Zeus and Poseidon have. The other gods have healing powers, but none of them can totally heal a badly injured person as the three older brothers can."

"So, Hades just walks in here, creates a mist and a few minutes later, that pile of arms and legs flies around and miraculously gets attached to the original bodies which are lying on the ground?" said Vesta sceptically. "You two aren't having me on, are you?"

Genghis and Attila both laughed and assured Vesta that wasn't the case.

"No," continued Genghis. "Later on today, I'll spend my time sorting through that pile, working out which arms and legs go where. Often Hades comes to help me. It's a long job, takes us many hours."

"Why do you do it like that?" asked Vesta. "When you pull the limbs off, why don't you just lay them by the side of each person on the ground? Then you'll know where they go later."

"Answer that one," said Attila with a large smile as he looked at Genghis's bemused face.

"Don't you put all the teeth you pull out in a large pile and then have to sort them out later?" Genghis asked Attila.

"I do," agreed Attila. "But from tomorrow, I'll be doing it the Vesta way."

"There must be a reason why we do it like this, but I can't think what it is."

"Probably because you've always put things in piles," Vesta suggested.

"Ah!" exclaimed Genghis. "More likely because we never went to school like you. You're a genius, young lady, and I'll follow your advice tomorrow and see how it goes. It will save me hours. It will also mean we don't have so many cock-ups. For example, a few weeks ago I couldn't find Shaka Zulu's right leg; all that was left was a leg six inches shorter, so he had to have that one. He's been hobbling around in a terrible mood until yesterday, when he came back. When we were putting him back together again, I managed to find him another right leg about the same length as the left. It's a white leg, but he doesn't mind. He can now run around normally, even if he is multi-coloured."

"Come on, Vesta," said Attila. "Let's go to my area."

Attila wasn't keen on spending long with Vesta in his torture room. There were people on racks but with their limbs still on; others were being crucified on the walls. A large group was moaning because of their thumbscrews and others were wandering around holding their jaws, which had been parted from their teeth. After having let Vesta look around for no more than a couple of minutes, Attila took her up the stairs back into their original room.

"Let's have another drink," he said, pouring water into the two goblets. "And let's sit down and have a chat. Any questions?"

By now Vesta had started to think of her own situation again. Having seen all the terrible punishments, she wondered which one had been reserved for her. It was time to become scared again – very scared – but it was better to know the worst than have nightmares because of the uncertainty. So, very nervously, she asked Attila what he was going to do to her.

Attila had been remarkably friendly during the whole guided tour but now looked at her sternly.

"Please take off your shoes and socks, Vesta," he said.

"Why? What's going to happen?"

"Do as I say."

Vesta slipped out of her shoes and pulled her socks off.

"Now lift your left leg up and close your eyes."

Vesta did as ordered, trembling at the prospect of what

awaited her. Was Attila going to cut off her foot, break her ankle, start removing the skin from her legs? These were all the thoughts that went through her brain at that time.

Suddenly, she burst into a fit of giggles, opening her eyes at the same time. "Stop it," she said. "You're tickling me." More giggles. "Stop it."

Vesta tried to pull her foot away, but Attila had it in an iron grip and she couldn't move. Meanwhile, he continued to tickle the sole of her foot.

"Done," he said after a few more seconds. "Now give me your right foot."

"What are you doing? I'm ticklish."

"Right foot, please," and Attila took hold of it and started tickling away, with Vesta wriggling and giggling all the time. "Finished," said Attila eventually. "Now put your socks and shoes back on."

"So, what was all that about?" asked Vesta as she got herself properly dressed.

Attila now gave Vesta a broad smile. "That's your punishment," he said.

"What, tickling my feet!"

"Fifteen seconds each foot every so often."

"That's not much of a punishment. I thought you showed me all the tortures there were upstairs. I didn't see anybody else having their feet tickled."

"We always show new arrivals the very worst punishments on their first day. Most people have much lighter punishments, but I agree, tickling feet is about the lightest. That's because you died young, so you hadn't had a chance to do too many really bad things. You should count yourself lucky. You never know, if you'd lived a long life you could have ended up in one of Ivan's cauldrons."

Vesta shuddered at the thought. "One last question, Attila," she said. "When I met Lord Hades and he was looking for a job for me, he suggested the Torturing Department. Supposing I'd said yes, what would I have been expected to do? I couldn't possibly do all the things you and the others do."

"Hades offers torturing as a job to everyone. He knows full well Satan would only accept someone who's done some really evil things in the past. I daren't tell you the terror I was responsible for, but I've mellowed a lot over the centuries. To me, it's just a job now. Sometime in the future I might give it up and ask for a transfer. I quite like the idea of becoming a builder. Keep that to yourself, Vesta; I don't want Satan knowing just yet. Anyway, we're finished – you can go."

"Thanks, Attila," and Vesta bent over and kissed him on the cheek.

VIII

'LIFE' IN
THE KITCHENS

MING HAD BEEN WORKING IN THE KITCHENS for many hundreds of years. She was originally from a village in what is now known as Sichuan province in China. In those days, famine was a regular occurrence and Ming, with many of her friends and family, had succumbed due to a string of bad harvests. Ming was small with straight black hair; she was a clever girl and as more people arrived in the Underworld over the years, she was always eager for information about new developments in the world above. She was possibly the only person born in the thirteenth century who actually knew what a computer was.

The Head Chef had asked Ming to bring Vesta to meet her after breakfast, since the two girls were in the same dormitory in the Girls' Quarters. They were just finishing their meal when Cerberus bounced into the dining hall. Many people glared warily at the three-headed dog since he was still universally unpopular, but he didn't seem to notice as he looked around for Vesta. On seeing her he scampered past various tables before appearing by the side of his new friend.

"Where have you been?" he asked Vesta. "I've been looking everywhere for you."

"Hi, Cerberus. I've been having breakfast with Ming," Vesta replied. "She's going to introduce me to the Head Chef. I start work in the Kitchens today."

"I was going to introduce you," Cerberus said peevishly.

"It's fine. Ming and I are in the same dormitory and she also works in the Kitchens."

Cerberus then looked up at Ming, who was eyeing him cautiously. He growled and started moving towards her. "Give us a Mars bar or I'll bite yer bum," he said.

Ming stood up and moved a couple of feet away. "Keep off, you horrible dog!" she shouted. "You shouldn't be in here."

As Cerberus was continuing to growl, Vesta jumped up as well. "Cerberus!" she exclaimed in a loud voice. "Don't you ever do that again. Ming's a friend of mine. Don't threaten her."

"I thought I was your friend?" Cerberus said, puzzled.

"You are," Vesta replied, sitting down. "You're my friend and Ming's also my friend."

"Can you have more than one friend?"

"Of course."

"Oh," Cerberus mumbled, backing away from the Chinese girl.

"How can you have that beast as your friend?" Ming asked in amazement, as she also sat down.

That question just got Cerberus growling aggressively once more, so Vesta had to pull him back by the tail.

"Ouch!" exclaimed Audrey as she was suddenly yanked hard.

"Cerberus, come and sit next to me for a while. Ming, I'll explain it all later."

The three of them sat quietly with none of them saying anything more as the two girls finished their breakfast. When it was time to go, Vesta looked at Cerberus and stroked one of his heads. Ming, who was watching her, pulled a rude face when the dog was looking the other way.

"You know, Cerberus, you don't have to threaten people to get a Mars bar," Vesta said as they all walked out of the dining hall. "If you asked politely, I'm sure you'd be just as successful."

"But my way sometimes works."

"Just start saying please and thank you, and stop growling when you speak."

"Are you sure?"

"Try it," said Vesta.

The Kitchens were next door to the dining hall. The central kitchen consisted of a massive oval-shaped room filled with huge metal vats about ten feet high, which were heated by individual furnaces. Each vat had a gantry around it with steps leading up to allow access. People were standing on the gantries holding long ladles that were used to stir the contents.

Ming led the way to the far side of the central kitchen where a large red-faced woman had just finished her early-morning briefing with her key section heads. She saw them approach and gave a friendly smile.

"Aggy, this is Vesta," Ming said.

"Pleased to meet you, Vesta," the large red-faced woman said, going up to her and giving her a motherly hug. "Welcome to the Kitchens. Just for the record, I'm Aggycraggywoggynog, the Head Chef, but everyone calls me Aggy."

"That's an interesting name," Vesta said. "Do you mind me asking where it's from?"

"I was an Eskimo," Aggy replied proudly. "Eskimoland's a large area without many people in it. There are only seven Aggycraggywoggynogs in the whole of the Underworld."

"Do you know them all?"

"Indeed, I do. I'm the only one you'll find in the Kitchens, though."

During all this time, Cerberus had stood a few feet away from the others, being very well behaved. He sensed it was now time to make his presence felt and show Vesta he was taking her advice.

"Woof, woof," he barked as he went up to Aggy. "Please give us a Mars bar or I'll bite yer bum."

Cerberus looked at Vesta for her approval, but all he saw was her hold her head in despair. Meanwhile, the Head Chef looked at him questioningly.

"Did I just hear you say please?" she asked the dog.

"Yes," he replied. "And if you give me a Mars bar, I'll say thank you."

"And if I don't, you'll bite my bum?"

"Woof, yes."

"Do you see that table next to me, Cerberus?"

"Woof."

"Do you see that big metal object on it? It's called a ladle."

"Woof."

"Do you want me to pick it up and hit you on your three heads with it?"

"Woof, woof, grrr, woof," Cerberus said, backing away. He then looked up at Vesta in a very confused state. "What did I say wrong?"

"You're not meant to threaten to bite people," Vesta replied, shaking her head.

"But how will they know I'll bite them on the bum if they don't give me a Mars bar?"

"Just stop all this about biting people on the bum. You're only meant to say please and thank you. Do what I say, Cerberus," Vesta snapped in an exasperated tone.

Meanwhile Aggy had opened a large cupboard behind her which was full of Mars bars. Cerberus looked at it greedily.

The Head Chef pulled out one bar, unwrapped it and gave it to Lefty.

"Thank you," said Middly politely.

"Now you're to go, Cerberus," Aggy said firmly. "We've got a lot of work to do and you can catch up with Vesta and Ming later."

All three heads looked up at Vesta, who nodded her agreement.

"Woof, woof. I'll go and do my job as well," Cerberus said. "I'm Head of Internal Security."

He turned round and walked off with a lot on his three minds. He was trying hard to do what Vesta was telling him, but it didn't always go right. He would have to have a long chat with her about how to ask for Mars bars without mentioning the biting on the bum. He wasn't entirely sure Vesta's way was going to be successful. Still, he was learning a lot. Today he had found out that you could have more than one friend. Vesta had both Ming and him as friends. He wondered if that automatically made Ming his friend as well; he decided to treat her as such. That meant that if Vesta got more friends, then he, Cerberus, would also have more. He thought that was good because Vesta seemed to be the sort of person who would be good at making friends. He knew he wasn't so good because he hadn't had any practice beforehand. Still, he would try, and this got him creating a mental list of likely candidates. Aggy would be a good person to be friends with because she had a cupboard full of Mars bars, so she was one. Cerberus knew Hades didn't want to be his friend, but that was only natural because he was the boss. Maybe Death could become his friend. Death was okay, but he wasn't going to be friends with the ferryman. No way! The banana fishes were also going to arrive in the next few days. Perhaps he and the banana fishes could be friends. Adding all those potential friends up, he thought Vesta would be pleased with him. She and Aggy were probably going to become friends anyway, but he was going to be the one to establish close bonds with Death and the banana fishes. He would tell Vesta of his plans when he next saw her.

While Cerberus was planning his future, Aggy was showing Vesta around the Kitchens. Ming also came along, although she knew everything already. The first thing that Vesta learned was that breakfast, lunch and dinner always consisted of the same dish – stew, just like lunch at school. She decided not to query this lack of variety at present but thought it was something she would be questioning sometime in the future.

The oval central kitchen consisted of large vats into which all the meat and vegetables were put for cooking once they had been prepared. There were a series of long rectangular rooms leading off from the central hub. Each one of these was dedicated to one particular item. This meant that there were separate rooms for the preparation of meat, carrots, potatoes, onions, sprouts, turnips and peas. In addition, there was a large workstation in the central area which had a number of stocks, gravies, spices, seasoning and the like, which a small team added to the vats at the appropriate time. Once the stew in a vat was properly cooked – Aggy had to approve each vat – it was carefully tipped over and its contents were poured into large basins, each of which were carried by two people into the serving room next door. From there, servers would ladle the contents into bowls for eating at the tables.

"So that is it," Aggy said as they came to the end of the guided tour. "I've got two positions to fill, Vesta. There's one in the Potato Section, where you'll be working on the same table as Ming. The other one is in Onions. It's entirely up to you. Neither's very exciting, but after a while, I'll give you a few projects for a bit of variety. Ming probably spends half her time on special projects."

"But I like potatoes as well," Ming said. "If we'd had potatoes in my village we wouldn't have starved."

Vesta chose potatoes and within a few minutes had a full understanding of how the Potato Section worked. The room consisted of masses of small tables where people sat in teams of four. There was a large bowl in the middle of each table with water in it, where people placed their peeled potatoes. On the floor, each peeler had a bucket of potatoes to be peeled and another one for the skins. Everyone had their own potato peeler and knife. In addition to the peeling teams, there were a large number of carriers going backwards and forwards. Their role was to refill the buckets with new potatoes, take away the unwanted skins, as well as removing the large bowls of peeled potatoes so they could be tipped into the large central vats. That was it; between now and eternity, Vesta would be peeling potatoes to go into the thrice-daily servings of stew. Still, it seemed better than working in the Torturing Department or being a miner. Also, Aggy had offered her some special projects sometime in the future.

Vesta joined a team which included Ming, Nelson and Mr Wong. With the exception of Ming, who already knew it, the others wanted to know Vesta's history, in particular how she had come to be in the Underworld at such an early age. The events of the school trip which went wrong, with the hot air balloon taking off and falling into the erupting volcano, were duly told. Vesta noticed at the end that no one commiserated with her; they just nodded their heads and thanked her for telling them. She realised that everyone had a sad story about how they died and it was of no benefit for people to make comments such as 'bad luck' or 'poor you'.

Ming's history was already known to everyone, so Nelson and Mr Wong volunteered their stories. Nelson was South African. He had been a trainee nurse in the 1930s in a hospital outside Johannesburg. One evening he went out for a walk along the nearby riverbank, when he tripped on the uneven footpath. The next minute he was floundering in the reeds, where a crocodile was concealed. The croc had been thinking about where dinner was going to come from that evening when Nelson's appearance provided the answer. There was a struggle, but as usually happens in such situations, the crocodile won.

Vesta made no comment, but she looked shocked. Nelson saw this and smiled. "It's no great shakes, Vesta," he said. "It happens quite often in my country. It was my fault for not taking care where I was walking." Vesta gave a small embarrassed smile back and returned to peeling her potato.

Mr Wong was far more voluble than Nelson about his history. He started off by explaining that he'd been born in Hong Kong but had then come to England as a young man with his new wife.

"We went to live in Alderley Edge in Cheshire which is nearly the North," he said. "Alderley Edge was a very posh place when I was there. It still is and now has many famous football players living in all the large houses. My wife and I worked in the restaurant trade as waiters, but once we got experience, we decided to set up our own restaurant. There were no good Chinese restaurants in Alderley Edge until I set up Mr Wong. Very good restaurant was Mr Wong."

"Did your wife also work in it?" Vesta asked.

"Not when it was first set up. She had the important job of having children. She performed well in that job: three children, but all girls. So, I gave her four out of five. Would have scored five out of five if one had been a boy. Do you agree, Vesta?" he asked, looking at the new recruit.

"No," replied Vesta.

"Neither do I," Ming added. "That's a very old-fashioned idea, Mr Wong."

"Well, I am old-fashioned. You two girls are young and don't properly understand."

"I'm older than they are and I don't agree with you," Nelson said.

"Huh! You're young too, Nelson," Mr Wong retorted.

"I'm doing the scoring and it's three against one," Ming said.

"Huh!" the former restaurant owner said again.

"Please will you continue with your history, Mr Wong?" Vesta said. "I'm interested."

"Very well, I will continue. Mr Wong Chinese restaurant was very successful. Very popular, especially with the famous footballers when they began to come and live in Alderley Edge. Excellent marketing slogan: 'Can't Go Wrong with Mr Wong.' We advertised in all the local papers, put on our menus, invoices, business cards, everything. The whole of Alderley Edge knew the slogan: 'Can't Go Wrong with Mr Wong.'"

"Did you make lots of profit?" Vesta asked.

"Very big profits for many years. In fact, we made super-profits. We decided to add 12.5% service charge onto all bills. Customers were happy, so they all paid this service charge. However, I had a very clever way of treating service charge. I kept it all as profit, so Mr Wong made super-profits. Very clever. You agree, Vesta?"

"No, that money was for the staff."

"I was working in the restaurant, so I was also one of the staff. To be a good businessman, Vesta, you need to do clever things like that." Mr Wong looked around but sensed no sympathy for this view, so he thought it best to continue. "Anyway, Mr Wong restaurant continued like that for many years. Both I and Mrs Wong got older; our three daughters were very clever – took after father – all went to university. Then one day, we had a problem at the restaurant. A busy Saturday evening with many bookings, but the chef had gone down sick—"

"What was wrong with him?" Vesta asked.

"Probably food poisoning, but no matter. Nobody to cook sixty Chinese meals that night, so I made an important management decision. Mrs Wong went into the kitchen to be chef. She was not happy, but I told her she must go, so eventually she did as instructed. Many problems then arose. She had never cooked for more than five people in her life, so sixty was a big problem. After three hours, she managed to do the first course; after another two hours, there was still no main course for anyone. Many customers became very unhappy and started complaining to me. After another hour, still no main course, so our customers now began to shout and walk out; didn't even pay for the first course and drinks. Very bad evening, especially since the editor of the local newspaper was one of the customers. Tuesday morning, when the new edition came out, it had as a headline on the front page, 'All Go Wrong with Mr Wong'. Very nasty words used in the article. I wanted to sue, but my solicitor stopped me. Apparently, you cannot sue if something is true. A very bad law, in my opinion."

"So, what happened next?" Ming now asked, although she knew the story.

"Popularity of restaurant went right down. Very few customers, so I made important next management decision. I changed wife."

"What!" exclaimed Vesta. "You changed your wife?"

"A very clever management decision. Old wife old and no more use, so I divorced her. I knew a young Chinese woman thirty years younger, so I married her. Old wife not happy; also three daughters took her side. In the divorce settlement I did not let on about all my money, so old wife did not get as much as she should have. Very clever again. You agree, Vesta?"

"No, I think that's awful," was the reply. "It's cheating."

"Ming and I agree," Nelson added.

"Well, I think it was very clever. Anyway, I continued with the restaurant. Business slowly got better as the very bad evening passed out of memory. Also, I had to drop prices to help get customers back. Not all going well in Mr Wong's life, though. My three daughters would not speak to me and the new wife started complaining. Just as I told the old wife I had less money than true, so I told the new wife before marriage I had more than I had. This caused big problems. I had offered to buy her a brand-new Ferrari motor car, but when married, I could only afford brand-new second-hand bike. She not—"

"How can a second-hand bike be brand-new?" Vesta asked.

"Brand new to the ownership of the Wong family. That was my argument, but new wife was not impressed and very annoyed. She decided on revenge, but I did not understand that at the time. As I said, she was a young woman and I was not a young man; also I had a heart condition she knew about. She suddenly became very demanding in the rumpy-pumpy area. Initially, I thought very good, but it went on all night, every night. I was very tired all the time; my heart was booming away as all this went on. I couldn't stop her; she was like a tiger. After two weeks, my heart came to my help and stopped. That was it, no more Mr Wong. New wife got all my money as the new will at time of marriage gave everything to her. She sold the restaurant, the house, everything, and went and married the editor of the local paper. He was her former boyfriend before marrying me."

"And are they still married?" Vesta asked.

"No; new wife's been in the Underworld nearly ten years. She is a good friend now with old wife. They both view Mr Wong as common enemy. Old wife because I told her I had less money than I had, and new wife because I told her I had more money than was true. Very unfair. Do you agree, Vesta?"

"No," Vesta again replied. "You should have told the truth about your money."

"I disagree. What good would that have done?"

"You might have lived longer."

"Huh!" Mr Wong responded, picking up a new potato to peel.

IX

THE SEA
GOD'S CAVERN

THIS WAS CERTAINLY NOT WHAT TOTTY
Turniptoes was expecting from her first visit to the
Mediterranean. Totty had turned 18 about six months
ago and shortly after her birthday, her elder cousin, Jade, had
approached her with a proposition. Jade was a couple of years
older than Totty and was really quite sophisticated. She was a
model, but not one of those who graced the pages of *Vogue* or
Cosmopolitan. No, Jade worked at select private events for small
groups. She did a lot of international travelling and often spoke
about meeting wealthy, older men, who were always nice and
generous to her. Jade would, of course, be nice back and Totty
was well aware that involved more than a smile and a kiss on the
cheek in the evening.

Jade's proposal to Totty was mind-blowing. It involved the
two of them going off to the South of France in June, where

they would join up with three other girls and spend a week on a luxury yacht, each being paid £10,000 in cash. All their expenses, such as flights, would be paid for and they would be transported to and from the airport in a luxury limo. Jade did admit that there would also be some men on the yacht, making the whole week more sociable. In answer to Totty's enquiry about what the girls would do all the time for their £10,000, Jade said that there'd be sunbathing and swimming as well as wining and dining. She also added that they would be expected to be nice to the men. Totty knew exactly what that meant.

Totty lived in Romford with her mum and two younger brothers. Her father had cleared off years ago with another woman and Totty didn't see much of him these days. Her mother was a part-time cleaner and Totty also had a job, but there was not a lot of money in the household, meaning that some weeks they had to rely on food banks to make ends meet. So, £10,000 cash later in the year was very appealing. Totty was an experienced girl and knew what would be involved. She'd had a number of boyfriends already and what was being proposed didn't seem very different to life in Romford. After all, if a boy took her out one evening to the local Pizza Express, it would be expected that she'd be nice to him afterwards. It's just how the world worked. All Totty would be doing by going off with Jade would be to go up a league; actually, many leagues!

Before agreeing, Totty wanted to clear it with her mum. She expected this to be fairly straightforward, and it was. After all, her mum had once mentioned that she'd done something similar as a young woman.

Totty and Jade took the EasyJet flight from London Gatwick to Nice. On the plane they found themselves sitting next to a girl called Chloe, who was also going to join their party. They were met by a chauffeur at Nice Airport and in the limo introduced themselves to the final two girls, Marie and Nicky, who were sisters from Manchester. The drive to the marina at Monaco was fairly short, and getting out of the car, they encountered a tall, elegant blonde woman in her mid-thirties. She introduced herself as Kirsty, explaining that she was Oscar's PA and would also be the girls' big sister during the week. Oscar was the American who owned the yacht and Kirsty was Canadian.

The yacht was called the *Princess BoomBoom* and each of the girls was shown to her own private cabin. After unpacking and changing, Kirsty took the girls upstairs to meet the male guests. As well as Oscar, there were two Russians, one Malaysian and Ahmed, who was from the Middle East. Everyone had champagne and they all sat around chatting and generally getting to know each other. Since it was quite late into the afternoon, drinks naturally led on to dinner, which was served by two white-coated waiters who were part of the ship's crew.

Dinner finished fairly early and it was agreed that everyone would turn in early. Totty had had a lot to drink, but she didn't think she had embarrassed herself during the evening. This was unlike Nicky, who, in a conversation about classical music, had let everyone know that she thought that meant Elvis and Cliff Richard. As she sat in her cabin, Totty wondered what happened next. She didn't have to wait long because soon there was a knock at the door and Kirsty came in for a chat. She made it clear that Totty, like the other girls, was to get a good night's sleep. She also said that Ahmed had really liked her and that the following day, especially in the evening, it would be really good if Totty and Ahmed could get to know each other a lot better.

The following morning involved the girls swimming and sunbathing on deck. The *Princess BoomBoom* was cruising along the French coast and Totty, wearing a red bikini, was leaning over the side looking at the various sights they passed. The yacht had just rounded Cap d'Antibes and was opposite Juan Les Pins when Totty's plans for the week suddenly changed.

At precisely the same time and in the same location, Moby

also found that his first trip to the Mediterranean was not turning out as expected. The Med was not really a sea that whales visited, but Moby had for many years had it on his list of things to do. When June arrived, he found himself passing through the straits of Gibraltar. Initially, he followed the parched North African coast until he came to Egypt. He nosed around the waters outside Alexandria but found he was too large to travel down the Nile to see the pyramids. So, he headed north and came to the Greek isles, which he swam around for a couple of days. After that, he headed up the Adriatic and fell in love with Venice. Returning along the Italian coast Moby rounded Sicily and then eventually came to the Italian and French Rivieras.

He spent a lot of time calling in at the various ports and marinas, which are so frequent along this coast. One afternoon, he was in the Monaco marina, when he saw a group of girls arrive at a large yacht. He was particularly interested in a ginger-haired girl in the party, who just happened to be Totty. The following day, Moby saw the *Princess BoomBoom* set sail at about the same time as the ginger-haired girl arrived on deck. He decided to follow the yacht, keeping just below the surface so as not to draw attention to himself.

Moby was near the side of the *Princess BoomBoom* when suddenly there was a loud roar as a speed boat shot over his tail. It caused him to jerk forward violently with the result that he knocked hard into the yacht. The boat swayed wildly from side to side and the ginger-haired girl toppled into the water. Totty was a good swimmer, so she kicked hard to reach the surface, but instead of moving upwards, she found her left leg caught in a net and was pulled deeper into the water. She struggled frantically to free herself, holding her breath as long as possible, but she had no success. After a while, water began to enter her lungs and then everything went blank.

Moby had caught the fishing net by accident off the Spanish

coast. It was only attached to his tail, but he hadn't been able to get rid of it. He hadn't been worried by the net and quickly ended up ignoring it. He would ask another whale to help him remove it sometime in the future when he met one. After hitting the *Princess BoomBoom* he thrashed around for a few minutes, trying to get away as far as possible from the yacht. It took him a little while to realise that the ginger-haired girl was caught up in the net and had drowned. As he looked round he could see Death diving into the water to follow him and take the girl away. Totty also regained consciousness at about the same time. She thought she might be having a dream, but then realised that she was under water and breathing was no longer a problem. She too looked behind her and saw Death following. "*I'm no longer alive,*" she thought. "*He must be coming to take me to heaven. I'll just have a little sleep while he catches up.*" And she closed her eyes and lost consciousness again.

Moby didn't much like Death, whom he'd known for many years. Once he saw him following, he made an immediate decision. He wasn't going to let Death have the ginger-haired girl. It had all been a terrible mistake, which he felt responsible for. No, what he intended to do was evade Death and take the girl to Poseidon, ask the Sea God to restore her to life, and send her back home.

Moby knew that his decision was going to cost him dearly. Poseidon's cavern was underneath the Indian Ocean and it would take weeks to get there. He'd have to swim out of the Med, down the African west coast, round the Cape of Good Hope before heading north-eastwards. This meant that he would miss his rendezvous with Bettina, a beautiful, petite beluga whale. Before going to the Med, he and Bettina had agreed that after his trip he would swim across the Atlantic towards the Antarctic, where Bettina would be waiting for him near Cape Horn. Now, she would accuse him of standing her up, leaving plenty of time for Helmut, an orca whale, to make love to her. Moby really disliked orca whales, especially Helmut, even more than his dislike of Death.

Moby set off on his journey, swimming as fast as possible. He was aware as the days passed that Death was still following him, but he couldn't keep up with the whale. Slowly, he began to slip further and further behind until he was lost to sight altogether. Moby did not think Death would give up; he would persevere and there would have to be a reckoning sometime in the future, but he needed to get the girl to Poseidon first. He was also conscious that his young cargo woke up at times during the long swim and would then fall asleep again. He just left her, unable to do anything for her until they reached their destination.

Eventually Moby was in the middle of the Indian Ocean above Poseidon's cavern. He dived to the ocean floor and approached a large cave, which he entered. After a number of firm strokes he emerged the other side into a huge cavern consisting of gleaming emeralds. Reaching the surface he swam halfway across the lagoon until he got to a large marble piazza, behind which was an immense golden palace with walls decorated with an emerald mosaic.

Moby bellowed as loud as he could, followed by more bellows. Shortly afterwards, a plump woman, wearing a blue frock and a brown apron, came running out of the palace. She was followed by a man in a butler's uniform. Both had long, straggly hair.

"What is it, Moby?" the woman shouted out in an American accent as she ran to the piazza edge.

"Dolores, please help. There's been a terrible accident. We need to free this girl who's attached to my tail."

"Oh, glory be!" Dolores said, seeing Totty for the first time. "Help me, Hashimoto."

Moby turned to his side while Dolores and Hashimoto bent down to free the girl from the fishing net. They also pulled the net off the whale's tail. They managed to get Totty, who was now awake, onto the piazza, where they sat her on the floor.

"My poor honey, it's alright now. You're safe."

"Where am I?" Totty asked. "Am I in heaven?"

"No, baby. You're in Lord Poseidon's palace."

"Who's he?"

"He's the Sea God."

"Oh," murmured Totty. "Why have I been brought here?"

"It was all a terrible mistake, all my fault," an anguished Moby called out. "What happened was—"

"Moby, we'll hear what happened later. Our number-one priority is to look after this young lady," Dolores said firmly before turning to Totty and asking, "Do you think you could stand up, my love?"

"I think so, but I'll need some help, please."

"We'll hold you," Dolores replied as she and the butler stood either side of Totty and helped her get to her feet.

"Thank you."

"That's okay, honey. Do you want us to keep holding on to you?"

Totty shook her head and steadied herself.

"That's great, baby," Dolores said, letting go of her. "Now, the first thing we're going to do is have some introductions here. Do you have a name, honey?"

"Yes. I'm Totty Turniptoes from Romford in England."

"Totty. I've not met any Tottys beforehand, but it's a mighty fine name. Yes, miss, a mighty fine name. I'm called Dolores, originally from Charleston in South Carolina."

"Pleased to meet you, Dolores," replied Totty, putting out her hand to shake, but Dolores had already taken hold of her and embraced her in a large hug.

The butler then looked at Totty and said, "Honourable Miss Totty. I am Mr Hashimoto and I am originally come from Tokyo in Japan."

Mr Hashimoto then bowed to Totty and she, rather hesitantly, bowed back after saying she was pleased to meet him.

"And I'm Moby," the whale called out.

"Hello, Moby," said Totty, waving at him.

"I'm really sorry," continued Moby. "What happened was—"

"Moby," Dolores interrupted again. "We'll hear all about it when Lord Poseidon comes."

"I'm upset," the whale said.

"I know you are, my love. Just wait a few minutes. I can see Lord Poseidon's coming now."

The Sea God came through the portico from the palace. He was very overweight and had long, dishevelled hair along with an equally unkept beard. He was shuffling along in his bedroom slippers, still wearing pyjamas, covered by a dark blue tatty old dressing gown. In his left hand was a trident, which he used to steady himself as he moved towards the group.

"What's going on here?" his booming voice called out. "Who's this young lady? What's Moby doing here?"

"I'll answer all your questions, Lord Poseidon," replied Dolores, taking charge. "There's been some terrible accident involving Moby and this young lady. We'll get all the details later, but we need to prioritise. The first thing we should do is introduce Totty to you. Secondly, I suggest I take her inside and get her changed and perhaps something to eat. While I'm doing that, you and Hashimoto can hear what happened from Moby."

"That seems a good plan, Dolores."

By now Poseidon was standing opposite Totty and was looking her up and down. He liked what he saw, thinking she was the sort of young girl whom he might like to have had as a daughter. Totty was also looking at the Sea God, thinking many things but especially the fact that he needed a haircut.

"Totty, honey," Dolores said, interrupting these thoughts. "This is Lord Poseidon, both God and King of the Seas. Lord

Poseidon, this is Miss Totty Turniptoes from Romford in England."

"Pleased to meet you, Totty," Poseidon said, putting out his hand to take Totty's to kiss.

Totty had never met a lord beforehand, let alone a king and a god, so she wasn't sure how to greet a person who was all three. However, she'd read somewhere that you should make a curtsy in front of royalty, so as Poseidon's hand moved forward and she was muttering, "Pleased to meet you too," back, she tried a curtsy. Unfortunately, this was all new to her and she ended up toppling over onto her backside.

"Oh dear," she muttered, embarrassed.

"Are you alright, my dear?" Poseidon asked, helping her to her feet.

"Yes, yes, thank you, sir. I'm all a bit shook up, if you know what I mean."

"Quite understandable. Now, you go off with Dolores and freshen up and have a change. Dol, I think one of your excellent hamburgers might be appreciated as well."

"That's what I have in mind, Lord Poseidon," Dolores replied as she led Totty off towards the palace.

Poseidon and Mr Hashimoto then listened attentively to Moby's tale about the mishap in the Mediterranean and how Moby had outrun Death to bring Totty to the cavern, while missing his date with Bettina in the South Atlantic. Poseidon asked the occasional question as the whale gave his report, but he was mainly in listening mode. When Moby had finished, he said nothing for about a minute as he thought how best to respond.

"So, what you're saying, Moby," the Sea God eventually said, "is that you want me to return Totty to the Mediterranean or Romford or wherever she wants to go to? Effectively, you want me to ignore the fact that she's drowned and restore her to life?"

"Yes, please," said Moby.

"But what I don't understand is why? People of all ages are dying every day of the year and we don't keep sending them back. In fact, Moby, you've caused a fair number of deaths. Just think of how many whalers you've been responsible for drowning."

"This is different," muttered Moby. "She's very young and nice and it was all my fault."

Moby looked so upset that Poseidon turned to Mr Hashimoto for some assistance.

"What do you think, Hash?" he asked his butler.

"I think Mr Moby's been involved in bloody big cock-up. Not easy to sort out. That's what I think, Lord P," Mr Hashimoto replied.

"That's a very accurate description," sighed Poseidon.

"But," continued the butler, "there are good arguments for Mr Moby."

"Oh, and what would they be?"

"Number one: I'm not convinced Miss Totty is totally dead. I think she's only properly dead once Death takes control of her, which he has not done yet. So, she's nearly dead, but not quite, which means she can become undead with a bit of help. I acknowledge that's a deep, philosophical argument, which only people with deep, philosophical brains will understand, but I believe a good point all the same. Number two: Miss Totty would be great help to Dolores and me in the palace. That's a good thing. Number three: the cavern's been getting a bit boring the last few years. Maybe, Miss Totty will cheer us up a bit because she's new. That's a good thing too. Number four: keeping her here and not sending her to the Underworld means putting two fingers up to Honourable Lord Hades. That's a very, very good thing. Number five—"

"Alright, Hash," Poseidon interrupted him. "That will do for now. Let me think for a while."

The Sea God wasn't sure about Mr Hashimoto's first point,

suspecting his brain was not deeply philosophical enough. However, he appreciated the other matters raised. He would have preferred putting up two fingers to his other brother, Zeus, but in the circumstances Hades would do. It was also right to say everything was getting boring; he knew he had been going to seed for a number of years, so a bright, bubbly Totty might liven things up in the cavern.

"Alright," Poseidon eventually said. "We'll keep Totty here for a while and make a decision sometime in the future. There's no need to rush it."

"Thank you," said Moby. "But what about Death?"

"How far behind you do you think he is, Moby?"

"He could arrive any time. I can't be sure when, but he won't give up."

"No, I agree," Poseidon said. "You leave Death to me."

"I'll also help," Mr Hashimoto added, while at the same time putting his arms and hands up in a fighting pose and then suddenly moving them in a series of frantically fast chopping motions in front of his face. "I'll give him many karate chops. He and I will have a good fight."

"I know you're a black belt in karate, Hash, but hopefully that won't be necessary," replied Poseidon. "Look, we've made our decision. Moby, leave it to us. You swim off and see Bettina; tell her you're late because you were on an urgent mission for me."

"I think I'll stay in the pool until Death's been," said Moby. "I'll be underwater on the far side and won't interfere."

"Fine, if you prefer it like that. Hash, let's go indoors now, but you're responsible for watching for Death from the palace."

"I'll give a big shout when he comes."

"Good man."

*

Death arrived the next day. He swam very slowly into the cavern and made for the piazza edge. He pulled himself wearily out of the water, looking tired and bedraggled. Mr Hashimoto saw him coming from a palace window and ran out to meet him.

"Ah, Mr Death," the butler said, giving him a bow. "An unexpected pleasure to meet you, sir. Are you lost or something?"

"Has that big white whale of yours been here in the last couple of days?" Death growled.

"Two days ago, no big white whale here, Mr Death."

"I said in the last two days."

"Why do you want to know? Have you been in a race with a big white whale? You hope to win a big prize?"

"Stop messing around, Hashimoto. You know why I'm here. Where's the girl?"

"Ah, the girl. Why did you not say so in first place?"

"Progress at last," Death sighed. "Where is she?"

"You want me to get her?"

"I do."

"I'll go to get her. You want me to ask her to make you a hamburger? It will give you lots of energy after your long swim."

"What are you talking about?"

"I'm asking if you want Missy Dolores to make you a hamburger before she comes to see you."

"I don't want Dolores!" Death shouted. "I want the girl!"

"For information, Mr Death, the residents of the cavern are Honourable Lord Poseidon, Honourable Missy Dolores and Honourable Mr Hashimoto – that's me. Lord P and I, we're not girls."

"Just get me the girl!" screeched Death.

"Ah!" said Mr Hashimoto, tapping his head as if remembering something. "I understand now. You mean Lady Amphitrite. She's not here at present. I think she may be in the Caribbean, but not sure. You'll need to turn around and swim there and make enquiries. Long way, though. Sure you don't want a hamburger before you go?"

Poseidon had now come out of the palace and was shuffling along to the piazza edge.

Death sighed with relief. "Perhaps I'll get more sense out of Poseidon," he muttered to himself.

"Hello, Death," the Sea God called as he got closer. "We don't often see you here."

"I've come for the girl, Poseidon," Death responded firmly. "Your butler's been talking all sorts of gibberish trying to fob me off. I hope you'll be straight with me. She is here, isn't she?"

Poseidon stared hard at Death for a long period. "I resent any assumption that I won't be straight with you, Death. Yes, the girl is here," he eventually said.

"Good. I'll relieve you of her straight away."

"No, you won't, Death," Poseidon growled. "She's staying here."

"But I have to take her to the Underworld," Death replied.

"Well, you can't. I said she's staying here."

"That's not how it works, Poseidon. She's dead and I have to take her to the Underworld."

"I don't necessarily accept your statement. I had understood that a person was only properly dead once you had taken control of her, which you haven't done yet. So, at the moment she can't properly be classified as dead."

Poseidon had decided to apply some of Mr Hashimoto's reasoning, just to see how Death would respond. All he got was a grunt.

"Eh?" said Death, totally perplexed.

"I agree I'm putting forward a deep, philosophical argument, which only people with a deep, philosophical brain will understand, but the point is still valid."

"Eh?" Death grunted again.

"So, that's settled. Nice to see you, Death. Do pop in any time," Poseidon said as he turned round to return to the palace.

"No!" Death shouted. "I don't know what you're talking about, but I'm here to take the girl away."

"Well, you can't have her," Poseidon said, turning round again.

"So, what are you going to do with her?" Death demanded.

"There are three options, Death. Firstly, I could return her to her former life. Secondly, I could keep her here long-term. Finally, I could let you take her to the Underworld."

"So, which of those options are you going to go for?"

"I haven't decided yet."

"When will you decide?"

"I haven't decided on that yet either."

"If you want to keep her here long-term, Poseidon, why don't you let me take her briefly to the Underworld and then she can come back to you? That's the way to do it."

"No," replied the Sea God. "I would then lose option one."

"This is most irregular. I must have her, Poseidon."

"Well, you can't."

"But I must!"

"Look, Death, the answer's no. If you don't like it, tell me what you're going to do about it."

"You can't do this!"

"I repeat, what are you going to do about it?"

Death was flummoxed and he just stood there growling at Poseidon. "I will speak to Hades," he said eventually.

"Good idea," Poseidon replied.

"This is not the last you will hear of this matter, Poseidon."

"I'm sure it's not. Do you want Moby to give you a lift, at least part of the way? He's going to the South Atlantic."

Death shook his head and turned round to the water's edge. Poseidon started moving back to the palace, but Mr Hashimoto went up to the hooded skeleton.

"I know why you're worried, Mr Death," the butler said. "If all dead people returned to life, then you'll no longer have a job. If unemployed, it's important to get a new job. I once was a fireman. Don't be a fireman; bloody hot work. Maybe you should become international swimmer, keep swimming round the world. Get lots of sponsorship, many interviews with media, that sort of thing."

"Shut it," Death growled.

Mr Hashimoto then raised his arms and hands and started moving them about at great speed in front of Death.

"Would you like to play a game of karate before you go, Death?" he said. "Plenty of good fun. See who breaks most bones?"

Death did not reply. Instead, he dived into the water and started off on his next journey.

X

TIME FOR
CHANGE

TOTTY HAD BEEN IN THE CAVERN FOR TWO DAYS and, to her great surprise, was really enjoying herself. Everything was new and completely different to her life in Romford. She had never met people like Dolores or Mr Hashimoto before and was fascinated by their histories. Even Lord Poseidon tried to be friendly, although she soon learned that he was not particularly happy at this time.

Totty knew she should be concerned about what was going to happen in the long term, but it just didn't seem to matter to her. Yes, it would be nice if she could see her mum and brothers again, but she suspected that was a bit of a long shot. Her mental attitude was now very much 'go with the flow'. She was also pleased that Dolores was open with her about the different possibilities. In particular, she let her know that if she did have to go to the Underworld with Death, then she could always return later to the cavern if she wanted to. Dolores was certain Poseidon would welcome her back. So, in her own mind Totty decided that the cavern could be her long-term home. There were a lot worse places, she thought, including the council estate where her mum lived, especially late on a Saturday night.

The palace was immense, consisting of more than a hundred rooms, most of which weren't used. Totty herself had been given a small suite which included a large bedroom with a double bed, a sitting room and a bathroom. It was probably about the size of her mum's house and was all for Totty. Dolores and Mr Hashimoto had similar suites.

Totty spent most of her time with Dolores, who was Poseidon's housekeeper. She had been a slave in South Carolina in the early part of the nineteenth century. Both her parents had been slaves and she was born, raised and lived on the same plantation all her life. She had worked in the house for the owner's wife, Mrs Albuquerque, who by and large treated her well. Dolores had been fond of a boy slave called Samson when she was young and the Albuquerques were quite amenable to letting them marry in due course. Unfortunately, Samson had died of a fever before any marriage took place and Dolores never met anyone else. She lived until the age forty-eight, which was a good age in those days, before herself succumbing to fever. In her last few years, she'd become Mrs Albuquerque's senior housemaid and effectively ran much of the household for her mistress.

Mr Hashimoto was not only Poseidon's butler but did the heavy work in the palace. Given the large number of rooms, much of this involved washing all the floors and windows in those rooms which had them. Mr Hashimoto had been a fireman in Tokyo in World War 2 and had been killed in a bombing raid in the latter stages of the war. He had developed his butlering skills by working part-time at receptions in the British Embassy before hostilities began, so he was happy to take on a similar role with Poseidon in the afterlife.

The Sea God was a concern to both Dolores and Mr Hashimoto. Many years ago, Poseidon had been a dynamic god, occasionally ferocious but very active, always travelling around the seas and oceans. However, he had now become sedentary, docile and was grossly overweight. He spent all of his time in the cavern, where he normally remained all day in his pyjamas, reading old books about marine life. Dolores put this down to the departure of Poseidon's wife, Lady Amphitrite, who was the Sea Goddess. She had been rather forced into the marriage against her will and had little in common with her husband. She now spent most of her time visiting different islands, where she had various palaces, only returning to the cavern for short periods every few years. The last time she had been here, she had taken Poseidon's horses and chariot, which he used when he was travelling around his kingdom.

Another factor behind Poseidon's weight was that every meal in the cavern consisted of hamburgers and chips. This also explained why Dolores and Mr Hashimoto were exceedingly tubby. Totty liked a burger about once every three months, but not every day for breakfast, lunch and dinner. She was concerned that if this diet went on too long, then she would not only become as large as Dolores but maybe even Lord Poseidon!

"Totty, honey," said Dolores on the third morning as they were washing the breakfast dishes. "Lord Poseidon's very keen for you to say what we should be doing differently. We're all a bit set in our ways, you know. Also, are there any things you would like us to get for you, my love?"

Dolores had raised this matter a couple of times before and Totty had been thinking about it. She just wasn't sure what would be acceptable to suggest or ask for.

"I don't really know what to say, Dolores," Totty said hesitantly. "Life here seems sort of organised as it is."

"You say what you want," said Mr Hashimoto, walking into

the kitchen. "We want big changes in the cavern, so you need to tell us."

"That's true, honey," agreed Dolores. "You tell us again what your work was in Romford and if you want to do any of that work here."

"Well," said Totty. "I had two jobs. The main one was as a hairdresser and a beautician. But I was also a fitness instructor in a gym."

"You a beautician, Miss Totty. Sure you were good at that. You're very beautiful yourself," Mr Hashimoto said.

"Thank you," replied Totty, blushing.

"Hold on," Dolores interrupted. "What's a hairdresser and a beautician? We didn't have such folk in South Carolina in my day."

"A hairdresser is a person who cuts hair," Mr Hashimoto replied before Totty. "But done in a high-powered professional way, not like when you and I cut each other's hair every two years. Hairdressers use proper cutters called scissors, not garden shears."

"So, what's a beautician?" Dolores asked.

"Someone who makes people beautiful," the butler continued. "Does nails, eyebrows, creams on the face for skin, also plenty of good lipstick. Turns pigs into queens."

"Is that right, honey?" Dolores asked Totty. "There are actually people who do this for a living?"

"Oh yes," Totty replied. "You can earn a lot of money if you've got the right clients."

"Like you had in Romford?"

"Not exactly. Romford's like a first step to greater things."

"So, what's a fitness instructor?" Dolores asked. "And let Totty answer, Hash."

"That's my intention. I'm not so up to date on modern terms like fitness instructor. Also, the only gym I know involved jumping over a thing called a horse all the time."

"Glory be!" exclaimed Dolores. "Jumping over a horse."

"I don't think Mr Hashimoto meant a real horse," Totty said, smiling. "I'll explain what a modern gym involves."

"You do that," the butler replied. "I hope modern gyms do not have a horse. I remember now, if you don't jump high enough, you have a big crash with legs apart. Very painful for a man. While recovering, no longer a proper man, if you know what I mean."

"I think so," Totty said, smiling. "Well, a modern gym is a place you visit to get fit. It has all sorts of equipment like exercise bikes, cross-trainers, rowing machines, equipment to strengthen knees and different weights for muscle building. A fitness instructor, which is what I am, helps people to use these machines, choosing what level of resistance or difficulty they need and then monitoring their progress over time."

"I have a question," said Mr Hashimoto. "For rowing machines, I assume there is a need for a lot of water, so can only have row if a lot of water nearby. Is Romford by the sea or a big river?"

"No," Totty replied. "This is a rowing machine you keep indoors. It doesn't actually move anywhere."

"Why do people row if don't move?"

"To keep fit. The machine mirrors the effort involved in rowing a real boat."

"Seems very crazy to me. Do all the hard work of rowing, but go nowhere," the butler commented.

"What I don't understand, honey," said Dolores, who had been listening intently to Totty's description of a gym, "is why people do this for fitness reasons? Don't they get fit working during the day in the fields or factories or whatever they do?"

"I think things have changed," Totty replied. "A lot of people's work now involves sitting around in offices all day, so they don't get much exercise."

Before Dolores had a chance to comment, Mr Hashimoto leaped in with more observations.

"You are right, Miss Totty," the butler said. "In Japan many people do nothing but sit around. Often means bad things happen. Government ministers and generals, they spend much of their time sitting. When sitting, they do too much thinking and talking. Result is they make decisions like going to war. That's a really stupid idea. All wars are stupid. What's even more stupid is to make a decision to fight wars which lose. Fighting a war which you lose is really very, very stupid. If you have to go to war, make sure you win. Best, though, not to go to war at all. That's my view."

Everyone was silent for a while after Mr Hashimoto's pearly words of wisdom on war; words which should be included in every school curriculum in every country for future government ministers and generals. Eventually, Dolores decided on some practical action.

"I think it would be good if you could keep up your skills while you're here, honey. Hebe's due tomorrow and if you can think of a list of things you want, like proper scissors and some of those machines, which go nowhere, then we can put an order in and she can bring them in a few days' time. I really like the idea of you doing some proper hairdressing on me."

"Who's Hebe?" Totty asked.

"Lady Hebe is a hard-working goddess who brings us a regular delivery of whatever we want from the land of the living. She does the same for Olympus and the Underworld. You'll like her, she's what you call a Modern Goddess."

"Is she the one who brings us all the hamburgers?" Totty asked.

"She is, my love," replied Dolores. "Without Hebe we'd all starve here."

"Can I raise something else?" Totty asked hesitantly.

"Of course, honey."

"While I really like hamburgers, is it possible to have something else from time to time?"

"Ah," said Mr Hashimoto. "I get the feeling you're going to tell us to eat differently; that's good thing. Lord Poseidon, he likes hamburgers, but about time we tried to have different food. Hamburgers make us very fat."

Dolores smiled. "I think I agree, Hash. What would you like us to eat, honey? We'll give it a try."

The three of them got into a detailed discussion about different types of foods. Everyone agreed that to have some fruit would be a good idea, so they decided on apples, bananas, oranges, peaches and melons. Totty then put her big foot in it by suggesting fish. It was lucky that she hadn't made that suggestion in front of Poseidon, the God of the Sea. Fish were viewed as his children and you certainly didn't eat them. Totty apologised profusely but was quickly forgiven because she was new. Instead, they decided to order some chicken and lamb. Dolores was interested to hear about all these vegetables that she knew nothing about, so peas, carrots, sprouts and broccoli were added to the mental list. When Totty raised the issue of pasta, the other two didn't know what she was talking about, until she also mentioned risotto made from rice. Mr Hashimoto was very keen on rice, so that was included. Finally, Totty suggested they should treat themselves and order a chocolate cake. Again, Dolores did not know what was meant, but Mr Hashimoto got very excited.

"Yes!" he shouted. "I once had chocolate cake when I visited an aunt in Kyoto. American lady sent her this cake before the war when still friends. I was allowed two pieces as Aunt's favourite nephew. Her other nephew, my cousin, not favourite. He only got one slice, not two. Serves him right."

"Then we'll try this chocolate cake, whatever it is," Dolores said. "Now, can I suggest we stop there? Totty, can you remember all these things we've decided to get so you can tell Hebe tomorrow?"

"It would really help if I could write them down," Totty replied.

"Oh, um, I'm not sure," Dolores suddenly said defensively.

"No embarrassment, Dolores," Mr Hashimoto intervened. "Miss Totty understands in your day, many people were not taught to read and write. I'll get pen, ink and parchment from Lord Poseidon. Totty can make a big list for Hebe and then we can all discuss when she comes tomorrow."

"Thank you, Hash," Dolores said, and then looked at Totty. "We didn't have much education in my day, honey."

"Don't worry, Dolores," Totty replied, and gave her a little hug. "You know millions of things I don't know. I'll spend a bit of time this afternoon making a list."

"Today all is good, Missy Dolores," Hashimoto commented. "You see, Miss Totty is a Modern Young Woman. She'll change things for the better in the cavern. I'll go get writing stuff now. Will also tell Poseidon what we're doing. He'll be very pleased, I know."

Totty was ensconced in the large library on the ground floor for the whole afternoon. Mr Hashimoto showed her how pen and ink worked since she was only used to a biro. Dolores again emphasised she was to put down on her list whatever she wanted. She started off by creating the hair and beauty list which ended up running to two pages. It wasn't just a question of a pair of scissors, but different types of scissors, cutters, brushes and combs. She also needed shampoo and conditioner, and all this was before she got onto a manicure set, addressed eyebrows, thought about face oils, shaving cream and razors for Mr Hashimoto, lipsticks, nail varnish, and so much more. At the end she decided to include small bottles of Calvin Klein, Estee Lauder and Yves St Laurent perfumes.

Totty then panicked when she thought of the cost of everything she had written down, so she raced off to the kitchen to ask what her budget was.

"Don't worry about money, honey," Dolores replied. "You just put down what you want. The gods, they have plenty of money. I don't know where it comes from; maybe they make it whenever they need it. Hebe will sort all that out."

Totty started drawing up a list of gym equipment and then tore it up. She remembered being told that Hebe came every two weeks and decided it was best to focus on one thing at a time. She also realised she needed some proper clothes. She was wearing a very large skirt belonging to Dolores, which could only be kept up with a tight belt, as well as a shirt about ten sizes too large for her. She also needed some proper shoes since she was going around wearing four pairs of socks so she didn't slip in Dolores's bedroom slippers.

This necessitated her running out again to see Dolores to ask if she could create a list of some clothes for herself. Dolores agreed that was a good idea and confirmed there was no dress code in the palace, so she could wear what she wanted. Despite this, Totty decided to be quite conservative and only order a few grey skirts and white tops as well as plenty of underwear. For footwear, she just wrote down 'shoes'. She then ran out again to ask Dolores if she could order any clothes for her and Mr Hashimoto. Dolores was quite interested but thought she'd look at how Totty dressed first before making an order next time.

The food list was relatively easy. Totty decided to add some lettuce, tomatoes and eggs for salad, and also orange and cranberry juice as refreshing drinks. She was not sure how much food to order but would consult Dolores later on that matter.

In the evening there was a meeting of the entire palace as Totty, Dolores, Mr Hashimoto and Poseidon sat in the Sea God's study discussing Totty's many lists. Discussion really involved Totty reading out all the things she'd put down and having to explain what things like hair conditioner were. Everyone was impressed, especially Lord Poseidon.

"This is really excellent, Totty," he said at the end. "Just what we need to move into the modern world. Could I please ask if one more item could be added to the food list?"

"Of course, My Lord," Totty replied, inwardly feeling pleased with her day's work.

"I remember once eating sausages," Poseidon said. "I liked them a lot. Do people still eat them?"

Totty nodded and added them to the list.

"All very good," Mr Hashimoto said as they broke up. "Plenty of healthy food. I'm looking forward to a big meal of sausage and chocolate cake. Very good for us; will make us all fit!"

*

Early the following morning, Hebe arrived. There was a large wave as her four white winged stallions came through the cave entrance into the lagoon. They drew a golden chariot and galloped rapidly over the water before smoothly jumping onto the piazza and coming to a halt. Hebe got out of her chariot, drying off in a matter of seconds, and walked the horses round the side of the palace and into the empty stables at the back. She unharnessed them and pulled out some large sacks of oats for their feed. After seeing them settled, she crossed the square to Poseidon's quarters to see her uncle.

An hour later, Hebe was sitting around the kitchen table with Dolores, Mr Hashimoto and Totty. The goddess was wearing a dark blue designer tracksuit and bright yellow trainers drinking a glass of wine as she went through Totty's various lists.

"I pretty well understand all this on the hairdressing and beauty list," she said. "I'm not sure I can get everything in one go but I'll see what I can do. By the way, Totty, you need a hairdryer as well. I'll get one of those hand-held ones."

"I did think of that," replied Totty, "but I didn't know what to do about electricity."

"We probably need to get a generator in the cavern, but that's a project for the future. I'll get a battery-driven dryer. I've only ever seen rechargeable ones, which hits the same problem long-term, but I'll talk to some people and see if they have any ideas."

"What are these electricity and battery things, Hebe, honey?" Dolores asked.

"You don't worry about that at the moment, Missy Dol," Hashimoto replied before anyone else. "They're very complicated modern things, which you let the rest of us modern people deal with."

"Hash, I am trying to become a modern person," Dolores replied in a firm, raised voice. "I'll never get to be modern unless I learn about all this new stuff."

"I'll explain afterwards," Hashimoto replied.

"No! Totty will. I want to be proper up-to-date modern, not old modern like you."

"I'm only a bit old modern," the butler retorted. "What's more, I will become very quickly new modern. When Miss Totty finishes making me beautiful, you will see. I'm sure Honourable Miss Hebe here will fall in love with New Modern Mr Hashimoto. You and Miss Totty will then have much competition for me. I suspect when Lady Aphrodite hears about me, she'll come and visit the cavern and fall in love with me too. I'll have a big pick of ladies, you see."

"I'm sure you're right," Hebe said to general laughter round the table. "I'll let my mother know and you'll probably find that Hera wants to make wild, passionate love to you as well."

Hashimoto, who was also sipping at his glass of wine at that instant, spluttered, "No! No, Hebe! You must not tell Lady Hera. I'll be in big trouble if she takes a fancy to New Modern Mr Hashimoto. She's not an easy woman. Also, your father, Zeus, he'll then get angry with me. He'll turn me into a mouse and feed me to a big cat. No, you must keep me secret; only tell Lady Aphrodite."

"Let's see what you look like first," Hebe said, tongue in cheek. "Come on, let's look at the food list."

Again, Hebe quickly understood everything that was needed. "Two additions," she suggested at the end. "If you're going to have sausages, you should have bacon."

"Yes," Totty agreed.

"And plenty of sausages for Lord P," added Mr Hashimoto.

"Secondly, I think I should bring some more hamburgers as well. Although Uncle Posy's very keen on trying all this new food, he might just hanker after a hamburger from time to time."

"Yes," Dolores said. "He's set in his ways and they involve eating hamburgers for breakfast, lunch and dinner."

Totty's clothes list was short and understandable. It was, however, boring, so Hebe added all the fashion wear Totty had deliberately omitted because she didn't want to appear to be too forward. The result was that it included track suits, jeans, dresses, T-shirts, trainers, a pair of high-heeled shoes and much more.

"So, what are your measurements?" Hebe asked.

"I'm a C cup, twenty-three inches around the waist, weight just over eight stone and I'm five foot five high, size six shoes," Totty replied.

"Hold on a minute," Hebe said, and raced out of the kitchen to the stables. She shortly returned with a tape measure. "I'm not doubting you, but let's check."

Totty stood against the wall, which Hebe marked so she could check her height. She then ran the tape around her waist and let Totty know that it had expanded by half an inch, laughing that it was likely down to all the hamburgers she'd eaten in the last few days.

"What about new clothes for you two?" Hebe asked, looking at Dolores and Mr Hashimoto.

"Honey, we thought we'd wait to see what Miss Totty looks

like first, then maybe get some new things a bit later," Dolores replied.

"I would like a tracksuit like yours, Hebe," Hashimoto added. "But an important question before you buy. Can I wear a bow tie with a tracksuit?"

"I don't think so, Hash, but we'll consider it next time. Look, if I see something for either of you, I'll just go ahead and buy it. But I agree with Dolores, new clothes for the two of you when we've seen what Totty looks like. One thing we can usefully do now, though, is take your measurements since I've got my tape here."

Dolores and Hashimoto stood by the wall so their heights could be checked and then Hebe ran the tape measure round each of them.

"Good," she said when she'd finished. "Dol, you're the same height as Totty, and Hash, you're five foot ten. As far as waist size is concerned, it's sixty-one inches and fifty-six inches respectively."

"And Totty's what?" Dolores asked sheepishly.

"Twenty-three and a half inches," Hebe answered.

"Glory be," muttered Dolores.

"Hah, you're not slim like me, Missy Dol," Hashimoto said with a broad grin on his face. "I've not got far to go to be modern man with modern waist." The butler duly received a hard tap on the head for his remark from the sixty-one inch housekeeper.

Hebe decided to change her plans at the end of the discussion. She had been planning on returning to Olympus for a few days but now decided to get on with all these new purchases. Bringing change to the Sea God's palace was something she was keen on, so she arranged to spend the night in the cavern before setting off for Yorkgate the following morning. With any luck, she would be back in a couple of days.

Later in the afternoon Hebe took Totty to see her stallions.

"They're beautiful," Totty commented after being introduced

to them. "And you say they can swim underwater and fly through the air as well as running on land. How do they do that?"

"Totty," Hebe said in a friendly tone. "Over time, you'll realise there are a few things that are gods' secrets. That's one of them."

"And what are their names again?"

"Donk, Tonk, Bonk and Zonk. They're all brothers, born as quads. They call me Honk, by the way. They think I'm their sister."

"You're not, are you?" Totty asked incredulously.

"Don't be daft." Hebe laughed at her. "Come on, let's go and put our hamburger orders in. It must be time to eat soon."

XI

THE BOULDER
AND THE HILL

"WOOF, WOOF," WENT CERBERUS AS HE approached Aggy in the central kitchen. "Please can I have a Mars bar?"

The head chef looked at him. "Very good, Cerberus," she replied. "And what will happen if I say no?"

Cerberus looked puzzled. "Woof, woof," he went again. "Woof. I'll… er… have to go and ask Vesta. I'm not sure what comes next if that happens."

Aggy smiled. "Here you are," she said, opening the cupboard and taking out a Mars bar for Cerberus. "Vesta will be here in a few minutes. She's carrying out her first special project for me after she finishes lunch."

"Thank you," Cerberus said as he started munching the bar. After he finished he sat quietly on the ground staring at Aggy as she reordered all the spice jars on her table.

"You're very thoughtful today," Aggy said after a few minutes of Cerberus staring at her.

"Woof, I've got something to ask you," the dog replied.

"Go on then."

"Vesta's my friend and I've now found out that you can have more than one friend."

"That's true. So…?"

"So, Aggy, I was wondering if you and I could become friends?"

"Were you?" Aggy said, continuing her work. "And why, after all these years, do you suddenly want to be my friend, Cerberus?"

"That's easy to answer. You've got a cupboard full of Mars bars and if we were friends, you'd always give me one."

"That makes sense, I suppose. That's a good reason why you would want to be my friend. But now, tell me, Cerberus, why would I want you as a friend?"

"Woof, woof," Cerberus barked, thinking hard. "Woof, woof."

"I'm still waiting," Aggy said after a few more 'woof, woofs'.

"Woof, woof. I… er… would never bite your bum again," he replied hopefully.

"That doesn't seem a very powerful reason, Cerberus. You see my big metal ladle over there? You and I have known each other many decades. In all that time you've managed to bite me on my bum once, and that was in my first week before I got to know you. Now, how many times have I hit your three heads with my ladle?"

"A lot," was the meek reply.

"Two hundred and seventy-four, to be precise," said Aggy. "So, your offer not to bite me isn't one I'm too concerned about. Try giving me another reason."

"Woof, woof. I think I'll have to ask Vesta that one as well," Cerberus muttered disconsolately.

"I think you will. Still, you've been much better behaved recently, so I will go part-way to becoming your friend, Cerberus. For a few weeks, why don't we treat each other as 'temporary, associate friends on probation'? We can then see how it goes, and if it works we can move on to the next stage."

"What would the next stage be?"

"We drop the probation."

"Woof. Let me say it – 'temporary, associate friends on probation'. That sounds alright. Woof, let's do it."

At that moment Vesta appeared. She had been briefed earlier that day on her first project. She was to deliver a large plate of stew to a man called Sisyphus, who spent all his time trying to roll a boulder up a hill. Aggy had drawn her a map, but this was unnecessary as Cerberus offered to show her the way.

"Can you please bring back yesterday's plate and spoon?" Aggy called after Vesta and Cerberus as they were going out of the central kitchen.

It was about a twenty-minute walk through a part of the Underworld Vesta had never been to before. This was principally an area where a lot of building work was taking place as new quarters were being built for the ever-enlarging population. During their walk, Cerberus told Vesta about his conversation with Aggy and in particular about their new temporary, associate friendship on probation that he was very proud of. Vesta was pleased for him and also gave him valuable advice on how to answer Aggy's difficult questions.

"You mean I'm to tell people that one reason they should want to be friends with me is that I'm kind and helpful?" Cerberus queried doubtfully. "Is that really the case?"

"Well, I think you are," Vesta replied. "Try it and see, but make sure you don't threaten to bite any bums as part of the same conversation."

Eventually the two of them passed all the building work and came to a large, steep hill. There was a man about halfway up pushing a huge boulder towards the summit. As he was about to achieve his goal, the boulder suddenly spun off to the left and came tumbling down the hill. The man followed it at a more leisurely pace.

"That's Sisyphus," Cerberus said, and then barked loudly to get the man's attention. "Woof! Woof!"

Sisyphus walked over to Vesta and Cerberus. He was huge, with immense muscles, especially in his arms and legs, but also with powerful shoulders and thighs. Vesta viewed him as the strongest man she had ever seen. He had hair down to his thighs and a long grey beard which reached his stomach. In fact, he was covered in hair – back, chest, arms and legs. All he wore was a pair of old shorts, allowing the rest of his bronze body to perspire freely.

"Woof, woof," barked Cerberus. "Give us a Mars bar or I'll bite yer bum." He then added "please" after a few seconds' thought and a reproachful look from Vesta.

Sisyphus looked at him. "Bugger off, Cerberus," he growled back angrily. "You try to do that and I'll push that large boulder right up your bum. Don't you believe it won't fit; I'll make it!"

Cerberus looked at the boulder, which was about ten feet high and decided he didn't like Sisyphus's proposal, so he gave a quiet woof, backed away and sat on the ground, deciding to keep quiet.

Vesta decided to change the subject. "Excuse me, Mr Sisyphus," she said. "I've brought your lunch."

"Are you a new lassie?" Sisyphus asked, not unkindly, looking at Vesta for the first time.

"Fairly new. This is my first special project for Aggy. My name's Vesta, by the way."

"You know my name, but you don't have to call me Sisyphus. Richard's my first name, so a lot of people call me Tricky Dicky."

"Why do they do that? Is it linked to you pushing that big heavy stone up the hill?"

"Hah!" He laughed. "I'll say. You clearly don't know my story, so if you give me my dish and sit down next to me, I'll tell it to you as I'm eating. Why's the dog here, by the way?"

"Cerberus was showing me the way. I'm sorry about him threatening to bite you on the bum."

"Woof," said Cerberus, not wanting to be left out.

"That's alright, lass. He's not succeeded in the three thousand years I've been here, so he's unlikely to do so now."

"Three thousand years!" Vesta exclaimed. "Have you been here all that time?"

"So Hades tells me. He comes to visit me every hundred years or so, and last time he was here, he mentioned I was coming up to the three thousand mark."

"Cool," Vesta commented, waiting for Sisyphus to begin his history.

Sisyphus took a few mouthfuls of stew with the spoon before continuing. "I used to be a king, you know," he eventually said. "King of Corinth. I was quite a clever lad in those days, sometimes thinking I was smarter than the gods. But by the time I got to the Underworld, they had me classed as a Big Bad Lad."

"Why? What did you do?"

"First of all, I upset Zeus big time. In those days the gods had instituted a law of hospitality. What that meant was that when travellers visited places, they should be looked after and entertained by the locals, especially the rulers. Well, I didn't very often comply. I would be good at the beginning when a wealthy merchant turned up, inviting him into my palace for a large banquet. After he was relaxed, eating my fine food and drinking the best wine, he would tell me about all the riches he was carrying. At that point, I would summon my executioner who would surprise the merchant by chopping his head off, followed by the heads of all his retinue. His riches then became mine, which was very satisfactory."

"That's really horrible," Vesta replied in disgust.

"Maybe, maybe not," Sisyphus said. "I didn't really believe in this hospitality law. After all, entertaining all these travellers was very expensive. Zeus wasn't paying, so where was the money going to come from? At least my way allowed the first lot of travellers to provide me with the funds to put on a banquet for the second lot and so on. It was all self-financing, which seemed good economics to me."

"I'm not sure," Vesta remarked pensively.

"Let me continue. So, not complying with the hospitality law got me into Zeus's bad books, but what really angered him was when I disturbed his hanky panky."

"Hanky panky?"

"Yes; Zeus was – and still is, I'm sure – a randy old devil, always seducing members of the female sex wherever he goes. There was a particular occasion when he ran off with a nymph. I forget her name, but she had a loving father who wasn't at all pleased. He was also a god and came looking for her. I happened to know where Zeus was heading, so I did a deal with the nymph's father when he was passing through Corinth. I disclosed Zeus's whereabouts and the god made significant improvements to the city's water supply. I don't think he was successful in getting his daughter back, but Zeus really had it in for me after that."

"Is that why you have to push the boulder up the hill?" Vesta asked.

"Yes, but it's more complicated than that. Once Zeus found out I'd given away his whereabouts, he ordered Death to bring me to the Underworld and to chain me here. That's where I got really tricky. When Death pulled this big chain out, I asked him to show me how it fitted before putting it on me. The fool chained himself up to demonstrate, and at that point, I turned the key and locked him up before escaping back to the real world. Well, all sorts of gods went ballistic, especially Mars.

With Death chained up in the Underworld, no one could die. Wars would be fought, but there was no fun as far as Mars was concerned if everyone ended up alive. Eventually, Mars made it down here and released Death, so things returned to normal."

"What happened next?"

"After that I had to watch myself for a while. When I did eventually return to the Underworld, I found out that my wife hadn't given me a proper funeral. I complained to Lady Persephone, Hades' wife, and she agreed to me returning to the world for the proper rituals. To be fair, it's possible Persephone got Hades to agree, but I'm not sure. It didn't matter because once I was up above again, there was no question of a funeral; I was going to stay alive. Unfortunately, I had involved myself in so many tricks by then that the gods ensured I returned to the Underworld pretty pronto. There was no opportunity for future escape. Instead, Zeus determined that my punishment should be pushing this gigantic boulder up the hill. The bastard put an enchantment on the rock, so just as I'm about to reach the top, it slips away from me and tumbles down the hill. I have to follow it down and then start again."

"And you've been doing that every day for three thousand years?"

"All of the day and all of the night. No rest except for a short break for lunch. I don't have breakfast and dinner, which is why you've brought me such a large bowl. It's supposedly got double portions in it."

Vesta didn't say anything for a while, leaving Sisyphus to complete his meal. When he was done, they both stood up and Vesta took the bowl as well as yesterday's.

"Can I just ask you, Mr Sisyphus, or Tricky Dicky, if you prefer, a very simple question?"

"What, lass?"

"What would happen if you just stopped?"

"I'm not sure I understand."

"I'm just asking what's to stop you just leaving the boulder where it is and you having a good rest?"

Sisyphus looked stunned by Vesta's question. Cerberus, however, got up and started woofing.

"I don't think you're meant to suggest that, Vesta," Cerberus said, somewhat alarmed for his friend.

"Maybe not," Vesta replied. "But all I'm interested to know is what would happen?"

"I really don't know," Sisyphus said, still in deep thought. "Let me carry on and think about it and I'll tell you tomorrow if you come."

"You could always try what I suggested and see," Vesta replied.

"Woof, woof," barked Cerberus. "This is dangerous territory, Vesta. Come away. You shouldn't be interfering with the gods' affairs."

"Cerberus is probably right, lass. Come back tomorrow and I'll tell you what I've thought," Sisyphus said as he once more moved over to the boulder.

*

The next day Vesta followed the same route to the hill with Sisyphus's lunch. As she approached it, she could not see any sign of him, but heard a loud rumbling noise. Getting closer, Vesta saw the former king lying on the ground fast asleep while emitting regular snoring sounds.

"Hello," she said, standing next to him. There was no response, just loud snores. Vesta spoke in a louder voice, but the snoring continued. After further attempts to wake Sisyphus, which included shouting at him, Vesta put the bowl of stew down, then bent over him and shook him very hard.

"What? What?" Sisyphus growled as he awoke, while at the same time waving his arms in the air.

"It's only me, Mr Sisyphus, Tricky Dicky," said Vesta. "I've brought your lunch."

Sisyphus had now opened his eyes. "Hello, lass," he said, recognising Vesta. "Thank you. Let me get up."

"I see you've decided to see what happens when you stop pushing the boulder up the hill."

"That's right," he replied, taking the bowl of stew. "I thought a lot about it for a few hours and then decided to take your advice – try it and see."

"Cool. Did anything happen?"

"Not to my knowledge. I thought I'd have a bit of a lie down and must have fallen fast asleep. I'm still feeling tired," he said, yawning. "But I suppose that's only natural. I've three thousand years of sleep to catch up on."

"Have you decided what you're going to do when you're not sleeping? Are you going to push the boulder up the hill again and then have breaks every so often for a sleep?"

"No, I don't think so. It's all pretty pointless, really. I think I'll just stay around here resting for a few years. I might sometime start exploring the Underworld, but I'd rather take it easy for a while."

"That seems like a good idea. You don't mind me waking you up with your lunch?"

"Not at all. If you didn't, I'd probably have a few hundred bowls of cold stew waiting for me by the time I awoke. Anyway, nice to have a bit of company."

"I'd like to ask about one of the things you said yesterday. Who is Lady Persephone, Hades' wife? I didn't know he was married and no one ever mentions her."

"Persephone's a nice lady. She got abducted by Hades a long time ago and he forced her to marry him. She doesn't like it here much, so it's been agreed that she spends most of her time on Mount Olympus with her mother and only a few months each year with Hades."

"All the gods seem to get involved in very violent things," said Vesta. "It's not at all like what my life was like when I was alive."

"I suppose the problem with gods is that they can do whatever they like. It goes to their heads a bit. If they want something, they just take it or do it."

"No self-control," Vesta commented.

"No self-control," agreed Sisyphus.

*

For the next few days Vesta continued to bring Sisyphus his lunch. Every time she had to wake him up as he still had a lot of sleep to catch up on. The two of them always managed to have a chat about what life had been like when he was a king. Vesta was particularly interested in the different gods, many of whom Sisyphus knew, since they seemed to be much more in evidence on the earth three thousand years ago compared to now.

Then one day Vesta heard loud voices as she approached the hill. As she got nearer, she saw Sisyphus standing up with Satan shouting at him. Attila was also there, standing in the background with Cerberus nearby.

"No more sleeping! Sleeping no more!" shouted Satan. "The boulder must up the hill go. Up it must!"

"No, it mustn't!" Sisyphus shouted back. "Every time it goes up the hill, it comes back again. It doesn't stay there, see, so it's pointless pushing it up."

"It must go up! Up the hill, it must!"

"Listen, you slimy creep. I've just bloody told you, haven't I? It doesn't stay there. It rolls back down again. If you don't believe me, you try it. Go on." Sisyphus pointed at the boulder.

"It's not meant to stay there!" a very agitated Satan screeched. "It's meant to come back! Back it's meant to come! That's the whole point of it! The point, that is!"

"Well, it's bloody stupid!" Sisyphus shouted back. "I'm not doing it anymore. Waste of my time. I've got better things to do!"

"Better things to do! Things better to do! This is what you do. The boulder up the hill you push. Up the hill it must go!"

This argument continued for some time, with Satan getting increasingly animated. Vesta went and stood near Attila and Cerberus.

"What's going on?" she asked in a quiet voice.

"Satan decided to have one of his occasional tours of the Underworld and dragged me along. We were way over there," Attila said pointing in the distance, "when he looked over at the hill and couldn't see Sisyphus. So, we came to investigate."

"Woof. I was also on one of my tours and saw Satan, so I thought I'd follow him. That's why I'm here," Cerberus explained his presence. "I think we should just stay here and watch. Best to keep out of it."

"I agree," Attila said.

As the shouting got louder, Satan pulled out a whip which he had been carrying in his shoulder bag. He limped over to Attila.

"My whip you must take, Mr Attila. You must apply it to his back. To his back it must be applied. He must be made to push the boulder up the hill. Up the hill it must go."

"No, Satan. Sisyphus isn't my responsibility," Attila replied.

"But I order you. It is an order!" Satan screeched.

"You do it."

"I order you!"

"No."

"I shall remember this, Mr Attila. Remember I shall," Satan snarled, turning round and moving towards Sisyphus.

"If you touch me with that whip," growled the former king. "I'll crush you under my boulder, you grubby little fiend."

"You must go back to work. Now you must!"

Sisyphus didn't move with the result that the next minute Satan cracked the whip at him, striking him on his chest. Sisyphus roared, yelled out a series of curses and charged at Satan. He knocked Satan over like a force 5 hurricane racing through a flower-bed. With Satan on his back, totally winded and so unable to speak, Sisyphus dragged him a few feet towards his boulder, turned him over on his stomach and then lifted up the boulder.

"No!" Vesta shouted, moving towards the pair.

Before she got to them Sisyphus had placed the boulder on Satan's back, pinning him to the ground. There was the sound of cracking ribs and moans from a very squashed Satan.

"I'm going to have my lunch now," Sisyphus said, taking the luncheon dish from her hands. He then proceeded to move about five metres away, sat down on the ground and started eating.

Vesta knelt down by Satan's head. "Are you alright, Mr Satan?" she asked. All she got in reply was a moan and a slight shake of the head.

"Come on," said Attila, who had also come over. "Let's move this rock off him... Sisyphus," he called. "You've made your point. Come and help."

"Not me. Let him stay like that," was the reply.

"I'll help," Vesta said, standing up. "Come on, Cerberus."

Attila, Vesta and Cerberus together tried to push the boulder off Satan's back. They pushed from many different angles, but it just would not move. Vesta and Attila kept pleading with Sisyphus to help, but he refused. Meanwhile, Satan kept making pathetic moaning sounds.

"It's too heavy for us," Attila eventually said, standing back. "Sisyphus has been building up his muscles for thousands of years. He's probably the only person in the Underworld who can move this boulder. I'll have to go and get some help."

"I'll stay here with Cerberus," Vesta said.

"Woof, woof," Cerberus agreed.

After Attila had left, Cerberus approached Satan and bent down trying to look at his face.

"He's got really bad breath," he commented.

"Let me look," Audrey said, so Cerberus turned round and let his tail investigate Satan. "I'll just give him a little bite on the nose!"

"Aaaaaagh!" screamed Satan, trying to move but unable to do so.

"That's woken him up a bit," Audrey said as Cerberus went and sat by Vesta.

Meanwhile, Attila had returned to the Torturing Department. Only Ivan was there, the others still being at lunch. Attila and Ivan set off for the dining area to look for them. When they arrived, Attila was feeling hungry, so he decided to have a plate of stew, while he explained to his three associates what had happened to Satan.

"I'm finding it difficult not to laugh," Genghis said once Attila had finished.

"It's not a laughing matter," the Hun replied.

"Then why are you struggling to keep a straight face?" Vlad asked.

"I'm not. I..." Attila burst into fits of laughter and was immediately joined by the others. It took them all a couple of minutes to calm down.

"I think we should hurry up and go," Vlad said. "I wouldn't want someone else to free Satan without me seeing him first."

"We'll need a board to carry him on," Attila commented as he stood up.

Satan's four able assistants went back to the Torturing Department and took one of the doors off its hinges. They then carried it as a group to Sisyphus's hill.

Vesta was kneeling down by Satan, trying to keep his spirits up when they arrived. "Mr Satan, they're here now. We'll soon have you free," she said.

Satan only responded by moaning.

"How are you doing, Satan?" Genghis asked, bending down to look at his boss. He received another moan in reply.

Both Ivan and Vlad joined Genghis and also asked Satan about his health. By this time, Vesta was getting frustrated.

"Stop talking to him!" she shouted. "Just get the boulder off him. NOW!"

The four of them stood on the same side of the boulder and pushed for all it was worth. Initially it didn't move, but then gave way just a little. At that point, it was given a mighty shove and rolled over on the side. Satan screamed out as another rib broke. Vesta went over to him again and tried to calm him down. Now he was blubbering, and although she didn't like Satan, Vesta gave him a little hug.

"Yack," Cerberus went.

Matters were speedily resolved from then onwards. Satan was lifted onto the board and his four assistants carried him off.

"What's going to happen?" Vesta asked as they were setting off.

"We'll put him in his room," Attila replied. "I'd then better go and tell Hades."

"I'll come with you," Cerberus added, and bounded after the ambulance party. "See you later, Vesta."

After they'd gone, Vesta turned round and looked at Sisyphus, who had continued to sit on the ground watching all the proceedings.

"I know what you're going to say, lassie. I shouldn't have done that, but then he shouldn't have taken that whip to me."

"That's the trouble with you men. You're always fighting. Tell me, what are you going to do now, Mr Sisyphus?"

"I think I'd better go back to pushing the boulder up the hill. It was good, having a break for a few days, though."

"I'm going to go and peel some more potatoes," Vesta said, getting up.

"At least there's some point to that," Sisyphus commented, beginning to push the immense rock.

"I agree," Vesta murmured as she walked off.

XII

SHOPPING
IN YORKGATE

A S HEBE'S CHARIOT SLOWLY DESCENDED OVER THE
Yorkshire countryside, she turned her smartphone
on and made a number of quick calls to set up her
appointments for the day. She then went onto her online
banking app, where she checked her balance, which at £24
million she thought was quite adequate for a day's shopping
of sausages, sprouts and jeans. She confirmed that she had her
debit card and that the expiry date had not passed, otherwise
she would have to make a quick adjustment which only she
knew how to do.

Hebe had set up her banking arrangements many years
ago when people began using debit and credit cards instead
of cash. Previously, she had minted her own Bank of England
notes from the Royal Mint offshoot she had set up on Mount
Olympus without the UK authorities knowing about it.

Hebe's bank account was with one of the UK's major banks in the name of Lady Hebe Olympiakos, which was printed on her debit card. Whenever her balance needed topping up, she would create a mysterious credit. This was never investigated because Hebe had placed a shield over her account, preventing anyone from asking any questions or taking any notice of it. This applied to clerks, senior management, auditors and the regulatory authorities. Hebe had been unable to avoid providing a correspondence address, so she rented a shed belonging to her friend Trevor, which had its own postal address.

After landing the chariot in a field about a mile outside Yorkgate, Hebe set off along the quiet country road into the town. Bonk, Donk, Tonk and Zonk trotted along merrily and invariably drew waves from people passing in their cars. Hebe and her stallions were well known in the area, as she had been doing much of her shopping in Yorkgate for many years. The town had a mixture of traditional and modern shops. Hebe was friends with many of the shop owners and in a number of instances was their best customer. They believed Lady Hebe Olympiakos was an international businesswoman and philanthropist. She personally shopped for a number of the institutions she supported. Mount Olympus was understood to be a luxury hotel overseas, the Underworld was the world's first underground boarding school and her purchases for the cavern were explained as relating to a much-loved elderly uncle and his care staff.

At the top of the high street Hebe turned the chariot down a narrow lane and then immediately left into a large yard. This was at the back of Loosebottom's General Store, run by Trevor Loosebottom, BA. The yard had a large warehouse along the far side and a small shed near the entrance which was Hebe's rented address. The goddess unharnessed the horses and took them into the shed, which was full of straw, oats and a large tank of fresh water that Trevor had filled when he got Hebe's call. Hebe left the stallions, picked up her Prada bag from the chariot and went through the store's back door into the stock room and then into the shop.

"Eh up, Trev," Hebe called, putting on a Yorkshire accent for a bit of fun.

"Eh up, Hebe," Trevor replied, looking up from the counter where he was reading the instructions for a battery hairdryer. "How you doin'?"

"Fine," she said going up to him and giving him a gentle peck on the cheek. "So, you've got one."

"Yea, but the battery only lasts up to forty-five minutes max. Merv's still in bed, but I'll get him up soon."

"No probs. I'm seeing Stella in fifteen minutes, back a couple of hours later."

"Have you got your lists? I'll copy them and dish them out while you're at Stella's."

"Here," said Hebe, pulling out the various lists Totty had prepared. "I've spoken to everyone, so they all know what's coming. The food list is between you and Stanley – I'm assuming you'll get all the fruit and veg; also a chocolate cake, please. Clothes for Doreen and I'll take the beauty list to Stella myself. I'll come back here after my hair's been done, meet up with you and Merv, then call in on the others. I'm staying at The Anchor tonight, so beers on me this evening."

"Champion," said Trevor as he walked over to the photocopying machine.

Trevor was about forty years old, medium height, medium weight, medium brown hair, bright rosy cheeks and large ears which stuck out at ninety degrees. He had a BA in marketing from some college in Wales, which was the only time he had ever ventured outside Yorkshire. He quite fancied Hebe but was too shy to ever make a move, which was a relief to her. She viewed Trevor as a mate and any prospect of a relationship might involve her having to make unwanted disclosures such as her age. She was old enough to be his great-great-great –

write down several pages full of the word great – grandmother, which might be a bit off-putting for any man. Equally, Hebe was deeply unattracted to the idea of ever ending up with a name like Mrs Loosebottom.

A few minutes later Hebe walked into Stella's Beauty Emporium, proprietress – Mrs Stella Sidebottom, a peroxide blonde woman in her mid-fifties.

"So, what gives, Hebe?" Stella asked as Hebe was sitting in a chair opposite a sink and mirror while she was checking the water temperature.

"As I explained on the phone," Hebe replied, "I've got a new carer for my elderly Uncle Posy. She was a hairdresser and beautician before and she's keen to keep up her skills, despite wanting a change to caring for a while. I promised, as part of her employment, to fully kit her out. She can practise on my uncle and all the other staff."

"Let's have a look at the list you mentioned on the phone."

Hebe pulled out Totty's two-page beauty list and handed it to Stella.

"Very detailed," said Stella. "Look, if it's okay with you, I'll get my niece Angie to start off on your hair and I'll work on this. You know our Angie, don't you?"

"Fine," replied Hebe as Stella went off to call her niece. Thirty seconds later Angie Rowbotham, a younger version of Stella, was attending to Hebe.

"Eh up, Hebe," Angie said. "Shampoo and set, in't it?"

"Eh up, Angie," the goddess replied. "That's right. How's your young man, Cyril?"

"Ooooh, I dropped 'im, didn't I? Got meself another feller, 'aven't I?"

"And what 'bottom' is he?"

"What ye mean?"

"Doesn't everyone in Yorkshire have a bottom in their name?"

"Ooooh, er. Never thought of that, did I? Come to think on it, yer right, ye know. 'Is name's Norman Goodbottom."

"So you've swapped a Longbottom for a Goodbottom?"

"Yea, I suppose I 'ave."

"Is the water ready now?" Hebe asked, deciding to change the subject.

"Yea. Bend forward, will ye?"

At this point, Hebe and Angie became that small team which exists in all ladies' hairdressers, of a stylist and her client, working together to create whatever image they jointly decided on. All this while invariably talking about sundry world affairs, largely focused on the stylist's love life.

Nearly two hours later, Angie was just finishing off and Stella drew up a chair, having brought a coffee for herself and Hebe.

"I've got spares of all this stuff on the list," Stella said. "I'll let you have an apprentice pack for hair stylists and also a full manicure set. Is that okay?"

"Sounds fine."

"I need you to come and choose the different perfumes and lipsticks. These luxury brands have lots of different types. Also, I see you want a few things for men, like aftershave."

"I've finished now, Hebe," said Angie at that moment.

"Thanks, Angie. You've done a good job," replied Hebe, looking at the finished product in the mirror. "Here, this is for you," and she handed the young stylist a £10 note she'd taken out of her bag.

"Ooooh, thanks, Hebe," Angie gushed, taking the note.

"Oh, you spoil her," Stella said.

"It's fine," Hebe replied, getting up. "Let's go and look at those perfumes. I'm going to largely take your advice, Stella."

It didn't take Hebe and Stella long to decide on a range of lipsticks and perfumes. When it came to the men, Hebe's view was to take whatever was recommended.

"I was thinking," said Stella. "Your uncle's a very old man, I gather. Why not take him some Brut? It was all the rage for men forty or fifty years ago. It might remind him of when he was a younger man."

Hebe nodded her assent. It was easier than explaining that when Poseidon was young, there were probably dinosaurs walking around and the smells were very different to those in the modern era. Anyway, she doubted Uncle Posy would be using anything bought from Stella's; the focus would be beginning to turn Hashimoto into the Modern Man.

"Finally, what do you think of this?" Stella took the top off a bottle she had on her desk and put it to Hebe's nose.

"That's wonderful. You're wearing it, aren't you?"

"It's a new brand that's just come out. It's called Naughty Girl. Do you want a bottle?"

"Please. I'll give it to the carers," Hebe replied, looking at the display behind Stella. "I can see there's also a Naughty Boy. I'll take a bottle of that as well."

"For your uncle?" Stella questioned.

"He has some younger male staff. It will be a treat for them."

"You'll have to watch all these people in your uncle's house, Hebe. If they're all going around with Naughty Girl and Naughty Boy scents, you don't know what they'll get up to."

"I'll take the risk," Hebe replied with a laugh.

Over the next few minutes, Stella drew up the bill, which Hebe settled with her debit card. They agreed that everything would be packaged up and delivered to Trevor's by 5pm. Saying good-bye to Stella, Angie and the other girls, Hebe went out into the high street. After a few yards down the road, she turned round and went back into Stella's.

"I'll take another bottle of Naughty Girl," she said to the owner.

"Who's this one for? Yourself?"

Hebe blushed. "Possibly," she said. "How much?"

Stella handed it to her. "Pay me next time. And Hebe – be careful," she said with a wink.

*

Back at Loosebottom's General Store, Trevor and Mervyn were looking at the dryer and listening to the radio.

"What's on?" Hebe asked as she went to join them.

"Test match," Trevor said. "Been played down the road at Headingley."

"Are we winning?"

"No, Aussies are, worst luck."

Hebe sat down on a chair and looked at Mervyn. "Eh up, Merv," she said.

"Aye," was the reply.

Mervyn Loosebottom was a slightly larger version of his cousin, Trevor. He carried another couple of stones of weight and still had the same rosy cheeks, but with bigger ears. He wore extra-strength spectacles due to being extremely short-sighted.

Mervyn ran a shop fifty yards along the high street which was called 'Merv the Nerd'. It was a gadget shop, dealing with the repairs and maintenance of all sorts of technology and electrical gadgets. Mervyn was always busy because he could fix anything, so whenever people had a problem with their TV, smartphone, laptop or whatever, they would take it to him, fully confident it could be picked up the next day in full working order. The reality was that Mervyn was a genius; he had once taken an IQ test where the average score was 100, with anything in excess of 150 being exceptional. Mervyn had scored 487 and the computer-generated response was, "You Are an Alien from Outer Space." Hebe had often thought that if she were a grasping capitalist, she would take Mervyn off to Silicon Valley and create a multi-billion-dollar business around his inventive brain. Instead, being a goddess, she left him in his Merv the Nerd shop. At least he was happy there; Silicon Valley was not Mervyn territory.

Mervyn was not a great communicator, tending to use few words; in fact only one. He couldn't handle a conversation involving himself and more than one person, which caused difficulties with new people who met him for the first time. Hebe had known Merv for many years and so knew how to speak with him.

"Trevor's explained the problem, has he, Merv? I need a hairdryer that's got a very long-lasting battery. It can't be recharged because it's going to be used in a place with no electricity."

"Aye," Mervyn responded.

"This dryer's only got batteries that last for forty-five minutes. Can we get longer lasting batteries?"

"Aye."

"Have you got any?"

Mervyn stared at Hebe, blinking at her behind his glasses.

"No aye?" she said, meaning no.

"Aye."

"Can you get some?"

"Aye."

"Will you be making them yourself?"

Mervyn smiled. "Aye," he said.

"Good. How long will they last – twenty-four hours?"

Mervyn blinked again.

"No aye?"

"Aye."

"Six hours?"

"Aye."

"Eight?"

"Aye."

"Nine?"

"Aye."

"Ten?"

Another blink.

"Okay," said Hebe. "So, you can create a battery that lasts nine hours for this dryer?"

"Aye."

"It needs four at any time, doesn't it?"

"Aye."

"So, as well as fitting four in it, I could have four spare?"

"Aye."

"When can you make them by? This evening?"

Mervyn blinked.

"No aye."

"Aye."

"Tomorrow at 4pm?" Hebe said, deciding to give Mervyn much of the night and the next day.

"Aye," the genius said with a smile.

"Deal done," and Hebe high-fived Mervyn and Trevor.

Twenty minutes later, Hebe was inside Titebotham's Quality Butchers, run by Stanley Titebotham and his son, Albert.

The father, who was very much the boss, was one of the more difficult people that Hebe had to deal with when in Yorkgate. He was in his early seventies, had a totally bald head and a face which bore a strong resemblance to those of the pork carcasses hanging from hooks behind the serving counter.

"Young Albert's busy making up the order now, Lady Hebe," the butcher said, nodding at his forty-five-year-old son who was chopping up lamb steaks in the far corner of the shop. "I have already prepared the invoice for your perusal and settlement."

"Thank you, Mr Titebotham," Hebe said. "I'll look at it."

"Before you do, I hope you won't mind me raising a matter with you."

"Of course not," Hebe said with a smile but expecting a spot of bother.

Stanley Titebotham began with a sigh. "Your order for your uncle's residence, Lady Hebe, is very different to what you normally purchase. Very different, indeed." Another sigh. "Yes, Young Albert and I both independently concluded that it was very different. It was also received at such short notice too. Mr Loosebottom handed it in mid-morning. Yes, very short notice and it does create some difficulty for us."

"Are you telling me, Mr Titebotham, you don't have everything I asked for?"

"No, no, no. Not at all, Lady Hebe," the butcher replied, shaking his head. "Everything you asked for will be delivered as requested to Mr Loosebottom's fridge by 5pm this evening. No fear on that account. No, the difficulty is elsewhere." This was followed by another sigh.

"Where?" Hebe asked.

"As you know, Lady Hebe, we are quality butchers and we are used to dealing with customers of the highest standing. Our customers have many excellent attributes, the most important one being—"

"The most important one being they pay their bills?" Hebe interrupted helpfully.

"That was not what I was going to say, no."

"So paying their bills isn't important?"

"Of course it is, Lady Hebe. However, what I was going to say in this instance is that we and our customers generally have a high level of trust in each other. They trust us to supply them with high-quality meats and we trust them to keep us informed about their requirements in a timely manner. There is a mutual understanding between us based on shared values and common courtesies. This allows us to meet their requirements and to avoid issues in our supply chain and unwanted stock levels and such matters. Our customers are normally of such a standing that they understand how these matters work and so—"

"Cut the crap, Stanley," Hebe said firmly. "What you're

trying to say is that you've got a ton of hamburgers that you were expecting me to take and now you're stuck with them."

"I wouldn't quite put it like that," the butcher said defensively. "I—"

"But that's what you mean, isn't it?"

"Yes."

"Right. I'll take my normal order for burgers as well this time. Please get them out and put them on the bill."

"Thank you, Lady Hebe. I knew you and I would be able to resolve this matter in an amicable way."

Hebe ignored him and pulled out her smartphone to check the news, while Mr Titebothom prepared the revised bill. She wasn't concerned about taking the extra burgers since she could take them to Olympus. Bacchus and Heph would probably eat most of them. After a short while, Hebe went and stood by the butcher as he was working on his calculator.

"Why do the lamb steaks cost so much?" she suddenly asked. "That's more than three times what the supermarket up the road is selling them for."

"Lady Hebe," replied Stanley Titebotham in a slightly offended tone. "The lambs for our steaks are of the highest quality. They are reared in a special way; their diet is of the best. This is naturally reflected in the price."

"I thought lambs just frolicked around eating grass all day," said Hebe. "Do yours have shepherds serving them caviar and smoked salmon every evening, rinsed down with a glass of Veuve Clicquot?"

"They are of the highest quality, I can assure you," was the firm response.

Hebe looked at the next item on the list. "What's this? One pound sterling for each sausage? The supermarket's got a special offer of eight for a pound."

"I cannot emphasise enough how much importance Titebotham's gives to quality. If you are interested in cheap food, you go to the supermarket. For quality, people come to us. Now, please, I really must finalise this bill for you, Lady Hebe."

Hebe moved away from Mr Titebotham so he could continue. She pulled out her smartphone again and tapped away. Unbeknown to the butcher, the goddess's tapping had resulted in his calculator automatically reducing her bill total by twenty percent.

Mr Titebotham finished adding up the bill, looked at it and frowned. It was less than he was expecting, so he cast it again with the same result. "Strange," he muttered.

"Is there a problem?" Hebe asked, looking up.

"No, no, not at all."

"Shall I check it?"

"That won't be necessary, Lady Hebe."

"What about Young Albert? Didn't he once get a B grade in a maths exam?"

Mr Titebotham called over his son who, using the same calculator, got an identical result. His father still looked perplexed but handed the bill to Hebe, who settled it with her debit card without any further comment. She then smiled pleasantly, took her leave of the Titebotham family and set off once more down the high street.

Hebe spent the next hour drinking tea and eating cream buns with Doreen Higginbothom, who ran Doreen's Fashion and Sportswear for Ladies. They went through Hebe's list and chose a number of items. Doreen's husband, Harold, who ran the equivalent shop for men next door, called in with some super-large shirts and two new bow ties for Mr Hashimoto. Hebe felt she needed more time than she had, so she and Doreen agreed to meet up early the following morning to finalise matters.

On the way back to Trevor's, Hebe passed a scruffy boy of about fifteen years old who was holding a handkerchief covered in blood against his mouth as well as limping on both legs. He was clearly distressed and very agitated, mouthing a string of four-letter expletives as he shuffled along.

Back in the general store Trevor was still listening to the radio.

"How's it going?" Hebe asked.

"We're still losing big time," Trevor replied, referring to the cricket. "I've got most of the stuff down to me on the lists, so that's champion. Also, here's your case," and he pointed to Hebe's overnight case on a chair. "You left it in the chariot."

"Silly me."

"Nearly lost it and all."

"Why? What happened?"

Trevor proceeded to recount the alleged events of the last half an hour. The boy Hebe had passed in the street was Oswald Titebotham, the grandson and son of Stanley and Albert respectively. He had been nosing around Trevor's back yard when he spied Hebe's case she had accidently left in the chariot. He grabbed hold of the case, intending to run off with it, but as he began to move, he claimed the case opened up and a large black fist emerged, punching him in the mouth, knocking three of his front teeth out. The next minute, one of Hebe's stallions came out of the shed and kicked him on both knees. The stallion then told him to 'bugger off' before returning to his companions. By this time, Oswald was screaming like mad, alerting Trevor, who ran out and found him. The boy told him what had happened, to which Trevor replied "Yea, and pigs do fly," and then pushed him out of the yard.

"A real-cock-and-bull story," Hebe commented.

"Yea," Trevor replied. "Whoever heard of horses talking and cases which punch people?"

"Precisely," said Hebe. "The boy's probably been on drugs. I think I'll phone up his grandfather, though. The pompous fool's been getting on my wick this afternoon."

Hebe pulled out her phone and phoned the butcher's.

"Is that Mr Titebotham?— Mr Stanley Titebotham?— Mr Titebotham, this is Lady Hebe Olympiakos— No, nothing to do with my order. It's another matter. Do you have a grandson called Oswald?— You do. I thought so. Well, I have to inform you that he has been involved in a very unpleasant incident this afternoon— Yes, I'm about to tell you. He appears to have been lurking around the general store's back yard. Apparently, I had left a case in my chariot and he tried to run off with it— I fully understand you can't believe it, but he was found by Mr Loosebottom— You're not doubting Mr Loosebottom's word, are you?— Good, I would hope not. Anyway, in getting off my chariot he must have fallen because he's badly injured his mouth and both his knees— No, there was no need to call an ambulance. I didn't know who he was, but I passed such an individual along the High Street— Please let me continue, Mr Titebotham. Not only did this incident occur, but young Oswald is making up some fantasy tale about a big black fist coming out of my case and punching him, as well as one of my stallions kicking him and telling him to 'bugger off.'— Yes, yes, Mr Titebotham, I am well aware that horses can kick, but are you seriously telling me they can speak English?— You're not. Very good. Similarly, do you think I have an overnight case with a large fist in it that's got a mind of its own?— You don't. Good again. Speaking as two adults, Mr Titebotham, I have to ask if your grandson takes substances?— You don't know what substances are? Let's try drugs, especially of the hallucinatory kind?— You're shocked at my suggestion. Well, I'm shocked that your grandson is a thief. What's more, why's he not at school? Has the local juvenile detention centre given a half day's holiday?— He's not at a detention centre, you say. At the local comprehensive, I'm surprised.— I understand your concern, Mr Titebotham. I have to say to you that I am used to only dealing with suppliers of the highest standing. They must have impeccable manners, and family businesses, in particular, must be judged by the behaviour of all their members. I am seriously going to have to consider my relationship with Titebotham's in the future. I will— What was that, Mr Titebotham? You interrupted me— You are offering a heartfelt and unreserved apology on behalf of your family for your grandson's behaviour?— That's what I thought you said. Is that all?— I see. You feel it would also be appropriate to make an ex gratia monetary recompense for the distress and upset I have been caused?— That seems most appropriate— A credit note against my last bill will be most acceptable. … I'm sorry, I didn't get the amount. Did you say fifteen percent?— Not a good line; I keep hearing something beginning with a T— Twenty percent?— Calm down, Mr Titebotham, I'm sure it began with a T. Do you mean thirty?— The line really isn't very good. Look, I think fifteen percent would be entirely appropriate; you don't have to go as high as twenty or thirty— You want to pay more? Surely not— Don't have a fit, Mr Titebotham; fifteen percent is perfectly fair— That's what you meant all along. Good, that's agreed. The line's much clearer now. I knew you couldn't have meant ten percent— One further thought, Mr Titebotham. What about all of Trevor's distress? How do you propose we deal with that?— A large piece of fillet steak will be delivered later for him with my order, you say. Very appropriate. What's he going to drink?— A bottle of best bitter, you say. Don't you mean a crate?— Very well, a six pack— And what about Mervyn's distress? He was here earlier— The same again. Very good, Mr Titebotham— I knew you and I would be able to resolve this matter in an amicable way— Goodbye."

"You are a one, Hebe," Trevor said at the end of the call.

The goddess smiled before going to see her stallions to thank them, especially Bonk.

XIII

THE CRICKET
MATCH

DOREEN HIGGINBOTHAM WAS STELLA'S BEST friend. They had gone to school together more than forty years ago and their families had known each other ever since. Their two businesses complemented each other well, with Doreen focusing on fashion while Stella's interest was on the beauty side. Between them they were responsible for developing the image or persona of many members of the female community in Yorkgate.

Doreen's shop catered for two main aspects of the market – smart casual as well as a sportswear section, although with the athleisure trend these days, there was a certain amount of crossover between the two. Doreen had three daughters in their late twenties and early thirties who were respectively responsible for these two business sections as well as purchasing. Doreen herself had long-standing contacts with a number of the major fashion houses in Europe, such as Versace, Hermes and Yves St Laurent, and she was able to access the major luxury fashion labels for her more select clients.

The other arm to the business was a workshop at the back of the main shop. This not only dealt with alterations but was also capable of manufacturing a limited range of clothing under the 'Hebe Loves Yorkgate' label with a logo of a chariot, a small blonde figure and four white stallions. This was an arrangement agreed a few years ago between Doreen and Hebe over three bottles of wine, with Hebe taking five percent of all sales as a credit against her future purchases.

The workshop was run by Kasia, who had come over to Yorkgate from Poland nearly twenty years ago. Kasia's first job had been with Doreen, who was just starting off at the time. She had remained with her ever since, having married the deputy headmaster of the local school, where their two children were currently pupils. Although Doreen retained the full ownership of the business, she treated Kasia as one of the family with equal shares of twenty percent of the profits for herself, each of her daughters and Kasia.

Kasia was entirely responsible for all the employment in the workshop. She always recruited girls from Eastern Europe, in particular from Poland, Ukraine, Belarus and Romania. They tended to be in their early twenties and usually followed one of two routes over the next couple of years. They either settled down with a local young man and became long-term residents of Yorkgate, or they preferred to return to their home country with a range of design and manufacturing skills as well as fluent English. Needless to say, Kasia was a mother hen to her entire team and the Higginbotham family were also very supportive.

Hebe had met up with Doreen at 8am and by shortly after nine was largely finished. She had got everything on the list for Totty; Mr Hashimoto was already taken care of with his new shirts and bow ties, and the workshop was busy enlarging three already super-sized skirts for Dolores. They were also in the process of designing and making a couple of super-sized tops for the South Carolinian to match the skirts.

Hebe was looking through a rack of T-shirts that were being offered at a fifty percent discount. She pulled out one which was white with the slogan 'Bollocks to Brexit' on it. Hebe knew that Brexit had been a controversial subject in the country a few years ago, but she didn't know much about it. However, she rather liked the word 'bollocks', so she thought she would buy the shirt for herself.

"I'll take this one as well, Doreen," she said to the proprietress. "You've got a lot of them on offer."

"Yorkgate's very pro-Brexit. Those T-shirts are for the other side," Doreen replied. "I have to say, I was torn come the vote, so I abstained. On one hand I believe in this country having full control of all its affairs, but then look at the wonderful girls I employ in the workshop."

"I like the word 'bollocks'," Hebe said. "If I wanted a T-shirt which said 'Bollocks to Mars', could it be made for me to take this afternoon?"

"Don't know why not, luv. Let's go and see Kasia."

All the girls greeted Hebe when she and Doreen walked into the workshop. They sat down at a table with Kasia, who called Gosia, Viktoria and Svetlana to join them. Kasia was a great believer in her team being involved in everything.

"Yea, dead simple," Kasia said in response to Hebe's wish to have the 'Bollocks to Mars' T-shirt by mid-afternoon. "How many do you want?"

Hebe had only thought of a small one for herself but suddenly realised there might be quite a demand on Mount Olympus. "What about six in total? Two small, two medium and two large."

Kasia looked at Gosia, who nodded.

"You know what," Kasia continued, "an even better design

would be to have a picture or drawing of this Mars thing on the front. We couldn't do it for this afternoon, but could show you a sample next time you're here."

"That's brilliant," Doreen commented. "Have you got a photo on your phone, luv? I assume it's not the planet?"

Hebe looked through her photos and came across a particularly nasty picture of Mars's snarling face. "I'll forward it to you," she said to Doreen, pressing various keys. "Mars is not actually a thing, definitely not a planet, but a person."

The photo came through the next instant on Doreen's phone and all the girls crowded round to look at it.

"Oh my god!" Doreen exclaimed. "What an evil-looking man."

"He a fiend," Viktoria added. "Where he from?"

"A long way away," Hebe replied. "Definitely not British."

"We don't let people like that live in my country," Svetlana, who was from Belarus, contributed.

"Nor mine," added Viktoria. "Strangle them at birth."

Doreen gave a little cough. "Where did you meet him, Hebe?" she asked.

"It's a long story," replied Hebe. "I don't really know him well."

"He must have horrible family," Svetlana said. "Parents must be very wicked. Any brothers and sisters, they too should have been strangled while little. Better for world."

"I agree," Viktoria added.

Hebe was beginning to feel slightly uncomfortable. Without them knowing it, the girls were speaking about her family and Mars's only full sister was herself. "Well, I have met some of his family occasionally," she said slightly defensively. "They don't seem to be too bad."

"Do not be taken in, Hebe. They all wicked people, I know!" Viktoria asserted.

"Let's move on," Kasia intervened. "If you're happy, Hebe,

we'll make six 'Bollocks to Mars' T-shirts for you today and will prepare a sample with his face on for next time you're here."

"Agreed," the goddess replied.

Shortly afterwards, Hebe was walking down the high street to the general store. The previous evening Trevor had drunk four beers in the Angel, while Hebe had had a half of shandy. He didn't want to stay for dinner because he had Mr Titebotham's fillet steak at home, together with more beers. Trevor's sole conversation that evening was about the test match, which England was losing very badly. In fact, it was expected to be over in about an hour the following morning, so the authorities were giving out free tickets. Trevor wanted to go and he talked Hebe into joining him. They had to leave by 10am, as the match began at eleven.

Hebe had dinner brought up to her room. She knew little about cricket; it seemed to be such a boring game, the gods had never been interested in it, unlike football. However, since she was going to a match, she wanted to research the rules that evening and also understand how far ahead Australia really was.

By the time she turned off the light, Hebe had become a leading authority on the rules of the game. She also realised that England's cause was dire. To win, Australia only had to score thirty-seven runs the following day with all their second innings wickets standing. Since they had scored 435 runs in their first innings, this looked like a piece of cake.

Hebe and Trevor set off for Headingley in the chariot. Trevor had long given up lecturing Hebe about the need for seatbelts; he now just accepted there weren't any.

After a few miles, they joined the slip road for the motorway.

"You can't drive on the motorway!" Trevor exclaimed.

"Yes, I can," was the confident reply. "There's nothing in the Highway Code saying chariots can't be driven on the motorway."

"Eeee; it's not right," Trevor squealed, but Hebe ignored him.

They were very quickly riding along in the outside lane. Hebe had a horn attached to her chariot and she kept honking it to make cars move over and let them continue. After five minutes, her speedometer showed they were travelling along at 130 miles per hour.

"Hebe, slow down!" Trevor shouted.

"Trevor, please stop panicking. It will be alright."

Just at that moment they passed a stationary police car that had drawn up on the bank. It quickly started its sirens and set off in pursuit.

"Hebe, the police are following us! You've got to stop!" Trevor squealed again.

"Don't worry, Trevor," Hebe replied calmly.

Another police car joined the chase and then a third one intervened. All the cars were finding it difficult to keep up with the chariot. After a few more miles, flashing lights on the overhead signs were telling all the vehicles to slow down as there was a roadblock ahead. The chariot continued until coming round a bend; it encountered a row of police cars blocking off the entire motorway. Trevor was having a complete nervous breakdown by now, but Hebe ignored him. She gave a slight tug on the reins as they got close to the roadblock. The four stallions in unison took off, pulling the chariot about twelve feet off the ground. They sailed over the barrier, landed smoothly on the other side and continued on their way. Meanwhile, the three chasing police cars, coming round the same bend, were unable to break in time and smashed into the barrier at about fifteen miles an hour. No one was injured, but a large number of police vehicles were badly damaged.

The chariot came off the motorway a few minutes later and then continued at a gentle pace until they reached the cricket ground. Hebe found a quiet spot to park and left the stallions to look after themselves. She then pulled a very stressed Trevor along towards Headingley's main entrance.

By the time the two of them took their seats, Hebe had managed to calm Trevor down. She might have used a bit of gods' magic to do this, but he was now focused on the match, providing Hebe with a detailed analysis of all Australia's strengths and England's many weaknesses.

Trevor pointed out a gangly young man in the field awaiting the start of play. He was Eustace Uselessbottom, the only Yorkshireman in the team. Despite their fierce pride in their county, most of the locals, especially Trevor, preferred to disown Eustace. Eustace was a fast bowler in his third test. In the previous two he had taken no wickets and scored no runs. In the current match, his bowling figures were 0 for 211 in the first innings and 0 for 23 so far in the second. Despite having managed to score one run with the bat the previous day, he was generally known as Useless Eustace.

The England captain had not meant Useless to bowl that morning, so he couldn't explain to himself why he threw the ball to him to begin the first over. The crowd groaned and Useless set off to deliver his first ball. It was cracked to the off-side boundary and the crowd groaned again. Four runs were rattled up on the score board; Australia now only needed thirty-three to win.

The next ball was travelling wide of the off stump and the batsman left it alone. It passed the stumps, but then mysteriously came to a halt after travelling a further two feet. It then proceeded to double-back at an angle and hit the stumps. Wicket to Useless Eustace! The England fielders were stunned with disbelief for a few seconds, before giving a roar and running over to the bowler to congratulate him. The Australian opener could not understand what had happened, which was also the case with the two umpires, but he was out and he had to walk back to the pavilion.

The new batsman played the next two balls very carefully. When Eustace started running up to the wicket for his fifth ball of the over, the batsman at the bowler's end suddenly started sprinting to his compatriot.

"What the bloody hell are you doing?" the facing batsman said when the other arrived at his crease.

"I don't know," replied the runner, scratching his head.

While a fair number of four-letter words were used by the two batsmen at the far end, Eustace, with ball still in hand, sauntered up to the wicket nearest to him and knocked the bails off. The Wallabies had lost their second wicket.

The sixth ball of the over was left alone by the batsman and the following over, bowled by Eustace's fellow fast bowler, resulted in a further two runs to Australia, but no more wickets were lost.

"Do you understand what's going on?" Trevor asked Hebe as the players were getting ready for Eustace's next over.

"Sort of," said Hebe, deciding to keep quiet about her research of the previous evening. "But shhh, I'm trying to concentrate."

Eustace's first ball was so fast at 150-mph that the Australian batsman didn't have time to raise his bat. It didn't matter because the ball broke the bat before smashing into the wicket. Everyone in the stadium went wild, especially Trevor, who jumped out of his seat and waved his arms around. The crowd eventually settled down in their seats and play continued. For the next fifteen minutes, not a lot happened. Australia lost no more wickets but scored five more runs. They now needed twenty-six to win.

Hebe had read about a hat-trick, being three wickets in successive balls, and how rare they were. She thought it would be good to witness such an event. It was the sort of thing you could tell your young nephews about in twenty years' time.

The third ball of Eustace's fifth over was directed at the middle stump. It was quite a tame delivery and the batsman was about to block it, when for some unknown reason he lifted his bat and let the ball hit the stumps.

"Why did I do that?" he said to himself, shaking his head as he walked back to the pavilion.

The next ball was firmly driven by the new batsman. While he thought he had driven it to the off-side, for some reason it flew straight into the groin of his fellow Wallaby at the far end. It caused him to topple over on his back, the ball still lodged between his legs. Eustace went over to him and picked the ball out of his groin before helping him to his feet. Since it hadn't hit the ground, the new batsman was given out – caught and bowled, Eustace Uselessbottom.

By now the crowd was in a state of perpetual frenzy and excitement. Large numbers, including Trevor, were on their feet chanting "Eustace the Greatest," followed by three loud claps, then, "Eustace the Greatest," clap, clap, clap, and so on.

The next delivery was on middle and off. It had to be played, but just as it was about to be struck, it swung slightly and nicked the edge of the bat, before being caught by the wicketkeeper.

Again, a period of calm followed and Australia accumulated a few more runs. When they only needed sixteen to win with four wickets standing, Eustace struck again. He delivered a fairly straightforward ball wide of the off-stump which the batsman padded away. It was clearly not going to hit the stumps and was not leg before wicket. All the England team knew this, but inexplicably, everyone appealed. The umpire shook his head, but the England captain, still unsure what was driving him, insisted on it being put to the third umpire. This involved the final arbiter who was in the pavilion looking at a television replay, which was also shown on a large screen in the ground. The replay, to everyone's surprise, showed the ball hitting the pads plumb in the middle of the stumps. It was as if the screen was showing a different delivery to the one people thought they had watched. That, of course, was nonsense, so the batsman had to be given out. He argued with both umpires on the field before leaving, but off he eventually went.

Three balls later, Eustace unleashed another trick he didn't know he had. He bowled straight on a good length. When the ball was about a foot away from the bat, it shot up in the air at ninety degrees, then travelled over the batsman's head, before coming down vertically to hit the wicket. Eight wickets down and the English crowd was going wild. "Eustace the Greatest," clap, clap, clap became louder and louder.

During the morning's proceedings, the Australian dressing room had become increasingly incensed at what was going on. They were sure that mystery forces were at work and when the eighth wicket fell, they snapped. The captain went on the balcony, calling the remaining batsman and the one who had just lost his wicket towards the pavilion. He then went down the stairs with his vice-captain and team manager for a consultation on the edge of the pitch. The crowd started to get restless, yelling at them to get on with it, poor losers and such like. Lots of the vernacular were spewing forth from between the Wallaby lips, so after a while the two umpires and the third umpire joined the group. It was clear, with arms being waved around, and fists being shaken, that the Australian team was in a fury. This was not just down to them having lost so many wickets, but the way those dismissals had occurred. However, as the umpires pointed out, the rules of the game had been strictly followed. If Eustace Uselessbottom had delivered a ball at 150-mph, even though this was nearly 50-mph greater than any other recorded delivery in the history of the game, it was not illegal. His action was entirely normal and he had no external assistance, such as a sling, to assist him in this matter. The Australians were left with wild allegations of voodoo magic being applied but could not provide any evidence. As one of the umpires, R J Gomez from the Caribbean, noted, voodoo was not known to be practised in England, especially not in the county of Yorkshire.

As the crowd became increasingly restless, it was agreed that there would be a twenty-minute break in play. Both teams returned to their respective dressing rooms, with the umpires joining the Australians. After some more debate about voodoo magic, Australia was given an ultimatum. They either resumed the match or the test would be awarded to England. After about fifty million four-letter words were uttered, they decided to carry on.

Trevor had been on his feet during all this break in play, singing, "Eustace the Greatest," or jeering at the Australians with the rest of the crowd. As he sat down, when the game was about to recommence, he looked at Hebe, who had been sitting quietly all this time.

"I told you that Eustace were brilliant, didn't I, Hebe?" he said.

The goddess smiled at him. "Something like that, my dear. Now, sit quietly and enjoy the rest of the match."

Australia progressed to within six runs of victory. Everyone was getting tense when Eustace set off on the final delivery of his over. A fast ball straight at the stumps bounced up a few inches more than the Wallaby batsman had expected. It looped in the air and Eustace took a straightforward catch in front of him. Nine wickets down and nothing unusual about that wicket. The outgoing batsman looked at the pitch, saw a slightly rough patch where the ball had landed, and cursed himself for not allowing for it. No voodoo magic there.

During the next over, Eustace was fielding on the boundary. Another run was scored and this brought Australia's number 11 to the crease. His nickname was Knocker and he was also a fast bowler who really disliked pommies. He was convinced that there was voodoo magic at work and had decided that the only way to counteract it was to whack the ball as hard and high as possible to get a six. Then it would be game over.

Knocker twice tried to wallop the ball but missed entirely. The next delivery involved a firm connection and the cricket ball shot high towards the boundary. It looked as if it was going to clear Eustace, but he leaped six feet in the air, higher than he had ever leaped before, and caught the ball in his left hand. He dropped to the ground, trying to ensure he kept hold of the ball as well as not touching the boundary rope. He was fine and the stadium erupted. The England team raced over to Eustace, lifted him on their shoulders and carried him round the entire boundary. The crowd kept chanting, "Eustace the Greatest," clap, clap, clap. After a while a number of them invaded the pitch, including Trevor. Hebe stayed where she was and decided to phone Mervyn.

"Aye," said a voice on the end of the phone.

"Merv, it's Hebe here."

"Aye."

"Are we still on track for later this afternoon?"

"Aye."

"Good man. By the way, we've just won the test match."

"Aye."

"See you later. Bye."

"Aye."

Hebe went off in search of Trevor. He wasn't too difficult to find with his bat ears. She had to pull him away from the crowd on the pitch as he was busy trying to arrange to go for a piss-up with a number of them.

"No, Trev. Not yet," Hebe replied. "You can go and get drunk this evening. We're going back to Yorkgate now. I want to be there for when Doreen brings her stuff and to link up with Mervyn. Also, it will take us some time to pack the chariot, so I can leave as soon as I've got everything."

"Just one drink, Hebe," Trevor pleaded.

"No," was the firm response.

"You sound like a wife," Trevor muttered.

"More like your mother."

"Her and all."

When they turned in to the street where the chariot was

parked, Trevor suddenly remembered the police chase and started panicking.

"There are two coppers walking by," he said.

"Don't worry, Trev," Hebe replied, knowing that she had put a shield around the chariot so everyone would ignore it.

"Good afternoon, officers," Hebe said with a smile as they all passed each other.

"Good afternoon, madam," one of them replied.

"We've just won the test match," Hebe continued.

"Who? England!" the same officer exclaimed.

"Indeed. Champion, in't it?"

"I'll say. Champion. Did you hear that, Doris?" he said to his fellow officer.

Hebe assured Trevor that they would ride back along the scenic route, so avoiding the motorway. As they were jogging along, she asked for his views on the match.

"Do you believe in all that voodoo magic stuff the Aussies were on about?" she asked.

"No way," Trevor replied.

"Perhaps it was me bringing England luck?"

"Nah." Trevor dismissed Hebe's theory. "It were Eustace. I told you he were brilliant beforehand, didn't I? Eustace The Greatest. He were the one that did it."

"If you say so," Hebe said with a smile.

XIV

BECOMING
BEAUTIFIED

―――――――――

"SO, AREN'T YOU SCARED OF MY BIG BROTHER BEATING you up if he sees you wearing this T-shirt?" Hebe asked Hashimoto.

"Mars never comes to the cavern," Hashimoto replied. "But if he does and starts a fight, I'll do karate chops on him. Break many bones as I do chop, chop. As the new shirt says, 'Bollocks to Mars.'"

"Okay, if you're sure, you can have it," the goddess said, handing Hashimoto a T-shirt. "But I think it's going to be too small for you. It's a large size, but you probably need a super-large one."

"I'll make me fit in it," Hashimoto asserted, pulling in his stomach. "I will soon be Super Fit New Modern Man."

"Fine," she said with a smile.

After Hebe had left for Olympus, Dolores, Hashimoto

and Totty put the large food delivery away into various kitchen cupboards as well as the ice room, which Poseidon had created more than a hundred years ago. All the hair and beauty products were taken up to Totty's suite for her to sort out over the next couple of days. That only left the clothes, which were divided up between the three of them, with ninety percent being for Totty.

"Totty, hon," Dolores said. "Both Hash and I would love to see you in your new clothes. Can we see you in them now?"

"We'll have a fashion show. That's what it's called, Missy Dol. New Modern Man, he knows about things like that," Hashimoto helpfully intervened.

They had a couple of hours before dinner, so it was agreed that they would all try on their clothes to show each other. Dolores went off to call Poseidon so he could also watch proceedings. All the clothes were put in the library which was next door to the main reception room, where the four of them congregated.

The next hour was spent by Totty putting on the various new clothes in the library and then presenting herself for inspection next door. Totty was delighted with Hebe's purchases and this was echoed by the others. In particular, her outfit of red high heels, black jeans and a cream pullover with a cheetah's face on the front was voted number one by everyone.

"I think we should give Totty a break for a while," Poseidon said after seeing her in the last of her three tracksuits. "Dol, why don't you go and show us what you've got?"

Dolores slipped into the library and returned wearing an emerald green skirt and a dark blue top, which resulted in general applause.

"I got other ones too, but this is the best," Dolores said. "I've really never had new clothes before. Always third-hand if lucky."

It was then Hashimoto's turn. He put on a new white shirt, which compared favourably with the very worn, dull-looking one he was previously wearing. He then adorned his neck with a large maroon bow tie. He looked at himself in the mirror approvingly before joining the others.

"You see, Lord P, you now have a New Modern Butler. Special dark-red coloured bow tie and super clean white shirt. I've also got a blue tie; have a look," Hashimoto said, waving his other bow tie in front of the audience.

"I'm very pleased to see my New Modern Butler," Poseidon replied, laughing. "You must only wear coloured ties from now on, Hash."

"You wait, everyone. I'll now go and put on the new T-shirt that Lady Hebe had specially made for Mr Hashimoto."

The butler trotted off next door, stripped off his shirt and put the 'Bollocks to Mars' T-shirt over his head. Unfortunately, Hebe was right. It was too small, being so tight he could only get it half on when it got stuck about three inches above his belly button. His arms were high up in the air and he also couldn't get the sleeves down. What was worse was that he couldn't pull the shirt off. After a few minutes of panic, he called out, "Help; help," in a loud voice. Dolores burst into the library and started laughing.

"I'm stuck," Hash said.

"So, this is what a New Modern Man looks like?" Dol said.

"No laughing matter," Hashimoto replied, seriously. "I cannot get on and cannot get off. It's stuck, and I need help from you, Missy Dolores. Don't call others; Lord P and Miss Totty will think I look mighty big fool."

"Come here and bend forwards, so I can pull it."

Dolores grabbed hold of the two arms of the T-shirt, which she yanked. Unfortunately, the garment didn't move at all, except to pull the butler towards Dolores. She tried again, but with no more success.

"I've got to get the others," Dolores said, after her third attempt.

"You ask them, please, Missy Dol, not to laugh," Hash answered.

Whatever Dolores said, Poseidon and Totty couldn't help laughing at the sight of Hashimoto. After various unsuccessful attempts, they decided to get Hashimoto lying on his front on the rug, with Poseidon holding his legs and the housekeeper and the beautician pulling at the sleeves.

"Pull your stomach in, Hash," the Sea God ordered. "Take a deep breath and hold it. Now, pull, everyone."

This time Hashimoto was released as the T-shirt came away. Unfortunately, in the process the shirt ripped, but at least the butler was free.

"Put one of your new white shirts on Hash," Poseidon said. "Hebe can always get you another T-shirt. I quite approve of the message. Nasty thug, my nephew. Perhaps she can have a Bollocks to Mars top made for me as well."

The focus of the next two days was on cooking. There were no more hamburgers. Instead, breakfast involved bacon, egg and a small sausage; lunch consisted of chicken or lamb and plenty of green vegetables. In the evening people either ate pasta or salad with plenty of fruit. Everyone was pleased to have a change of diet and Poseidon enjoyed his beloved sausages. It was agreed that the chocolate cake should wait for a few days.

The third day after Hebe left was set aside for Totty to start work on beautifying Dolores and Hashimoto. She had spent the evening before setting up her beauty salon in Lady Amphitrite's large bathroom, so when Dolores walked in the following morning she was presented with a number of tables covered with all the purchases Hebe had made in Yorkgate.

"You sit here on this chair in front of the mirror, Dolores," Totty said. "We'll begin with the hair and then move on from there."

"Gee, I've never been professionally beautified before,

hon," Dolores replied. "A brand-new experience for an old slave girl."

Totty had to take it very slowly with Dolores. When she asked her about how she wanted her hair to look, there was a blank expression. Totty raced off to her room and returned with a pad and pen to draw a few different styles. Dolores actually had very long, rich, curly hair which was a mixture of black and grey, so many different looks were possible. After their joint deliberations, the two settled on hair just touching the shoulders with a few curls. The next two hours were spent creating this image as Totty washed the hair, used conditioner, applied rollers and many different scissors before turning on the long-life battery dryer.

"Wow!" exclaimed Dolores at the end. "I sure look swell now."

"You do, Dolores," Totty replied. "But we've only just started."

"Hon, I'm in your hands. Hash is gonna be real impressed."

"And Lord Poseidon, I hope, at the end of all this."

"Let's go for it."

Totty then moved on to eyelashes, face cream for the skin and then showed Dolores a series of lipsticks.

"I've never worn lipstick before," she said.

"Well, let's choose one and see what you look like."

"What do you recommend?"

"This one," replied Totty, picking up a deep red colour. "It's called Passion Red."

"Passion Red! Go on, hon," Dolores said, giggling.

Totty applied it to Dolores's lips and was given ten out of ten for her choice. The two of them then set to work on hands and feet, starting in both cases with nails, which were far too long. Totty managed after quite a long time to get them cut, filed and cleaned. She decided not to suggest varnish on the fingernails, since a lot more work over the coming weeks would need to be carried out on both hands and feet. She did, however, apply skin cream and suggested to Dolores that she should take the tube and use it herself each morning and evening.

"I think that's nearly done for the time being," said Totty, reviewing her handiwork. "There's just the ladies' perfume to be applied."

Dolores and Totty sniffed the various bottles and decided on the Yves St Laurent. Dolores also liked the Naughty Girl scent which Hebe had included but decided it would be better if Totty wore it. She was shown by Totty how to apply the Yves St Laurent before taking the bottle off to her room, where she changed into her new emerald green skirt and a dark blue top.

It had been agreed beforehand that Hashimoto would cook lunch while the ladies were involved in beauty matters. Since he was only an expert at making hamburgers it was accepted that the old fare should be brought back that day. He also included a sausage for Lord Poseidon whom he served at the regular time.

Hashimoto had lunch with Dolores and Totty and spent all the time complimenting the former on being such a 'beautiful lady'.

"It's down to the two of you," he said. "You're a naturally beautiful lady, Missy Dol, and Miss Totty brings out best features. Now we've finished lunch, Miss Totty going to turn me into the New Modern Man, so Lady Aphrodite will fall in love with me."

"Go on, then," said Dolores. "Leave the washing-up to me."

When Hashimoto sat down opposite the mirror in Totty's beauty salon, he proudly said, "You see, Miss Totty, I've put on new clean shirt and blue tie for you today."

"Well, the first thing you're going to have to do is take the bow tie off and undo the top buttons of your shirt," Totty replied. "I need to put this towel round your neck."

"Is this the new modern way of making me beautiful?"

"No. This is called common sense. I'm going to start by washing your hair and it's to stop your new tie getting wet."

"Very well. Mr Hashimoto will do what Miss Totty says."

"Good. Now what do you want me to do with your hair and beard?"

"You mean style? I want to look like people a hundred years ago in Japan. Short hair and no beard."

"That's clear," said Totty. "Let's start. Please bend forward over the sink so I can wash your hair."

Hashimoto was far easier for Totty to do than Dolores. He had long, straggly hair and she cut away large chunks of it before carrying out the more intricate styling. It really was a traditional short back and sides. When it came to the beard and moustache, she covered him with shaving cream and then used two different razors. She couldn't help cutting Hash's skin in a few places because it hadn't been exposed to the air for many years. He didn't mind and a tissue soon stopped the bleeding.

"It feels very raw," was all Hashimoto said at the end of the shaving.

"It will do so for a few days. I suggest you wash your face regularly during the day and put on this face cream in the morning and in the evening," Totty replied, handing the butler a new tube of cream. "Next time Hebe goes shopping for us, I'll ask her to get you some aftershave."

It was agreed that Hashimoto would take one of the razors and shaving cream away with him so he could shave himself every morning. Totty showed him how to change the blades since he was only used to a cut-throat razor. After that, Totty cut Hash's nails, which were in much better condition than Dolores's and then they were finished. Hashimoto buttoned up his shirt, put his bow tie back on and looked at himself in the mirror.

"Brilliant, Miss Totty," he said. "I am now New Modern Man. You agree?"

Totty laughed. "I do, and I have a final gift for you. Here's a bottle of Naughty Boy, it's men's perfume," and Totty handed Hashimoto the bottle that Hebe had brought.

"Men do not wear perfume!" Hashimoto exclaimed.

"New Modern Men do," Totty replied. "Here, take the bottle and go and put a little on. Dolores will show you how to do it."

"Ah, she's got perfume, I know. Her scent is even stronger than hamburger's. That I could tell over lunch. I'll do what you say, Totty. I will become Naughty New Modern Man."

Later that afternoon, Hashimoto was in the palace's large entrance hall. He had applied the perfume under Dolores's guidance and was now wandering around the palace, doing no work but looking at himself in all the mirrors. The hall had two extremely large mirrors and Hash was standing opposite the one to the left of the entrance. He held his head up and moved from side to side looking at himself in different profiles.

"Honourable Mr Hashimoto," he said aloud as he admired himself. "New Modern Man." He then turned to change his profile. "Naughty Boy," he muttered. "Hash is very Naughty Boy." A different profile again followed by, "Who's a Naughty Boy?" in a squeaky voice, to which he replied in a deep manly tone, "Hash. Hash is a Naughty Boy."

Poseidon had been shuffling along the first-floor landing in his pyjamas, an old dressing gown and his bedroom slippers, supporting himself with his trident. At the sound of Hashimoto's voice he stopped and looked over the bannister, listening to all this talk about New Modern Man and Naughty Boy.

"Are you alright, Hash?" he called out before the butler had a chance to change his profile again.

"Ah, Lord Poseidon. I am just looking at myself after Miss Totty has been spending the afternoon making me beautiful."

"Well, come up here and let me look at you," Poseidon said.

Hashimoto trotted up the stairs. "You like the style?" he asked. "New Modern Man, I hope you agree?"

"I can't remember ever seeing you without a beard, and your

hair's so tidy. I do agree, a great improvement. But what's all this Naughty Boy stuff?"

"You've been watching me, Lord P?"

"It is my palace."

"Very true. Naughty Boy is men's perfume Miss Totty gave me. You smell." He moved closer to Poseidon.

"Very enticing, I'm sure," the Sea God said. "But I don't need any scent to tell me you're a Naughty Boy."

"It's not for you, My Lord. It's for Lady Aphrodite."

"Aphrodite. What's she got to do with it?"

"I'll let Lady Hebe tell you. She knows all about special big plans for me and Lady Aphrodite."

"Really?" Poseidon said sceptically. "Still, the important point is that Totty has done a really fine job on you, and Dolores also looks marvellous. She came and showed herself to me while you were having your hair cut."

"Miss Totty is a very skilled young lady. What do you think about her making you beautiful too? I'm her booking manager and can make an appointment for you over the next few days. Will have to consult the diary, but sure we can find time for Honourable Lord P."

"I've already been talked into it by Dolores. It's arranged for two days' time."

"Already arranged. That's good. Missy Dolores is my assistant. She is assistant booking manager. Very well trained by Hashimoto."

"Clearly so," replied Poseidon, turning round to return to his own quarters.

*

In the evening Totty was in the piazza reflecting on the day. She was feeling tired but really happy that she was able to apply her hairdressing and beauty skills in the cavern. She was looking forward to tackling Lord Poseidon, but he would be a very considerable challenge. She suspected it could take most of the day because the two of them would need to have regular breaks.

As she got close to the water's edge, she heard a female voice.

"Hello," the voice said. "Are you Totty?"

Totty looked down into the water and saw a girl of about her own age with blonde hair.

"Yes," said Totty. "But who are you?"

"I'm Kinky," the girl said with a giggle.

"What are you doing here?"

"I live here," Kinky replied. "With my friends. We're mermaids," and Kinky suddenly dived, showing her golden and blue tail to Totty.

"Mermaids!" Totty exclaimed when Kinky had surfaced. "I never thought you were real."

"Of course, we're real. I'll introduce you to my friends later. One day, if you like, you can come and visit us in our palace."

"You've got a palace! Where is it?"

"It's not really a palace, but we call it that. We live behind the rocks in that far corner." She pointed to the left of the lagoon. "There's a hidden passage at the side to get in. Half our palace is underwater and the rest is above the surface. There are little windows you can't see from here. We mermaids normally sleep on our nice comfy beds of warm sand with our fins in the water."

"So how long have you been here?" Totty asked. "I've not seen you before."

"We only got back a couple of days ago. We've been on holiday in the Seychelles with the boys."

"The boys?"

"Yes, we have mermaid boys, you know. They like to be called mermen, but they're really boys. Old Posy won't let them into the cavern without his permission, so when we want to see them we have to go out. Every so often we'll arrange a holiday together, but after a couple of weeks we're glad to get back. We love them a lot, but they're really silly at times, always showing off. Are people boys like that?"

"Yes," said Totty, smiling. "So why haven't I seen you in the last two days?"

"You're seeing us now. We heard about you on the way back from the Seychelles and—"

"How did you hear about me?" Totty interrupted.

"Gerrard told us. He gave us a lift back. He's a whale and is Moby's best friend. They bumped into each other when Moby had left the cavern and he told Gerrard all about you. So when we got back we girls thought we'd keep out of sight and watch what you were doing for a little while."

"But I've been indoors most of the time."

"Yes, but we've got very good eyesight and can see through the windows even if they're a long way away. Also, both Doly and Hash come out in the piazza sometimes. We've seen their new hairstyles. Did you do that?"

"I've been spending all day working on them. I'm a hairdresser."

"Super!" Kinky said. "That's my new favourite word, by the way. Super! I just love saying it. Super! So, you do people's hair. Will you do my hair one day, please?"

"If you want me to. But I'll really only be able to cut it because it's in the water all the time."

"That's okay. I like what you've done to Doly, so I'd like to try shorter hair. If I don't like it, I suppose it will always grow. Tell me, are you going to cut Old Posy's hair?"

"In a couple of days' time."

"Good. He needs smartening up. He's not been looking after himself for years. He used to come swimming with us some days, but now he never gets into the water. Do you swim, Totty?"

"Yes, but I'm not very fast."

"Don't worry, we'll teach you to go faster. If you started swimming, maybe that would get Old Posy to take it up again. Doly and Hash don't swim at all. We've offered to show them how, but they keep saying no."

"Perhaps I can encourage them to start," Totty said.

"That would be really good. Look, it's time you met my three friends. Stay here a minute."

Kinky disappeared under the water and then resurfaced with another mermaid who had ginger hair.

"This is Pinky," Kinky said.

"Hello, Pinky," was Totty's response with a little wave.

"Hello, Totty," Pinky replied. "We've got the same colour hair, haven't we? Ginger's best."

"No, it's not," Kinky said. "Blonde's best. Let me get the other two."

Kinky dived again and brought up Linky and Minky to meet Totty. Linky had brown hair and Minky had black. They both giggled, said, "Hello," and waved at Totty.

"Totty's going to cut all our hair, just like Doly's," Kinky informed the group.

There was a lot of giggling and splashing by the mermaids.

"That's Totally Top," Minky eventually said to Totty. "Kinky always does the organising for us. She likes talking a lot." This was followed by more giggling and splashing.

"Totally Top's Minky's favourite word, just like Super's mine," Kinky explained after the splashing had subsided.

"Totally Top's two words," Minky corrected her friend. "Linky and I say Totally Top, and Kinky and Pinky say Super."

"I think both are good," Totty replied.

"Do you sing, Totty?" Kinky asked.

"A little. My voice isn't all that good."

"We love music." Linky spoke for the first time. "Is Doly around? She's got a beautiful voice. What's that song we all like?"

"'Amazing Grace,'" Kinky replied. "Totty, could you please call her and ask if she'd sing it to us now?"

"I'll go and look for her."

Totty turned round and walked back into the palace. A couple of minutes later she emerged with Dolores.

"Hi, hunnies," Dol said. "Did you all have a swell vacation?"

There was a lot of everyone speaking at the same time about holidays, Dolores's new hairstyle, how Poseidon and Hash were. After a while, Dolores hushed everyone up.

"Look, we'll all speak more over the next few days. I've still got some tidying up to do inside, but I've come out specifically to sing 'Amazing Grace' to you all. Miss Totty's asked me because you've apparently recommended it to her."

"Hush, everyone," Kinky said. "Let's hear Dols."

Dolores stood in front of the lagoon, took a deep breath and then filled the cavern with her beautiful voice:

Amazing grace. How sweet the sound
That saved a wretch like me!
I once was lost, but now am found
Was blind, but now I see.

After the second verse, the mermaids joined in, but no voice could compare with Dolores's rich mezzo-soprano. Totty also started singing gently, while Hashimoto came into the piazza and even he began to hum. Poseidon's figure appeared at one of the windows and, while he did not contribute to the singing, a small tear fell from his right eye as the last verse came to an end.

"That's what we need in the cavern," Totty said to herself, joining the applause for Dolores. "Music!"

XV

NUMBER 5
CARNATION DRIVE

Iris and Hebe lived in a bungalow on the west side of Mount Olympus. Although they were both goddesses and each entitled to have a large palace made of gold and ornamented with rich stones, they preferred much simpler living arrangements. Their bungalow consisted of four bedrooms, two of which were en suite, separate living and dining rooms, together with a large modern kitchen with an island and stools in the middle. The property was constructed of brick but covered with white cladding. It was in grounds of about three acres, which would generally be considered excessive for a bungalow of that size. However, Hebe kept her four horses in a small paddock at the back, which included stables both for the animals as well as providing space for her chariot.

Nobbly Butt, formerly known as Norbert, had been provided with a map of Olympus by Hephaestus, so he was able to find Carnation Drive relatively easily. As he turned into the road, he was surprised to see only one property. Carnation Drive did not have a number 1, 2, 3 or 4 before coming to number 5, where Iris and Hebe lived. Nor was there a 6, 7, 8 or 9 and so on afterwards.

He walked up the driveway and, to his surprise, saw an electric doorbell which he pressed. This emitted a loud buzz and a short while later the door was opened. Nobbly Butt looked down and saw a small boy wearing a Manchester United T-shirt, blue shorts and a helmet on his head. In his right hand was a wooden sword which he was pointing at the visitor.

"Friend or foe?" said the small boy.

"Er, friend, I think," Nobbly Butt replied.

"Good," was the response. "Now, who are you?"

"I'm the maintenance man, come to fix the leak you've got. Are either Lady Iris or Lady Hebe in?"

"Auntie Hebe's round the back with the horses. I'll ask Auntie Iris if she's in," the boy said, and then turned round and shouted, "Auntie Iris, are you in?"

"Yes," was the reply from one of the rooms. "Who is it?"

"The man to fix the leak."

Iris appeared behind the boy and looked at the newcomer. "Do come in," she said. "You must be Nobbly Butt? Heph told us you'd be along sometime today. I'm Iris."

"Pleased to meet you, Lady Iris," said Nobbly Butt.

"Call me Iris. There's no standing on ceremony in Carnation Drive. You've met Fearless, I see."

"We haven't been formally introduced," the young boy interjected.

"Oh!" responded Iris, laughing. "Fearless, this is Mr Nobbly Butt; he works with Uncle Heph. Nobbly Butt, this is the renowned Fearless Frupert, aged six, who proudly protects Hebe and me from the many dangers to be found on Olympus."

"Pleased to meet you, sir," said the young warrior, putting out his hand.

"Likewise," replied the builder as he shook Fearless's hand.

Fearless Frupert followed the two adults into the kitchen. He had been living in 5 Carnation Drive for about fifty years. He was a casualty of the Thirty Years War that had devastated Central Europe in the seventeenth century. His original name was Ruprecht, but in the Underworld people started calling him Rupert, which was more common than the German equivalent. Because he'd spent much of his young life trying to survive, he was used to standing up for himself and so inevitably got into scraps with boys older than himself. On one occasion, after he'd won a fight with an eight-year-old, an adult commented that Rupert was really quite fearless; hence the name Fearless Frupert came into being.

Having been living in the Children's Quarters in the Underworld, without much to do, he had begun to take an interest in Hebe's regular visits, especially her four horses. After a while, being naturally fearless, he had plucked up courage to go and speak to the goddess and asked if he could look after the animals. From then onwards, it became a regular arrangement that Fearless would take charge of the horses for Hebe while she busied herself with various affairs in the Underworld. In due course, Hebe spoke to Iris about her young friend and the two of them, with Hades' approval, invited Fearless Frupert for a two-week holiday on Mount Olympus. The result was that Iris took to him as much as Hebe had, and so he became the third member of their household.

"Before we get on to the leak, would you like a coffee?" Iris asked.

"Coffee!" Nobbly Butt exclaimed. "I would, but how do you get coffee here? Everyone seems to either drink wine or water, although I've heard that somewhere you can get beer."

"We're very modern in this household," replied Iris, leading the way into the kitchen. "I'm afraid it's only instant, since we only get the coffee machine going at weekends."

"Coffee machine! Hold on; blimey, Lady Iris, what have you got here? This looks like a modern twenty-first century luxury kitchen. You must have electricity and all."

"We have, can't you hear the kettle heating up?"

"But how?" asked Nobbly Butt. "Everywhere else on Olympus and in the Underworld, it's all fires with coals and wood. No one's got electricity, let alone all these appliances. Top brands from what I can see."

"Let me show you," said Iris, moving around the kitchen and pointing things out. "Large oven, hob, microwave, coffee machine, washing machine, dishwasher – which we rarely use – American fridge freezer and plenty of storage space. Hebe spends a lot of time down below and so is able to bring back all the latest gadgets."

"But what about the electricity?"

"Oh, we have our own generator at the back. It works by sunlight or something like that. We got a Mr Farraday from the Underworld to spend a few weeks here setting everything up. He seemed to know a lot about electricity, which is gobbledegook to me."

"And it works the television," Fearless added to the conversation.

"Blimey! You've got a television?"

"In the living room," Iris responded. "Fearless is a Manchester United supporter, so we have to watch all the matches when they're on."

"I'm Hungarian, so I used to support Ferencvarosi in Budapest, but I followed the English game as well. West Ham was my team."

"Rubbish," was Fearless's definitive response.

"Before you two fall out on your respective teams, let me show you this leak," said Iris, smiling.

The goddess went over to the sink and explained that every time the tap was turned on, water started dribbling from the pipe which was in a cupboard underneath the sink.

"I see what you mean," said Nobbly Butt, bending down and watching the water seep through as Iris turned on the tap. "It's probably that the U-bend's become a bit detached at one of the joints. It might even have a slight crack in it. I'll check, but it looks as if it can easily be fixed."

"That's good. Let me pour out the coffee for you and then leave you for a few minutes; I've got to pop round the back and see Hebe. Do you want some coffee as well, Fearless?"

"Yes, please, Auntie Iris. Also, can I stay in here and watch how to mend the pipe?"

Iris looked at Nobbly Butt, who smiled, turned to the young boy and said, "Of course you can, Master Fearless. You help me out this time and then maybe you'll be able to fix the problem if it ever happens again."

"Good," said Fearless. "Let's get to work."

After Iris had poured out the coffees and left, Nobbly Butt and Fearless got onto their hands and knees and undid the U-bend completely before reattaching it securely.

"That's fine," said Nobbly Butt. "Let's see if that's all we have to do. Fearless, can you please turn the tap on while I look at the pipe?"

Fearless did as requested. The water no longer came out from the joint, but a few drops leaked out from the bottom of the pipe.

"Look at this, Fearless. There's a very small crack there which we need to mend. I think the best thing is to completely replace the pipe, but I don't have a spare one with me; so, we'll have a temporary fix. We'll put some sealant tape around it today which should last for about a week. I'll take some measurements, create a new pipe this evening and will bring it round tomorrow to replace this one. Does that sound like a good idea?"

Fearless studied the pipe and then, putting on his most important voice, replied, "I think that is an excellent idea."

Just at that moment there was a loud incessant hammering at the front door.

"I'll get it," said Fearless.

On opening the front door, Mars strode in and slammed the young warrior hard against the wall. "Out of my way, squirt," the God of War growled. "Where's that Nobb scumbag or whatever he's called?" Without waiting for an answer, Mars marched into the kitchen and found Nobbly Butt on his knees with his head under the sink. "You, come with me now."

The builder looked round and stood up. "Are you speaking to me, Lord Mars?"

"Of course!" Mars growled. "Come with me now, scumbag. I've got a cracked window and you're to fix it now."

"But I've got to finish here and then Lord Hephaestus has arranged for me to go to Lord Zeus and Lady Hera's because they've got a problem with some of their tiles."

"I don't care!" screeched Mars. "I say come now, so do as you're told, you snivelling wretch!"

"I'm sorry, My Lord," said Nobbly Butt, "but I really have to follow the instructions from my boss. He's made that very clear to me."

Mars was now standing directly in front of Nobbly Butt. "You will come now," he said menacingly, and at that moment started to move his right fist to thump the builder in the solar plexus to reinforce the point.

During this altercation, Fearless Frupert had recovered from being crashed against the wall and returned to the kitchen. Now, Fearless had always hated Mars; he was the one god on Olympus whom he did not call Uncle or Aunt, instead he always referred to him as the Pig. As he got nearer to Mars he held his wooden sword firmly in front of him.

Just as Mars drew his fist back to hit Nobbly Butt, a series of things happened at the same time. Firstly, Fearless's sword jabbed into the back of Mars's right knee with all the might that a six-year-old warrior could muster. Secondly, Nobbly Butt, who had been a bit of a street fighter in his days in Budapest and had seen Mars in action with Mr Bumble, ducked and shifted his weight to one side. Thirdly, Iris and Hebe walked into the kitchen, having heard the raised voices, and Iris let out a sharp scream.

Mars's right fist moved forwards, but his knee gave way, just as Nobbly Butt managed to move his body to the side. The result was that the right fist missed the builder but slammed into the side of the sink. Also, Mars toppled over and bashed his head on the sink edge and slumped to the ground. Hebe, who was behind Iris, raced forward and threw herself on top of Mars. He was groggy, but Hebe yanked his head back and then slammed his face down hard against the kitchen floor. There was a loud cracking sound, but Hebe repeated the exercise and there was another crack.

"Well done, Fearless. You okay, Nobbly Butt? Sorry, can't shake hands at the moment as I'm busy," Hebe said, continuing to sit on Mars, who was now unconscious.

Iris had quickly recovered from the initial shock and raced out of the room, returning with various restraints.

"Fearless, an important job. I want you to kneel down behind the Pig and keep shoving your sword up his backside," Hebe instructed.

"Yes, Auntie Hebe," the six-year-old warrior replied and eagerly did what he'd been told, putting as much energy as he could into the sword thrusts.

"I'll do it," Hebe said, taking a pair of handcuffs from Iris and pulling Mars's hands behind his back and securing him firmly. As she was doing that Iris knelt down and attached a pair of leg irons to his ankles, with a chain about a foot long.

"We need some tape to shut his gob up," Hebe commented.

"Will this do?" asked Nobbly Butt, as he showed her the sealant tape.

"Ideal," replied Hebe, taking it and putting it all over Mars's mouth. "Right, let's have a look at him." She half turned him over and they all looked at the god's face; even Fearless temporarily stopped his sword thrusts to view the results of their combined handywork.

"Blood everywhere," Iris commented. "His nose is clearly broken, left eye looks damaged and I'm sure his skull has cracked."

"Tuff buns. Anyway, it's quite an improvement from before," Hebe commented as she dropped Mars's head downwards on the floor.

"Hi, Nobbly Butt, I'm Hebe," she said to the builder as she stood up. "We're really sorry about what happened. We heard it all from the outside and came racing in. Are you hurt in any way?"

"No, Lady Hebe."

"That's good. Now, everyone, what should we do with him?" she said, looking at Iris.

"I want to say," interjected Fearless, "that the Pig pushed me really hard against the wall. I've got this big red mark on my elbow."

"The rotten sod!" Hebe exclaimed, looking at Fearless's arm. "I'll put some cream on that later." She then kicked Mars in the ribs as retribution.

"The first thing I suggest," Iris said, just as Fearless had moved back into position with his sword, "is that Master Frupert stops shoving his sword up Mars's backside."

"Oh, Auntie Iris," moaned Fearless. "Just one more hit."

"Just one more," Iris responded firmly. Fearless looked at Hebe, who nodded, so he gave one mighty last thrust before getting up.

"Next, let's move him out of here into the hall, while we

discuss... I'm sorry, I'm not sure what words I'm looking for," Iris said hesitantly.

"While we discuss how to dispose of him?" Hebe suggested.

"Not quite, but you know what I mean," replied Iris more confidently. "Come on, let's move him. Can you please help, Nobbly Butt?"

The three of them, with some assistance from Fearless, pulled Mars into the hallway. He remained face down on the floor, so Hebe decided to give the young warrior his instructions.

"Right, Fearless, I want you to take charge of keeping Mars under control while we go back into the kitchen."

"Yes, Auntie Hebe."

"What you're to do is sit on his back like this," and she sat on Mars's shoulders, "and watch his head. If it moves at all or there's any sign of him waking up, you're to do this." Hebe again pulled his head back and slammed it down face first on the floor. "Now, you try."

The two swapped places and the young warrior pulled the hair back and then bashed the head down with all his might.

"Not too hard," Iris said. "You might damage something."

"There's not a lot to damage," Hebe interjected. "There's no brain for a start. Anyway, keep him quiet, Fearless."

"Yes, Auntie."

Iris, Hebe and Nobbly Butt returned to the kitchen. The two goddesses assured the builder that he had acted perfectly properly and he wasn't in any way responsible for what had happened. Mars was well known for causing trouble wherever he went. It was agreed that as soon as he'd finished sealing the pipe, Nobbly Butt should go directly to Hephaestus, even before Zeus and Hera, and tell him what had happened. The two goddesses would follow once they'd sorted Mars out, although they weren't quite sure yet what that involved.

Five Carnation Drive was a busy place that day because at that moment the doorbell rang again.

"That will be Athene. I completely forgot she was coming round," said Iris getting up. "You stay where you are, Fearless; I'll get it."

Athene walked in and stared at the spectacle of Mars manacled and unconscious on the floor with Fearless sitting on top of him. She'd stopped being surprised by anything Mars had been involved in over a thousand years ago, so she merely asked, "What's he been doing now?"

Fearless leaped in with a quick-fire explanation. "The Pig hit me, Auntie Athene, and then he went to hit Mr Nobbly Butt and then I got up and hit him back and then Auntie Hebe also hit him and then we tied him up. So, you see, we won."

Athene smiled and bent down to kiss the six-year-old. "I can see that, Fearless. You've clearly done a very good job."

"Thank you, Auntie Athene," he replied, kissing her back from his sitting position.

"Come this way, Athene," Iris said, "and Hebe and I will give you all the grisly details. You stay where you are, Fearless. Call if you need any help."

"I won't," Fearless replied firmly.

In the living room, the three goddesses discussed the events of the morning. Nobbly Butt knocked at the door after he'd finished in the kitchen and joined them for a few minutes. He and Athene already knew each other because he'd recently repainted the study in her palace. Athene repeated the assurances given by the others that Nobbly Butt was not responsible for any of this situation – it was Mars's normal behaviour. She also offered to go and see Hephaestus later, although possibly after Iris and Hebe.

"I suppose that Fearless's short explanation, Iris, was pretty accurate," Athene said after the builder had left.

"What was that?" Hebe asked.

"I'll shorten it even further. Mars started a fight with Fearless Frupert, aged six. Fearless fought back and he won."

They all laughed.

"That's what we'll tell everyone," said Hebe jokingly. "But what are we going to do with him? Much as I would like to, we can't leave him on the hall floor forever with Fearless knocking him out whenever he wakes up."

Iris sighed, "I suppose one of us will have to use her powers and partially heal him, leaving the rest to time. For obvious reasons we can't take him to Zeus. You've got the strongest powers out of all of us, Athene. How do you feel about it?"

"I've got another idea," Athene replied. "If we heal him here, he's likely to go berserk and there'll be more trouble. I think our best bet is to wake him up and I'll take him as is to Paean, who can do a proper professional job on him. It will give the two of you time to get to Heph and he can then come along to Paean's and collect his troublesome brother."

"And beat him up again!" Hebe exclaimed, pleased at the idea. "Let's do what you suggest."

The goddesses returned to the hall and told Fearless what the plan was. He wasn't very keen, preferring to keep Mars under his firm control for a lot longer. However, he was persuaded by the prospect of a full bucket of very cold water being thrown over Mars's head to wake him up.

"Can I throw it?" Fearless asked.

"You can help me," replied Iris as she walked into the kitchen.

It took two full buckets to completely awaken Mars. As soon as he became conscious he started struggling violently, trying to get up and clearly uttering a torrent of abuse from his sealed mouth.

Athene knelt down and, pulling him by the hair, so their faces were a few inches apart, started lecturing him.

"I'm here now, Mars," she said. "You've caused a lot of trouble today and it's to stop now. Understand?" Mars glared at her but gave no response, so Athene yanked his head back. "Understand?" she shouted. He gave a slight assent with his eyes. "Good. What's going to happen now is that I'm going to take you to Paean for some patching up. Meanwhile, Hebe and Iris are going to your brother Heph to tell him about your disgraceful attack on a six-year-old boy and one of his staff members. I've no doubt you'll have to settle your account with him later. Whether Zeus is then informed is a matter which we will all need to consider later. Understand?" Again, Mars just stared at Athene, so she pulled his head back again. "I said, understand?" Once more, a slight movement of his eyes. "It would be better for you, Mars, if you started understanding first time round. Still, you're clear so far. I'm now going to stand up and we're all going to pull you up. You and I will then go out of the front door and walk to Paean's. You'll start walking with these restraints still on, but I'll have the keys. If I feel you're behaving yourself, as we go along, I may decide to remove some of them. If you start struggling or being aggressive in any way, they'll stay on. Understand?" This time Mars gave his immediate assent.

The goddesses pulled Mars up and Athene marched him to the front door. She turned down Hebe's suggestion of a metal clamp around his neck with a chain so she could pull him along, preferring to hold him firmly by the arm. Iris handed her the keys, while at the same time holding Fearless back from making one final thrust with his sword into Mars's posterior.

They could only shuffle along because of the leg restraints on Mars's ankles. He did try to struggle, but Athene kept him firmly under control. He also attempted to speak but could only utter 'mmm... mmm... mmm' noises. Athene said nothing to him until they were away from the bungalow and about half-way down Carnation Drive.

"Next time, Mars," she eventually said in a softer tone than previously, "you should pick on someone your own size. There was such a mismatch between you and Fearless Frupert and then Hebe, that you didn't have a chance. You should only fight people your own size."

"Mmm… mmm… mmm."

"I'm sorry, I didn't get that," said Athene. "No matter. It would probably have annoyed me. Seriously, though, Mars, you are a total idiot. You know you're on a yellow card with Zeus, who's just sick and tired of your bullying behaviour. Every time you hit Bumble, his good wife tells Hera, who then passes it onto Zeus. It upsets the household for the rest of the day. Your parents are very fond of the Bumbles in their own way. They're a bit quaint, I know, but the palace works smoothly with them in charge."

"Mmm… mmm… mmm."

"You know what will happen if today's events get back to Zeus. He'll give you the red card and that involves you being banished to an asteroid for a thousand years. Perhaps you deserve it, but for reasons I can't explain, I'm going to try to persuade Iris, Hebe and Heph to keep it quiet."

"Mmm… mmm… mmm."

"I suppose I ought to hear what you're trying to say," Athene said, sighing, "and we're walking too slowly with your leg irons on, so stand still and I'll take them off as well as the tape."

Athene partially released Mars but kept the handcuffs on him.

"Get these off as well!" he shouted as soon as the tape was torn off his mouth.

"Perhaps later," replied Athene, again taking a tight hold of his arm.

Mars said nothing for a period of time and then growled, "Zeus will never banish me. There'd be no wars, so there'd be no fun."

"I don't think I want to have a philosophical discussion with you on whether war is fun, Mars. Just think of whether you want to risk sitting on an asteroid for a thousand years."

"It's my job to create conflict. I am actually the God of War, or had you forgotten? You used to be a Warrior Goddess yourself in the past."

"I still am, but I don't create chaos for the sake of it. Anyway, I agree that you are the God of War, but Zeus's gripe with you is that you should focus your activities on mankind, not on Olympus."

Mars snorted in reply. "Come on, Athene," he growled. "Just take off these cuffs and then heal me yourself. I don't want to go to Paean's."

"You're going," Athene firmly stated. "After all, you'll be able to see Nurse Nightingale again. You like her, don't you? Do you remember she stuck that big needle into you last time and filled you up with all that calming liquid? After five minutes you were in a nice, quiet mood, almost behaving as a normal person for once."

"Shut up, you bitch!" shouted Mars and started to struggle. "Let me free."

"Right," said Athene angrily. "I've had enough of you," and she quickly got behind Mars and replaced the tape over his mouth. He tried to kick Athene, but she jumped out of the way. "No, you don't," and the goddess once more grabbed Mars's arm and marched him forwards.

Paean was the Healing God. This involved not just applying the inherent powers arising from him being a member of the deity but also the latest medical developments. Paean's great interest was science and he was well up to date with all the changes in modern medicine, which he applied on Olympus. He was ably assisted by Nurse Nightingale who had joined him with all her experience in the Crimea and various London hospitals. Like Paean, Nurse Nightingale had kept up to date with the latest nursing practices, avidly reading a wide range of nursing journals with which Hebe supplied her on a monthly basis. She also brought a high degree of professionalism to Paean's palace, setting up a consulting room, a clinic and had plans for a maternity unit if ever the gods started breeding again. During the day, she wore a blue nurses' uniform and supplied

Dr Paean, as she insisted on calling him, with a regular supply of white coats. Both of them always referred to the palace as the Surgery.

"We're nearly there," said Athene as she and Mars walked down the pathway to the palace. "Look at the window on the right, Mars. Can you see Florence? She's seen us and is waving. I'll wave back for the two of us. Oh, and she's already prepared. She's holding up that nice big needle which she's going to jab into you, the one with all that lovely, calming liquid."

"Mmm... mmm... mmm..." mumbled Mars frantically trying to pull away from Athene, who continued to grip him firmly.

"Don't be scared, my dear. Florence really likes you; I'm sure you're one of her favourites. There was a time when I thought she might make a good wife for you, but then I thought it would be a bit unfair on her. She really is too intelligent and attractive for you."

"Mmm... Mmm—"

"Come on," and Athene shoved the God of War towards the blue-coated Nurse Nightingale with her large needle.

XVI

EVEN GODS
NEED SORTING

K INKY HAD BEEN WAITING FOR HASHIMOTO TO appear at the front of the palace, so she could ask him to carry her inside to see Old Posy. The butler was used to doing this for the mermaids; he quickly fetched a towel for Kinky to dry herself with, before lifting her into his arms.

"You're puffing and panting a lot today," the mermaid said. "It's because you're unfit."

"You're right, Crazy Girl," he replied. "Miss Totty, she will get us all fit. We are going to do exercises with a boat to row which does not move. Very modern."

"I don't know what you mean, Hash, but no doubt I'll find out in good time. By the way, I like your new hairstyle and also that nice smell you're giving off."

"That is Naughty Boy perfume. It comes from Miss Totty

193

and Lady Hebe; special delivery to make Mr Hashimoto a New Naughty Modern Man."

"Well, I approve," Kinky said.

"Why do you want to see Lord P? He's a very busy god. I know; I keep his appointments diary. A very responsible job."

"No, he's not busy. Anyway, I've got an important question to ask him."

"Important high-powered question. I understand. I will let you ask him and then no doubt he will consult me before giving an answer. I'm his number-one advisor."

"You're always talking nonsense, Hash, but you make me laugh."

The Sea God was sitting in his study with the door open when they arrived.

"Can I bring Crazy Girl in, Lord P?" Hash asked at the study entrance. "She's got an important question to ask you."

"Of course," Poseidon answered. "Hello, Kinky, please sit on your normal chair."

Hashimoto gently lowered the mermaid into a comfortable maroon armchair.

"Thank you, Hash," she said when she was settled.

"You can call me Naughty Boy now," the butler replied.

"Have you got names for everyone?" Poseidon asked.

"Yes, Lord P. Everyone now has got a new name as we become modern with Miss Totty here. Miss Kinky is Crazy Girl, although she's been Crazy Girl for a long time. I am now Naughty Boy, Miss Totty is Clever Girl and Missy Dol is Mother Hen. All very modern."

"And what do you call me behind my back?" Poseidon asked.

"You're Big Chief, Lord P."

"Big Chief. Where does that come from?"

"American President is sometimes called Chief. You are more important than him, so you called Big Chief."

"There are probably worse names," Poseidon replied.

"And what about Minky, Pinky and Linky?" the mermaid asked.

"They are all Crazy Girls too. I haven't yet worked out separate names for them; will apply New Modern Brain to the problem in near future."

"Don't you mean Naughty Boy Brain?" Poseidon asked.

"Will get him involved as well," Hash said. "Enough gossip. I will leave you both to deal with Crazy Girl's important question. See you both later."

Hashimoto left leaving the door open, so Poseidon got up and shuffled over in his pyjamas and dressing gown to close it. The Sea God was very fond of Kinky, whom he viewed as the most intelligent and communicative of all the mermaids. Over the years he found he could have conversations with her on all sorts of matters, which he couldn't with others. These invariably needed a degree of privacy.

"You look well, Kinky," he said after sitting down again. "Have you come to tell me all about your holiday or is there really an important question you want to ask me?"

"It's a bit of both," the mermaid replied. "The holiday was super, but I'll come to it later. I really want to ask you to please take up swimming with us as you used to years ago."

Poseidon smiled. "What makes you bring this up?"

"Aren't there changes beginning to take place in the cavern, Posy? I've met Totty and seen what she's done to smarten up Dol and Hash. She's going to do all us girls' hair in a short while, but only after she's done yours."

"It's happening tomorrow, but I'm a bit surprised you want yours done. After all, you're under water half the time."

"That's what Totty said. No matter, we'll give it a go. She's going to come swimming with us and we're going to teach her to swim really fast. That got me thinking you might like to come back into the water again. We used to all have a lot of fun trying to outrace you, but you just stay indoors in your palace now. You are the God of the Sea, you know, Posy."

"Have you been talking to my niece, Hebe, recently?"

"No. Why?"

"You sound just like her the last time she was here. She was delivering new food, new clothes, all this hairdressing and beauty stuff for Totty. She didn't have time to stay in the cavern long, but she made sure she was here long enough to have a good heart-to-heart with me. I thought the two of you might have some conspiracy going."

"I've honestly not seen her for weeks. What did she say to you?"

"This is for your ears only, Kinky?" The mermaid nodded. "She was not in the least bit polite; actually, she was bloody rude. She told me I was a fat lazy bum, who should get off my big backside and do some work. By that she means carrying out my responsibilities as the God of the Sea, which she's interpreted as travelling around my kingdom, dealing with any problems that arise. She gave all sorts of examples, the most concerning one being open warfare between the shark and orca whale populations off the coast of Japan, which she seems to know about, but I don't."

"You're right, Hebe wasn't very polite. What did you say?"

"I told her she should have some respect for the older generation, but she just went pooh-pooh to that. Said we were both many thousands of years old and so any age difference was no longer relevant."

"I suppose that's true," Kinky said.

"Maybe," Poseidon replied. "What's more relevant is the substance of what she said. She's right, isn't she?"

"Yes," the mermaid agreed. "But I wouldn't have put it the way Hebe did."

"Hebe's always direct. It comes of dealing with a brother like Mars."

"Why did she bring it up now?"

"Presumably for the same reason as you. Totty's arrived and is beginning to change things. It's opened the door."

"Do you object to what she's doing?"

"Not at all. I support it, but I have my pride. I'm one of the three gods who rule the world, if not the universe. It's not easy to accept I've let myself become almost irrelevant."

"That's not true, Posy. We need you back with us as you were, even if there were times when you'd become very angry and we'd all be scared of you. Remember those tidal waves you'd create, battering us all against the rocks?"

"Yes," Poseidon said reflecting, before continuing. "Look, Kinky, let's not say much more on the subject. I do understand what you're all saying and I accept I've got to change. Please let me do it in my own way."

"Does that mean you will come swimming again?"

"Yes, but leave the timing to me."

"Super!" Kinky exclaimed. "One thing, though. You're so much tubbier than you were, so will you please enter the water gently? If you jump in like you used to, you'll end up emptying the lagoon."

"You're a cheeky little monkey, you know. Now, tell me about your holiday."

*

The following morning, Poseidon shuffled into Lady Amphitrite's bathroom, which had now become a hair and beauty salon. Dolores had agreed to help Totty for part of the time so she could learn how to cut Totty's hair in the future. The first thing they did was to agree with the Sea God what style he wanted. He was very clear on this. He still wanted long hair and his beard, but everything needed a massive tidy up. The other issue was addressing his hands and feet. Both had calluses and very long nails, but fortunately, there were no signs of ingrowing toenails. Instead, they were just a mess, especially the feet. Totty was sure that Poseidon spending all day in his bedroom slippers was a large part of the problem.

After Dolores had left the two of them to see to lunch, Poseidon spent a lot of the time telling the new arrival about the other gods and their history. Totty learned about the struggle between the Titans and Zeus, Poseidon and Hades, who were all brothers. Eventually the Titans had been defeated and sent to Tartarus, which was deep in the bowels of the earth, much lower than the Underworld. The three brothers then drew lots to decide who should reign in the various parts of their empire. Poseidon drew the Seas and the Oceans, Hades claimed the Underworld, and Zeus became God of the Sky, which also included the land.

Poseidon explained that Zeus lived on Olympus, which was in the sky, where many of the other, mostly younger, gods lived. He talked about the different personalities, being very complimentary about Athene's wisdom, Hephaestus's building and creative work, Aphrodite's beauty, and also the quality of Bacchus's wine. He clearly didn't like Mars, but then the Sea God claimed no one did, although he acknowledged the important role the God of War played. "If we didn't have a Mars, we'd have to invent one," was Poseidon's dry comment.

Poseidon spoke very affectionately about Hebe, not mentioning the fact that a few days earlier she had called him a fat lazy bum. The one member of the deity that Totty was aware he didn't mention was his wife, Amphitrite. In view of what Dolores had already told her, Totty felt it was prudent not to make any enquiries about the goddess. She had a strong feeling that if she stayed in the cavern long enough, she would be seeing for herself how the Sea God's marital relationship played out.

Poseidon was keen to hear about Totty's life in Romford, so

he was given a brief version of her family and what she did, much of which the Sea God had already heard from Dolores. Both of them avoided addressing the difficult question of Totty's future, the Sea God because he wasn't sure what his decision was and Totty because she just wanted to carry on 'going with the flow'.

"So, Totty, tell me about what you did as a fitness instructor," Poseidon said.

"There's not a lot to say, really. I did two days a week, mainly dealing with GP referrals," she replied.

"What are they?"

"GPs are general practitioners, that's doctors. A lot of people's health problems revolve around their lifestyle – eating the wrong food, too much alcohol, no exercise, that sort of thing. The doctors would send them to me for sorting."

"You mean these people had become lazy and fat like me?"

"No!" Totty squealed. "I didn't mean that, Lord Poseidon. You're a god; the rules are different for you." Totty blushed and became slightly flustered. "Oh dear, I don't know what I'm saying. I didn't mean you were lazy and fat— I mean obese. We're not meant to use the F word. Honestly, I really—"

"Don't worry, Totty," Poseidon intervened in a kindly manner. "I know what you meant. Why don't you carry on and tell me what 'sorting' involves?"

Totty took a deep breath and regained her composure. "It basically involves me developing a programme of exercises for them; some are done in the gym, some at home. It can go on for weeks and months and I show them at the start how to do the exercises, and then monitor how they're getting on once or twice a week."

"What about the food and drink?"

"They're not really my responsibility, but I always advise people. There's no use people doing loads of exercise if they then eat hamburgers three…" Totty blushed again. "Oh no, I've put my big foot in it again."

Poseidon laughed. "I understand and I actually agree with you," he said. "Tell me, does all this sorting of people actually work?"

"It depends. If someone wants it to work, it will. If they don't, it won't."

"That's the story of life," Poseidon commented. "So, are you going to be getting Hash and Dol sorted?"

"They want me to. Dolores says I can order some fitness equipment, if that's okay with you? Also, I want to keep up my own fitness."

"Of course – and what about different clothing for all this exercise? We can't have Hash doing press-ups in his butler's uniform and bow tie."

"No, we'll have to get sportswear for everyone. I've already begun creating a list for next time Lady Hebe comes."

"And what else is on the agenda for change in the cavern?" Poseidon asked.

"Dolores and I thought we would explore an even more varied diet. Also, more clothes for her and Mr Hashimoto. Something else I only thought about when I heard Dolores sing is music. Would you mind if we had some music? It's really good for listening to when we do the gym exercises."

"Good idea. Will this be the modern stuff?"

"Fairly modern, if that's okay?"

Poseidon nodded his head and reflected for a few seconds before continuing. "And how do you see me fitting into all this, Totty?" he asked.

"I'm not sure what you mean," Totty said hesitantly.

"Very simple. Don't you think it would be good if I had some new clothes and you devised an exercise programme for me? After all, even gods need sorting at times."

"That's great," Totty replied with a smile as she finished clipping the Sea God's last toenails. "If you really want me to, I'll get Your Lordship sorted."

*

The mermaids wanted to have their hair done on the piazza near the water's edge. This was because they were keen to watch Totty at work on each other's hair, which they wouldn't be able to do in the Sea Goddess's bathroom. The result was that Totty, Hash and Dol carried the tables with all the scissors, brushes, etc, onto the piazza, together with a chair as well as a large mirror that Hash propped up at the front. It was agreed that Totty would do Kinky's and Linky's hair one day and then Minky's and Pinky's the next. After that, the maids wanted to show Totty their palace.

The five of them had had a long discussion the previous evening on hairstyles. Totty was not entirely confident in the choices which the mermaids had made, but she was unable to dissuade them. They had apparently seen girls wearing their hair in all sorts of different ways while on holiday and each one of them was adamant about her own particular requirements. Totty took the view that she had tried her best to advise, but now was the time to give them what they wanted. After all, their hair would eventually grow back again if they ended up not liking what she'd done.

Kinky was sitting in the chair opposite the mirror. The three other mermaids were all in the water leaning on the edge of the piazza, watching proceedings that were about to start.

"Right," said Totty. "Just to recap. Kinky, you want your hair to look like Dolores's; Linky wants a bun like Lady Hebe's got, whereas you, Minky, want pigtails; finally, Pinky wants really short hair in the punk style. Have I got that right?" They all said yes and Totty then continued. "I've mentioned that once you get your hair wet, it won't look the same. That's especially true of buns and pigtails, so if anyone wants to change their mind before I set to work, that's fine."

"We won't," Minky said. The others agreed with her.

"And then after that we all want bras," Kinky added.

"Or bikini tops," Pinky said.

"Yes, bras or bikini tops," Kinky continued. "We'll ask Hebe to get them for us."

"She'll have to measure you," Totty replied. "Although you all look about the same size as me."

"I've got the largest," Minky boasted.

"No, you haven't," Kinky responded. "Mine are—"

"Sssh!" Totty intervened. "Let's get started," and she began to brush Kinky's hair.

After a few minutes in which all the mermaids talked about how smart Old Posy looked now his hair had been cut, his beard trimmed and his whole face generally tidied up, Totty decided to ask for their views on the next part of her project.

"We're going to get some music in the cavern," she said.

"Music!" Kinky exclaimed. "That's super."

"Super," said Pinky, with Linky and Minky, giving the idea a "Totally Top."

"How up to date on music are you all?" Totty asked. "I thought with a recent holiday in the Seychelles, you might have some favourite tunes."

"We all love music," Kinky replied. "Whenever we go off on holiday, we just adore listening to all the different sounds. We normally have three long holidays a year, so we know what's going on. Also, we often go out of the cavern and follow the cruise ships. The best time's in the evening, especially if they've got a band playing."

"So, what music do you like?"

"Abba," Kinky answered in a shot. "That's my favourite."

"That's mine as well," Linky said. "Especially 'Dancing Queen' and that one about a man after midnight."

"'Gimme! Gimme! Gimme!'" Pinky and Minky both chipped in at the same time.

"And 'Super Trouper,'" Kinky said when the others had stopped singing.

"And 'Money, Money, Money,'" Pinky added to the list.

"Great," Totty intervened in a loud voice before the mermaids tried to name every one of the Swedish group's songs. "Any other music?"

"Simon and Garfunkel," Kinky replied, "and Madonna and that Hotel California song."

"I like Queen," Minky contributed. "Especially that 'We Will Rock You' one."

The maids started chanting about rocking you in unison.

It continued like this over the course of the next two days as Totty styled all the mermaids' hair. Totty realised that all the music which the maids liked dated back to the 1960s, '70s and '80s, but found that understandable. Many of the tourists at a lot of the places they visited on holiday, as well as on the cruise ships they followed, would tend to be middle-aged or older and would want to listen to the sounds of their youth.

After all their hair was done, the mermaids said they also wanted perfume, which Totty was able to talk them out of because they were always in the water. The maids did insist on lipstick, promising to keep their heads above the surface for the rest of the day, so Totty gave them Passion Red, which was Dolores's choice.

As soon as they had put on their lipstick, the mermaids insisted on taking Totty to see their palace. She hadn't yet ordered any swimwear with Hebe, although it was on her list, so she just stripped off to her underwear and gently lowered herself into the water. It was surprisingly warm and she began to do breaststroke. She wasn't fast, but she was strong. The maids swam with her to the far left-hand corner of the lagoon. When they reached it, they swam round a rock which stuck out and entered a large cave. Just like the lagoon, the water came to an edge about halfway into the cave, which was the mermaids' living room.

"This is wonderful," Totty said, pulling herself out of the water.

The cave was very wide and filled with sand. At each side were a number of cubicles which had wooden boards to seal them off from each other but allowing entry from the water.

"These are our four bedrooms," Kinky said. "Old Posy arranged for Lord Heph to come here and put up these screens so we all have some privacy. As I said when we first met, we like to sleep with our fins in the water and our bodies on the ground."

"You've all got mattresses," Totty commented.

"And blankets in case it gets cold, but that's not often."

"And I see in the main living room, you've got a wine rack with bottles of prosecco."

"That's our favourite drink. We've also got lots of crystal wine glasses," Linky added.

Totty nosed around the maids' palace for a few minutes before suggesting they should all return to the piazza. She and Dolores had agreed that once everyone in the cavern was beautified, it would be time to eat the chocolate cake.

When the five of them had swum back to the piazza they found Dolores, Hashimoto and Poseidon waiting for them. Dolores had already cut up the cake and placed slices on plates for everyone. Totty got out of the water and pulled her jeans and T-shirt on. She wasn't worried about her underwear being wet; it would dry soon enough.

Dolores loved the different mermaids' hairstyles, which Totty admitted to herself had come out better than she expected. The effect of going underwater was still to be seen, but so far, so good.

"This is really good cake, Dol," Poseidon said with his mouth full.

"It is, Lord P," the housekeeper replied. "Hebe's made a mighty fine choice for us."

"It's scrumptious," Kinky said. "Really super!"

"Umm… yummy. Totally Top!" Pinky agreed. The other two maids had their mouths too full to speak.

"There is one big problem, Mother Hen," Hashimoto said, raising a discordant voice.

"What?" Dolores asked. "And stop calling me Mother Hen."

"That's your new name. You must now call me Naughty Boy."

"No, I don't. I call you Hashimoto and you call me Dolores. Our old names don't need changing."

"What do you think, Big Chief?" Hashimoto asked Poseidon.

"I think you should do what Dol says. But what's your big problem?"

"Where's my second piece of cake? I told you before I always have two pieces."

"There is no second piece," Dolores said. "I cut the cake into eight slices because there are eight of us. Everyone gets one slice."

"That's not right," Hash said. "Someone has my second slice. Miss Totty, I think you are eating my cake."

"No, I'm not, Hash," Totty said laughing. "Anyway, I've eaten most of it."

"You maids," Hash said, looking at the mermaids. "There's been a very big mistake. You are all eating my cake."

"No, we're not," Kinky spoke for all of them. "Go away or we'll pull you into the water."

"Missy Doll?" Hashimoto looked hopefully at the housekeeper.

"No!" was the very firm response.

"Lord P?"

"All gone, Naughty Boy," the Sea God said while licking his lips.

"I am treated like my unpopular cousin," Hashimoto moaned.

"Come on," Poseidon said when they had all finished eating. "Let's clear up here. I'll help you carry all Totty's stuff indoors."

Dolores and Totty spent the next day preparing for Hebe's return, which was expected at any time. Totty prepared all the lists herself on fitness equipment and music, although she knew she and Hebe would have to have a detailed discussion about how the music was to be played. She and Dolores worked on the clothes together, Totty taking most responsibility for the sportswear. Again, they agreed they would have to talk to Hebe about shoe sizes as well as measuring Poseidon for clothes. Finally, food was also a joint effort, with Dolores triggering Totty to have another bright idea.

"Gee, honey," said the housekeeper. "That chocolate cake sure was good. I wish someone could teach me to make it in the cavern. Do you think Hebe will know?"

"I don't know," Totty replied. "But why don't we buy a cookery book? That will allow us to cook all sorts of new dishes."

"What's a cookery book?" Dolores asked.

"What its name says. It's a book that teaches you how to make different foods. We'll work together on it."

"Gee, you modern people have all sorts of modern things. Let's go ask Hebe to get us one."

Probably two or three, Totty thought to herself, putting 'cookery books' on her list.

XVII

COMMUNITY
MATTERS

ATTILA AND GENGHIS HAD JOINED VESTA AND Ming at the luncheon table.

"How's Mr Satan?" Vesta asked.

"Coming along slowly," Attila replied. "Which suits us fine."

"What I don't understand is why Hades didn't heal him completely after his fight with Sisyphus?"

"Hades really hates Satan. There's a long history between them. Satan once tried to lead a revolution to take over the Underworld. He also tried the same with Olympus. Unsuccessful both times."

"Which all means Hades likes to see Satan suffer a bit from time to time," Genghis added. "He also makes sure he keeps a close watch on him in case he tries any funny business again."

"Presumably the two of you help him in that?" Ming said, more as a statement than a question.

Genghis and Attila had a quick look at each other. "Smart girl," was all Genghis replied with a slight smile.

"Hades knocked out two of Sisyphus's teeth as a punishment," Vesta said. "He's keeping them, hoping Hades will put them back one day."

"He probably will," Attila commented. "In a couple of hundred years' time."

"I'm waiting for him to do something similar to me," Vesta added. "You probably don't know that I'm the one who suggested to Sisyphus he should stop pushing the boulder up the hill."

"We do know. After all, I was there when Cerberus told Hades."

"Cerberus was a fool giving you away, Vesta," Ming said. "Talk about friends!"

"It's okay," Vesta replied. "Cerberus was only trying to be helpful when he asked Hades not to blame me. That naturally led to Hades asking what I had to do with the matter and it all came out."

"Cerberus should have kept his three big mouths shut."

"It's easily done," Attila said. "Cerberus meant well and we've all put our big feet in it at times. But to put your mind at rest, Vesta, I don't think Hades will punish you at all over Sisyphus. You're actually in his good books."

"I can vouch for that," Genghis added. "Hades is still marvelling at how efficient my section is since we introduced your proposal on keeping the arms and legs next to their actual bodies. The same applies to the teeth and nails Attila pulls out."

Attila nodded his head. "That's another thing Satan did to annoy Hades. He claimed it was all his idea, but Genghis and I had already let Hades know it was your suggestion."

"Which reminds me," Genghis interrupted. "Ivan and Vlad want you to come and do something they call a management consultancy job on their two sections. I think that means looking for better ways to boil and impale people."

"Ugh!" went Ming, screwing up her face in disgust.

"When am I meant to be coming along for my next torture session?" Vesta asked, looking at Attila.

"When would you like to come?"

"Surely you've got a schedule or a plan?"

"Of course they haven't," Ming interrupted. "It's all random."

"What does that mean? The Torturing Department must have a plan."

"Well, it hasn't!" Ming retorted and then looked at the two torturers. "Has it?"

Attila and Genghis looked sheepishly at each other. Eventually Genghis said, "Well, it's... er... not quite as formal as it could be. A lot's in our heads because... er... we've been doing it for a long time. Isn't that so, Attila?" he asked looking at his friend hopefully.

Attila shook his head. "No, Genghis. Let's be honest. We don't have any plan or schedule or anything."

"So, how does it work?" Vesta asked.

"I'll tell you how it works," Ming responded. "Half the people in the Torturing Department just turn up from time to time because they think they ought to. They've got used to their tortures and sometimes it's a chance to meet up with their friends. You told me about Harold and William, well they'd be in that category. The rest of the people are rounded up at random by Genghis, Attila and the other two early in the morning. If they see you and think you haven't been tortured for some time, they take you in. Recently, Genghis has also been grabbing hold of people with mismatched arms and legs, so he can pull them off and then try and create better fits elsewhere."

"What!" Vesta exclaimed. "That's rebuilding people's bodies. You could be creating monsters!"

"I'm just trying to give people better bodies like that Shaka Zulu I was telling you about," Genghis replied.

"This is so uncool," Vesta said.

"What it all means," Ming continued, "is that lots of people hide from Satan's four assistants and never go to the Torturing Department, while others are being done every few days. Ivan, for example, always seems to find Lord PompousAss, who spends half his time being boiled."

Attila looked at Vesta. "You're not impressed, are you?" he said to her.

"No. You need a proper system."

"How would that work?"

"First of all, how often should people be tortured if it's done properly, or is it all different periods for different people?"

"We've never been told," Attila replied. "But I think about once a month would be about right." He looked at Genghis, who nodded.

"Right," said Vesta. "You take a piece of paper and on the left-hand side put down everyone's name in the Underworld. You—"

"That's going to be a very long piece of paper," Genghis interrupted. "There are billions of people here. Also, Attila and I aren't very good at reading and writing."

"They're details we can get round," Vesta continued. "You then write along the top all the numbers from one to thirty in a row, each number representing a day. Next, you put a mark against each name in the day column when the torture is due to take place. So, against my name, there might be a mark against Day 7, which is the day I have to come in and have my feet tickled."

"I'm already confused," Genghis said. "Do you understand any of this, Ming?"

"I think I get what Vesta's trying to do, but there are lots of problems."

"Like what?" Vesta asked.

"Like the fact that we don't have days, weeks, months and years here in the Underworld. One day finishes and the next begins and that's going on forever. So that means no one will know which day it is. There's also a big communication job to explain all this and people will forget which day they're meant to come in. Then, it will take ages to create this schedule and it will have to be checked. But having said all that, I think it's a really good idea. I'm just not sure how to make it work."

"I can answer your first question now," Vesta replied. "What you do when everything is ready to go, is to say this is Day 1 and you put up a big notice or a sign with the number 1 on it. The next day the sign says 2 and so on."

"We can get Cerberus to paint the signs," Genghis commented flippantly. The others just stared at him in silence. "Maybe not," he added after a few seconds.

"Yes, that would work," Ming said after reflecting on Vesta's proposal. "But you've still got the other problems as well as what Genghis said about people not being able to read and write, so they won't recognise the day on the sign."

"There's also compliance," Genghis interrupted. "As you said earlier, Ming, lots of people hide from us to avoid being brought in for their tortures."

"May I make a suggestion?" Attila said, contributing for the first time. "Instead of having numbers for the days, why not have letters instead? It will mean everyone visiting the Torturing Department every twenty-six days, but that's not a problem. If you use letters, then everyone's torture day is the same as the first letter of their name. So, Ming, on day M, that's when you come in."

Vesta was thinking deeply and the other three were watching her, waiting for a response.

"Attila, that's really brilliant," she eventually said. "If we use letters, then we don't have to spend time preparing massive schedules, at least not at first. We just know that everyone whose name begins with A comes in on the A letter day, B on the B letter day and so on. What's more, most people who can't read or write probably know the first letter of their name."

"I agree," Ming commented. "Having letters solves a lot of problems. Not all, but a lot."

They continued discussing the subject for a few minutes before Attila drew it to an end.

"There are still lots of issues," he said. "But it's the way to go. Let's stop there now. Genghis and I need to discuss things with the others who might have some ideas. What I can say is that we can start following the letter idea very soon. I suggest we put a big sign up each day on the Department's roof. I also want to speak to Hades on the matter and get his support before Satan comes back. Let's all meet up for lunch again in two days' time and see where we are."

As they walked back to the Torturing Department, Attila and Genghis reflected on the discussion they had just had.

"Why didn't we have clever girls like Vesta and Ming when we were alive?" Genghis asked.

"We did," Attila replied. "We just didn't listen to them."

"It might have avoided a lot of problems if we had."

"As far as you were concerned, that's correct. My kingdom fortunately had me as its leader and I've just been called brilliant by Vesta, so no argument," Attila said with a broad smile on his face.

*

While the Torturing Department was eagerly exploring a change in approach, Aggy was mulling over the future of the Kitchens. Most new arrivals in the Underworld spoke to her about why they had to have stew every day for breakfast, lunch and dinner. Vesta had had more than one conversation with her on the matter. Aggy actually agreed with the wish for greater variety, but every time she had raised the matter with Hades, he had refused to sanction a change. Why he wanted the entire Underworld population to eat stew all the time, she could never understand. It couldn't be a punishment because he also only ate stew.

Aggy, however, was now sensing an opportunity to try again. She had been observing various changes in the Torturing Department which Hades had approved and wondered if he was now in a mood for progress in the Kitchens. She was well aware that many of these changes had been suggested by Vesta and knew from Attila that Hades had a lot of respect for her new young lady. Another card she could play was her own friendship with Lady Hebe, who delivered all the food for cooking on a regular basis. How she could fit an order for many billions of hungry mouths into her chariot, Aggy could not understand. However, she always succeeded in doing so and Aggy accepted that she should just view this as Gods' Business. Now, Hebe was a very progressive goddess, always open to new ideas. She was also Hades' favourite niece, so Aggy felt that if she could enlist her support, together with Vesta's involvement, it was possible that some headway could be made. At least it was worth a try.

Aggy had arranged a small group to get together with Hebe during her next visit. They met up in the back room off the Central Kitchen. It consisted of Vesta, Ming, Gigliola, Cerberus and herself. Gigliola was Italian, having run her own restaurant in Palermo. She was currently the Sprouts Section Head, which frustrated her because, more than anyone over the years, she had been arguing for variety in the menu. However, she was excellent at her job and Aggy viewed her as her informal number two. Cerberus had not been on the original invite list, but when he heard about the meeting he asked to be part of it. His basic argument was that being Aggy's temporary associate friend on probation entitled him to a seat at the table, which Aggy agreed to because he had asked very politely.

The meeting had been going on for about an hour, with most of the talking being done by Aggy and Gigliola. Hebe had agreed with Aggy beforehand to be in listening mode for most of the time. She was joined in this by Vesta, Ming and Cerberus, the latter primarily concerned about ensuring there were to be no changes to the supply of Mars bars to the Underworld. Much of the discussion had been about how the Kitchens would work if a variety of meals were allowed. Everyone agreed that the focus should be on lunch as the main meal of the day; breakfast and dinner could be addressed later. Aggy believed that there should be a different dish each day; for example, pasta one day, chicken and veg the next, fish the third, and so on before rotating back to pasta after about a week. This meant that the whole kitchen would be focused on producing one main dish each day and then another dish the next. Gigliola took the contrary view; she believed that there should be a variety of dishes every day, so people could have a choice. It would also allow individual sections in the kitchen to specialise as they did now. So, the potatoes section could become the fish section, the sprouts section could focus on pasta and so on.

After a while, Hebe interrupted the discussion. "What do Ming, Vesta and Cerberus think?" she asked.

Ming thought both Aggy's and Gigliola's proposals were good and didn't mind which one to go for. Cerberus was concerned about how Mars bars fitted into this plan.

"Have you heard of other types of chocolate, Cerberus?" Hebe enquired. "You could one day have Hershey bars, another day Galaxy bars, then KitKat, Cadbury flakes, a whole mass of delicious goodies."

"Woof, woof. Are they better than Mars bars?" he asked.

"They're all good. It depends on what you think. You won't find out unless you try."

"Woof. Can I have Mars bars on the menu as well?"

"Of course you can."

"Woof, woof. Let's go for it."

"What about you, Vesta?" Hebe asked.

"I think two things. Firstly, I'm like Ming; I think both proposals will work. Whatever we do, we're going to have to have a trial run."

"How would that work?"

"Probably have a small group of ten or twenty from the Kitchens making three or four different dishes to begin with. They then decide which one to try out more widely, so one day that dish gets cooked for all the kitchen workers. If that works, you then have a day when it's available for everyone. I suspect we'll have to have stew on the menu as well because a lot of people will feel uncertain about eating, say, Spaghetti Bolognese."

"Why?" Gigliola interrupted. "Spaghetti Bolognese is very good for you."

"We know what Vesta means," Aggy said. "So, what you're saying is we have a trial run with one dish, get that to work, so we can serve that either every day or once a week whatever we decide? We then do the same with a second dish and so on."

"That's right," replied Vesta.

"Makes sense to me," Hebe said. "But I think you've got another point?"

"Yes. It's simply that it's no good talking about all the detail if Lord Hades doesn't allow us to do it. What I don't get is why we have to eat stew all the time and we're not allowed to eat anything else?"

"Woof," Cerberus went. "Except Mars bars."

"Except Mars bars," Aggy repeated. "Vesta's right, though. Unless we can get Hades to change his mind, we can't move forward. But why he always stops us is beyond me."

"I've been with you many times, Aggy, to see Hades, and I too don't understand why he always says no," Gigliola added.

By now everyone was looking at Hebe, hoping she would have an answer to their question about Hades.

"I've never actually asked him directly," Hebe said after a

few seconds' reflection. "But I think I know why it might be. Uncle Hady is a very traditional god; he doesn't really believe in change or any sort of progress. That's certainly how he looks on the Underworld. His view is that humanity has a life on earth when they can do all sorts of things, often in the name of progress, but not always successfully. Once a person dies, though, everything relating to that person becomes frozen. So, Vesta, you remain as you were when you came here and you'll never grow up anymore, even though centuries will pass. It means that Uncle Hady views his kingdom as being static; he's not interested in change or progress here. The Underworld's been eating stew since it came into existence, so he thinks it should just continue to do so."

"But, Lady Hebe, that's daft." Vesta said. "Yes, I understand that none of us grow any older in human terms, but we do change. Since I've been here, I've developed new friends, I've seen lots of building work take place, I've even become an expert in peeling potatoes. Cerberus has become Head of Internal Security with his sign and dangerous fish—"

"They're the banana fishes," Cerberus interrupted.

"That's right. Also, the Torturing Department's introduced new procedures as you can see from the big notices with letters all around the place. The Underworld clearly isn't static. It might be full of dead people, but it's still a dynamic society or community, if you like."

"Gosh!" Hebe said with a big beam on her face. "That's really well put. What do the rest of you think?"

"Vesta's right." Gigliola leapt in ahead of everyone else. "We might be dead, but we're very active dead. When Aggy hits you on the head with her ladle, Cerberus, that's an active hit, not a static hit, no?"

"Woof, woof. It's a hit that hurts. Is that an active hit?"

"I should think so," said Hebe.

Both Aggy and Ming agreed that they were a society that

didn't stand still. Aggy was particularly focused on the changes in the Torturing Department and felt she should be allowed to make similar changes in the Kitchens.

"Right," Hebe said, standing up. "I'll go and see Uncle Hady now. All I can do is try my best."

*

When Hebe arrived at the palace she found Hades alone in his throne room.

"Hebe," he said, standing up and moving towards her for an embrace. "How nice to see you. Let's go into my private apartments, which are more comfortable than this austere setting."

"No need, Uncle Hady. I'll just sit on this stool and you go back to your throne."

"Are you sure?"

"Yes. This is fine."

"So, have you seen my wife recently?"

"I see lots of her on Olympus and she's well."

"And did she have a message for me?"

"She always sends her love."

"Which means you have no specific message," Hades said, sighing. "Does she ever mention me at all?"

"She's aware she's to return to the Underworld in a few weeks so will soon be making arrangements."

"Reluctantly, no doubt. She views the Underworld as a prison and me her jailer."

"Let's talk about something else, Uncle Hady," Hebe said, thinking it best to change the subject. "How have you been and what's going on in the Underworld?"

"Oh, I'm alright, I suppose. I have one particular problem, though, that you might be able to help me with. Have you been to Poseidon's cavern recently?"

"Yes."

"And do you know about a Miss Totty Turniptoes?"

"Ah," said Hebe. "You've had an earful from Death, I suspect?"

"A very agitated Death, who wants me to go to Olympus and call a full Gods' Council Meeting on the matter."

"That sounds a bit extreme."

"It is, but I'm still deliberating with myself about what to do. Death's right, though. Why on earth is Poseidon holding onto the girl? She's dead and needs to come to the Underworld. If my brother wants her back, I'll let him have her. What is it? Has he got a crush on her or something?"

"No, he hasn't. My advice is to leave matters as they are for a while. If you don't mind me saying so, all you three brothers are in a bit of a rut at the moment. Poseidon, though, is in the worst condition of all of you. He shuffles around in his pyjamas, he's terribly overweight and unfit, he never leaves the cavern to travel the seas and oceans as he used to. Totty has arrived out of the blue and has started to bring changes to life in the cavern. She's altered their diets, begun to smarten everyone up and plans are afoot to start fitness classes to get everyone healthy. She's a real force for good, and Poseidon, Dolores and Hash are responding to her. Let her keep going for a while and then try and see Poseidon face to face and sort it out."

"Hmm, I'll think about it," was all Hades would reply. Then after a few seconds he continued, "So, you think Zeus and I are in a rut as well, do you?"

"Aren't you? I know Father is. He's always racing around everywhere, giving this impression that he's a bundle of energy, but what's he actually achieving? Not a lot. He's also got all the problems of the other gods to sort out and that's often a full-time job. Mars is a source of continuous grief to both him and Hera, to say nothing about the stirrings of Artemis and her little group."

"I've heard, but it's all very well analysing, Hebe. The question is, what's to be done?"

"For a start, Uncle Hady, you, Father and Poseidon should have a meet-up. You're the senior male gods and yet you never share your concerns."

"Actually, I agree with you, but do my two brothers?"

"I think they might. I've a feeling Athene might be playing a role in bringing you all together, so if she descends on you sometime in the future, please respond positively."

There was a short silence between the two of them as Hades was deep in thought. Hebe felt it was best to wait for him to speak. Eventually he looked her between the eyes.

"And why am I in a rut? A bit stale, maybe, but am I really in a rut?"

"Tell me, Uncle, do you find stew an aphrodisiac?"

"What are you talking about, Hebe?" Hades responded shirtily. "I thought we were having a serious conversation. Go and ask your half-sister Aphrodite about such matters."

"I am being serious," Hebe replied. "Every time I come here, the only thing to eat is stew – every day, morning, noon and night. What I don't understand is, why? It's just like the cavern. They've only been eating hamburgers for years, but now Totty's changed that and they've got some variety in their diets."

"What's triggered this? Have you been speaking to Aggy, who's been pestering me on this matter for decades?"

"I happened to be sitting in on a meeting with Aggy and some of her team, and the issue did come up at one point, yes. Having seen the changes in the cavern, I thought I might raise the point with you if the opportunity arose."

Hades stared sternly at his niece, who looked back equally sternly at him.

"Please answer me a question – yes or no. Was a recent arrival called Vesta also sitting in on this meeting of Aggy's?"

"I think the name might have been mentioned in the introductions."

Hades continued to stare sternly at Hebe and then sat back and burst out laughing.

"You've found out I too have a Totty Turniptoes. What do you think of her?"

Hebe laughed as well. "A very smart young lady. I gather she's behind some recent changes to the Torturing Department and other areas."

"She is. She's also become the first person to make a friend of Cerberus. I take it Vesta's in Aggy's camp on wanting some alternatives to stew?"

"Of course. Shall I put forward her arguments?"

"It's not necessary. I'm now a little more sympathetic to the need for some changes. Would you mind asking Aggy to come and see me on her plans for the Kitchens? I haven't decided finally on the need for change, but you can say the door's slightly ajar."

"Aggy alone or accompanied?"

"Aggy alone, I think."

"Okay. Something you might like to consider before you see Aggy is the impression varied foods might make on Persephone when she comes. I know as a fact she doesn't view eating stew all the time as one of the great draws to her time in the Underworld."

"Good point. Perhaps you could speak to Bacchus about a few fine wines, but only for the palace."

"Will do," said Hebe, getting up to leave.

"Before you go, Hebe, thank you for coming to see me. If you could try and call in a little more frequently, that would be appreciated. One thought, though. The Underworld's got Vesta, Poseidon's got Totty, but doesn't Olympus need a similar bright young lady?"

"Olympus is just fine," Hebe answered with a cheeky smile. "Don't forget, it's got me."

XVIII

DISCOMBOBULATION
AT THE PALACE

ZEUS WAS IN HIS LIBRARY REFLECTING ON THE past twenty-four hours. He had told Hera the previous day that he was going to Northern Europe to review the political scene. He did this from time to time so he could keep up to date with current events. Knowing full well that his wife would decline, he'd asked her if she would like to accompany him since he planned to be away overnight. As expected, she'd shaken her head which meant he was off her leash for a while.

He immediately headed to Hamburg with the express purpose of tracking down the two frauleins in the Hanseatic Headbanger poster. He walked around the city centre looking to see if he could catch sight of them, but after an hour he realised this was a pretty useless exercise. After all, Hamburg had a population of nearly two million and he wasn't entirely certain that they lived in the city anyway. He then decided to look for HH's head office. Unlike Hebe, who was well versed in the internet, Zeus knew nothing about computers and online searches, so he started asking people in the street where Hanseatic Headbanger's office was. No one knew, but someone pointed him to a tavern which sold Headbanger. Fortunately, it had few people in it, which gave him the opportunity of getting into conversation with the tavern keeper, who not only gave him a large glass of beer on the house but also drew him a map giving directions to HH's head office.

On entering the reception Zeus thought the attractive young lady at the desk looked like one of the girls in the poster. Admittedly, she was wearing a dark blue suit instead of a bikini, but she did have blonde hair. Her name tag had the words 'Heidi Fassbender' printed on it, so Zeus proceeded to ask her if she was indeed one of the young ladies; if not, he would be very grateful if she could kindly give him the addresses of the two models. Heidi asked Zeus to wait a minute as she got up and went into the room behind her. Shortly afterwards she returned with two large security officers, who asked Zeus very politely to leave. He started to protest, but they each firmly gripped one of his arms and escorted him out of the front door into the street outside.

Zeus, being Top God, could have used his powers to resist the security officers. However, he was reluctant to do so because of past experiences. He was aware that whenever he became annoyed among humankind, he found it difficult to moderate his temper. In one South American country about fifty years ago he had over-reacted and caused a massive explosion over some trivial matter. This had left a large hole one hundred metres in diameter and five hundred metres deep where previously there had been a pleasant park. Certain eyewitnesses near Zeus at the time had given the police a detailed description of his features with the result that a sketch of his face was still on various Most Wanted Terrorist lists in Latin America.

Zeus spent the rest of the day roaming around Hamburg looking for the two poster girls, but with no success. By the evening he found himself near the docks where there were a number of young ladies hanging around. Zeus had now given up on the poster girls and decided that any sort of female company would be welcome. He approached a young busty brunette in high heels, wearing a T-shirt and a short black leather skirt. Her face was covered with makeup, the lipstick on her lips was bright red and she was chewing gum.

"Hello, Granddad," the girl said. "Looking for some company?"

Zeus replied that he was.

"Why've you got on your dressing gown?"

Zeus explained it was a robe.

"Looks like one of them night gowns you get down the second-hand market for five euros. How much money you got? It's a hundred for a quickie, two hundred for longer."

Zeus suddenly realised he had come out without any money. Although Hebe kept him well supplied, he'd forgotten to bring some. He tried to explain to the girl, telling her that he was the great Lord Zeus and his credit was good.

"Oh yea," she said. "And I'm the German Chancellor, I am."

Zeus kept claiming he was the Top God, but it wasn't having any effect on the girl.

"Yea, yea. And I keep telling you, I'm the German Chancellor." She called over to a small redhead nearby, "Inga, I'm the German Chancellor, ain't I? And you're the Queen of England."

"Yea, Judit, if you like. Have you got one of them kinky weirdo types?" replied Inga. "Is he looking for two girls?"

"Yea, probably, but he's got no money."

"Well, stop wasting time with him. There's a bunch of fellers in suits over there," said Inga, pointing down the street. "Let's look 'em over."

"Yea," the other girl said, and then looked at Zeus and gave him a slight push. "Clear off, pervert, and stop trying to molest respectable girls." With that comment she walked away with Inga.

Zeus did think of returning to Olympus but knew that cutting short his trip might cause Hera to start an inquisition. Much of the time she was not interested in his visits to the world, but whenever plans got changed, she would get suspicious and start asking him questions. He didn't fancy having to invent a story for her which she would pick holes in, so he decided it was best to stay overnight in Hamburg, even though his trip had been pointless.

Shortly afterwards it began raining and Zeus looked for shelter. He went down a narrow alleyway and stood in the far corner underneath a balcony. After a while the rain became increasingly heavy and a fierce wind swept down the alley, blowing the water horizontally towards Zeus. He was becoming increasingly wet and was eyeing a dark blue tarpaulin which was lying on the ground nearby, wondering if he could find shelter underneath. He did not have to ponder for long because all of a sudden one of the tarpaulin's corners was raised and a grizzly face appeared.

"You'd better come under here," the face said as he invited Zeus to get under the tarpaulin.

"Thank you," Zeus replied, hurrying over to the tarpaulin.

When both Zeus and the face were under cover, the face said, "My name is Fritz. This is where I live. Have a drink of schnapps." Fritz took a large swig himself and then handed the bottle to Zeus.

"Thank you again," the Top God replied. "I'm Zeus, that's Lord Zeus."

"I don't doubt it," said Fritz. "To be entirely truthful, I'm actually Kaiser Wilhelm, but I prefer to be known as Fritz."

"You're really the Kaiser?" Zeus said, somewhat puzzled. "I thought you went to the Underworld decades ago?"

"A popular misconception," Fritz answered. "But I'd appreciate you keeping it between the two of us. I prefer to be incognito these days. Take a swig of the schnapps; that's what it's there for."

Zeus put the bottle to his lips and took a long drink. "Very tasty. Thank you," he said, handing the bottle back to Fritz.

"Plenty more where this came from, so I suggest you and I finish off the bottle. If I were you, I'd settle down here for the night. This rain comes from the east. It's sent over by those pesky Russians, so it will likely go on till morning."

Fritz again had a swig of schnapps before handing it once more to Zeus who took another drink before returning the bottle to his companion.

"Tell me, Zeus, what are you actually doing in Hamburg?"

"Some research into Hanseatic Headbanger, that local beer of yours."

"I don't drink it myself, but isn't that the one with the two blonde models on all the advertising?"

"It is," replied Zeus, suddenly perking up. "Do you know where I can find the two young ladies?"

"They're nieces of mine," said Fritz.

"Nieces!" Zeus exclaimed. "Are you sure? If you really are the Kaiser, you must be over 160 years old. These girls look as if they're in their early twenties. What age were your brothers and sisters?"

"Well, maybe they're great nieces or great-great nieces; I don't really remember. I lost contact with my family ages ago, so I'm not sure where you can find the girls. Look, finish off the schnapps and let's turn in."

Fritz handed the bottle to Zeus once more, lay back and immediately started snoring. Zeus had a final drink, put the empty bottle down by his side and closed his eyes. After a few moments he became drowsy, but just as he was about to nod off, he felt something soft and wet touching his face.

"What's that?" he asked, jerking his head.

Fritz instantly woke up. "That's Gropuddle," he said. "He won't harm you."

Zeus looked at a small ugly mongrel dog, who tried to lick his face again. "Why's he called Gropuddle?" he enquired.

"You'll soon found out," Fritz replied, turning over again to go to sleep.

Zeus didn't sleep much during the night. Despite being under the tarpaulin, a mixture of rain seeping in and Gropuddle managed to ensure he got totally soaked as the hours progressed. He was, therefore, thankful when the morning came, by which time the rain had eased off. He took his leave of Fritz and Gropuddle and, while no one was looking, created a small cloud and zoomed back up to Olympus.

It was shortly after Zeus's return that Mrs Bumble knocked on the library door and, hearing a grunt of sorts from the inside, walked in. Mrs Bumble was a female version of her husband. Like him, she was a portly lady who was dressed in blue. She also had a big red face, although her nose and ears were not quite so red, being more of a dark shade of pink.

"Good morning, My Lord," said the Head Housekeeper. "Have you any instructions for me this morning?"

Zeus looked up from his desk. "What makes you think I'll have any instructions for you, Mrs Bumble?" he replied.

"I am simply making an enquiry, My Lord."

"Why?"

Mrs Bumble frowned. "I have seen Lady Hera for her instructions and, as is usual practice, I have now come to you to ask if you have any particular requirements."

"Why?" Zeus asked again.

Once more Mrs Bumble frowned. "Why, My Lord, because I've been doing the same thing every day for a hundred years."

"Have you?" Zeus replied while giving a yawn. "I've never noticed before."

Mrs Bumble gave an even bigger frown. "Well, I'm sorry to disturb you, My Lord. If you have no particular instructions, I will go and continue with my normal duties."

As she turned round to leave the library, Zeus stood up and moved away from his desk. "One minute, Mrs Bumble. I see there's some mud on the floor here," he said, pointing to a small lump of mud in the middle of the room. "That's not very satisfactory, is it? How has that been allowed to happen?"

Mrs Bumble looked at the mud and then at Zeus's sandals. "Your footwear is all muddy, My Lord," she said. "It looks as if you have been outside and have brought the mud in."

Zeus looked down at his feet. "I have been out, Mrs Bumble," he agreed. "But why don't we have a mat by the front door so people can wipe their feet before coming in?"

"But we do, My Lord. It's a very good mat we've had for a number of years."

"If you mean that old thing out at the front, it's really just a rug. Totally unsatisfactory. Who chose it?"

"I believe you and Lady Hera did, My Lord. However, if you are unhappy with it, I will speak to Her Ladyship on the matter."

"Please do," said Zeus. He looked around the room before continuing. "Another thing, Mrs Bumble, these net curtains need a good clean. Why have they been allowed to get so dirty?"

Mrs Bumble went over to the nets and couldn't see anything wrong with them. "Perhaps my eyesight is not as good as Your Lordship's, but I am unable to see that they need a clean. We have a system of cleaning them every 150 days, which so far we've found to be very satisfactory."

"So, what day are we on now?"

"Ninety-seven," replied Mrs Bumble.

"And who decided on this every 150 days?"

"You and Lady Hera, My Lord. It was at a meeting with me and Mr Bumble some time ago on household matters."

"Was it?" Zeus replied. "And why do we have nets in the first place? Seems a ridiculous idea. I can't get to look outside properly."

"I believe it was discussed at the same meeting. The concern was people looking in, if I recall correctly."

"And who was concerned about that?"

"From memory, you were, My Lord. However, I shall go and discuss the matter with Lady Hera, if you wish."

"That's a good idea."

"Will there be anything else, My Lord?"

"Not at the moment, thank you, Mrs Bumble."

Just as the Head Housekeeper was about to leave the room, Zeus called her back again. "You know, Mrs Bumble, I really shouldn't be involved in these petty household matters. It is a great responsibility being Top God. Are you aware of that?"

"I can well believe it. I'm sure the demands must be very great, Lord Zeus."

"Quite right, Mrs Bumble. Every day brings new problems. One is in a state of near-permanent discombobulation."

"I'm very sorry to hear that, My Lord. To be discobobblebelated must be very upsetting."

"It's actually discombobulated, Mrs Bumble. You do know what it means, do you?"

"Not as precisely as I would like," the Head Housekeeper replied. "Discobobblebelation is not a word Mr Bumble and I use in everyday conversation."

"It means confused, unsettled, frustrated, that sort of thing," said Zeus. "A very good word. I would advise you and Mr Bumble to start using it."

"I will speak to my husband on the matter, My Lord."

"Very good, very good." Zeus sat back in his chair and reflected for a few seconds. "Tell me, Mrs Bumble, if you were Top God, what would you do?"

"I don't rightly know, My Lord. It's not a matter I've given any consideration to."

"Well, there must be certain things you've thought about. You know, changes which you and Mr Bumble would like to see."

Mrs Bumble thought hard before speaking again. "There's certainly one matter I would consider addressing, but I fear you will think me impertinent for mentioning it, My Lord."

"No, I won't. I really want to hear what you have to say; in fact, I insist," said Zeus. "Assume you're Top God. What would you do?"

"As I say, I'm hesitant to mention it, My Lord. But if you insist, it relates to your son, Lord Mars. I would stop him bullying people and creating all sorts of unpleasantness on Olympus. If he's the God of War, he should be starting wars on planet Earth, not up here. I hope I haven't caused offence by saying this."

Zeus took a deep breath. "No, Mrs Bumble. As you've said, we've known each other about a hundred years and I did insist on you speaking frankly. Mars's disagreeable behaviour is well known. I take it there haven't been any recent incidents I should hear about?"

"Not that I'm aware of, My Lord."

"Let me ask you a follow-up question, Mrs Bumble. If you were in my shoes, would you send Mars away somewhere? I'm thinking of a particular asteroid, for example."

"I don't know much about asteroids. Are they near here or quite far away?"

"A long way away in outer space," Zeus replied, waving his right arm towards the skies.

"While it might be pleasant for us to have a break from Lord Mars for a while, I would be concerned about him causing problems for the people living on this asteroid. Aren't we just shifting responsibility elsewhere?"

"What people are you talking about, Mrs Bumble?"

"The ones who live on the asteroid, My Lord."

"There aren't any people on an asteroid. It's a large piece of barren rock. That's the whole purpose of sending Mars there."

"Oh dear," Mrs Bumble replied. "But who will do Lord Mars's laundry when he's there? Who'll cook him his meals, change his bed, clean his palace?"

"No one," Zeus replied. "He won't be changing his clothes or eating any food. As for a palace, he'll be sitting on a hard rock all the time."

"Oh dear," Mrs Bumble said again in a concerned voice. "Won't he get lonely, My Lord?"

"Mars doesn't have any friends, except perhaps Hephaestus. As my daughter, Hebe, would say, 'Tuff Buns.'"

"Yes, that is one of her expressions," Mrs Bumble agreed. "And how long might Lord Mars be sent to this asteroid for?"

"I'm thinking of a thousand years."

"A thousand years!" exclaimed Mrs Bumble.

"Yes. How long were you thinking of?"

"I was thinking of about a week."

Zeus shook his head. "Being Top God involves having to make hard decisions, Mrs Bumble. That's why I feel discombobulated a lot of the time."

"Yes, I see, My Lord."

"You know, Mrs Bumble, I've found this conversation very interesting. Perhaps you and I should carry out an experiment and swap roles for a few days; ten days would be a sensible time. How do you feel about that?"

Mrs Bumble frowned and then blinked, followed by another frown. "I'm not sure I'm with you, My Lord," she replied in due course.

"I'm suggesting a job swap, Mrs Bumble. You will become Top God for ten days and I'll be Head Housekeeper in that period. We can then compare notes on how we've both got on. We might learn a few things."

"Would it not be better if you did this with Mr Bumble instead, My Lord?"

"Not at all; I specifically want to do it with you. I'll transfer a limited number of my powers to you, so you feel you have the authority to act. Similarly, I'd welcome a quick teach-in from you on what the role of Head Housekeeper involves."

"Will I be able to throw thunderbolts, My Lord?"

"I'm not sure; I'll have to think about it. Possibly some of the smaller ones. Any more questions, Mrs Bumble?"

"Probably an awful lot, Lord Zeus. But one matter I don't understand is, what my relationship will be with Lady Hera?"

"If you're taking my place, Mrs Bumble, you'll be her husband."

"Her husband! But I'm a woman, My Lord."

"No problem, it's only for ten days."

"And what, My Lord, will your relationship be with Mr Bumble?"

"I'll be his wife."

"Goodness gracious me! That will be quite a shock to him, Lord Zeus."

"Again, it will only be for a few days."

"Ummm," went Mrs Bumble.

"So, what do you say about this job swap idea, Mrs Bumble?"

"I'm still not really sure, My Lord. I feel a need to discuss it with Mr Bumble, if you don't mind."

"I fully understand," the current Top God said.

"And will you be speaking to Lady Hera about this proposal?"

Zeus looked a bit sheepish. "Possibly," he replied uncertainly. "In fact, you raise a good point. I think it would be best if you and Mr Bumble said nothing to Her Ladyship. Best to let me deal with her."

"Yes, My Lord." There was a silence between the two of them, so Mrs Bumble decided to take the opportunity of leaving

Zeus before he thought of any more interesting proposals. "Are there any other household matters you wish to raise with me, My Lord?" she asked. "Because if not, I will return to my duties."

"No, thank you, Mrs Bumble. You may go now," Zeus replied. As she got close to the library door, the Top God called her back once more. "Oh, Mrs Bumble, one last thing. I think it would be a good idea if each morning, after having seen Lady Hera, you also came to see me. I might well have some matters to raise with you. Will you please put that into your routine?"

"Yes, My Lord," Mrs Bumble replied before leaving.

Once Mrs Bumble was in the hallway, she hurried off towards the pantry to find her husband.

"I feel so tizzy after that discussion," she said to herself. "I really don't know how Mr Bumble's going to take all this, especially the bit about me being Lady Hera's husband for a few days and him having Lord Zeus as his wife. Actually, I do know: he'll be well and truly discobobblebelated – and what's more, that will be two of us!"

XIX

FIGHTING
FIT

POSEIDON, DOLORES AND HASHIMOTO WERE standing on thick grey mats in the piazza. They were all in a row a few feet between each other. They were dressed identically in blue shorts, Bollocks to Mars T-shirts and trainers on their feet. Hebe was also standing in the row next to Hashimoto; she was similarly attired, as was Totty, who stood facing the group.

This was the first session in the fitness programme they had all signed up to. Hebe had arrived the evening before with all the new clothes that Totty and Dolores had requested. She had also brought a large number of mats to lay on the piazza floor for exercise purposes. She would be bringing the new gym equipment on her next visit since Trevor and Mervyn needed more time both to source it and also to ensure it was in proper working order.

Totty had decided that now everyone had proper sportswear and with the large supply of mats, it made sense to start doing some stretching and other simple exercises. Hebe, who quite rightly felt she was an integral part of the fitness project, decided to stay overnight, so she could join in on the first session.

The action in the piazza was being watched by the four mermaids, who as normal were leaning on the piazza edge. They were all wearing bikini tops, which Hebe had brought them the previous evening. Kinky and Pinky had black tops and the other two were in red.

"I want a 'Bollocks to Mars' T-shirt," Kinky said to the others.

"So do I," Minky replied, immediately followed by Linky and Pinky.

"We'll speak to Hebe later," Kinky said. "But let's shush now; they're about to begin."

"Okay, everyone," Totty spoke in a loud voice. "We're just going to go through a few easy routines. First of all, I'd like everyone to bend down to see if they can touch their toes. You've got to keep your legs perfectly straight with no bending of the knees. Like this."

Totty slowly bent forwards in an arch and touched her toes, before standing upright again.

"Now you try it. Go as far as you can and then hold it for a few seconds."

The four others proceeded to bend forwards, all trying to keep their legs perfectly straight. Poseidon could only get as far as the top of his thighs, Dolores was halfway down her thighs, while Hashimoto was struggling to reach the top of his knees. He couldn't resist a slight bend of his knees to get a little bit further.

"No, Hash," Totty said. "Knees entirely straight."

"It is too difficult," the butler said, straightening his legs, so his hands went back up his thighs a few inches. "Hashimoto's back isn't built to bend so much."

"Let's all straighten up now and relax. Well done, Hebe," Totty said looking specifically at the pocket-rocket who, like Totty, had managed to touch her toes.

The mermaids all turned round in the water and bent over at the waist to touch the end of their fins. Having done this successfully, they resumed their position at the piazza's edge to continue watching proceedings.

"We're now going to have a try at doing squats," Totty said. "Can everyone please stand with their feet slightly apart? You need to put your arms out in front of you to provide some balance. It's fine to hold your hands in the front, if you prefer. Your backs must be kept entirely straight and then you slowly lower yourself down as if you're about to sit on a chair. Like this."

Totty bent her knees until she was in a sitting position, which she held for a couple of seconds before raising herself straight again. She then proceeded to go up and down a few times before coming to a halt.

"In time, I'd like us to do a dozen squats in succession, but let's all try to do just one to begin with. Please remember to keep your backs straight; no leaning forward. If anything, lean very slightly backwards as you go down."

Totty's four pupils proceeded to try a squat for the first time. Unsurprisingly, Hebe did hers perfectly. The others unfortunately took Totty's advice about leaning slightly backwards too literally with the result that they all toppled over onto their backsides with three pairs of legs sticking up in the air.

"Oh dear," Totty said. "Let's all try that one again. What I suggest is that we don't go down fully; we'll do half or three-quarters squats."

Over the next few minutes, Totty managed to get her team doing reasonable three-quarters squats with no more tumbles. As she was doing this the mermaids decided that they would do a series of somersaults before settling down again for Totty's next exercise.

"I'd now like us to do a simple balance exercise. It involves standing on one leg for ten seconds. As with squats, you might like to hold your hands out in front of you. Watch me."

Totty stood on one leg and counted aloud to ten before reverting to two legs.

"Have a go. It doesn't matter which leg you choose. I'll do the counting."

All four of them managed to get onto one leg. Poseidon held it for two seconds, whereas Dolores got to four seconds. Hashimoto was doing very well and got as far as six seconds before he began to topple over. Instead of immediately putting his other foot on the ground, he continued to topple. A second later Hash had fallen against Hebe, who was still on one leg, and the two of them fell onto the floor.

"What are you doing, Hash?" Hebe shouted. "Get off me."

"Very sorry, Honourable Lady Hebe," the butler said as he lifted himself off the goddess. "Hashimoto's no good on one leg. That's why he has two legs. Please don't turn me into frog as a punishment."

"Come on, help me up," Hebe said.

As they were untangling themselves, the mermaids decided to pass a few comments on what they had seen so far.

"I think Totty's got a very big job on her hands with this lot," Kinky said to the others.

"They're not very good, are they?" Linky replied.

"A lot of sorting needs to be done," Kinky continued.

"Why do you call it sorting?" Linky asked.

"That's what Totty calls it. She says people come to her for 'sorting'. When they can do all their exercises properly and they're really fit, she says they're 'sorted'."

"Does that mean they're Totally Top?" Minky asked.

"Totally Top and Super," Kinky said.

"Well, today they're all definitely Totally Untop," Linky replied.

"And Unsuper," Pinky contributed.

"Totally Untop and Totally Unsuper," Kinky agreed.

After Hebe and Hashimoto were on their feet Totty decided to focus on some very easy stretching exercises. These principally involved upper-body stretching with a lot of emphasis on improving mobility around the neck and shoulders. The mermaids all joined in as well. All that went pretty well, so after a few minutes without mishaps, Totty thought she would be a little more adventurous with the final exercise of the day – press-ups. She showed her class of four how to do them properly and then asked everyone to get into position and start off. The scores were pretty much as Totty had expected. Hebe did ten press-ups straight off; she could have carried on but thought that was probably enough, given the progress of the others. Poseidon and Hashimoto managed to do two each before their arms gave way, whereas Dolores did not even have the strength to complete one.

Totty suggested they should stop at that stage. The plan was to repeat the process the following day and then to continue daily. By the time the gym equipment arrived, she hoped everyone would start feeling just a little looser. The problem was that everyone's bodies were incredibly stiff through lack of exercise over many years. They also didn't have much muscle.

"It's a pity we don't have a bookie in the cavern," Kinky said as the trainee gymnasts were walking back into the palace.

"What's a bookie?" Minky asked.

"He's a person who takes bets. If we had one here we could all go and place bets on who would do the most press-ups in, say, ten days' time."

"I would always bet on Hebe," Minky replied.

"She's leaving soon. She only joined in today because she was here."

"So, it's between the other three. They're all pretty useless."

"At the moment. Let's see what Totty can do with them over a few weeks. Then we can start placing our bets."

"But we haven't got a bookie," Minky said.

"We could always bet amongst ourselves," Kinky replied.

"What would we bet with? We haven't got any money."

"I'll go and ask Old Posy if he'll let us have some emeralds. He's got plenty spare."

*

A few days after the first gym class, the Sea God got out of bed very early while everyone else in the palace was still asleep. He put on a pair of dark green swimming trunks that Hebe had brought back from Yorkgate, having had them specially made in view of his size. It was a struggle to fit into them, but he managed to do so. Hebe had actually brought three pairs of everything for Poseidon, Dolores and Hashimoto, all of different sizes. She was working on the assumption that as the palace's inhabitants got fitter, they would lose weight and so would need smaller sizes. Naturally Poseidon had chosen the largest pair of trunks; the others were there as an incentive to follow Totty's instructions.

Poseidon walked across the piazza and sat on the water's edge. Slowly, he lowered himself into the lagoon and started swimming towards the middle. Although he was unfit, overweight and had not been in the water for many years, he felt quite comfortable making gentle breaststrokes. Poseidon had normally preferred to do the crawl or even the butterfly, but they were not for today. He had now overcome the psychological barrier of getting back into the water and, like Totty's daily gym classes, he believed a swim early each morning would do him good.

Kinky had also woken up early that morning. Although

she was still lying on her bed, her fins felt miniscule ripples of water, suggesting that something was moving in the lagoon. She lowered herself off her bed and quietly swam out of the maids' palace. She saw Poseidon in the middle of the lagoon, so she swam deep underwater until she was just below him. Kinky then launched herself vertically at speed, coming to the surface immediately in front of the Sea God.

"Boo!" she shouted as she popped up and started splashing him.

Poseidon stopped swimming and started splashing Kinky back. His splashes were far greater than hers so she stopped and went back under water again. When she resurfaced he was waiting for her.

"Trust you to catch me on my first day in the water," he said, laughing. "Are you spying on me?"

"No, Posy. I was awake and felt something in the lagoon. How is it?"

"Good, I'm glad you suggested it."

"Totty also swims most days. We maids are teaching her how to do the crawl. She'll be able to go faster. Perhaps we can all swim together and have a race one day."

"I don't know about racing, but it would be good to all swim at the same time."

"I've suggested to her we have another go at trying to teach Dol and Hash," Kinky said. "It's never worked in the past, but Totty's a good teacher. She's also got legs so will be able to show the others what to do with them. That's always been a problem for us mermaids; we can only teach the arms side of things."

"I've got legs as well, so maybe I can help," Poseidon said. "Yes, it would be a good idea to get everyone here swimming. I'll talk to them about it."

"Why don't you let Totty speak to them? If you do it, they'll view it as an order. We want them to start swimming because they want to, not because they're forced to."

"Alright, we'll do it like that. Will you speak to Totty or shall I?"

"Why don't we both do it? Now you're back in the water, you can suggest that Totty comes swimming with you this afternoon. I'll join in and we can have a powwow."

It was not too difficult to get Dolores's and Hashimoto's agreement to learn to swim. The housekeeper was now totally into the fitness project and, in particular, losing weight. She had the three different sizes of dresses, skirts and tops that Hebe had brought for her. Naturally, she was currently wearing the largest, but every time she went to her room she looked enviously at the two smaller sizes. She was determined to get into them as soon as possible. Since Totty had 'sold' swimming to her as being an integral part of getting fit, she didn't need too much persuading to agree. She was also assured that the collective group of the four mermaids, Totty and Poseidon were to be involved in helping her.

Hashimoto had been more reluctant to take up swimming at the beginning. Totty couldn't understand why, so she challenged him.

"I don't understand what your reluctance is, Hash," she said.

"Hashimoto can see no benefit in swimming. He does not intend to swim anywhere on holiday like the mermaids. Hashimoto will stay in the cavern."

"You're not scared, are you? If Dolores, who's just a girl, can do it, why can't a black belt at karate?"

Dolores looked peevishly at Totty for calling her 'just a girl' but didn't say anything because she knew Totty was trying to provoke Hashimoto. She was spot on in this regard. The butler pushed out his chest and then said in a defiant tone, "Honourable Mr Hashimoto is not scared of anything. He is bravest of the brave. He will show you he learns to swim. You teach Missy Dol first, Miss Totty, then you teach Hashimoto. He will learn in double quick time. You'll see."

"Good. That's agreed then," Totty said. "We'll begin tomorrow afternoon, if that's okay, Dol?"

"Sure is, hon," the South Carolinian said.

"Mr Hashimoto will come and observe. He wants to check quality of teaching," Hashimoto said, wanting the last word.

*

When Dolores and Totty came out of the palace in their swimwear the next day, the four mermaids were waiting for them. Poseidon was also swimming in the lagoon; it had been agreed he would leave the teaching to Totty and the maids but would be around if needed. Hashimoto, who was in his butler's uniform, had already set up his observation post, having brought out a chair to sit on by the water's edge.

The previous evening Totty had swum out to the mermaids' palace to discuss the best way to teach Dolores to swim. The following afternoon, they implemented their agreed plan.

The first thing that happened was for Totty to get in the water and start swimming with Dolores watching from the piazza edge. All the maids were calling to Dolores to watch how Totty's legs were moving because they thought this might be the most difficult part to get right.

"Miss Totty does not swim very fast," Hashimoto unhelpfully commented. "When Hashimoto learns to swim, he will go super-fast."

"Quiet, Hash," Dolores said. "At least Totty can swim. You and I can't."

"I only say—"

At that moment a mass of water was splashed at the butler by the four mermaids.

"Oh!" he exclaimed, looking down at his wet jacket. "Mermaids are very misbehaved today. Need lessons in manners."

"Quiet!" Dolores now shouted at him. "Not another word."

"Yes, Missy Dol. I'm only trying to be helpful. I will keep quiet now. Promise."

"Good."

Totty pulled herself out of the lagoon and then spent the next few minutes with Dolores on the piazza. She got her pupil to do the swimming arm movements while standing up. This was followed with Dolores lying on her front on the piazza edge with her legs hanging directly over the water. She then practised the leg movements, with Totty correcting her at various points.

It was now time for Dolores to get in the water. It was agreed that she would lower herself very gently into the arms of the four mermaids, who would hold her up. Poseidon was about ten metres away just in case he was needed, while Totty would supervise matters from the piazza edge.

Everything went according to plan, despite Dolores being nervous when she first slipped into the water. It was then a question of getting Dolores into a horizontal position, which the maids did easily by having two of them on either side supporting her upper torso. Totty called out to start moving her arms and legs and Dolores began to swim for the first time in her life with the maids holding her above the surface.

By the end of the first day, Dolores was swimming quite confidently with the support of the mermaids. On the second day, all four maids again started by holding Dolores, but without saying anything, one on either side slipped away. A few minutes later the other two released their hold but continued to stay by Dolores's side. The housekeeper was now swimming by herself without realising her support had gone. This carried on for a few strokes until she became aware that she was swimming alone. She then had a minor panic, stopped and began to sink. Kinky and Minky immediately grabbed hold of her and held her up.

"You've done it," Totty shouted. "Dol, you've actually swum by yourself."

"Gee, but I started to sink."

"Only because you became aware you didn't need any help. That happens to everyone first time round. You did it; you can swim."

"You're a star, Dol," Kinky said to her. "Now start off by yourself, but Minky and I will be right next to you in case you need us."

A short while later, Totty helped Dolores to get out of the lagoon after a thoroughly successful lesson. Hashimoto was still sitting in his chair; he had been remarkably quiet since his telling-off the day before, but decided it was now time to open his mouth once more.

"You've done well, Missy Dol," he said. "Also, you have done quite well, Miss Totty. I give you seven out of ten."

"Why not ten?" Dolores asked.

"Staff indiscipline. Mermaids splashed observer's jacket; they need lessons in good behaviour," Hashimoto replied. "However, I consider Totty just good enough to teach Mr Hashimoto, provided staff kept under control. When do we begin – tomorrow?"

"No," Totty said. "I want to keep working with Dolores tomorrow to make sure everything's okay. I suggest the day after."

"I will check my diary," Hashimoto said.

*

By the time Hebe returned to the cavern, both Dolores and Hashimoto had learned how to swim. A fitness routine had already been established, which consisted of exercises in the early morning after breakfast followed by swimming in the late afternoon. In the in-between period Dolores, Hashimoto and Totty did their work, which involved all the cooking as well as keeping the palace clean.

Hebe's stallions and chariot splashed through the cave entrance into the cavern just as everyone was getting out of the lagoon after their afternoon swim.

"It's Hebe!" shouted Kinky as the stallions galloped across the top of the water before jumping smoothly onto the piazza and coming to a halt.

"Eh up!" Hebe said to everyone as she got down from her chariot. "You're all swimmers now, I see."

"Miss Dol and I are number-one swimmers in the cavern," Hashimoto replied, going over to pat the stallions. "We always beat Lord P, Miss Totty and mermaids in the races."

"Rubbish!" Kinky called, and was backed up in the rubbish comments by the other maids.

"What have you got for us this time, Hebe?" Poseidon asked.

"All the gym equipment and lots of cookery books for Dol and Totty."

"Gee, that's great," Dolores said.

"What I suggest we do," Hebe continued, "is unload everything from the chariot now, leave it in the piazza overnight and then assemble it tomorrow. It's going to take us all day to put it together, so we'd better get going bright and early."

"Who will be guard overnight?" Hashimoto asked.

"What are you talking about?" Hebe replied. "No one, of course."

"Very mischievous mermaids in cavern. Might cause sabotage."

"Boo! Boo to Hashimoto!" Kinky called. "Just because we splashed him when he was being cheeky about Totty's swimming."

"Hash is a very Naughty Boy," Poseidon added.

"I am," the butler agreed proudly.

"We'll take a chance on security," Hebe said conclusively.

Hebe's assessment was entirely accurate since it did take all day to assemble the gym equipment. Poseidon worked with the others because he was determined to show his niece he had no intention of remaining a fat lazy bum. Hebe took the role of project manager since she knew how everything was put together. Trevor and Mervyn had spent a lot of time in Yorkgate showing her how to assemble each piece of equipment and then packing it up again. There were also manuals on the matter which she and Totty kept referring to.

"The biggest issue we had was creating really powerful long-life batteries because in a normal gym all this stuff works by electricity," Hebe said. "It was just like the hair dryer issue but magnified dozens of times. Anyway, Merv the Nerd, whom I think I've mentioned before, is a real genius, and he's managed to create these super batteries which I'm going to plug in soon. They're like car batteries, but better."

"Won't they run down eventually?" Totty asked.

"Yes, we're only talking about you getting a few weeks out of them before they need recharging. I've brought a full set of replacements, but every time I come backwards and forwards, I'll have to bring new ones and take the old ones away for recharging. It's a bit of a drag, but one day we'll see if we can get that generator into the cavern. We might be able to get it working by wave power."

"When's that likely to be?" Totty enquired.

"Probably in years, not months. It will be up to other gods and they sometimes work at a snail's pace," Hebe replied. She didn't mention that there was no way Hades would let Mr Farraday, the electrician, come to the cavern until he and Poseidon had worked out their differences over Totty's status.

After everything was assembled, Hebe and Totty spent the evening checking that all the equipment was working properly. They then went and had a final glass of wine before turning in for the night. Hebe had to leave early in the morning since she needed to collect a large food order for delivery to the Underworld.

All the day's proceedings had been watched by the four mermaids. The new gym had been resurrected on the right-hand side of the piazza next to the water's edge. This had been agreed between Totty and Kinky because there were certain pieces of equipment that they thought the maids might be able to use.

"We can sit on the piazza edge and do exercises with those weights," Kinky said to the others.

"What about those funny-looking machines over there?" Minky asked, pointing to the exercise bike and cross-trainer.

"We can't use those. We haven't got legs."

"What about that one with a seat and a big ring thing that goes round?" Pinky asked.

"Maybe," Kinky replied. "We'll have to speak to Totty."

During the next two days, Totty showed Poseidon, Hashimoto and Dolores how the different pieces of equipment worked. She divided it into four main sections. There were machines to improve the cardio-vascular system, which really meant fitness. These were an exercise bike, a treadmill, a rowing machine and a cross-trainer. Then there was equipment for strengthening the lower-body muscles such as a leg-press machine. Similarly, there were separate pieces of equipment for the upper body, focusing not just on the arm muscles but also the shoulders and back. Finally, there were weights, which were also for strengthening the upper body.

Totty agreed a separate programme of daily exercises with each of her pupils. They were all of a similar format, with five minutes of stretching, followed by ten minutes on one of the cardio-vascular machines. Everyone then had six upper- or lower-body routines to complete before a final ten minutes on another CV machine. She wanted people to mix up the different pieces of equipment each day; so, for example, if Dolores was on the exercise bike, Hash might be on the cross-trainer at the same time, with the two of them reversing the next day. Totty also agreed specific levels of intensity and resistance with each person depending on their current strength. The aim would be to slowly make matters more challenging as they progressed.

Eventually, Totty felt that it was time to begin the daily routines. By that time, her team had made reasonable progress with the stretching and other simple exercises. They were now all able to squat ten times in succession without tipping backwards, they could all stand on each of their legs for ten seconds and could also do a minimum of five press-ups. It didn't look like they could get much closer to their toes when they bent down, but that would take some time and a considerable amount of weight loss by each of them. Totty would also be monitoring everyone's weight since Hebe had provided them with a set of scales.

"I am going to go on the boat that does not move," Hashimoto said at the beginning of the first proper gym day. "It is not really a boat. That's why it does not go anywhere."

"No one ever said it was," Totty replied. "It's called a rowing machine."

"That's what threw me. All things to row, which Hashimoto has come across before, were boats. Rowing machine is a new modern term I've just learnt. I will start to use such words, since I am New Modern Man. That's how I want people to describe me – Mr Hashimoto, New Modern Man."

"I thought you were to be known as Naughty Boy?" said Totty.

"I prefer New Modern Man. Anyway, must stop gossiping. Others have begun so I must catch up."

Hashimoto sat down on the rowing machine, set the resistance level, strapped his feet and began to row without going anywhere.

"Totty," Kinky called from the side of the lagoon where she was watching with her three friends. "Now all the people have got their exercise plans, can you please do the same for us?"

"Hi, Kinky. Do you really need plans? You're incredibly fit anyway with all your swimming."

"But we want to use the weights and some of those machines, like the one with the wheel that goes round. We are part of the cavern population and it would make us feel involved."

"Okay," Totty said, laughing. "I need to do a lot of monitoring of my three other pupils for a few days, but then I'll sign you all up to a new class."

"Super!" Kinky replied.

"Totally Top!" Linky and Minky said in unison, followed by another, "Super!" from Pinky.

XX

BECOMING
POSHIFIED

CERBERUS WAS VERY IMPRESSED WITH ALL THE changes he had witnessed in recent weeks in the Underworld. Nothing like this had happened in thousands of years. In his opinion, it was all down to Vesta, and he realised that her advice to him on friends and Mars bars was all about him changing. No one had ever suggested that to him before. While he paid attention to everything Vesta said, he also wanted to do some research himself and so worked out a plan. Before implementing it, though, he decided to secure a couple more friendships, which he thought should be fairly straightforward.

Death came out of Hades' palace in a bad mood. He had once again spoken to the god about Totty Turniptoes, but Hades had been evasive in his response. This meant he was not in a positive frame of mind when Cerberus bounded up to him as he was walking back to the ferry.

"Woof, woof," went Cerberus. "I've been waiting for you, Death."

"Shut it, Cerberus," Death responded, continuing to walk with the dog at his side. "I've not got any Mars bars on me."

"Woof, that was not what I wanted to see you about."

"Whatever it is, I don't want to know. Just clear off."

"That's not very friendly, Death," Cerberus said. "This is to your advantage."

"What is it then?" Death growled.

"I'm collecting friends and I wondered if you and I should become friends? What do you say?"

"What are you talking about, Cerberus? You and I don't have friends."

"Speak for yourself, Death," Cerberus replied. "I have loads of friends. If you agree, I could be your first friend."

"Shut it."

"Is that a yes or a no?"

"Shut it, I said, and leave me alone."

"You're obviously having a bad day, Death. I will honourably withdraw for the time being and approach the subject on another occasion when you're in a better mood."

"Shut it!" Death growled again and walked on at a faster pace.

Cerberus didn't follow the black coated skeleton. "I'll put that down as a maybe," he said to himself after a little reflection.

Later that morning Cerberus also visited the ferry jetty. His sign was still there and he looked into the water for the banana fishes. He couldn't see them, so he wondered if he should make a speech in a loud voice to draw their attention. An even better idea came to him: he would put one of his heads into the water for a good look around. Since the whole issue of friendship was such an important matter, he decided that Righty, Lefty and Middly would all go partially into the water together. He took deep breaths, bent down and submerged his three heads so he could have a good look around for the banana fishes, who were about to learn that they were to become his friends.

Initially, Cerberus could not see anything because the water was murky, but after a few seconds he saw lots of banana fishes swimming towards him. He thought they were going to give him little kisses, so he kept his heads in the water as a sign of their new friendship. Things stopped going to plan at that point, as the next instant he jumped back and started yapping in pain. All three of his faces hurt and blood was streaming from each of them, where the banana fishes had taken small bites out of his flesh. He continued to yap as the pain wouldn't go. He was angry with the fishes, so he kicked the water with his right foreleg, which only resulted in another series of yaps as a small chunk of flesh was taken out of his leg.

For the next few minutes Cerberus moved around in small circles, continuing to yap. After a while, the pain subsided and his yaps became angry barks. It had no effect on the banana fishes, who merely swam around waiting for some more lunch to reappear. Cerberus realised that all his faces were dripping with blood and his eyes were watery with tears. He moved over to the water once more and gave a series of angry barks and snarls before finally turning round and heading for the Kitchens.

"What have you been doing with yourself?" Aggy asked when a very miserable Cerberus came up to her.

"I'm hurt, Aggy," a tearful Cerberus moaned. "It was the banana fishes. I put my heads in the water to ask them to become friends and they've done this to me."

"Come this way," the Head Chef said, taking him into a pantry where she kept her first aid box. "Let's get you tidied up."

Aggy spent the next fifteen minutes washing Cerberus's three faces, then putting some cream on them before covering the wounds with a series of plasters. Vesta came in during this and heard what had happened, so she spent some time stroking his three heads while speaking kindly to him.

"Do you think a Mars bar will help to heal the wounds?" Vesta asked. Aggy agreed that Mars bars were very good medicines for fish bites, so Vesta went off to get one from Aggy's cupboard.

When Vesta returned, Cerberus's tail reared up in front of her. "I told them not to do it," Audrey whispered. "But they didn't listen. No brains at all."

"That's all done now," Aggy said when she had finished patching Cerberus up and he had a Mars bar in his mouth. "Now, I suggest you take it easy for the rest of the day and no more talking with banana fishes for a while. Come back tomorrow and I'll take your dressings off. You won't have healed properly, but the bleeding will have stopped and it's best to let some air get to the wounds."

"Thank you, Aggy. Thank you, Vesta," a happier Cerberus said as he turned round to leave.

*

Cerberus had a couple of lazy days before getting on with his self-improvement plan. Early on the third day after the banana fishes incident, he was standing outside the Underworld's library. It was a large three-storey building next to Hades' palace. It had been constructed by Lord Hephaestus more than two thousand years ago when the builder god spent a lot of time in the Underworld setting up a building team for all the construction work that was an important feature of life underground. Cerberus had only ever been into the building on one occasion, which was to have a look round to see if there were any Mars bars. There weren't, so he took no further interest in the place.

There was no one on the ground floor when Cerberus entered, so he bounded up the stairs to the first floor. No one was there either, but on the second floor he saw two very old men sitting at a table at the far end. Both had white hair and white beards, and they were wearing identical white tunics. They were remarkably similar, except, on getting closer, one of them had an aura about him of having been in the Underworld approximately seven hundred years longer than the other – which was actually the case.

Cerberus knew that the two old men were Mr Homer, the Head Librarian, and Mr Virgil, the Assistant Librarian. These were the two people Cerberus had decided could help him to change for the better. He was unsure how to raise the subject so thought it best to go in for a bit of intimidation. This involved forgetting everything Vesta and Aggy had taught him, with the result that as he approached their table he began to growl to get their attention.

"Give us a Mars bar or I'll bite yer bums," he snarled in his most snarly way. This was followed by more growls and him opening all three mouths to show his large jaws. "Grrrr. Give us a Mars bar or I'll bite yer bums," he repeated.

By now both Homer and Virgil were very aware of Cerberus's presence, and they both stood up and backed away into the corner. Cerberus followed them and kept snarling.

"It's the... the dog," Homer stammered.

"The dog," Virgil repeated, trying to cower behind Homer.

"Good morning, Mr Cerberus," a frightened Homer said. "I'm afraid we... er... don't have any M... Mars bars in the library." Cerberus snarled again. "I... I... could go and loo... ook for one and le...eave Mr Virgil here as a ho... ostage"

"No, no, no," Virgil said. "I... I'm youn... nger. I would g... go and get back fas... ster. Mr Ho... omer could stay as a ho... ostage."

Cerberus looked at the two frightened old men. He then smiled. "Don't worry about the Mars bar," he said in a polite, friendly voice. "I was only showing you the old Cerberus. You can help me in another matter, but first of all please sit down at your table. I would like us to be friends."

"Friends?" Homer repeated, clearly confused, as he sat down.

"Friends?" Virgil also repeated, equally confused.

"Yes," Cerberus confirmed, moving round to the front of the table so they could all get a good look at each other. "What I've just demonstrated is the old Cerberus that you've known for thousands of years. But you should know I'm beginning to change. I've already got one definite friend and one temporary associate friend on probation. I've also got a couple of maybes, but I'm keen to get some more friends. I'm here because I want to learn how to communicate better with people, so they want to become my friend."

"Bless my soul," Homer said, quite shocked. "Have you ever heard anything like it, Virgil?"

"Never," the other old man replied. "But it's a fascinating challenge."

"It is," Homer agreed. "I think we're talking about behaviour. Is that what you're driving at, Mr Cerberus?"

"It is, if that involves saying the right thing at the right time."

"It's manners," Virgil intervened. "What's that word to describe good manners, Homer? Is it etiquette?"

"That's the word, Virgil. Etiquette. Is that what you want to learn, Mr Cerberus – etiquette?"

"Exocet," Cerberus said. "I think it could be. Is it the same thing as poshiness? Because that's what I really want. Poshiness."

"Poshiness," Virgil repeated, and looked at Homer. "I think we could agree that's what etiquette is about."

"I agree," Homer said. "Let's go with poshiness. I think what you really want to know, Mr Cerberus, is how to behave in polite society. Is that correct?"

"That's what I want," Cerberus agreed, nodding his three heads. "I wish to be poshified."

"How are we going to go about this, Virgil?" Homer asked, looking at his fellow librarian.

"Do you read, Mr Cerberus?" Virgil asked.

"Yes, but I'm not very good at it. I'm better at reading than writing, though. It's the spelling which is difficult."

"Books, Virgil. An excellent idea. Let us spend a few minutes looking for some books on etiquette."

"Poshiness," Cerberus emphasised.

In the next half an hour everything was set up for Cerberus. Virgil went off to look for some books on poshiness, while Homer pulled up a second table next to the one the librarians used. A large bench was procured for Cerberus to sit on at his table and Homer lent him a spare pair of spectacles to enlarge the print. When Virgil returned with half a dozen books, Cerberus was already waiting to start studying.

There were a few mechanical problems to be resolved at the beginning. The most important one was how Cerberus was to turn the pages. After a few minutes a solution was found. Audrey would bend round and use her long, thin tongue to do the turning, which had the advantage that the pages were not marked. When this was resolved Cerberus set to work on Debrett's. The reading was done by Middly, with Audrey turning the pages, and Lefty and Righty got their brains working on what all of this meant.

The first day was slow and tiring for Cerberus, who kept asking Homer and Virgil questions. When they all packed up in the evening, the two librarians walked off together to the Old Men's Quarters as they discussed how to assist Cerberus. It was clear that just giving him a load of books to read was going to take him a long time before he became properly poshified.

The following morning, the three of them agreed an action plan. At the beginning of each day, Homer and Virgil would have a polite conversation in front of Cerberus for a few minutes, so he could see how well-mannered people spoke. Cerberus would then do some reading of selected pages, which Virgil had chosen as the most helpful. After that the two librarians would run tutorials for Cerberus either side of lunch. Some more reading would follow while the two old men had their afternoon siesta, followed by a final discussion at the end of the day on any matters Cerberus felt unsure about.

The early-morning conversations between Homer and Virgil inevitably led to all sorts of questions. On the first day it went like this:

"Good morning, Virgil, young chap. I hope you had a good night's sleep."

"Thank you, old boy. An excellent night. How did you fare?"

"Also, first class. I suspect today will be a fine day – the weather is looking particularly clement."

"It is. No sign of rain, I'm pleased to say."

"I wish we could say the same about the political weather. Trouble once more in the Peloponnese. Sparta's throwing its weight around again."

"And we have trouble brewing for Rome. Hannibal has just completed his crossing of the Alps and—"

"Woof, woof," went Cerberus. "I'm already confused. What's weather and what's rain?"

The two old men looked at each other.

"Of course," Homer said. "Cerberus has only ever lived in the Underworld. We don't have weather here."

"Nor will the histories of ancient Greece and Rome be of any relevance, however dear they are to the two of us," Virgil agreed. "I'm sorry, Cerberus, we'll keep our morning conversations focused on the Underworld."

"Woof. That's okay, young chap. I'm already learning," Cerberus replied.

The next few days went well as the three of them followed the plan. Cerberus really liked the teach-ins, which often led to long discussions.

"So, in polite conversation I'm to call Hades, Lord Hades. Also, you are Mr Homer and Mr Virgil. Is that right?"

"And you are Mr Cerberus," Homer replied.

"But sometimes you call each other Homer and Virgil with no Mr. Also, no one except you two calls me Mr Cerberus. Does that mean they're not being polite?"

Virgil shook his head. "No. For polite conversation read formal conversation. Homer and I know each other well, so we don't use Mr between ourselves. However, if someone else walks in, whom we don't know very well, then we become formal for a while until we're all relaxed."

"What about females?"

"Lady Persephone is Lady Persephone. Aggy is Mistress Aggy. Young girls are called Miss."

"So, old women are mistresses and young women are misses?"

"I wouldn't describe it quite like that, but in broad terms that's not a bad way of looking at it."

"Woof. Got it."

Homer and Virgil spoke a lot about the common courtesies, in particular using please and thank you in conversation.

"That's what Vesta keeps telling me," Cerberus said.

"Who is Vesta?" Homer asked. "You've mentioned her before. Do you know her, Virgil?" The assistant librarian shook his head.

"Miss Vesta is my friend," Cerberus replied very proudly. "She's only recently arrived but is already looked on as the cleverest person in the Underworld."

"Really," Homer said. "Is she even more clever than Aristotle?"

"Definitely cleverer than Harry Totle," Cerberus replied firmly.

"And what about Confucius? Is she cleverer than him?"

"Yes; cleverer than Confused Bus."

"What about Einstein?"

"Heinz Time is just not in her league."

"By Jove, Virgil. We must meet this young lady one day," Homer said.

"I'll introduce her to the two of you sometime," Cerberus said. "She's very busy reorganising the Underworld at present, but I'll make sure she gives you a few minutes."

"Reorganising the Underworld. What does that involve?" Virgil asked.

"She's already sorted out the Torturing Department and is now onto the Kitchens with Aggy. I expect she'll be getting on to the Library in due course."

"What!" Homer exclaimed. "Why do we need reorganising?"

"No one has ever complained," Virgil added.

"No one ever comes here," Cerberus honestly stated, unaware that he was unsettling the two old men. "But it's surprising what Vesta finds when she starts looking."

"What does Hades say about all this?"

Cerberus was now in full swing on the merits of his friend. Unfortunately, he started to get a bit carried away. Actually, very carried away.

"Hades relies on Vesta almost entirely. In fact, I'll let you into a secret just between the three of us." Cerberus looked around and the two librarians bent their heads closer as he continued in a quieter voice. "Not to be disclosed to anyone. Promise?"

"Promise," whispered Homer.

"Promise," whispered Virgil.

"It's becoming understood amongst the elite in Underworld society that Vesta will take over from Hades when he retires."

"When Hades retires!" Homer exclaimed. "I—"

Cerberus interrupted him sharply. "Ssssh," he said. "Keep your voice down."

"I'm sorry," Homer said in a quieter voice. "I didn't think gods retired."

"Neither did I," Virgil contributed.

"Nothing's yet set in stone," Cerberus replied. "But there have been conversations. After all, Vesta is the first person to have arrived in the Underworld with the skills to do Hades' job."

"Well, I'm shocked," Homer said. "Is she a goddess in disguise?"

"Vesta is a being above all the gods and goddesses. She is unique!"

Both the librarians looked at each other with astonishment on their faces.

"Are you thinking what I'm thinking?" Virgil asked Homer.

"I am," was the reply. "This is 'The One', the ultimate creator."

"Yes, 'The One'," Virgil repeated.

"I think you've hit it on the head," Cerberus said, thinking it sensible to agree with the two old men, despite not knowing who 'The One' character was. "But don't forget, this information is highly confidential. No speaking to anyone but me on the subject."

"Agreed," Homer and Virgil said in unison.

Over the next few days, Cerberus continued to learn many things about being poshified. He was taught about the importance of understanding the other person's point of view in any conversation. This reminded him of his talk with Aggy about becoming friends when she asked him why that would benefit her. He had been stumped for a reply at the time, and though Vesta had given him some good reasons afterwards, that was too late. 'Think first, speak second' was what Virgil kept emphasising.

This linked into a long tutorial from Homer on objectives. Cerberus was told that he had to know what he expected from a conversation before beginning it. This was difficult for him at first because he thought conversations just happened. It was only when Homer gave him an example relating to Mars bars that the penny dropped.

"When you first came in here, Cerberus, and threatened Virgil and me with bites on the bum, did you think you would succeed in getting a Mars bar?"

"What do you mean?" Cerberus asked.

"Did you honestly believe we would have a spare Mars bar in the library for you?"

"Well…," Cerberus muttered hesitantly. "I'm not really sure I thought about it."

"And if you had thought, what would your answer have been?"

"Probably no. The library's not the sort of place for spare Mars bars."

"Precisely!" Homer emphasised. "Which means you came in asking for something which you weren't going to get because it wasn't here. Put another way – your objective was a Mars bar, but you had no hope of achieving your objective."

"Not very clever," Cerberus muttered.

"Not very clever," Homer agreed in a firm voice.

"But I did get to meet you and Virgil, which was what I wanted to do as well."

"Agreed, but then why talk about Mars bars?"

"I don't really know," Cerberus said disconsolately. "I suppose that's why I'm here."

"And we are already making great strides in poshifying you," Homer replied, deciding to instil some confidence into his pupil.

"Woof, woof," was the somewhat more eager reply, with Audrey also giving a friendly wag.

The next day Homer had to go off to the Torturing Department because it was an H day, so Virgil and Cerberus spent the day together.

"What's Homer's torture?" Cerberus asked the Assistant Librarian.

"He has to sit on a spike all day," was the response.

"That's not nice. What did he do to deserve that?"

"He wrote a book about the Greeks beating the Trojans in a war."

"If he'd let the Trojans win, what would have happened?"

"He'd have been put in a tub of boiling water."

"How do you know?"

"Because I also wrote a book, but mine was pro-Trojan."

"Did you let them beat the Greeks?"

"No, that was already decided. I wrote about some Trojans who after the war went off and founded the Roman empire."

"And that was pro-Trojan?"

"Definitely."

"Interesting," said Cerberus. "What poshiness subject are we covering today?"

The two spent the whole day working on the difference between soft power and hard power. Again, Cerberus initially had a lot of difficulty understanding what this was all about, until once more the Mars bar came to his rescue by way of an example.

"So, soft power is being nice, is it? It's like saying, 'Virgil, I'm really hungry, I wondered if you could please let me have a Mars bar?'"

"Precisely; it involves you being sensitive and tactful in your request."

"Whereas hard power involves me saying, 'Give us a Mars bar or I'll bite yer bum'?"

"That's it. Hard power might also include the physical biting of the bum."

"But how do I know which to use – soft power or hard power?"

"You always use soft power first. If that doesn't work, you can then consider hard power. You may actually decide not to apply it. As you once explained, threats to Aggy often result in you being bashed on your heads with a ladle. That's something best avoided."

"Can't I use hard power first and then go to soft power if that doesn't work?"

"Generally not. Would you want to be friendly with someone who had previously bitten you on the bum?"

"I suppose not," replied Cerberus. "But when I first came to the library, I applied hard power first, threatening to bite you on the bum, and then I became friendly."

"There are always exceptions to the rule, Cerberus," sighed Virgil. "It's called life."

"Except you're dead."

"Thank you for reminding me."

At the end of two weeks of intensive tutoring, Homer and Virgil felt that Cerberus had been suitably poshified and was now fit to apply his skills on the rest of the Underworld. On the final afternoon, the three of them all had a celebration with Cerberus providing three Mars bars, courtesy of Aggy, so a graduation feast could be held in the library. They all swore everlasting friendship to each other during these festivities, which meant Cerberus had now accumulated two more friends.

XXI

THE EQUALITIES
COMMITTEE

I T HAD TAKEN ARTEMIS AND HERA A LONG TIME TO agree the working party to review the issue of women's equality in sport. There were many reasons for this but underlying everything was the fact that the two goddesses did not get on. This was entirely Zeus's fault since Artemis was his daughter by another goddess, Leto, which naturally was a source of considerable discontent to his wife Hera. This was quite a frequent occurrence as far as the parentage of many of the younger gods was concerned, but Hera felt a particular enmity towards Leto who was carrying Artemis and her twin Apollo at the time of Hera's marriage to Zeus.

The two also had different ideas on what the review body should be trying to achieve. Artemis was an ardent feminist who wanted to bring about sexual equality everywhere as quickly as possible, whereas Hera largely favoured, if not the status quo, change which was exceedingly gradual. The result was that Artemis was trying to pack the working party with gods and goddesses who would agree with her progressive views, whereas Hera wanted members of the deity who would exercise restraint on Artemis's wilder ideas. Since they both knew what each other was up to, this inevitably led to trade-offs between the two of them.

Eventually a committee of four goddesses and three gods was agreed. These were Artemis (as Chairperson), Aphrodite, Athene, Hebe, Hermes, Hephaestus and Bacchus. Hera had made it very clear at the beginning that she viewed both Aphrodite and Apollo as being under Artemis's thumb, so she could only have one of them. While Hermes was also viewed as largely being in Artemis's camp, he was viewed by Hera as 'balanced', so the quid pro quo of including him was to also have Hephaestus. Athene was simply non-negotiable – she was the Goddess of Wisdom and had proposed the working party at the Council Meeting. Artemis knew she would have to be included at the beginning, so did not dissent. Hebe was viewed as neutral, with neither Artemis nor Hera knowing what line she would take. However, in her favour, she knew humankind better than anyone else on Olympus, so that experience was viewed as a positive. Finally, there was Bacchus, who would not normally have been anyone's choice for any committee. Hera was entirely upfront with Artemis about his inclusion; it was at Zeus's insistence and the Top God had made it clear to his wife that he would be letting off thunderbolts all over the place if Bacchus's name was not included. So, he was the final name on the committee.

Hera had made a point of not joining the committee. This surprised Artemis at first until she realised that this allowed Zeus's wife to have influence, as her counsellor, without taking responsibility for the eventual proposals. It meant she could openly disagree with them at any subsequent Council Meeting when they were discussed.

Before calling a committee meeting Artemis decided to have separate talks with the individual members. She hoped to be able to persuade a majority to agree with her proposals in one-on-one talks, so meetings would just be a formality. She knew Aphrodite would do what she was told, so she didn't spend any time with her. The key seemed to be the two other goddesses. She needed to know how radical they were likely to be, especially Athene, who would be a significant influence on all the others. This included Hermes, who was not entirely under Artemis's control, despite their close friendship.

The grounds of Artemis's palace were extensive and included an archery range. That morning she and Athene were practising their shooting skills. Artemis was the Goddess of the Hunt and had a tall, slender build with well-developed muscles. She had darker hair than Athene but was of a similar build. They each had their own targets and were perpetually hitting the bullseye.

Hebe came round the side of the palace on her mountain bike. She peddled along the pathway to reach the archery range.

"Eh up," she said in her Yorkshire accent, as she came to a halt. "Sorry I'm late."

"We haven't started our discussion yet," replied Artemis. "Come and practise your archery skills, Hebe. We've brought a spare bow and there are plenty of arrows. We can talk as we shoot."

Hebe got off her bike. Whereas Artemis and Athene were both wearing white smock dresses, Hebe was in jeans and a T-shirt. She picked up the spare bow, took some arrows and stood opposite a third target which had been set up for her. For a few minutes the three of them didn't converse but instead focused on their archery skills. The two taller goddesses continued to hit the bullseye every time. However, Hebe's first shot flew off to the right of her target and hit a tree. She adjusted her position, but the second shot now flew to the left and in to the shrubbery. She tried again, but this time her arrow fell short and ended up in the grass about six feet from the board.

"This isn't working," she said, and walked towards her target. She pulled off her T-shirt and carefully placed it over the target.

"What are you wearing?" Artemis demanded as she stared at Hebe's upper body.

"It's a bra," Hebe replied. "I may be only little up top, but it keeps everything in place. Stops them jiggling around. Do you like the bright red colour? It's the first time I've worn this one."

"What do you want to wear one of those things for? You're a goddess; you should expose yourself to nature," Artemis replied scornfully. "You don't wear bras, do you, Athene?"

"I do actually," Athene said. "I've got one on now," and she pulled her smock dress to one side to expose her white bra.

"And you're bigger up top," Hebe commented. "Without a bra, yours would jiggle around a lot more than mine."

Artemis didn't say anything. She just gave a little sneer and picked up another arrow to shoot.

Hebe did the same. She stared hard at the target before drawing the bow back slowly and then letting loose.

"Yea! How about that?" she shouted. "You see, I've now got an incentive."

The arrow had clearly hit the bullseye beneath her T-shirt. Her incentive related to the face on the T-shirt which belonged to Mars, underneath which the words 'Bollocks to Mars' were printed. Hebe had deliberately placed Mars's large red nose over the bullseye and had hit between the two nostrils. Her next two shots matched the first and Hebe felt she was now in the rhythm.

"You've ruined your shirt," Athene said to her.

"No matter," Hebe replied. "I've got plenty more where they came from. Fearless now wears one all the time. Would the two of you like one? I've got a range of sizes."

"A bit provocative," Athene replied.

"I'll have one," Artemis said.

"I'll send Fearless along with it later," Hebe said.

The goddesses continued their archery, Hebe now joining Artemis and Athene in continually hitting the bullseye.

"Are we meant to be discussing this equalities thing?" Hebe asked after a couple of minutes.

"Yes," Artemis said. "I thought it would be helpful if the three of us had a preliminary discussion before the whole group gets together. I'll be speaking to the others as well. I'm keen to know where we're all coming from and to see if we can agree some matters beforehand."

"Aha," said Hebe. "We girls are going to try and stitch everything up first; I get it."

"That's certainly not the case!" Artemis replied, slightly affronted. "After all, Aphy isn't here."

"She doesn't have to be," Hebe said. "You've got her vote anyway. Don't get me wrong, Arty, if I were in your shoes I might do the same. I'm just trying to understand where we're all coming from."

"I assure you, there's no intention of a stitch-up," Artemis again protested.

"I bet there is, but it doesn't matter. Let's move on." At this point, Athene, who had remained silent, looked directly at Hebe, raised her eyebrows and gave a knowing smile to show she agreed with her.

Artemis shot off a couple more arrows in a fit of pique without saying anything more, so Athene decided to try to progress matters.

"Do we have a name for this working group, Arty?" she said.

"I was thinking of calling it 'The Female Equalities Committee'," was the reply.

"That seems fine," Athene responded. "Any views, Hebe?"

"Seems good to me too."

"Putting aside all ideas of a stitch-up, Arty, it would be

helpful to know what you would like to achieve as the end result? What are the main decisions you'd like us to come to, fully accepting that matters might change after the committee's had its various discussions?"

"That's simple. I want to see in a short period of time, say, five years, total equality between the sexes. That means equal pay and fifty per cent of all positions, especially the senior ones, being held by women right across society," Artemis replied, now fully engaged once more.

"Do you mean the whole of society?" Hebe asked. "I thought we were meant to be just talking about sport."

"We have to address both," Artemis said. "Inequalities in sport arise from inequalities in society."

"I agree with Artemis," Athene intervened ahead of Hebe. "However, when I proposed this committee, I envisaged focusing on sport initially but acknowledging that wider issues would be raised. I was thinking these could be addressed subsequently. If we try and change the whole world in one go, we'll fail. If we address bits at a time we might get somewhere."

"If you're saying sport is a pilot run for other matters, I can live with that," Artemis said. "What about you, Hebe?"

"I'm okay with that as well."

"Good," Athene commented. "So, picking up Artemis's points, are we saying that there are firstly pay issues and secondly matters relating to equality of positions?"

"I think it's really all about money," Hebe commented. "But what I'd like to understand is what equal pay really means?"

"Isn't that obvious?" Artemis replied. "If you have a country that has a men's football team and also a women's team, then the players should earn the same amount of money when they play, whatever their sex."

"What about affordability?" Hebe asked.

"What do you mean?" said Athene.

"If more people go to watch the men than the women or the

men's game gets more advertising, greater TV rights, that sort of thing, then the men's matches earn a lot more money than the women's. Surely the men should be paid more?"

"But men's and women's matches both last the same time; the training is the same," replied Artemis.

"All the same, you've got the men subsidising the women."

"What's wrong with that?" Artemis demanded. "Women have been doing unpaid work for men for centuries."

"So, your argument is that if in sport, women work just as hard as men, then they should be paid the same, whatever?"

"Yes," Artemis stated firmly.

"What about tennis championships?" Hebe asked.

"What about them?" was Artemis's reply.

"Let's take Wimbledon as an example. The men and the women get the same prize money, but the men play the best of five sets, while it's the best of three for the women. The men have to work harder but don't get any more money. It may be equal, but what's fair about it?"

"Look, Hebe," said Artemis putting down her bow. "Do you believe in women's equality or not? You're putting forward all the reactionary, fascist arguments I'd expect of Mars."

Hebe also put down her bow. "No, I'm not, Arty. I'm asking the sorts of questions which we are going to have to answer. If the men, who represent half the population in the world, don't buy into this equality thing, then it's dead in the water. Just because you proclaim things should happen doesn't mean they will."

"I am not pro—"

Athene clapped her hands. "Quiet, the two of you," she interrupted in a raised voice. "Let's all understand the real purpose of us getting together today. We're not going to get the answers to everything now. What we're doing is highlighting some of the issues for further debate. By the way, Arty, just accept Hebe's being deliberately provocative."

"No, I'm not!" Hebe responded.

"Yes, you are," Athene replied. "You're always arguing."

"No, I'm not!" Hebe continued to defend herself.

"There you go again," Athene said, pointing at her.

"What? No, I'm not!"

"And again. You're arguing with me."

Hebe looked at Athene and burst out laughing. Athene did the same.

"Okay, you got me there," Hebe acknowledged.

"Let's move on to this issue of positions," Athene said once she'd settled down.

"That's another thing I'd like to understand," Hebe immediately piped up. "Are we saying that in every sport we should have combined teams? So, in football, to have equality, let's say the right back would be a man, but the left back's a woman and so on? I don't know what we do about the eleventh player, but is that the general idea?"

Artemis shook her head. "I accept in many sports, for purely physical reasons, you can't mix men and women up. Where you can, like archery and chess, you should do so, but in most sports you'll have separate men and women's teams."

"So, what's this positions thing all about then?" Hebe asked.

"Let me say something," Athene intervened. "Football's a good example. What I think we might be suggesting is that a lot of the non-playing jobs, which can be carried out by either sex, should be open to both. That means you can have women referees at men's matches and men referees at women's."

"That's what I believe," Artemis said.

"And will the best person always be chosen, whatever their sex? If so, how do you get equality if all the best referees are always men?" Hebe asked.

"Women have got to be given the opportunity," Artemis replied. "I think that means at times a woman should be chosen, even if she's not the best."

"That's mighty controversial," Hebe commented.

"Yes, it is," Athene quickly responded before Artemis had a chance to say anything. "Positions is really the wrong word. We should be looking at equalising opportunities between the sexes."

"But you'll still get many situations where the men are better than the women," Hebe said.

"I agree," Athene responded. "But that's often because women have lacked opportunities for years, if not decades, in many sports. Look at football again. Across the world, much more money has gone into the men's game than into the women's. The best way to level things up between the sexes is to put a lot more money into women's sport. For a time, maybe more than into the men's."

"So, is it all about the money, as Hebe said at the beginning?" Artemis responded.

"Not quite," replied Athene. "Money's incredibly important, but there are other factors."

"I assume this applies to all sports everywhere?" Hebe asked. When the other two goddesses nodded, she continued with one of her tongue-in-cheek comments. "So, presumably, there will be a lot of oil money going into training hundreds of female sumo wrestlers in Saudi Arabia?"

"That's one for you to champion, Hebe," Athene responded with a smile.

"Thanks."

The discussion then proceeded to get into a number of the non-money factors. It covered countries where the culture was against women playing sport, the effect of having children and how LGBT issues should be taken into account. Artemis had to admit that she didn't really know much about what LGBT was about, so this had to be explained to her.

"I'm running out of issues to address on women's equality," Hebe eventually said, "but I'm also questioning why we aren't addressing lots of other inequalities in the world as well?"

"Maybe we should be," Athene responded. "But I still think we should focus on the sports area initially or our discussions will just be too broad."

"What other inequalities are you thinking of?" Artemis asked.

"Race inequalities, income and wealth disparities, poor and rich areas of the world, educational inequalities, to name a few," Athene said. "Many of these inequalities are inter-linked."

"I'd like to include short people and tall people," Hebe added. "When I was growing up my big tall brothers always used to push me around because of their size."

"They're still taller than you, Hebe," Athene said, "but now you push them around. Anyway, the politically correct term for short people is vertically challenged."

"Alright, but I still think vertically challenged people should have greater rights," Hebe responded. "Also, what about horizontally challenged people?"

"What are they?" Artemis asked.

"Lumps of lard."

"Hebe!" Athene said, scolding her, but finding it hard to keep a straight face.

"Okay, fat people then."

"The word is obese," Athene said.

"I'll stick with horizontally challenged."

"So, we're saying we should be addressing all these equality issues as well?" Artemis asked, slightly perplexed.

"They're all very important," Athene replied. "Although vertically and horizontally challenged inequalities are probably quite low down the list."

"Vertically challenged are higher up then horizontally challenged," Hebe piped up. "But more seriously, if our committee's going to look more widely, shouldn't it just be called 'The Equalities Committee' and not have Women in the name?"

"Probably, yes," Athene replied, and then looked at Artemis. "Any views, Arty?"

"I suppose so," she said, feeling that by now the entire discussion had largely been taken over by Athene and Hebe.

The three goddesses broke up shortly afterwards, agreeing they would each reflect on matters before the first committee meeting. Also, Artemis needed to have her separate discussions with the other members, especially the three male gods.

As they were walking back from the archery field, Hebe said, "By the way, why do we want all this equality stuff? What's wrong with just leaving everything as it is?"

"That's a good point," Athene replied. "Perhaps that's the first question the committee should address before we start changing the whole world."

When the others had left, Artemis went and lay down on one of her sofas. She was used to getting her own way, but matters had turned out very differently to what she had planned beforehand. Her head was buzzing and she was initially a mixture of being a bit depressed as well as irritated. However, as she continued to reflect during the day, she began to get things more into perspective. After all, she was now operating in the big league with Athene, who was much higher up the Olympian hierarchy than she was. Chairing this committee was clearly not going to be the same as leading a pack consisting of Apollo, Aphrodite and sometimes Hermes.

The first point Artemis accepted was that the whole matter of equality, whether women's or more generally, was a lot more complicated than she had expected. Originally, she had thought a few quick edicts would resolve a lot of matters but now accepted that wasn't going to happen. The next point that struck her was that it was a lot easier being a rabble rouser and asking difficult questions at meetings than actually trying to find answers that would work. This was the first time she had been given real responsibility as a committee chairperson. It was her job to make sure the answers were found.

Artemis was clever but knew she hadn't had the experience

of many of the other gods and goddesses. It was clear to her that the best person to chair the committee was Athene and she did seriously think about going to the Goddess of Wisdom to suggest they should swap places. Artemis, however, had some pride and she wanted to see if she could make a success of being in charge. Instead, she would go and speak to Athene to request her help, being quite prepared to acknowledge Athene's greater experience in these complicated matters. As far as Hebe was concerned, she was sorry she'd used the word fascist. Artemis liked Hebe and would go and see her to put things right; she now understood what the pocket-rocket had been trying to do. In addition, she wanted to ask if she could accompany her on some of her trips. When she visited the world, Artemis spent most of her time hunting in the forests of South America, Africa and South East Asia; she needed to get to know towns and cities a lot more, especially the people who lived in them, including the LGBT community.

Finally, Artemis went back in her mind to one of the first things Athene had raised, which was the need for focus. It was pretty clear to her now that the focus should not begin with the subject of women's sport. A better starting point would be one particular sport in one country. Her grandiose plans when she had woken up that morning had become much more limited as the day had progressed.

*

As promised, Fearless Frupert arrived at Artemis's palace later in the afternoon.

"I've brought you two T-shirts of the Pig, Auntie Artemis," Fearless said. "Auntie Hebe sent a spare one if you want to use it for target practice."

"Thank you, Fearless," Artemis said. "Tell me, do you know how to use a bow and arrow?"

Fearless shook his head. "I know how to use a sword," he said, waving his wooden sword around.

"Would you like to learn?"

"Ooh, yes please. Will you teach me, Auntie?" Fearless asked eagerly.

"Come this way."

The young warrior had arrived just at the time Artemis had finished her deliberations on equality issues. She felt she needed a break from her thoughts and giving Fearless an archery lesson would be a good distraction. The two of them initially went off to the bows and arrows cupboard and found a small bow which Fearless could handle. They then went to the archery range and Artemis taught her young pupil the basic techniques. It was then a question of practice, with the goddess adjusting his positioning and technique with each shot.

After a few false shots which went in every direction except towards the target, Fearless began to get his range and direction. Although the two of them stood quite close to the target and the shots were getting nearer, none of them were actually striking the board, so Artemis told Fearless to stop while she quickly ran back to the palace. She returned a couple of minutes later with one of the 'Bollocks to Mars' T-shirts, which she hung over the board.

"Now try that," Artemis said.

Fearless took another shot and hit the outer edge of the board, but not Mars's face.

"Much better, Fearless. Now try again."

The next shot missed the target completely, but the third punctured a hole in Mars's left ear.

"Success!" Fearless shouted. He tried again, but another miss. This was followed by a direct hit in Mars's right eye and then the next shot was a bullseye right into Mars's large red nose. "Hurrah!" the young warrior shouted.

After a few more minutes, Fearless was beginning to lose his strength, so the two of them decided to stop.

"Would you like to have a lesson tomorrow, Fearless?" asked Artemis.

"Yes, please."

"Come about the same time."

"Right-ho, Auntie! Shall I keep the bow and a few arrows and bring them back tomorrow?"

"No," Artemis said. "You can leave them here."

"But if I see the Pig, I'll be able to shoot him if I keep them with me."

"Fearless, you shouldn't do that without getting permission from Auntie Iris or Auntie Hebe."

"Can't you give me permission?"

"No, it's got to be one of your other aunts."

"The Pig isn't a friend of yours, is he?"

"He certainly isn't."

"That's good," Fearless responded. "Because I couldn't be your friend anymore if you liked the Pig. But since he's not your friend, I'll let you join my gang."

"What's your gang?" Artemis asked.

"I'll tell you all about it tomorrow. I must go now or I'll be late for tea," Fearless replied, and started running across the lawn on his way back to 5 Carnation Drive.

Artemis watched his little legs move. He turned round at one point to wave before setting off again. Artemis waved back. She'd had a really tough day, but there were compensations. After all, she was now a member of Fearless Frupert's gang!

XXII

IMPRESSING
THE BOSS

CERBERUS LOOKED INTO THE THRONE ROOM AND saw Hades was alone. This was his opportunity to show off his poshiness to the Boss. He slowly walked into the room, giving a little cough to draw the god's attention to his presence.

"Have I permission to approach Your Gracious Majesty?" Cerberus asked in a very posh voice.

Hades frowned and beckoned Cerberus forward with his right hand, wondering what all this was about. Cerberus got as far as the stool before coming to a halt.

"My Lord," he said, and bowed all three heads to the god. Audrey also bowed despite looking the wrong way.

"What is it, Cerberus?" Hades asked.

"I have come to deliver my report as Head of Internal Security. Have I your permission to proceed?"

Hades frowned again, but then nodded his head. *What's he on about?* he asked himself.

"Thank you, My Lord. By way of general observations, I note that the weather today is most clement. It is the same as yesterday and forecast to be the same tomorrow."

"What are you talking about, Cerberus? We don't have any weather in the Underworld."

"Which confirms my statement about yesterday and today being the same and also provides strong support for tomorrow's forecast, My Lord."

"I suppose it does," Hades muttered. "Go on."

"It should also be noted that the political situation in the Underworld is worthy of my close attention."

"What political situation?"

"The one to which I am giving my close attention. There is no need for you to trouble yourself on such matters. The Internal Security team is forever alert."

Hades sighed and decided not to press the point. Clearly, Cerberus was in a strange mood today and he would just listen. What he really wanted to hear was some barking. Where were the 'woof, woofs' that he was used to?

"Getting down to the specifics, My Lord, the banana fishes are well and continuing to do their job diligently. The warning sign remains intact as a deterrent, but I have agreed to have a professional replacement made. I am using Mr Nelson, who as well as being an excellent trainee nurse and potato peeler, also has hidden design capabilities."

"Very good," Hades muttered, nodding his head.

"As far as the Torturing Department is concerned, Mr Satan has now returned after his lengthy rehabilitation. If I may make an observation, the Department performed admirably in his absence. I make my observation purely as a matter of interest."

"I know," Hades muttered.

"The various procedural changes proposed by the excellent

Miss Vesta have all been introduced and have led to important efficiencies, which are much appreciated by all. I understand there are further issues to be addressed in due course, which I am confident the excellent Miss Vesta will resolve with ease."

"I know," Hades muttered again.

"The Kitchens have been experimenting with new food and today, Spaghetti Bolognese is to be made available for the first time to the entire Underworld for lunch. There is considerable excitement about this matter which has been spearheaded by Mistress Aggy, Miss Gigliola and the excellent Miss Vesta. I myself am to be offered a Galaxy bar as an alternative to my normal Mars bar, which I am very much looking forward to. I should note that the excellent Miss Vesta will be here shortly to show you a special menu which has been created as a token of the Kitchens' high regard for Your Gracious Majesty."

"Thank you, Cerberus," Hades sighed. "Anything else?"

"At a personal level, My Lord may be interested to know that I have not only established a formal friendship with the excellent Miss Vesta but also recently with Mr Homer and Mr Virgil. Mistress Aggy and I have decided to become temporary associate friends on probation, which I envisage will lead on to a closer relationship. I also have high hopes of Mr Attila, Miss Ming, Mr Nelson and possibly even Mr Death and the banana fishes. I do not intend to pursue a friendship with either Mr Satan or Mr Wong, who in particular talks too much."

"Fine," said Hades. "Are we finished?"

"Yes, My Lord. I am happy to answer any questions, but in their absence, I would beg your leave to withdraw."

"What's happened to you, Cerberus? Why the posh voice and where's the 'woof, woof'?"

"My Lord, it is still an important part of my conversational armoury."

"Show me then."

"Wooaf, wooaf," went Cerberus. "Is that satisfactory, My Lord?"

"Wooaf, wooaf," Hades repeated with a sigh. He decided not to press Cerberus any more on why he was behaving in this extraordinary manner. He'd get more sense out of Vesta later on, so he just said, "That's fine. You may go now."

"Thank you, Your Gracious Majesty," Cerberus said, followed by all his heads and Audrey bowing once more. Cerberus then proceeded to walk backwards to the entrance to the throne room before repeating his bow and then leaving.

*

Later that morning, Vesta was sitting on the stool in front of Hades.

"So, Vesta," the god said. "Today's the big day. I gather it's Spaghetti Bolognese for everyone?"

"There's still the choice of stew, if people prefer it."

"And have you come to ask me which one I would like – spaghetti or stew?"

"Not quite, Lord Hades," Vesta answered. "We've actually prepared a special menu for you with Lady Hebe's help. It's a way of the Kitchens team saying thank you for letting us experiment with new dishes. I've got it here, so if you wouldn't mind looking at it and telling me what you'd like, I can put your order in."

Vesta stood up and handed a sheet of parchment to Hades.

Special Luncheon Menu for Lord Hades
(To commemorate Our First Spaghetti Bolognese Day)

Starters
  Duck Liver Parfait
  Smoked Salmon
  Chargrilled Asparagus

Mains
   8oz Fillet Steak
   Sole Meuniere
   Half Roast British Chicken
   Spaghetti Bolognese
   (Choice of French Fries, Mashed Potatoes, Spinach,
   Peas, Broccoli, Mixed Salad)
Desserts
   Apple and Rhubarb Pie
   Chocolate Profiteroles
   Fruit Salad
Wines
   Prestige Chablis
   Cave de Fleurie

Hades studied it for a couple of minutes and then pulled out a quill pen from his robe to mark Smoked Salmon, Spaghetti Bolognese, Fruit Salad and Chablis wine. He then got up and handed it to Vesta.

"Tell me, Vesta," he said, sitting down again on his throne. "Am I to have this special menu every day?"

"If you would like it, I'm sure that would be okay," Vesta replied hesitantly.

"But I sense that wasn't the plan?"

"You can obviously have whatever you want, Lord Hades. But what Aggy thought was that we would prepare a special menu for you to celebrate particular occasions."

"Let's do that then," Hades said with a smile. "Will Aggy bring my meal as usual or will you?"

"Aggy will."

Hades nodded. "Then that gives us an opportunity to have a chat about a few matters now," he said.

"Cool," Vesta replied, but not feeling at all confident because she was certain Sisyphus would be brought up.

"First of all," Hades said, launching off without noticing Vesta's nervousness, "can you please tell me what's happened to Cerberus? I've had him in here bowing and calling me My Gracious Majesty and reporting on various matters in the poshest voice I've ever heard. He's also stopped barking and being aggressive, which isn't exactly what I want from the Underworld's guard dog."

"Oh," Vesta said with a laugh. "He's been spending the last two weeks in the library trying to be poshified. He thinks it will help him become more socially acceptable; he wants to make more friends and get people to give him more Mars bars. He calls it using soft power instead of hard power, whatever that means."

"In the library!" Hades exclaimed. "What's he been doing there?"

"He's been reading various books on something he calls exocet. I think it refers to manners and making polite conversation. Also—"

"Exocet," Hades interrupted. "I suspect Cerberus means etiquette. So, has he actually understood what he's been reading? He's not exactly a scholar."

"He somehow managed to persuade the two librarians, Mr Homer and Mr Virgil, to give him lessons as well. I've not met them yet, but I gather both of them have written books."

"Very famous books," said Hades. "That will explain why he claims Homer and Virgil are friends of his."

"I think so."

"Vesta, I'm amazed at the changes you've inspired in Cerberus in the last few weeks. While it's good he's not threatening to bite everyone on the bum if he doesn't get a Mars bar, I think he's gone completely overboard with this excessive politeness and posh voice. As I said earlier, that's not how a guard dog should be behaving. Look, you seem to have more influence over him than anyone else, so would you please try and get him to adopt some sort of halfway house? I won't specify precisely what that is because I don't know. I'll leave it to your judgement."

"I think I know what you mean. I'll try my best. I take it you don't want any more bowing?"

"And no more Gracious Majesty. I'm called Lord Hades or just Hades occasionally when we're being informal."

"Cool," Vesta muttered.

"Next on my list is the Torturing Department. Let me say up front how pleased I am with the changes you've suggested. They've saved us all a lot of time and created some sort of structure, which we should have had a long time ago. Still, I suppose, we all get a bit stale and everyone's been there for centuries. Sometimes it needs a fresh face. Are there any other ideas you have for that area?"

"I gather that Vlad and Ivan want me to look at what they're doing and I've promised to do that sometime. I've been really busy in the Kitchens recently."

"Yes, I'll come on to the Kitchens in a minute, but let's stay on torturing for a while. What about this point that some people avoid being tortured at all? Have you any ideas to prevent that?"

"Lord Hades, if I'm honest I don't really like the idea of torture. I'm quite happy to make common-sense suggestions about keeping arms and legs next to their original bodies, but I would have difficulty suggesting ideas which result in catching people so they can be tortured."

Hades looked sternly at Vesta. "Tortures are decreed by the gods," he said eventually. "Are you saying that you support people disobeying the gods?"

"No," said Vesta. "I just don't think it's a matter for me to resolve. It's what Satan should be doing."

There was a lengthy silence and Vesta became increasingly nervous at what she had said. The longer the silence went on, the more certain she was that Hades would punish her for her comments. Eventually he gave a little smile.

"You're very brave," he said in a friendly voice. "Very few people in the Underworld would dare to speak to me like that. However, I happen to agree with you. It's Satan's job as the Director of the Torturing Department and I'll speak to him about it. I do still want you to look at Vlad and Ivan's areas. Are you happy to do that?"

"Of course," Vesta replied with a big sigh of relief.

"Let's talk about the Kitchens now. Is today going to be a success?"

"We hope so. We've practised a lot and when we served Spaghetti Bolognese to all the Kitchens' team, it went really well. Only a small number wanted to continue with stew and the feedback was really positive. Our biggest difficulty today is working out how much spag bol and how much stew to produce, so we've decided to cook too much of everything. What's left over can always be served up this evening or tomorrow."

"Very wise," Hades commented. "So, assuming today is a success, what's the next dish to be produced?"

"We thought we'd go for fish and chips. Do you have a view or another suggestion?"

"Fish will really upset my brother Poseidon, but that's no reason not to do it. No, I'll leave it up to all of you. Aggy knows what she's doing and she's got a good team."

"Thank you," Vesta replied because she knew Hades was including her in that compliment.

"That's all I've got on my list. Are there any matters you want to raise with me?"

Vesta thought very hard about whether to raise Sisyphus. Deep down, she knew she had been worrying about her involvement with his 'strike action' ever since it had happened. She decided it would be better to clear the air now, especially since Hades had not blown her up for her earlier comments on the Torturing Department.

"Only that you've not spoken to me about Mr Sisyphus," she eventually said, somewhat hesitantly.

"No," Hades replied. "I gather you might have put the idea of stopping into Sisyphus's head, but I'm not blaming you for what happened. I've known him for three thousand years. He's one of the trickiest devils you'll ever meet. He's responsible for his own affairs."

"But isn't what he's doing totally pointless?"

"Yes, but that's the reason he's doing it. He upset a lot of gods when he was King of Carthage. Me, my wife Persephone, Mars, but in particular Zeus, to name a few. It's my brother that decreed what his punishment should be in the Underworld."

"Isn't three thousand years long enough?"

"No, it will go on forever."

"Have you ever thought Sisyphus could be much more useful doing other things?"

"What do you mean?"

"I'm sure he must be the strongest man in the whole of the Underworld; you only have to look at his muscles after all those years of pushing his boulder up the hill. He could work in the quarries instead or carry the stones which have been mined to the different building sites. He would still be doing heavy manual work, but at least he'd be productive."

"It doesn't work like that, Vesta," Hades responded. "Punishments are set for ever in the Underworld. They don't change."

"But other things change, don't they? Look at all the building work, the changes in Satan's area, the new food we're cooking in the Kitchens. Why can't punishments change? Think what could be achieved if people here could be rewarded for doing a good job or penalised for doing bad things. It's what happened when we were alive in society. The Underworld is just a different form of society."

"It's not what we do," Hades responded defensively.

"I bet you could if you really wanted to."

"I would be reluctant to go against Zeus's punishment for Sisyphus."

"Why? Is Zeus senior to you?"

"No!" Hades shouted and slammed his fist down hard on the arm of his throne. "Who's told you that?"

"No one," said Vesta. "It's just that you're reluctant to change something after three thousand years when it could benefit your kingdom. I'm sure if you really wanted to, you could change it. After all, you're both a god and a king, so you can do anything."

There was a long silence as Hades stared hard at Vesta. She tried to avoid his gaze by looking everywhere, except at his face. She knew she'd yet again gone too far and was awaiting Hades' reaction. She kept waiting and waiting until she felt compelled to say something more.

"I'm sorry, Lord Hades. I shouldn't have said all that. Please accept my apologies."

"Because you acknowledge I am a god and a king, you must accept that tomorrow you will find Sisyphus pushing his boulder up the hill and you will find him doing the same the next day." Hades spoke in a very stern voice. "Do you accept that?"

"Yes, Lord Hades," Vesta replied quietly.

"Good. Now we will say no more about Sisyphus," he said in a less stern tone. "Thank you for everything, Vesta, and please hurry back to the Kitchens. There's a lot of work to be done, today of all days."

Vesta knew she had been let off lightly, so she set about focusing all her energies with the others in making sure that the new Spaghetti Bolognese lunch was a success. She was particularly comforted by Aggy who, returning from delivering Hades his lunch, took her aside and said that Hades briefly mentioned their discussion and she was not to be concerned about what she had said.

"I think he rather appreciates having debates with you, Vesta," the Head Chef said. "Not a lot of people dare to disagree with him. You're a challenge and he enjoys that, even if he doesn't agree with you on everything."

"Thank you, Aggy," Vesta said, and as her eyes were about to well up with a few tears, she was taken into the older woman's arms and given a big hug.

By mid-afternoon, lunch had ended and it was clear that the Spaghetti Bolognese option had been a huge success. The majority of people had chosen it and all the feedback was positive. Aggy and the small team, who had pioneered the change, sat around a table and had a debrief. They decided on three things: firstly, spag bol would be served up about every ten days; secondly, and as expected, fish and chips was the next dish to be developed, and, finally, consideration should be given to either a Chinese or a pure vegetarian meal after that.

Cerberus, who attended the debrief in his capacity as Aggy's temporary associate friend on probation, also expressed his approval of the Galaxy chocolate bar. He suggested the team should celebrate what had been a good day, with everyone having a Galaxy bar on him, which really meant Aggy since she held the key to the chocolate cupboard.

*

About a week later, Vesta was walking back to the Girls' Quarters when she suddenly heard a shout.

"Ahoy, lassie!" the voice called.

She turned round and saw Sisyphus carrying two huge stones, one under each arm. She hadn't seen him for some time because after the incident with Satan, Aggy had felt it better to get someone else to deliver the former king's meals.

"What are you doing here?" Vesta asked in an astonished voice.

Sisyphus came up to her and put his two stones on the ground. "I've got myself a proper job now. I'm a carrier, transporting these large rocks from the quarries to different building sites. Lass, I've got you to thank for that. Hades actually listened to you and that makes you a star. I'm a bit hot and sweaty at the moment, otherwise I'd give you a big kiss."

"But Hades said he wasn't going to let you off. You'd keep pushing the boulder up the hill."

"Not quite," Sisyphus said. "He told me exactly what he said at the end of your conversation. He said you would find me pushing the boulder up the hill the day after your talk and also the day after that. He didn't say anything about the third day onwards, did he?"

Vesta smiled. "No, I don't think he did. Hades is as tricky as you are, Sisyphus."

"No way, that's impossible. I have taught him a few tricks over the years, though."

"So, what else has changed?"

"I now live in the Men's Quarters. I've got my own bed, but I don't like all these fancy mattresses and sheets and things, so I normally sleep on the floor. I have three meals a day now, and that dog of yours and I have agreed to become friends. Also, I now have regular torture sessions. Whenever it's an S day, I have to go back to the hill and push the boulder up it for the rest of the day. Attila and my new friend Cerberus have been given responsibility for making sure I do it. Don't worry, I won't give them any trouble; I'm just happy at the change. It was all getting a bit boring after three thousand years."

"Well, I'm very pleased," Vesta said with a big smile.

"Look, I'd better be off because the builders are waiting for these two big stones. Tomorrow's an S day, so I'll be back on my hill, but let's make a date and meet up the following day for lunch. We can then have a longer chat."

"Cool," Vesta replied. "I'll be in the central kitchen area with

Aggy. Why don't you come and look for me there when you're free?"

"Will do," Sisyphus said, picking up his stones and setting off. "Remember, that's a date, lassie. Just you and me," he called as he left.

Vesta watched Sisyphus march off with his gigantic load. She was thinking of that word, 'date.' She'd never been on one of those before and was concerned she was a bit young, especially with a much older man – three thousand years to be precise! Also, he did say 'just you and me', which sounded a bit worrying. She'd better ignore that last bit and bring Cerberus along as a chaperone, just in case.

With that decision, Vesta walked slowly to the Girls' Quarters, deep in thought about her 'first date'.

XXIII

DRINKS ON
THE HOUSE

EVERY FEW WEEKS BACCHUS AND MISTRESS Quickly would have a 'pub night'. Everyone on Mount Olympus was invited, whether they were gods or humans. There was a strict house rule on these evenings, which was that everyone was on equal terms. There was no use of the term Lord or Lady and, wherever possible, humans were to be referred to by their first names. The deity only had one name, so first names did not apply to them.

That morning Lennie had been sent off to deliver the invitations. All this involved was him flying to the various palaces, as well as 5 Carnation Drive, catching someone's attention and then screeching, 'pub night'. Word got around pretty quickly, since such evenings were really at the heart of Olympian social life. That day Lennie had taken longer than usual since he needed to enlist Apollo's assistance with a special project which he would reveal later in the day.

Artemis and her brother Apollo arrived when the evening was already in full swing. Artemis looked at the Hanseatic Headbanger poster which was outside the front door and became annoyed. She pushed it to the ground face down, muttering various disparaging remarks to Apollo as she did so. He just smiled and led the way into the pub.

"Nell," Artemis said, going over to the hostess, who was behind the bar. "How can you have that sexist poster outside the front door? It objectifies women; I can't believe you approve of it."

"What do you want, Artemis? Your usual dry white wine?" Nell replied.

"Please. And Apy will have…" She looked round for her brother, but he'd already gone off to the other end of the pub to mingle. "Forget him. Let's get back to this poster."

"Look, Artemis, it was sent to Bacchus when he put in a large order for this new beer, Hanseatic Headbanger. I've tasted it and it's really good; you should have some later. The poster's marketing material and I've got no problem with it."

"But it objectifies women!" Artemis repeated. "Two sexy young blondes in bikinis. You really can't approve, do you, Nell?"

"Well, I don't know what this 'objectifies women' means. It's meant to encourage men to come in and order pints of Headbanger because they see two attractive blondes drinking it. As far as I can see, it serves its purpose. It's a much better idea than having a picture of me and Brenda Bumble in our bikinis with pints in our hands. That would put any man off."

"But as I keep—"

"Let's stop there, Artemis. We're friends; let's say no more or we'll get this evening off on the wrong foot. Pub night is all about enjoying ourselves, not getting into disagreements. Here's your wine."

"Okay, and thanks. I should tell you that the poster annoyed me so much, I've pushed it over."

"Have you?" Nell said. "Well, I'll go and put it back up again. If you've damaged it, that drink will be your last and you'll have to go home. We can't have vandals in the Dog and Duck."

"I am not a vandal!" Artemis replied, but Mistress Quickly wasn't listening as she was already walking to the front door.

This conversation had been heard by Lennie, who was standing with Beetle on a table in a nearby alcove.

"Artemis," he called. "Could we please have a private word?"

The goddess moved over to the alcove. "Oh, hello, Lennie; hello, Beetle, I didn't see you there."

"I just wanted to say that I agree completely with your sentiments," Lennie said. "It's a disgrace to have that sexist poster outside the pub. Beetle agrees, don't you?"

"Do I?" Beetle said, looking up from his lettuce.

"Yes!" Lennie stated firmly. "You should know, Artemis, that there's a move afoot to totally rebrand this pub. Under the new branding, which involves changing the name to The Eagle, there will be an absolute prohibition on such advertising material. Women will no longer be objectified, whatever that means. That's an absolute guarantee."

"So, Bacchus has agreed to change the name of the pub to the Eagle, has he?"

"As I said, there's a move afoot. We've got this petition here, which I wondered if you'd kindly sign? It was Apollo who prepared it for me earlier in the day."

Artemis picked up and read a large parchment which was headed PETITION TO RENAME THE DOG AND DUCK PUBLIC HOUSE AS 'THE EAGLE'.

"Why's it not going to be called the Eagle and Tortoise?" Artemis asked.

"A totally inappropriate name," Lennie replied. "Beetle agrees."

"Do I?" said Beetle once more.

"Yes!" Lennie snapped.

"What does Nell say about all of this?" Artemis asked.

"Well, as you can see, Artemis, she's given us this table and is fully aware of our petition. That clearly suggests a lot of support from her."

"No, it doesn't," Beetle interrupted. "She got tired of arguing with you over two hours and she doesn't think anything will come of it anyway, so she decided to let you have your way."

"Beetle!" Lennie snapped again. "I wish you wouldn't involve yourself in matters which don't concern you. Please don't interfere!"

Artemis was looking at the various names on the petition. "You've already got quite a lot of names, Lennie," she said. "As well as Apollo's I'm looking at the King of Africa, the Duke of Detroit, the Man in The Moon, Pinocchio, Moaning Lisa. Who's Moaning Lisa?"

"A very beautiful Italian lady, I believe," Lennie replied.

"I see. The Prince of Thieves, the Queen of Utopia, even Beetle. How did you sign this, Beetle?" Artemis asked. "You can't write."

"Signed under proxy," Lennie hastily intervened. "All with a properly executed power of attorney."

"Really," said Artemis. "And then I come to Nell Quickly, which seems very strange given what Beetle just said. Does she know she's signed this?"

"Yes," Lennie replied confidently.

"Are there some additional words you should be adding after yes?"

"Yes, in the fullness of time."

"What does that mean, Lennie?"

"It means that when she reads the petition, she'll know she's signed it," the eagle replied.

"I'm sure she'll be very impressed." Artemis continued to

study the parchment. "Another thing I find interesting about this document," she said after a while, "is how everyone's signed in the same handwriting. In fact, it all looks like Apollo's writing."

"Does it?" Lennie replied nonchalantly, pretending to have a look. "I don't see it myself. Perhaps because it's the same quill pen being used. Also, Apollo has such lovely handwriting, the others probably wanted to copy him."

There was a silence as Artemis continued to study the list of names. Lennie was becoming increasingly frustrated with the time she was taking.

"Come on, Artemis," he eventually said. "Are you going to sign or not?"

Artemis smiled at Lennie. "Yes, alright," she said, picking up the quill pen and adding her signature. "I've signed after Santa Claus."

Meanwhile, Apollo had come to the pub night with the express purpose of both creating some mischief and also having some fun. He was currently talking to Marie Antoinette. With her head reinstated, the former Queen of France was tall and slim. Her curly hair was light brown, her nose was slightly too long and she had a permanent frown on her face. She was in a black dress and wore high-heeled red shoes. Apollo had been listening to her moan continuously about Hera and felt it was now time to change the subject.

"You know, Marie Antoinette," the god said, "while I have every sympathy for you, I find it highly unlikely that Hera will start calling you Your Majesty. After all, she does view you as her maid. Nor do I think she's going to provide you with your own maid, footman and butler."

"But it is not right," Marie Antoinette replied. "I was the great Queen of La France, n'est ce pas?"

"You did unfortunately have an unhappy ending."

"But it was not ma faute. It was my stupid husband. I told him to let the peasants eat cake, but he did not listen, no?"

"I'm sure you're right," Apollo agreed, trying to keep a straight face. "Let me, however, bring up more immediate affairs. How are you and Bacchus getting on?"

"*Pardon moi?* I do not understand what you mean by me and Bacchus getting on. I try my best to ignore him. He is a boozy, ugly, fat little man, who is *pas de tout sympathique*, no?"

"He's a god, not a man," Apollo replied. "But I was only asking because I thought you and he were mutually attracted to each other."

"*Comment?*" Marie Antoinette exclaimed. "There must be some *erreur*. How can we be, how do you say it, mutually attracted to each other? *C'est impossible.*"

"But I've heard that Lord Bacchus views you as the most beautiful female he's ever met. Far more desirable than Aphrodite or Athene or my twin, Artemis. He also adores your elegance, your fine manners and overall sophistication. He even admits to dreaming every night about you. I won't repeat any of the details of his dreams, except to suggest they indicate an all-consuming passion for you."

"Ooh la la, Apollo," Marie Antoinette replied, having turned a deep shade of pink. "I cannot believe, *c'est vrai*. You have heard these things, but from whom?"

"They're widely known amongst the deity. Many of us are waiting for the two of you to announce your betrothal."

"I am feeling slightly giddy, Monsieur Apollo. Could you please find me a chair?"

When Marie Antoinette was sitting down on a chair, she took some deep breaths before continuing. "And you have heard these words from Lord Bacchus yourself, *avez vous?*"

"You should know that Bacchus and I are very close," Apollo replied. "I won't disclose all our conversations, but I more than anyone know his mind."

"But he hardly knows me."

"It doesn't stop him from admiring you, Marie Antoinette."

"And what of Madame Quickly? What role has she?"

"Don't think about Nell Quickly. She's very competent, but Bacchus views her as just a servant. He needs a sophisticated lady to run his household."

"But his household is but a pub."

"If he had the right lady partner, a large palace would be built for him. The pub is just a side show, by the way. He spends most of his time as Zeus's principal advisor, being the one god that Zeus relies on. If it were not for Bacchus, Zeus wouldn't be able to cope. Being entirely honest, Bacchus really runs Olympus."

"I thought Bacchus spent most of his time in a state of being, how you say it, piss-headed?"

"I won't deny he likes a drink, but most of the time he's thinking deeply about all Zeus's problems. You know, it's said that if Zeus ever retires, Bacchus would take over as Top God."

"Ooh la la, Lord Zeus is to retire, *oui?*"

"Not just yet, but Bacchus is all positioned to be Top God when it happens. And you know what that means?"

"Please to tell me, Apollo. I am all the ears."

"Bacchus as Top God will need a queen to reign with him. You, Marie Antoinette, have been a queen. It is why all we other gods and goddesses believe you are the perfect match for him. Not just us, but Bacchus himself does."

"*C'est vrai,*" replied Marie Antoinette. "I am the most right lady to be Queen of Olympus, *n'est ce pas?* Lord Bacchus, for whom I have always had high regard *avec beaucoup d'intelligence,* does need me. Ooh la la, I see it now. *Mais oui,* he has made the right choice."

"That confirms his intelligence, doesn't it?" said Apollo.

"You are right. He is a most distinguished and handsome god, and he will have a beautiful, elegant wife as his queen. *C'est bon, n'est ce pas?*"

"Nothing could be better," Apollo replied.

While Apollo was advising Marie Antoinette on how to progress the Bacchus relationship, Lennie was continuing to drum up support for his petition. He hopped along the floor to where Zeus, Hermes and Mr Bumble were in deep conversation. Hermes had recently been studying nuclear physics and was busy explaining about the Second Law of Thermodynamics. Zeus and Mr Bumble knew nothing about the subject when Hermes began talking and after half an hour, knew even less. They were, therefore, mightily relieved when Lennie jumped onto their table with his petition and quill pen in his mouth.

"You seem to have a lot of names already," Zeus said, while studying the list of signatories.

"There's a powerful movement behind this change," Lennie replied. "Very strong feelings."

"It's just surprising I don't know most of these people," Zeus commented. "Where do the Duke of Detroit and the King of Thieves actually live on Olympus? Also, what jobs do they do here?"

"They tend to only come for short periods. If they need to stay overnight, we've various guest rooms on the first floor."

"And when were they last here having a drink?"

"Were you in the pub last night, Zeus?" Lennie asked.

"No," replied the Top God.

"That's when they last came."

"Extraordinary. And tell me, Lennie, how do they get here? Does Hebe bring them in her chariot?"

"That's one possible means of transport. Santa Claus has his own sleigh pulled by reindeers, so he comes under his own steam."

"And the others?" Zeus asked.

"Normally by space rocket," Lennie replied.

"Space rocket!" Zeus exclaimed. "Where does it land?"

"In the back garden."

"Even more extraordinary," Zeus again commented with a smile. "What do you two think?"

Hermes and Mr Bumble had a short consultation with Zeus on the matter, as Lennie listened. The end result was that Hermes signed the petition because he viewed it as a bit of fun. Zeus agreed it was a bit of fun but withheld his signature, so Mr Bumble naturally did the same. Lennie protested vigorously that it was a serious business and not a bit of fun, but having got Hermes's signature he hopped off to where Hera, Iris, Nurse Nightingale and Fearless Frupert were sitting. He decided to try his luck with them.

It was quite late in the evening when Mars walked in. Most of the guests were engrossed in their own conversations by this time so were not aware of his presence. Nell Quickly was busy pouring out two glasses of white wine, which Mrs Bumble was ordering for herself and Hebe, as well as another tankard of Headbanger for Bacchus. Mars marched over to the hostess and slammed his right hand down on the counter.

"Give me a Headbanger," he demanded in an aggressive tone.

"One minute, please, Mars," Mistress Quickly replied. "I'm dealing with another order first."

Mars's reaction was to bang his hand down even more fiercely before leaning over, grabbing Nell Quickly's shoulder and yelling, "Give it me now!"

Various events then took place in the space of a few seconds. Some of the male gods jumped up and started moving towards the commotion, Mrs Bumble stood back from the counter and let out a shriek while dropping her wine glass on the floor, and Zeus pulled out a small thunderbolt ready to launch. Perhaps the most noticeable matter was Mistress Quickly's reaction. She did not say anything but continued to pour out the second glass of wine with her free arm. When that was completed, her arm went under the counter and her hand took hold of a large frying pan. This pan then emerged and travelled in a full circle over her head and landed on Mars's skull. The pupils in the God of War's eyes suddenly enlarged, his grip on the hostess's shoulder relaxed and he slumped to the floor. Meanwhile, Nell Quickly started pouring out the tankard of beer for Bacchus.

The first person on the scene was Nurse Nightingale, soon followed by Hebe.

"He'll be alright," Nurse Nightingale said after a quick examination. "It looks like that's one of your two-hour blows, Nell?"

"I put a slight twist on it at the last moment," the hostess replied, "so there should be another quarter of an hour."

"Is that how long he'll be unconscious for?" Hebe asked, coming up.

"That's the plan," Nell said.

"Let's get him out of here, lay him outside," Hebe suggested, just as a number of able-bodied males arrived.

Hephaestus, Bacchus and Nobbly Butt between them lifted Mars up and carried him out of the front door, depositing him on his back by the rose garden. During this entire episode Hera, his mother, had not moved, other than to turn her head to observe events. She had seen so many similar incidents that she had ceased being concerned. Also, she had lost her maternal instincts towards Mars many thousands of years ago.

"I take it all will be well?" she enquired once Florence had returned to the seat next to her.

"He'll have a nasty headache when he comes round, but that's normal. I'll take him back to the hospital later and keep him under observation just in case."

"The headache will serve him right," Mars's unmaternal mother replied with a sigh.

Hephaestus and Nobbly Butt had been chatting with Athene and Aphrodite before Mars had come into the pub. When they returned they found Lennie on their table; he had already obtained Aphrodite's signature to his petition but had got nowhere with Athene. Lennie had never met Nobbly Butt, so he introduced himself to the builder. He was also realising that it was time to try a bit of trickery to obtain more support, since he had had a number of rejections during the evening.

"What an interesting name Nobbly Butt is," he said. "It would be very helpful to me if you could please just write it down on this little scrap of paper I have here. It's purely in case I forget it."

"Oh, do sign it, Nobbles," Aphrodite said eagerly, just as Athene, who had caught his eye, was shaking her head.

"Let's look at what this is," Hephaestus said, picking up the petition. After a few seconds he burst out laughing and put the paper into the eagle's beak. "Nice try, Lennie. Off you go; we're busy having a language lesson."

Lennie tried to protest but got nowhere, so he soon flew off to look for support elsewhere.

"I thought it was all a bit of fun," Aphrodite piped up after Lennie had gone. "But no probs; you were teaching us the language of eggy, Nobbles?"

"Yea," Nobbly Butt said. "This is a language that various gangs in Budapest used to speak to confuse the police. It involves saying 'egg' in front of every vowel."

"Were you a gang member?" Aphrodite purred.

"Only for a very short time when I was young. Everyone was on our estate."

"So, what's my name in eggy?" Athene asked.

"Atheggenegge," Nobbly Butt replied.

"What about putting egg in front of the A at the beginning?"

"It's optional if the word or name begins with one of them vowels. Likewise, it's optional to put egg in front of Y; it's like I, you see."

"It all seems incredibly complicated," Aphrodite commented. "What's my name in eggy?"

"Aphreggodeggitegge," was the response.

"It might be better to use my short name of Aphy. Would that be Apheggy?"

"Yea, very good," Nobbly Butt said.

"Let me try my name," said Hephaestus. "Is that Heggepheggasteggus?"

"Not quite. You missed out an egg. It should be Heggepheggaeggesteggus."

"Heggepheggaeggesteggus," the builder god repeated. "Is that it?"

"Right on," said Nobbly Butt. "But like Aphy, you might prefer your shortened name of Heph."

"That would be Heggeph. That seems easier."

"So is your name Neggobbleggy Beggutt?" Athene asked.

"It is."

"And is Nobbles, Neggobblegges?" Aphy asked.

"Very good again."

"See, I got that one right too," the Goddess of Love said with a beam on her face. "Let's take it in turn to name everyone who's here tonight."

The four of them then spent some time translating myriad names into eggy. The result was that the pub was full of individuals with names such as Zeggeeggus, Heggeregga, Mr and Mrs Beggumblegge, Neggell, Ireggis, Fleggoreggencegge, Heggebegge and many more. The only person who could get Marie Antoinette correct first time round was Nobbly Butt, with Meggareggiegge Anteggoeggineggettegge.

"You are so clever," Aphrodite said to Nobbly Butt admiringly. "But can we try some sentences? Pretend we're lovers, Nobbles, and please say 'I love you' in eggy."

"Eggi leggovegge yeggoeggu," was the prompt reply.

"Eggi leggovegge yeggoeggu. I think that's gorgeous," Aphy repeated.

The discussion then moved on to saying simple sentences to each other before Nobbly Butt was put to the test, with the three members of the deity giving him more and more complicated words for translation into eggy. He was clearly totally fluent in the language as no one could find any mistakes. Aphy was continuously saying, "you are so clever," as she kept looking at him admiringly.

"I've got a word to test you," Athene said with a tinge of mischief in her eyes.

"Nobbles can't be beaten," Aphy quickly spoke up for her hero.

"Supercalifragilisticexpialidocious," Athene said.

Hephaestus burst out laughing, at the same time as Aphy moaned, "That's not fair."

"Go on, give it a go," said Athene.

Nobbly Butt took a deep breath before beginning.

"Seggupeggerceggaleggifreggageggileggisteggiceggexpeg-gieggaleggideggoceggieggoeggus."

The other three all clapped, despite none of them being sure if he had got it completely right.

"You've done it, Nobbles!" Aphrodite said in a loud voice. "You're a star. Let me give you a kiss," and she leant over and kissed Nobbly Butt on the cheek.

Shortly afterwards, Nell Quickly rang her bell to indicate it was closing time at the Dog and Duck. Marie Antoinette had been unsuccessfully trying to catch Bacchus alone since her conversation with Apollo, but he had spent all his time with Hebe and Mrs Bumble. However, as everyone was packing up to leave, the former Queen of France saw an opportunity to catch Bacchus by himself.

"Lord Bacchus," she said, sidling up to him. "I am so *désolé* we have not had the time to speak this evening. I just want to say how much I admire you in hosting this wonderful evening. You are a man, *non*, a god, I mean, of many talents."

"Oh, thank you, Marie Antoinette," Bacchus replied.

"Yes, you have the many talents I admire so much. I am sure we have much to discuss sometime together."

"Have we?"

"*Mais oui, Monsieur*. To our mutual advantage, *tu comprends?*" she said with a saucy look on her face.

"Do I?" said Bacchus.

Marie Antoinette gave him a friendly nudge with her arm. "*Mais oui,*" she continued. "I think you do, you naughty god." This was followed by another nudge. "I propose one evening when here is quiet to come and visit. You and I can then have a tete a tete together, *n'est ce pas?*"

"If you like," replied a somewhat confused Bacchus.

"No, Lord Bacchus, it is if we both like. Remember, to our mutual advantage. I am now going, but I will soon return. *Au revoir*, My Gallant Lord Bacchus."

Marie Antoinette turned round and walked to the front door, where she found Apollo, who had seen her speaking to Bacchus. He offered her his arm so he could walk her home. They followed a number of other couples who had already left. Zeus was escorting Hera, while Mr Bumble had his good lady wife on his arm. Hebe was listening to Hermes giving her a brief lecture on the Second Law of Thermodynamics, with Iris on Fearless Frupert's arm just behind them. Artemis had stayed behind to berate Bacchus on the Hanseatic Headbanger poster, but he just smiled at her and talked her into trying it out. He actually wanted to catch her on what democracy was all about and, because it was a political subject close to her heart, she remained behind. She could always stay overnight in one of the pub's guest rooms if it got too late.

Aphrodite and Nobbly Butt were amongst the last to leave. They were casually strolling arm in arm, with the goddess continuing to try out her eggy. Her favourite expression was 'egge leggovegge yeggoeggu', which she repeated at regular intervals. As they left, they passed Hephaestus, Athene and Florence Nightingale, who were standing over Mars as he sat on the ground, holding his head.

"Do you want any help?" Nobbly Butt asked.

"No, thanks," Heph replied. "There are enough of us here to see Mars home."

"Okay, good night," the builder replied.

"Geggoeggod neggight," Aphrodite called as they walked away.

After a short consultation, Hephaestus and Athene pulled Mars to his feet and, each holding one of his arms behind his back, frog-marched the God of War along the pathway to the hospital. Florence walked behind them.

"Have you got plenty of that calming fluid?" Athene asked the nurse.

"Yes," Florence replied, "and a big needle to make sure it all goes in."

"Did you hear that, Mars?" Athene said. "Florence is going to stick a great big needle into you and then you're going to spend the whole night with her. It's the second time in a few short weeks. Lucky you."

Mars shook his head vigorously, but his mouth had been sealed up with tape, so nothing of any sense could be heard.

XXIV

THE RETURN
OF THE QUEEN

HEBE HAD AT LONG LAST DELIVERED A CD PLAYER to Poseidon's palace. It was battery-powered like everything else in the cavern which lacked any sort of wireless or cable communication. It had taken some time to put together because Merv the Nerd had had a number of technical difficulties creating the super long-life batteries for the player, but these had eventually been overcome. Hebe had also brought a mass of CDs which were on the list that Totty had made after consultation with the mermaids. The two of them decided to place the CD player, together with powerful speakers, at the edge of the piazza next to the gym area. This allowed music to be played while the team was exercising, as well as letting the mermaids work the player, so they could listen to music when they were swimming in the lagoon.

Totty showed the maids how the CD player operated,

especially how to change discs and alter the sound volume. The discs were kept in a box at the same location. For the first few days, the mermaids seemed to monopolise the music in the cavern, which meant that Abba's greatest hits were played continuously. The only time that there was any break from the Swedish group was when the early-morning exercise routine was in full swing, at which time Totty took responsibility for the music and ensured there was some variety.

Totty's nan had been a dance teacher when she was young. She had passed away more than a year ago, having been battling breast cancer for some time. Totty had been very close to her nan, who had taught her how to dance from a young age. She loved many of the dances from the '60s onwards and had three favourites, which had been the popular dances when her nan was growing up and in her later years as a teacher. Hebe had been able to get discs for these dance songs, which Totty had kept back when everything was delivered. She had an idea that it might be fun if she could get Poseidon, Dolores and Hashimoto to start dancing, but she wanted to remind herself of the steps before suggesting the matter to them.

About ten days after the CD player had been delivered Totty went into the piazza in the early afternoon with the three dance discs. Kinky was the only mermaid in the lagoon swimming by herself and listening to Abba singing 'Waterloo'.

"Do you mind if I change the disc, Kinky?" Totty called.

"What are you going to put on?" Kinky asked as she swam over to Totty.

"I've got some dance music which I thought we might try. I want to practise the steps before suggesting it to the others."

"I love dancing. Do you see us maids dancing to the Abba songs?"

"You've all got great rhythm. You can dance with me now. The first one's called 'The Loco-motion' by Little Eva. It's got lots of arm movements."

"Super!" Kinky said.

"Here goes. Watch how I move and then turn it into a mermaid dance. Ready?" Totty asked as she changed the disc and pressed the play button.

"Ready," Kinky replied.

Little Eva's voice began singing about a brand-new dance called 'The Loco-motion'.

Totty stood tapping her feet, but not otherwise moving. She bent down and stopped the music at the end of the first verse.

"You didn't dance," Kinky said.

"No, I just wanted to get a feel at the beginning. Let's start again and I'll start dancing. I think I've got the movements now."

Little Eva's voice began the first verse again and Totty started to rock from foot to foot; she then moved on to more complex steps, which involved crossing her legs followed by a turn, swinging her hips as she went. Her arms began to move backwards and forwards, like the chugga-chugga motion of a locomotive. Kinky joined in, especially doing the chugga-chugga with her arms. Eventually the song finished and Totty and Kinky stopped dancing.

"That was Super," the mermaid said. "Can we do it again?"

"We need to," Totty replied. "I need a lot of practice."

Totty and Kinky played 'The Loco-motion' half a dozen times in succession as they perfected their movements.

"Let me play you the other two dance songs I've got," Totty said to Kinky.

"What are they?"

"'Let's Twist Again' by Chubby Checker and 'The Lambada'."

"I know 'The Lambada'," Kinky replied. "It's really beautiful, and I remember the twist from years ago."

"Let's put them on. I want to focus on dancing 'The Loco-motion' first of all, so let's just listen to the other two."

By now the other three mermaids had come out into the lagoon. They wanted to know what was going on, so Kinky explained that Totty was going to get everyone in the cavern dancing.

"Super!" Pinky said, followed by, "Totally Top," from the other two maids.

Totty put Chubby Checker on first and the mermaids began to try the twist in the water as it was played. They then all started singing when the second verse came on and continued throughout the song.

"I like 'The Lambada' best," Minky said after everything had been played a number of times.

"That's my favourite too," Kinky agreed.

"'The Loco-motion' is mine," Pinky said.

"Mine's 'The Lambada', but I like doing the twist best," Linky contributed.

"We haven't all learned how to dance them yet," Kinky replied.

"No, but I remember we all did the twist when we went on holiday to Goa," Linky said.

"That's right," Minky agreed. "Goa was Totally Top."

"And Super," Pinky added.

For the next couple of days Totty continued to practise the dance steps of the three songs she had chosen. All the mermaids joined her as they worked out their aquatic movements. Totty had told Poseidon, Dolores and Hashimoto what she was doing, and they agreed to leave her alone until she was ready to give them all lessons.

"Gee, Totty, hon, I've not done this dancing thing for a long, long time. You sure must take it real slow with me," Dolores said as they were having lunch on one of the days when Totty was still practising.

"It won't be a problem for you, Dol," Totty replied. "You're naturally a musical person with your lovely voice. You'll pick it up fine."

"What do you think of my karate movements, Miss Totty? Will they help me do dancing?" Hashimoto asked.

"We'll soon find out, Hash," Totty replied.

"Perhaps you find some music which goes with karate moves. Needs to be a song with plenty of chop, chop in. Do you think we have?"

"The only one I can think of is Queen's 'We Will Rock You'. Perhaps we could change it to 'We Will Chop You.'"

"No need for we. Words can be changed to 'I Will Chop You'. Very good; Hashimoto likes that. 'I Will Chop You,'" and at that point, Hash made a hard karate chop on the table, which caused his near-full plate of spaghetti carbonara to fly onto the floor.

The days ran into weeks which then ran into months as the cavern became an increasingly lively place. Totty had eventually firmed up on an exercise routine which seemed to suit everyone. It involved gym exercises in the morning and swimming in the afternoon for four days on the run, followed by a full day's rest. Totty was very insistent on this rest day because bodies needed time to recover. The mermaids also exercised at the same time and made sure they were in the lagoon in the afternoon. At Kinky's suggestion, they all started playing water polo together, with Poseidon quickly becoming the best player.

Dolores and Totty also proposed certain changes to the meals that were eaten. This was because a major priority of all the exercise was to lose weight; it was accepted that it was fairly pointless burning off the calories in the gym if this was followed by a meal consisting of sausages, chips and chocolates. The result was that even Poseidon was persuaded to only have sausages with his breakfast every other day instead of daily. In addition, Dolores had become an expert at making many different types of cake – in addition to chocolate, there was coffee, lemon and fruit cake, as well as a range of pies, including apple, rhubarb and mince. The agreed deal was that on Day 5, the rest day, people could eat Dolores's patisserie but would refrain from doing so during the exercise days. This also applied to the maids, who had somehow managed to talk Dolores into including them whenever it was a cake-eating day.

Dancing had taken off slowly at first because, with the exception of Totty and the maids, everyone was still overweight and lacked any elegance on the dance floor. Over time, this was overcome and dancing became a natural feature of life in the cavern. The mermaids were always very enthusiastic and in particular they encouraged Poseidon to participate. 'The Lambada' was the most difficult dance for everyone and it really needed couples dancing together. Poseidon and Totty formed a natural pair and Dolores and Hashimoto another, with the mermaids always mixing and matching between themselves. As far as music for Hash's karate moves was concerned, this never really took off, despite initial attempts at adapting Queen's rock song to 'I Will Chop You'.

Hebe's scales were very popular since everyone could measure their progress in losing weight. Over the months, Poseidon, Dolores and Hashimoto each lost many stones under the new regime. They not only looked much better but felt fitter and stronger. Poseidon was becoming mentally sharper as well; he wanted to become active once more and was planning visits to the various parts of his sea and ocean kingdom. He had recently agreed with Hebe that Hephaestus would make him a new chariot on Olympus which would be delivered once complete. Hebe was confident she could find him four horses with all the qualities that the gods required.

As the residents of the cavern lost weight they needed smaller clothes sizes. The three different sizes which Hebe had brought them at the beginning had long ago turned out to be too large. The result was that Hebe was forever measuring them and having replacements made in Yorkgate. Poseidon had embraced the informal wear that Totty had introduced and now everyone wore either shorts or tracksuit bottoms with smart tops. Even Hashimoto had given up on his bow ties and butler's uniform; his favourite top continued to be the Bollocks to Mars T-shirt. Despite this lack of formality, everyone took pride in their appearance and Hebe began bringing designer tops for them all, but especially Poseidon. The Sea God was soon wearing Givenchy, Versace and many other luxury labels. With Totty continuing to look after his grooming, he increasingly looked like the all-powerful deity he had once been.

The mermaids also wanted new clothes and they all had their Mars T-shirts. However, their main items of wear were bras and bikini tops, with requests to Hebe for new colours and styles whenever she visited the cavern.

Totty had taken on one more task in recent months. She was teaching Dolores to read and write. This was largely driven by the South Carolinian wanting to read all the cookery books, but she also started taking note of the different books on the shelves when she was dusting Poseidon's library. Totty would often help her in this task, which took longer and longer on each occasion as Dolores would ask her what the maroon leather book on the top left shelf was about, followed by wanting to know the title of the black volume on the shelf below, and so on.

One afternoon the waters in the piazza suddenly became choppy. Shortly afterwards there was a loud bellow followed by a quieter bellow.

"It's Moby," Kinky shouted in the mermaids' palace after she had looked out of one of the windows. "Come on, everyone. Let's go and say hello."

The maids swam out of their home into the lagoon, just at the time Dolores and Totty were coming out of the front of the main palace.

"Hello, Moby," Dolores shouted as she and Totty hurried over to the water's edge. They were soon followed by Poseidon and Hashimoto. By the time they got there the maids were kissing Moby, jumping on his back and generally making a big fuss of him.

"Afternoon, Moby," Poseidon called. "What brings you here?"

"I've brought my fiancée, Bettina, to meet you all."

The head of a very small whale emerged from the water just behind Moby. He moved aside so she could swim closer to the water's edge.

"I know Bettina," Poseidon called. "Welcome to the cavern, my dear."

"Thank you, Lord Poseidon," Bettina said in a quiet voice. "Yes, Moby and I have only just got engaged and we've come to ask for your blessing."

"Which I readily give," the Sea God said, with a large smile on his face.

The next few minutes were taken up with everyone making a huge fuss of Bettina, especially the mermaids, who had never met her beforehand. While this was taking place, Moby quietly swam to the piazza edge where Totty was standing.

"Am I forgiven, Totty?" he asked her quietly.

"Of course you are," Totty replied. "Everything here is good."

"I've been so worried."

"Don't be. I'm really enjoying myself in the cavern."

The waters suddenly became choppy again as two other large shapes emerged from the cave entrance.

"It's today like Clapham Junction here," Hashimoto said. Although he had never been to Clapham Junction, he was aware it was a busy railway station in the London area, which was often referred to by Britons when places got crowded.

Poseidon looked at the newcomers who were a pair of fin whales. "It's Gerrard and Suki, isn't it?" he said when their heads had surfaced. "Are you two engaged as well?"

"Not yet," Suki, the female, replied. "Just boy- and girl-friend. We're taking it slowly."

"Very wise," Poseidon commented.

"We've come with Moby and Bettina," Gerrard said. "I'm going to be best man and Suki's chief bridesmaid."

"Then you'd better say hello to everyone here, if you don't know them already."

"I'll do the introductions," Kinky called as she swam over to Gerrard and gave him a big kiss.

Over the next hour a large number of other sea creatures found their way into the cavern. Totty met Dolly and Donald Dolphin and their four small children, Prudence Porpoise, Sidney the Shark, Olly Octopus and many more of the Sea God's subjects.

"Aren't they scared of each other?" Totty quietly asked Dolores when the two were alone. "I thought sharks lived on smaller fish."

"Hon, you're right, but not today. There are two rules Poseidon has. Number one, no eating or fighting each other in the lagoon. Number two, mermaids are protected in all the seas and oceans."

"That explains why all the maids are kissing the sharks, despite their sharp teeth."

"Oh, sharks ain't so bad once you get to know them," Dolores replied.

Given all the activity in the cavern, it was probably no surprise when four white stallions came charging through the cave entrance, pulling a large golden chariot with a diminutive blonde goddess at the reins.

"It's Hebe!" all the maids shouted as the stallions and chariot jumped out of the water onto the piazza. Hebe unharnessed the horses, pulled a bundle of hay from the chariot for them to eat and walked over to the others.

"Hiya," she said. "I was in the area and thought I'd call in to see how things are going. I've got a few bottles of champagne and some cake. I thought we could have some music, a dance and a small party."

"Excellent," Poseidon replied. "I'm in just the mood for a party. Look at all my lovely sea creatures who've called in to see us. Moby and Bettina have got engaged, so we should toast their good health."

"Good idea, Uncle Posy," Hebe said. "Come on, Hash; help me unload the champagne."

"How many bottles have you got, Lady Hebe?" the butler asked.

"Two dozen."

"Two dozen!" Dolores, who was nearby, exclaimed. "There are only four of us."

"Five with me," Hebe corrected her.

"Nine with us maids," Kinky called, having been listening from the water's edge.

"What about them?" Totty asked, pointing to what appeared to be another group of mermaids who were at the far side of the lagoon.

"The boys!" Kinky shouted. "Did Old Posy say they could come in?"

"I did," Hebe replied. "So that makes thirteen. Not quite two bottles each."

"Did you mention cake as well?" Totty asked.

"I've brought four large black forest gateaux."

"Super!" Kinky exclaimed. "We had that in the Seychelles."

"Come on, everyone, let's get it all unloaded."

"I'll go and get a large table to put it on," Totty said, walking back to the palace.

Within a short space of time the party was in full swing. Although Dolores had cut the black forest gateau into slices and Hashimoto had opened a few bottles of champagne, everyone was focusing on dancing. Totty was in charge of the music and initially played a lot of Abba songs to please the mermaids. The boys had been reluctant to participate at the beginning because they were wary of Poseidon. However, he waved them over and from then onwards they joined the maids in all the disco dances they had learned on holiday in the Seychelles and elsewhere.

As time went on, even the whales and dolphins and other sea creatures started moving to the sound of the music. The first time Totty played 'Let's Twist Again', Moby and Bettina were shaking their bodies from side to side, with Moby bellowing in delight at what he viewed as his engagement party.

After an hour, Totty and Dolores decided it was time for a break, so they stopped the music. Glasses of champagne were handed out to the maids and the boys as well as pieces of black forest gateau.

"This is Far Out, Man," one of the boys said to Totty with a mouth full of gateau, and a half-full glass of champagne in his right hand.

"Totty, this is my special friend Ted," Kinky said from nearby. "Far Out, Man is what the boys say, while we maids are still into Super and Totally Top."

"Far Out, Man," Totty said back to Ted and raised her champagne glass to him.

Shortly afterwards, Totty went to put the music back on.

"Come on, Totty," Hebe said, moving over to her. "Let's do 'The Loco-motion' together."

"Fine," Totty replied, pressing the play button on the CD recorder.

Little Eva had only just begun singing when there was a loud rush of water from the cave. Four black winged mares came bounding over the water, drawing a silver chariot embossed with emeralds and rubies. Like Hebe's stallions, they jumped easily onto the piazza and came to a halt. A tall, slim female with jet-black hair got out of the chariot and looked around. She was wearing an emerald cloak with a tiara on her head covered in diamonds.

Everyone stopped dancing and all the sea creatures silently moved closer to the water's edge so they could observe proceedings. Hebe turned the music off and Poseidon slowly began to walk over to the newcomer.

"Poseidon," the female said in a loud, confident voice. "You look incredibly well and more handsome than ever. What has happened to you? You're just like the king I married all those years ago."

"Amphitrite," Poseidon said slightly nervously. "Your arrival has taken us all by surprise."

"I hope a positive surprise. Come over here and kiss your queen."

The Sea God stood in front of his wife, but before he could do anything, she had taken hold of his shirt, pulled him to her breast and given him a passionate embrace.

"It's been a long time, My Lord, since we've done that. What are you all doing on the piazza? It looks like a party."

"It is," Poseidon replied. "One of those spur-of-the-moment parties, which Hebe initiated when she also arrived out of the blue."

"Hebe's here, is she?"

"Hello, Aunt Amphy," Hebe said, moving over to the Queen and giving her a kiss. "What a surprise, the two of us coming to the cavern at the same time."

"Isn't it?" Amphitrite said as she and Hebe looked knowingly into each other's eyes. "I wish you wouldn't call me Aunt. I can never remember which of us was born first; it was so long ago."

Amphitrite looked up and saw Dolores and Hashimoto.

"Dol and Hash. How good to see you again," she said, putting out her hand, which they both kissed. "You've clearly been looking after my Lord Poseidon very well while I've been away. I can see the changes in him are also reflected in the two of you. Perhaps you'll let me in on the secret over the coming days."

"My Lady," was all Dolores said.

Hashimoto was far more forward. "You see, Lady P, Hashimoto is now the New Modern Butler," he said. "He dresses in super-new, modern style."

"I like your T-shirt – Bollocks to Mars. Let's hope the God of War doesn't suddenly decide to come and visit us today as well."

"I will do karate chops on him if he come."

"That will be interesting."

"Amphitrite," Poseidon interrupted, beckoning Totty. "I'd like to introduce you to Miss Totty Turniptoes, who is our new resident in the cavern."

Amphitrite looked up and smiled at a slightly nervous Totty. "I have to admit to having already heard of your presence here, Totty," the goddess said, putting out her hand for kissing. "A force for good is the widespread opinion. No doubt you are the one responsible for rejuvenating both Lord Poseidon and Dolores, as well as giving me a New Modern Butler."

"My Lady," was all Totty could say, blushing.

"I'm sure you and I will have many long talks in the days to come, Totty. But let me not delay the party everyone's having. It looked as if you were all dancing as well. Perhaps I could join in?"

"I'll go and put the music back on," Totty said. "We also have champagne, if I could bring you a glass."

"Later, I think. Let's dance a little first. Dolores!" Amphitrite called when she saw Dolores walking back to the palace. "Where are you going?"

"I have to go and prepare your room, My Lady," Dolores replied.

"Leave it, Dol," the goddess said. "I'll be staying in my husband's room tonight. You can prepare my room over the next few days. There's plenty of time; I expect I'll be staying in the cavern for a long period and then Lord Poseidon and I might well be visiting different parts of our kingdom together."

When Totty reached the CD recorder, Hebe was already there.

"Let's have 'The Loco-motion' again," the diminutive goddess said, "followed by 'Let's Twist Again' and then 'The Lambada.'"

"Will Lady Amphitrite be able to do these dances?" Totty asked.

"We'll soon find out," Hebe replied.

Little Eva's voice began once again and everyone on the piazza started dancing 'The Loco-motion'. Hebe had gone and unbridled Amphitrite's mares and they moved over to join the white stallions. All of the horses suddenly began tapping their hooves to the beat of the music as well as shaking their bodies to the left and right. The mermaids and the boys were particularly lively, and they were soon joined by the other sea creatures who were also in the mood to sway around. All this activity, especially from the whales, caused the waters in the lagoon to become choppy and splash onto the piazza, but no one cared.

Although Totty was dancing with enthusiasm, she was also watching Amphitrite. She was amazed at how the goddess seemed to know the steps of 'The Loco-motion' even better than her nan. The same was true of the twist, where she was outdoing Totty and everyone else on the piazza with her style. When it came to 'The Lambada', Amphitrite and Poseidon became a natural couple as they began to dance closely in the middle of the piazza.

"We won't join in just yet," Hebe said to Totty while also pulling Dolores and Hashimoto back. "This is their moment; let them have centre stage just to themselves."

The mermaids, boys and other sea creatures seemed to know Hebe's mind. They also stopped dancing and again all moved to the piazza edge to watch their king and queen.

"You know what Hashimoto thinks," the New Modern Butler said, looking at Hebe in particular.

"No, Hash. What do you think?" Hebe replied.

"I think it's mighty big coincidence that all these different whales, dolphins, boys and other creatures, they all decide to turn up in the cavern at same time."

"Just coincidence, as you say," Hebe responded.

"Even bigger coincidence is that you turn up with all this champagne, soon after."

"I agree with you; it's a coincidence."

"Even bigger, bigger coincidence that later you are followed by Lady Amphitrite, who's not been here many years."

"Yes, it is. These coincidences do happen."

"Biggest coincidence of all is Lady Amphitrite knows how to dance all these dances we do. That's just about biggest, biggest coincidence going. That's what Hashimoto thinks."

"I couldn't agree with you more, Hash. As you say, just coincidence," Hebe replied as she winked at Totty.

EPILOGUE

WHEN TOTTY FELL INTO THE MEDITERRANEAN from the *Princess BoomBoom*, she little realised that she was about to be the catalyst for change in the life of one of the three most powerful gods of all time. Fortunately, she had fertile territory to plough. She arrived at the Sea God's Cavern at a time when Poseidon was at a low, both physically as well as emotionally. His two co-inhabitants, Dolores and Hashimoto, were also aware that the Sea God's realm was going backwards instead of making progress – it was simply not the right environment for Hashimoto to become a New Modern Man! Even the mermaids were conscious that all was not well with Old Posy, as Kinky affectionately called him. Totty was the ideal candidate to bring change to this environment. She was very much the Modern Young Woman with a strong interest in fashion, health and beauty, fitness, food and music. She also had a sympathetic personality and this allowed her to set about making personal improvements to Poseidon's household, without coming over as too 'pushy.'

There is little doubt that Hebe's assistance contributed to the changes in the cavern. The suspicion is that she was in regular communication with Amphitrite during this time and ensured that the Sea Goddess knew the dance steps to 'The Loco-motion', 'Let's Twist Again' and 'The Lambada' before returning to her husband. The reunion between Poseidon and his wife was the culmination of all this hard work by Hebe and Totty, although the latter was unaware of Hebe's additional motive in bringing some order back to her uncle's matrimonial affairs.

However, this is only the start. There are many unresolved issues, not least Totty's status as a deceased person, which needs clarifying sooner rather than later. In addition, Poseidon and Amphitrite have been apart for so many years, and they need time to settle down together once more. Then the really important stuff has to happen. Poseidon needs to get out of the cavern and spend time in the oceans and the seas. So much has been going on there in recent years with no involvement by the Sea God. It is time he started exercising his considerable powers once more for the benefit of his realm.

Just as Totty was the catalyst for change in Poseidon's realm, Vesta played a similar role when she arrived in the Underworld. However, her involvement was mainly in questioning the bureaucratic running of the realm. It was not that Vesta, at her young age, was a brilliant management consultant – although she was clearly very bright. It was quite simply that she asked the obvious questions, such as who guards the gate to the Underworld when Cerberus isn't there? Similarly, wouldn't it be more productive if Sisyphus carried large rocks and stones from the quarry to the building sites, instead of pushing a great big boulder up a hill just for it to run back down again? The changes to the Torturing Department fit into the same vein.

Unlike his Sea God brother, Hades was not at a psychological low, but he did acknowledge that he might be becoming stale and his kingdom could do with some sort of shake-up. He was, however, naturally conservative, but Vesta soon acquired important allies in support of her ideas. Aggy, Attila and Genghis were all respected by Hades, but above all

Cerberus soon became her principal fan. While most of Vesta's improvements were directed at organisational matters, the changes she brought about in Cerberus were very much to do with his personal development. Put simply, he became 'almost human'.

As with Poseidon's realm, there is still a lot more work to be done. Progress needs to be brought to all the other functions, ranging from the building sites, the laundry, house-keeping and much more. But there is a wider issue, which is whether the Underworld is simply too big for one god to oversee? Does Hades really know what goes on throughout his entire kingdom? It is so large that the suspicion has to be that there are groups of people who 'fell off the radar' a long time ago. Of even more immediate concern to Hades, is the imminent return of his wife, Persephone, who is required to spend a third of her time in the Underworld. All has never been well between the god and the goddess since Hades abducted her when she was young, and she has always resented her time away from Olympus. However, perhaps on her next visit she will begin to take an interest in the changes which have begun and will join with Vesta, Cerberus and the others to deliver further progress.

While both the Sea Cavern and the Underworld are beginning to adjust to the modern age, the same cannot be said of Olympus. Iris and Hebe may live in a 21st century bungalow with their own electricity supply, but none of the other gods have followed suit. Similarly, discussions may have begun about contemporary subjects such as equality, but even Artemis, who is their principal champion, acknowledges she knows little about towns and cities where such ideas flourish. Perhaps this reflects Zeus as a leader? Poseidon and Hades in their own different ways recognise that they are either in a rut or going stale, but Zeus has no such qualms. He expects to carry on as he has been doing for thousands of years, whether that involves visits to Hamburg looking for crumpet, or keeping a firm grip on Gods' Council meeting decisions.

Zeus does actually recognise he has some problems, but he perceives these as being caused by the other gods and goddesses – whether it's Hera complaining about her maid, Artemis's support for democracy or Mars causing strife wherever he goes. Dealing with Mars is perhaps Zeus's biggest challenge and he will soon have to decide if he really is going to banish the God of War to an asteroid.

The reality is that Zeus's realm needs a Totty or a Vesta figure to help it to adapt to the modern world. Hebe could play such a role, since she has the closest links to twenty-first century humanity. She hasn't done so to date, despite suggesting to Hades, somewhat tongue in cheek, that Olympus was fine because it had her! This is principally because she has been so busy elsewhere, especially in Poseidon's realm. However, for the good of Olympus, she may have to refocus her attention increasingly towards its affairs. Athene, as the Goddess of Wisdom, could also flex her muscles more and she and Hebe would make a powerful duo in their father's realm.

Perhaps the single most important thing that the three senior gods need to do is to meet up. They may have a slanging match and start fighting each other at first, but that's what brothers often do. Once they've calmed down, the three of them could well benefit from sharing their frustrations and experiences together. While it's unlikely that Hades' idea of a job swap will be realised, focusing three heads on problems is sometimes better than one. Just ask Cerberus!

Finally, there is one matter on which all the gods fortunately do agree – *what happens next must be recorded for posterity*. This was discussed at a recent Girls Night Out held at the Dog and Duck. These events happen every so often when a number of the goddesses are in the mood. When they occur, Mistress Quickly banishes Bacchus to his room upstairs with a large jug of Hanseatic Headbanger and the pub's doors are barred to all members of the male sex. There are, of course, exceptions and, on this particular evening, both Nobbly Butt and Fearless Frupert were allowed to join the party as 'honorary girls'. This was justified by virtue of Nobbly Butt having become a firm attachment to Aphrodite and Fearless being similarly attached to Iris and Hebe. Also, since some of his gang members were in attendance, it was considered imprudent to deny him entrance.

When the question of who should record these subsequent events was discussed, Athene indicated that she had a friend who would make a suitable candidate.

"I know whom you're talking about," said Aphrodite, who had spent quite a lot of time with the Goddess of Wisdom over recent weeks, since Nobbly Butt had been replacing the roof of her palace.

"Who's that?" Artemis enquired.

"He's called Reggupeggert Stegganbeggury," Aphrodite replied, giving his name in fluent eggy. As she did so, she looked at Nobbly Butt who gave her the thumbs up. Athene also nodded approvingly.

"Then he'd better get a move on," Hebe said.

"He's already begun," Athene responded.

At that moment, Nell Quickly and Iris appeared, each carrying a large tray with goblets full of Hanseatic Headbanger. There was also a glass of ginger beer for Fearless.

"If that's the case," said Nell as she and Iris handed out the drinks, "we should drink a toast to Reggupeggert and wish him luck."

Everyone raised their goblets and said in unison – "To Reggupeggert!"

"And get a move on, Reggupeggert, or we'll send Mars round to sort you out!" Hebe added before she downed her Headbanger.

"That's not very nice," Aphrodite said, standing up for the poor writer.

"No, but it's a good idea," Artemis commented to general amusement in the room.

 Matador